PENGUIN BOOKS
NIGHT OF THE DARK TREES

Abraham Eraly is the author of two critically acclaimed books on Indian history, *The Last Spring: The Lives and Times of the Great Mughals* (1997) and *Gem in the Lotus: The Seeding of Indian Civilization* (2000).

Born in Kerala, and educated there and in Chennai, Eraly has taught Indian history in colleges in India and the United States, and was the editor of a current affairs magazine for several years.

He now lives in Chennai, and is working on a study of classical Indian civilization. He can be contacted at abraham_eraly@ yahoo.co.in

W0232849

BY ABRAHAM ERALY

The Last Spring: The Lives and Times of the Great Mughals

Gem in the Lotus: The Seeding of Indian Civilization

Night of the Dark Trees

A Novel

ABRAHAM ERALY

PENGUIN BOOKS

PENGUIN BOOKS

USA | Canada | UK | Ireland | Australia
New Zealand | India | South Africa | China | Singapore

Penguin Books is part of the Penguin Random House group of companies
whose addresses can be found at global.penguinrandomhouse.com

Published by Penguin Random House India Pvt. Ltd
4th Floor, Capital Tower 1, MG Road,
Gurugram 122 002, Haryana, India

Penguin
Random House
India

First published by Penguin Books India 2006

ISBN 9780143061830

Typeset in Sabon by Mantra Virtual Services, New Delhi

Printed at Manipal Technologies Limited, India

www.penguin.co.in

MIX
Paper | Supporting
responsible forestry
FSC® C043100

This is a legitimate digitally printed version of the book and therefore might not
have certain extra finishing on the cover.

To be sure, I am a forest, and a night of dark trees;
but he who is not afraid of my darkness
will find banks full of roses under my cypresses.

—Nietzsche: *Thus Spake Zarathustra*

The Oracle

1

Zerubbabel. Zeruba for short. No one in India, perhaps no one in the world, had this preposterous Old Testament name. And no one knew what to make of it. Or even how to pronounce it. In the Kerala village where he grew up, everyone in school slurred his name to call him *Seruvaval*, baby bat, a toothless vampire. It was a standing joke for the witless. And later on in life, he was often greeted by strangers with suppressed smiles when introduced. Pardon? Cherub? Doesn't look the role, does he? More like Mephisto. Wrong casting. Change the subject.

Zeruba didn't give a damn. A loner, he was safe from the world, living curled up within himself.

'Oh, I love the name,' gushed Aditi, his future wife, doubling over with laughter, holding up in the crook of her left arm the *pallu* of her sari that had slipped from her shoulder, and in her right hand a glass of gin and lime that she shook to tinkle the ice as she laughed. 'Sounds like so many bells ringing together. Zerubbabel-*bell*!'

They were at a cocktail party hosted by a Madras socialite, and had just been introduced. Zeruba was there as a celebrity artist, and Aditi as a friend of the hostess. She, well into her fifth or sixth peg, was roaring drunk. As she shook with laughter, her full, firm breasts surged braless against the confining seams of her low-cut, skin-tight, white cotton-voile blouse, their dark, tumescent nipples nearly spearing through the gauzy fabric. Her eyes sparkled impishly. Magical, he thought.

The name Zerubbabel—the Biblical hero of Jewish resurgence—was the inspiration of his great-grandfather, in whose lap he was placed by his parents on the eleventh day of his life. The old man scowled into the baby's crinkling eyes, laid a copper hand on his downy head, and proclaimed in his gruff, loud voice: 'You are Zerubbabel. You shall lead us out of our misfortunes.' Saying this, he looked up at the child's parents standing nervously before him with folded arms, and, seeing their dismay, roared with laughter. Then, still laughing, he planted a prickly kiss on the baby's forehead, and blessed: 'May you grow up to be like me.'

'I don't know whether I really remember seeing and hearing this, or only imagine it from what my mother told me,' Zeruba said, recounting to Aditi the story of his naming. 'But right now I can see it all vividly, like a movie projected inside my head.' He could see his great-grandfather's blazing, tyrant eyes boring into him from his rugged face with its grizzly stubble and plummeting nose; he could even smell the acrid, tobacco-smoke infused thicket of hair on his chest, feel his stomach heave as he laughed, the muscles of his brawny arms flex as he cradled him. 'I squealed in terror,' he recalled.

Aditi doubled over again, shrieking. This man is a scream, she thought.

2

Zeruba did, in fact, grow up to be a bit like his great-grandfather— though, of course, to be only half the man that the old man was. Zero-baba: cipher-seer. Okay. A lesser age, a lesser creature. But he managed to make an even greater mess of his life than his great-grandfather did with his. And this was inevitable, an oracle had warned him. He had to bear the karmic consequences of his sins in previous lives.

'You were born at a time when there shouldn't have been any birth at all,' growled the oracle, savagely clawing at his beard and glowering at Zeruba with bloodshot eyes.

Zeruba had just finished college at this time and was at a loss about what to do with his life, so he was taken to the oracle for guidance by Gopi, a childhood friend.

'He's infallible,' Gopi said.

'I don't have a horoscope,' Zeruba protested.

'You don't need one,' Gopi assured him. 'He just looks at you and reads your life.'

The oracle lived in a village south of Kochi, in a tile-roofed, freshly whitewashed little cottage beside a shallow irrigation canal. A sandy path from the road through coconut groves led to his house. When Zeruba and Gopi arrived, there were about half a dozen men in the bare visitor's room, a nondescript group of townsmen and villagers on a bench at one end of the room. They sat tense and silent, each tightly wrapped up in his own problems. A scrawny peasant woman in a soiled white dhoti and faded red blouse stood at the door, quietly weeping.

At the far end of the room, next to a green-painted closed door, were a small, grimy wooden table and a straight-backed armless chair, and on the wall behind the table were several calendar pictures of gods and goddesses dangling from nails. Sunlight streamed into the room through a narrow, barred window on the side-wall, burning white stripes on the cow-dung daubed olive-green floor. From an inner room they could hear the tinkling of bells and the chanting of mantras. The smell of incense was thick in the air.

Presently the door was flung open and the oracle entered, a gaunt, bare-chested and ash-smeared old man of uncertain age, with beetling eyebrows and long, wispy grey hair and beard. He seemed to be in a trance, his movements jerky, his body taut as a drawn bow. He staggered to the table without even a glance at the visitors, and sat slumped in the chair for a minute or so, his hands tensely clenched together, his chin sunk into his skeletal chest, his eyes shut, muttering to himself, tears streaming down his cheeks. Zeruba sat transfixed, barely breathing. Then suddenly, as if jolted by an electric shock, the oracle's head snapped back, and he opened his wild, deep-sunken eyes. Zeruba was right in front of him, but it was on the peasant woman at the door that his eyes fell.

'Cry! Cry!' he screamed. 'What's the use! Your daughter will die. And it'll be a terrible, terrible death.'

'Help me, swami,' the woman pleaded in a quavering voice.

'Not even Brahma can change karma,' swore the seer viciously.

'Swami . . .' she wailed.

'*Podi, po! Po!*' he shouted at her, flailing his arms furiously—
You begone! Begone!

Then, as abruptly as he first spoke to the woman, he turned to Zeruba and spilled the horrid secret of his untimely birth. 'You shouldn't have been born at all,' the oracle said, lowering his voice and shaking his head. 'Having been born anyhow, you should have died in your first month. But since you have survived, it's not death that you have to fear, but life.'

'What do you mean?' Zeruba asked.

The seer fixed him with his hard, baleful, crazed eyes for a long, silent moment. 'You'll find out,' he said at last, almost in a whisper.

And that was that.

3

The oracle was not far wrong about Zeruba's first near-death, for he was born with the umbilical cord wound tightly around his neck in a prenatal suicide attempt. And, in an inventive variation of Zarathustra guffawing at birth, he choked and spat green bile into the face of the demoness attending on his birth as a midwife.

'It scared the shit out of her,' he told Aditi one day, regaling her with the droll misadventures of his life. 'She thought I was a monster from another world.'

'I don't believe a word of what you're saying,' Aditi laughed.

'Honest,' Zeruba said. 'Ask anyone. People still talk about it in my hometown.'

The midwife was a hideously, obscenely ugly woman, with pox-marked face and yellow buck-teeth. Attending on Zeruba's birth was the high point of her life, and she would never let him forget her. Even years later, whenever he was at home from college, she would somehow hear about it and drop in to gleefully rib him about his birth antics, as he cowered behind a newspaper and servants laughed.

What the midwife didn't know was that the baby, having blotched his first suicide attempt, tried again a couple of weeks later, wriggling out of the hands of his nurse and diving into the white enamelled water-basin in which she was bathing him at his mother's bedside. Before she could fish him out, he managed to breathe in a lungful of soap water, and would have died then if his maternal uncle Isahaq had not happened to be in the room. He held up the baby dangling by his feet and with a couple of firm slaps on his back made him cough out the water, and then wordlessly handed him over to his sobbing mother. And she in a great swell of relief hugged him so tightly to her bosom that he nearly died again. Zeruba was the only consolation of her joyless life, and not much of a consolation at that.

Mariam, Zeruba's mother, was a melancholy woman, but no one knew what it was that troubled her. She had once dreamed of becoming a doctor, and had, after school, joined a medical college for a few months, but was pulled out by her parents and married off to a mercurial, feckless lawyer, whom she could not respect or love. Could this be what soured her life, Zeruba used to wonder. Or could it be some unrequited love? Whatever it was, she had not ever spoken to anyone about her sorrows. But Zeruba had often seen her sitting all alone in the veranda of the inner courtyard of their dreary and ramshackle home, looking utterly forlorn, shrouded in the dark veil of some unspoken grief stoically borne.

'Why are you so gloomy, Amma?' he once asked her.

She did not answer, but turned her face away. She was a very private person, of quiet but inviolable dignity. She seldom spoke above a whisper, and never in anger or frustration. Zeruba had never seen her agitated or excited about anything, and had never seen her cry. A small-made woman, fine-boned and delicate-featured, she was quite pretty, except for the heavy shadows under her pensive eyes.

It was heartbreaking for Zeruba to see her in her old age, when he returned home after many years of stubborn self-ostracism. Ancient and shrivelled, her skin completely crinkled, like crepe, she lay on her back in bed, motionless, staring blankly at the ceiling, a crisp white sheet spread smooth over her, her hands folded limply on her chest. The light in her eyes had wholly faded, and the fine head of hair that she once had was nearly all gone; her toothless mouth had collapsed, so her chin seemed to jut out from the base of her nose. She had almost completely lost her mind, and could hardly recognize anybody or remember anything.

'See who's here, Amma!' Chacko, Zeruba's younger brother, said to her in his usual breezy, bluff manner, standing over her and shaking her shoulders, and pointing to Zeruba sitting on her bed.

She didn't answer or move.

Zeruba then leaned over and lifted one of her hands from her chest and cupped it in his palms. Overhead, an ancient, grimy ceiling fan creaked mournfully as it slowly, laboriously turned its immense blades.

'Look at me, Amma,' he said softly, leaning over her.

Her eyes shifted. A flicker of interest there. And when he spoke again, she raised her head slightly from the pillow and looked at him full in the eyes.

'Don't you recognize me, Amma?' he asked.

A fleeting smile now played on her lips and she said slowly, clearly, 'Zeruba.' Then she did something strange. She pinched his hand conspiratorially. This was the secret sign by which she in his childhood used to pacify him when his father ranted at him, or at her, and to reassure him that it was all pretty silly and was not to be taken seriously.

Eight years earlier when he had last seen her, she, seventy-three then, was already beginning to show signs of dementia, and would keep asking the same questions over and over, always prefacing each question with the apology, 'You mustn't mind me—it's just that I can't remember.' He used to wonder at that time whether she was not at least partly faking forgetfulness, to be done with remembering, so that her wounds would not hurt her any more. But, of course, he was wrong. Her brain was evidently decaying, though probably her wilfulness not to remember her woes also had something to do with inducing or hastening senility. This old suspicion rose in him again when she pinched him, so he pinched her back, as he used to do as a child. But there was no response. Her eyes had gone blank again.

'For a moment she was with us,' Zeruba said. 'Now we've lost her again.'

Chacko spread his arms in cheerful resignation. 'Sometimes she surprises us,' he said.

'Yes?'

Chacko visited her without fail once a month, driving all the way from Thiruvananthapuram, where he was a big-shot minister in the state government. He would spend about half an hour with her, chaffing her and trying to cheer her up, though she never responded or showed any sign of even hearing him. But one day, said Chacko, she suddenly flared up at something he said. 'Che dog! You trying to trick me?' she cursed him under her breath.

'Your profession, Chacko,' Zeruba said.

'What?'

'Conning people.'

7

Chacko laughed.

'One has to get on,' he said, turning the bedside chair to sit facing Zeruba.

'What else did she say?'

'I was amazed,' Chacko said, rubbing his palms together, pleased with the memory of his amazement. 'This was another time. I was teasing her that her heart was icy, and that she had no love for anyone. And she—would you believe this?—she put her hand on her chest and said: It's there, inside.'

'Really?' Zeruba too was amazed, but not so much by what she said as by that she had cared to say it at all, for she was not a demonstrative person, and held herself aloof from everything and everybody, even from him, her beloved firstborn. He could not recall himself as a child ever being fondled by her, and his only intimate memory about her was of her crooning a lullaby to him, holding him in her lap and rocking him gently:

Omana thingal kidaavoo
Nalla komala thamara poovoo
Poovil niranja madhuvoo . . .

She lived tightly rolled into herself, holding her joys and sorrows hermetically sealed within. There were no surface ripples. They were all like that in her family, her brothers and sisters, all taking after their introverted and reclusive father. And this was a trait that Zeruba had in turn inherited.

4

Zeruba's maternal grandfather was a tall, lean man, in the mould of his ancient Semitic ancestors. His habits were clockwork-precise. As soon as he woke up, he drank a bowl of coffee, and then, sitting in a deckchair in the broad front veranda of the house, his legs stretched out on its extended arms, he read the

Malayala Manorama newspaper from end to end, even every one of the advertisements. He was not, in his old age, interested in the news or anything else in the paper, but he was a man of habit and would not change his routine. His meals too were unvaried, every day the same fare: rice gruel with ghee and mango pickle for breakfast, and for lunch, four bun-sized country biscuits and a marble-sized ball of opium washed down with a large bowl of milk. After lunch, he smoked a bidi, the only one he smoked the whole day, and slept for an hour or so. When he woke up, he had a bath and wore fresh clothes, a white borderless dhoti, a half-sleeved white shirt and a neatly folded black-bordered shoulder cloth. Then he put off the *methiyadi*—strapless clogs with only a peg for toehold—that he wore at home, slipped on a pair of leather sandals, and went out for a stroll, carrying an ivory-headed walking stick. Always by himself. He had no friends. Dinner was his big meal of the day, and consisted of rice with buttermilk, fried vegetables and usually a fish curry, occasionally beef or chicken, rarely mutton.

On Saturday mornings he took an oil bath, and that was quite a ritual. He sat on a footstool in the kitchen veranda, wearing only a G-string, and massaged sesame oil over his whole body with great care and thoroughness, spending nearly half an hour on it. He then waited for an hour for the oil to soak in, before taking bath. Though he usually bathed in cold water, even in winter, on Saturdays he bathed in hot water, and was particular about using only a mixture of green-gram powder and turmeric, not soap, to wash off the oil, scrubbing his body with *inja*, the crushed bark of a medicinal tree. On the last day of every month he took an enema first thing in the morning, assisted by Grandma.

The high point of Zeruba's recollection of his grandpa was of the day he got on to the tiled roof of the kitchen veranda to clear the dead leaves fallen from the mango tree spreading over it. Zeruba was seven or eight then, and was in the veranda at this time, pestering his grandma for something or other while she was cleaning fish. His mother and her two sisters were also there, as they usually were, sitting idly side by side on the broad bench placed against the wall, their legs drawn up, hugging their knees and leaning against the wall, which even many years later bore the oil smears of their heads.

None of them at first paid any attention to Grandpa when he brought a bamboo ladder from the firewood-shed and leaned it against the roof. But when he picked up a broom and began climbing the ladder, Grandma spoke up. 'Why should you do this?' she called out. 'Let Chathan do it.' Chathan was their odd-jobs farmhand.

Grandpa didn't pause or answer.

'You'll fall,' warned Grandma.

She was wasting her breath. Grandpa climbed on to the roof and disappeared from sight. He made no sound at all as he worked, moving slowly, cautiously, sweeping down a steady shower of blackened, rotting mango leaves. Then suddenly, without even a warning cry, he himself came tumbling down the roof. He fell lightly, like a cat, and hit the sandy courtyard with a barely audible thud.

'*Ayo!*' cried Grandma and ran to him, and Zeruba with her. The three sisters also roused themselves from their reverie and ran up. But before anyone got to him, Grandpa was already on his feet. He got up casually, without hurry or bother, as if nothing unusual whatever had happened.

'You hurt?' asked Grandma.

'No,' he said without looking up, brushing off leaves and sand from his clothes. Then he took the ladder back to the shed. The next day Chathan cleared the roof.

5

'Do you remember Grandpa?' Zeruba asked Chacko.

'Who?'

'Amma's father.' They were still at her bedside.

'No. I was too young when he died. Why?'

'Amma is like him.'

'I thought he was a tall man.'

'The resemblance is not physical,' Zeruba said. He looked at his mother, lying there inert like a prehistoric mummy, as lifeless as one could be without being actually dead. Was he right in thinking that she and her father were alike in nature? Didn't a different body mean a different chemistry, a different psyche? Are there really any mind-body coordinates? Physically, Zeruba and his father were exactly alike, but how unlike each other they were as persons!

'You said something?' Chacko asked.

'No. I was thinking about Amma,' Zeruba said. 'Poor thing! She has not known a single day's happiness in life.'

'I know,' Chacko said.

Zeruba looked at him levelly. 'No, you don't, you happy imbecile,' he taunted. Eleven years the elder, he could take such liberties.

Chacko laughed heartily. 'Maybe I'm not intelligent enough to be unhappy.'

He had put on a lot of weight since Zeruba had seen him last, and had about him the sated look of contentment and well-being. His eyes were clear, happy, confident. In just a dozen years he had soared meteorically in politics and had fabulously enriched himself. But will it last, Zeruba wondered.

'Don't you ever worry that one day they might catch you out and pack you off to jail?' Zeruba asked.

'Who?'

'Your political adversaries.'

'If I go to jail, so will everyone else,' Chacko said, laughing. 'We are all equally corrupt, in all political parties.'

'What about public interest litigation? Civic activists can trip you up.'

'Oh, they have their prices too,' Chacko said dismissively. 'And so have the judges.'

'I know some who are incorruptible.'

'There's no such thing as an incorruptible human being, Chetta,' Chacko said with assurance. 'Our vulnerabilities might be different, but there's no one who is not vulnerable in some way or other. It's simply a matter finding out who has what weakness and exploiting it to secure one's interests.'

'Doesn't it trouble your conscience that much of what you are doing is wrong?' Zeruba asked.

'But much of what I'm doing is right,' Chacko countered. 'You think that I lead an odious life, but lakhs and lakhs of people think of me as a good man. Otherwise how could I have won elections time and again with some of the largest majorities in the electoral history of India? That too in Kerala?'

'Elections don't decide right and wrong,' Zeruba said.

'Yes, they do,' Chacko asserted. 'The world has changed. Values have changed.'

'Maybe. But the past still remains with us,' Zeruba said. 'We can't ever be rid of it.'

'Yes, we can. We must,' Chacko said. 'There's no future in the past, Chetta.'

Lakshmi

1

That was just posturing. Actually Chacko was quite attached to the family, and he loved and cherished his parents, unlike Zeruba, who had cut himself lose and had drifted away. But Chacko had also the worldly wisdom to know that the means to preserve continuity—indeed, to survive at all—was to change with the changing times. And this he did by deftly changing his colours to blend smoothly into the new socio-economic environment, while still remaining firmly rooted in the ancient soil and drawing abundant sustenance from it.

But Zeruba was rootless, and was doomed to feed on himself. 'There is no nurture in this soil for us any more,' he had once grandly told his uncle Mathu, his father's younger brother, explaining why he had to break free from family bonds. 'I'll be reduced to compost if I remain here.'

Zeruba had no particular feeling of identity with his family. Or with the community to which he belonged, a small and obscure clan of ancient Christians called Jacobite Syrian Christians, who proudly claimed descent from the few families of high-caste Indians converted by Apostle Thomas in the first century. A hyper-orthodox community, it was noted for its clan pride, even though this pride now stood, in the case of most families, on rickety legs of attenuated fortunes. Zeruba's father, Korah, was especially touchy about family status, and he was deeply offended when Zeruba decided to drop out of college to become an artist.

'Artist!' Korah exploded on receiving Zeruba's letter about his plan. In his view, artists were barely distinct from common artisans.

'Artists are highly respected in Western society,' Mathu told him. He was the only one in the family to support Zeruba's decision.

'It's alright as a hobby, not as a profession.'

'It's the professional artist that is respected in the West, not the hobbyist,' said Mathu.

'I won't stand for it,' Korah said morosely.

He particularly resented that Zeruba, instead of seeking his advice and blessing, had merely informed him of his decision. 'He does not even have the courtesy to consult me,' he grumbled.

'It's another generation, Chetta,' Mathu said. 'They are independent-minded.'

'Chacko discusses everything with me.'

'People are different,' Mathu consoled.

Zeruba had never been close to his father, and had hardly ever lived with him. He had spent his entire childhood in his mother's home, studying in the village school there, as Korah, a briefless lawyer subsisting on the niggardly allowance given by his scornful mother, could not at that time afford to pay even the child's school fees. Later, by the time Korah got his inheritance on his mother's death and moved into his ancestral home, Zeruba was in college, and was at home only for a few weeks in the year, during vacations. They were strangers to each other.

'It must have been a wretched childhood for you, to be left there like an orphan,' Mathu said to Zeruba one day. 'I've always felt very bad about it.'

'Oh, I don't know,' Zeruba said. 'I've no recollection of being particularly unhappy.'

His mother's people were good to him, and he was fond of them. Theirs was a liberal and cultured family, and the village itself was highly literate and progressive. It was a fine environment for the precocious child to grow up in. One of his mother's grand-uncles was a well-known poet in Malayalam, and her own father loved to work on wood, sculpting tiny figurines. When Zeruba showed an aptitude for drawing, his uncle Isahaq encouraged him, supplying him with drawing paper, crayons and a box of watercolours.

There was a good collection of Malayalam and English books in the house—a few hundred books, which was exceptional for a village home in Kerala at this time—and there was also an excellent public library in the village, which even had a Malayalam translation of Tolstoy's *War and Peace*. Zeruba read voraciously whatever books he could get hold of. But by the time he was about twelve, his interests turned from literature to politics and philosophy, especially to communism. Lenin was his special hero, and the two-volume English translation of his collected works his Bible.

No one supervised his reading. He was free to buy or read any books he wanted. These were the years just before Indian independence, and the village hummed with political activity of every spectrum. And Zeruba, a hyperactive adolescent, plunged into the vortex—determined to save the world from inequity and oppression, no less! He joined the Student Federation, a wing of the Communist Party of India, and when the party was banned in the state soon after Indian independence, he ran an underground, hand-written revolutionary magazine. Again, no one interfered.

When Zeruba finished school he was sent off to college in Madras, as Korah had by then come into his inheritance, and could afford to educate him. He joined the Madras Christian College, a lovely campus in a four-hundred acre wooded estate in a city suburb, where his father and grandfather too had studied. This was the turning point in Zeruba's life, for in Madras he lost his political contacts, lost interest in politics itself, and turned to science. 'It's science and technology that will transform the world, not politics,' he loftily told Mathu when he returned home on his first vacation from college.

Zeruba did well in college, and after taking his MSc degree in chemistry, he went on to enrol as a doctoral candidate in biochemistry. This was not exactly the career that Korah had planned for Zeruba—he, bearing in mind his own dismal failure as a lawyer, had wanted Zeruba to become a doctor. Doctors always made money, whether it was war or peace, and whatever be the state of politics or economy, he pointed out. Zeruba was not tempted. He could not stand sick people, he said. Korah then acquiesced to Zeruba's decision, though without enthusiasm. But all hell broke loose when Zeruba decided to give up research after a couple of years and take up art. So Mathu, who was very fond of Zeruba, took on himself the mission to deal with the crisis and set out for Madras.

'I thought you were keen on biochemistry,' Mathu said, trying to dissuade Zeruba from abandoning his research.

'I was. I still am,' said Zeruba. 'But I'm not cut out for the academic world.'

'What's wrong?'

'It's drab and stifling, crowded with pompous mediocrities,' Zeruba said. 'It'll destroy what little originality and creativity I have.'

'It'll be even more frustrating in art,' Mathu warned.

'Why?'

'Because there are no objective criteria by which a painting can be valued,' Mathu said. 'Your success will depend on the whims of critics.'

'I'm not looking for fame in art, but for self-fulfilment,' Zeruba said. 'Besides, I want to live outside society, without social ties and constraints. And that's possible only for an artist.'

'But you've to earn a living.'

'I'll manage. My material needs are very simple.'

'Suppose you don't sell at all?'

'I don't think it'll come to that,' Zeruba said. 'I've already sold a couple of paintings. And I'm going to work very, very hard.'

Zeruba had been painting regularly ever since he took up research, to relieve the tedium of lab work, and found it immensely enjoyable, its pleasure direct and immediate. He had also participated in a couple of art exhibitions, and had received favourable critical attention. His artist friends were appreciative of his work, and that gave him the confidence to become a full-time artist.

'I may yet make something of my life,' he told Mathu.

'Your father is very upset,' said Mathu.

'He'll get over it.'

'Shouldn't you be thinking of his feelings? After all, you are the eldest son. You have special responsibilities.'

'My primary responsibility is to bring out what is struggling to be born from within me.'

'What do you want me to do?'

'I want to set up a studio,' Zeruba said. 'Buy a small plot of land on the beach in the suburb, and build a cottage there, where I can live as I please and paint as I please. I've some savings, but I would need financial support for a couple of years.'

'How much do you want?'

'I don't know. Land is very cheap in the area I'm thinking of, about ten or fifteen thousand rupees an acre. I need only half an acre. Then there's the building cost, and living expenses for a couple of years, till I start selling my paintings. Altogether maybe about fifty-sixty thousand rupees, maybe less.'

'I'll see what I can do,' said Mathu. 'But what if he doesn't agree?'

'Then I'll live in a mud hut,' Zeruba said firmly. 'But I'll not swerve from the course I've chosen.'

In the face of Zeruba's stubbornness, Korah finally yielded, but with sullen resentment and foreboding. He sold a small tract of land and sent the money to Zeruba.

'Who can stop him if he's set on ruining his life?' he said in resignation. 'It's all fate.'

Zeruba built his dream cottage on the beach in a remote southern suburb of Madras, just a large, slope-roofed, sunny hall, twenty-four feet by twenty-four feet, with an attached bathroom and a kitchenette, and a broad veranda along the front, facing the sea. The hall served as his studio-cum-living-cum-bedroom. It was a Spartan cottage, comfortable but basic, its only luxury being a ceramic bathtub. 'I absolutely need it,' Zeruba told Mathangi, his architect friend who designed the cottage.

Extending from the veranda and on level with it was a large platform enclosed by a low railing. This was covered with lush, marvellously springy Korean-grass, and served as a patio. In the inner left corner of the patio, right alongside the veranda, Zeruba planted a scarlet-flowered temple-tree, with a couple of its branches reaching into the veranda itself, integrating the cottage with the lawn and the landscape. The tree was known in folklore as the roost of goblins, and this association pleased Zeruba. Good company for the demons within him, he felt.

In the outer corner of the patio, diagonally across from the temple-tree, he planted a low shrub of gardenia, bordered with a semicircular bed of chrysanthemum, dahlia and zinnia, to draw the eye towards the sea and the horizon. He loved pottering about in the compound in a sort of throwback to the ways of his remote farming ancestors, and planted all sorts of fruit and flower trees and shrubs around the cottage. The cottage itself nestled under a giant rain tree, the most maternal of all trees—in fact, the tree was the reason why he chose that particular plot of land.

'This is perfect for me,' Zeruba said to himself when he moved into the cottage. But he had at one time very nearly scuttled the project, despairing over the endless hassles involved in registering the land in his name, in obtaining the various permissions required to build the cottage, and in getting electricity and telephone connections. What saved the project was the help of a genial tout who attached himself to Zeruba at the registrar's office, seeing him sitting weary and miserable on a bench in a corner.

'Don't worry about a thing,' the tout said, on finding out what it was that Zeruba wanted to get done. 'I'll take care of everything.'

'I won't give bribes,' Zeruba warned.

'You don't have to,' said the man. 'Leave everything to me.'

The tout was true to his word. He took five hundred rupees from Zeruba and set to work with expertise and finesse. The registrar's office was in a dilapidated old building, which was immediately identifiable as a government office by its distinctive musty odour of mouldy files and damp wooden furniture. Forlorn supplicants and eager touts were milling around, besieging officials, pushing papers, pleading in undertones. It was a grey, rainy day, and water from the leaky eaves of the building oozed down its grimy glass windows, like pus from putrid running sores. The registrar, a bespectacled and mild-mannered gent dressed in crisp, white khadi clothes, read Zeruba's purchase deed with ponderous deliberation, clucking softly every now and then in gentle disapproval. Finally, he dropped the papers on the table in weary disgust, and informed Zeruba that he could not register the deed, as there were many flaws in it.

And Zeruba, ignorant of the ways of the world, rose from his seat and told him, 'Alright, I'll get it redrafted.'

The officer looked up at him in surprise.

'Please do sit down, sir,' he said softly. 'There is a solution.'

Indeed there was, as the tout whispered in Zeruba's ears. The tout dropped two hundred rupee notes into the open table drawer of the officer, who then smiled at Zeruba benignly and endorsed his document. There was nothing furtive about it at all. The bribe was given openly, in a room with a number of people moving about in it. No one paid the slightest attention to the transaction.

Zeruba and the tout then moved on to the officer's deputy, and then to the upper and lower division clerks, each of whom had left a table drawer helpfully open. The prescribed ritual was repeated at each table, with only the money dropped diminishing as they moved down the official ladder. The office peon, who did not have a table, stretched out his shirt pocket, barely glancing at the tout when he dropped a tenner into it.

'Everybody taken care of,' the tout informed Zeruba cheerily.

'Why the peon?' Zeruba asked.

'Very important person,' said the tout. 'He can misplace or lose your papers.'

3

Moving into the cottage, Zeruba soon fell into a tight and unvarying routine of work and play. He woke up very early in the morning, at four, and had two cups of steaming tea sitting in a deckchair on the patio, watching the slow blushing of the horizon over the sea. It was a time of absolute peace and quiet, and was the most valued moment of his day. He then spent an hour on yoga and meditation, after which he went for a stroll on the beach till sunrise, taking slow, deep breaths of the crisp pre-dawn air rich in neural nutrients, and working out ideas for paintings. Returning to the cottage, he had a shower, and then read the day's newspaper sitting in the veranda.

He prepared his own breakfast, which was his heaviest meal of the day, with plenty of fish or meat, a huge bowl of raw vegetables tossed in vinegar and salt, several slices of buttered toast, a half-boiled egg, and a glass of milk. After breakfast he set to work, painting steadily till lunchtime. The lunch was prepared and served by his maid, and usually consisted of two chapathis served with lentils and fish or meat, a small scoop of rice with curds and pickles, topped off with a cup of pazha-pradhaman, his favourite dessert, made of sliced banana fried in ghee and then boiled in milk and sugar. He rested for an hour after lunch, and then painted till sundown. Every day at dusk he went for a jog along the beach, and afterwards immersed himself in the bathtub for about half an hour—to cool his body and launder his mind, as he told Mathangi, explaining why he needed the tub. Then, reclining in a deckchair on the patio, he had a drink or two with a small bowl of peanuts. He had no dinner, but ate some fruits, usually a pomegranate or a bunch of grapes, and relaxed till bedtime, reading a book. He had very few friends, and hardly any social life.

The maid who prepared his lunch was godsend. He had noticed her while the cottage was being built, and was struck by the extraordinary brightness of her eyes, as she stood watching the construction work from the doorway of her mud hovel in the slum colony behind Zeruba's compound. Then one morning soon after he moved into the cottage, when he was sitting in the veranda reading the newspaper, she came to see him, dressed in a dirty yellow sari and blouse, her face unwashed, hair uncombed.

'Have you any work for me?' she asked.

He lowered the newspaper and regarded her silently for a long moment. She had an oval face with an open brow, a pert nose, and a soft, slightly pouty mouth. Her waist was slender, her breasts full. But her most striking features were her eyes— enormous and limpid under thick, long lashes, they shone with mesmerizing luminosity. As he looked her over, she stood calm and relaxed before him, entirely unselfconscious, neither pleased nor displeased with his scrutiny. But there was a faint hint of amusement in her eyes, and seeing this, he smiled back. Instantly the twinkle in her eyes vanished.

'Come close,' he said.

She frowned and did not move.

'Don't be uneasy,' he said. 'I only want to look at your hands.'

She went over and stretched out her hands to him. The lines on her palms were fine and sharply etched, the headline stretching straight across the entire width of the palm. Her fingers were long and beautifully tapered. This girl does not belong to the slum, he thought.

'Turn over your hands,' he said.

Her nails were smooth and pink, but caked with dirt.

'What's your name?' he asked.

'Lachmi.'

'Lakshmi,' he corrected her. 'Your name is Lakshmi, not Lachmi. How old are you?'

'Eighteen,' she said. 'Are you a *josyan*?' A fortune-teller?

'I know a little of everything,' he said. 'What work can you do?'

'What work do you have?'

'Sweeping, washing and cooking.'

'I don't know any cooking.'

'I'll teach you.'

'How much will you pay?'

'We'll decide that later,' he said. 'But first I want to talk to your mother and father. Ask them to come and see me.'

'I've no father,' she said.

'What happened?'

'He ran away somewhere.'

'Alright. Bring your mother.'

4

Lakshmi's mother, an emaciated little woman with dead eyes, came immediately. Her husband, a mason, had disappeared some years ago, and she did not know where he was or what had happened to him. She had four daughters, two older than Lakshmi and one younger, and all of them eked out a living doing odd jobs. None of them had gone to school even for a day, and none of them were married.

'We have no money,' she said wearily. 'How can I marry them off without money?'

'Alright,' said Zeruba. 'I'll employ Lakshmi.'

'How much will you pay?'

'I'll pay well,' he said.

'How much?'

'I'll pay her two hundred rupees a month,' he said, and Lakshmi gasped in astonishment, covering her mouth with her hand. It was a princely sum in the late 1950s, and was in fact about the same amount as the stipend that Zeruba had received as a research scholar. Lakshmi's mother remained impassive.

'What's the work she has to do?' she asked.

'All the housework—sweeping the compound, cleaning the house, washing clothes, and cooking,' he said. 'She should come in the morning at eight, and leave at four in the afternoon, after serving me tea. She can have one meal here and have tea twice.'

'Where's your wife?' the woman asked.

'I'm not married,' he said.

'You're alone?'

'Yes.'

'How can I send Lachmi to a young man who lives alone?' she asked. 'I won't do that.'

'Listen to me carefully and then decide,' Zeruba said. 'I'm going to speak to you openly, concealing nothing. Lakshmi is a very bright girl, and I can save her from her squalid life. You have four daughters, give this one to me. I'll take care of all her needs, and she'll come to absolutely no harm from me. And, apart from the salary, I'll give her a bonus of a thousand rupees for every full year she works for me, which you can save for her dowry.'

'What'll people say?' she demurred.

'What does it matter what people say?' he asked. 'Are they helping you in any way now?'

'It's not right.'

'Alright, we'll leave it, then,' he said, rising. He looked at Lakshmi.

'I'll work,' she said, intervening in the conversation for the first time.

'There's no need for you to decide now,' he said. 'Go home, think it over, discuss it with your mother, and let me know tomorrow.'

They turned to go, but Zeruba called them back.

'If you decide to send Lakshmi,' he told the mother, 'she should bathe and wear clean clothes when she comes here.'

'Every day?'

'Yes.'

'That'd be difficult,' the woman said. 'Where'll she bathe every day?'

'She can use the workmen's lavatory and bathroom in that corner of the compound,' he said. 'And I'll buy her two sets of clothes right away.'

The woman remained silent.

'One other thing,' continued Zeruba. 'I'll deal only with Lakshmi. No one else should come to me to ask for anything or interfere in my life in any way. If that happens, that very day I'll dismiss Lakshmi. Think over all this and let me know tomorrow.'

'When should I start working?' Lakshmi asked.

'Do you go to temple?' he asked.

'Sometimes,' she said.

'Go this Friday. Oil your head and take a bath, and wear fresh clothes. And ask for god's blessing for your new life. Then come to me.'

Lakshmi came early next morning to say that her mother had agreed to let her work for him. She had oiled her hair and had taken a bath, and even wore a clean though threadbare sari.

'Good,' said Zeruba.

'But I too have a condition,' she said.

'Condition! What?'

'Of the two hundred rupees a month you have promised me, give seventy-five rupees to my mother for family expenses, and give twenty-five rupees to me for my personal expenses. The remaining money you should save for me.'

'Excellent,' said Zeruba. 'In fact, I'll do more than save the money for you. For every rupee you save, I'll add an equal amount. This is in addition to the thousand-rupee yearly bonus I have promised you.'

'*Nandri*,' she said gravely. Thanks.

'But ask your mother to come and speak to me.'

'I'm the one to decide about my life,' she said.

Zeruba smiled. 'True,' he said. 'But bring her just this one time.'

So she went and brought her right away.

'Do you agree?' he asked.

'She has decided,' the woman said, nodding peevishly towards Lakshmi. 'What is there for me to decide?'

'You know the arrangement about the salary?'

'Yes', she said.

5

On Friday morning, Lakshmi came to the cottage directly from the temple, wearing a clean sari and a bright smile. Her hair was combed back tight and braided into a thick plait at the back, and was adorned with a small string of jasmines. Her dark-brown skin, oiled and scrubbed, shone like burnished rosewood and she wore a neat red tilak on her forehead. Coming into the veranda to where Zeruba stood, she bent over and reverentially touched his feet with her fingertips.

'Save me, Iyya,' she said.

'I'll save you,' he said, touched by her earnestness. 'And you'll save me.'

Taking her inside, he presented her with the two saris and blouse-pieces that he had bought for her, and placed on them a pair of tiny gold earrings, conforming to his family tradition that any new beginning should be marked by a gift of gold. He then showed her around the cottage, and told her of the work she had to do.

'Don't try to do everything today itself,' he told her. 'Begin slowly and learn along the way.'

'Yes, Iyya.'

'By the way, what did you say your name is?' he asked.

'Lakshmi,' she enunciated clearly.

'Not Lachmi?' he asked, laughing.

'No, it's Lakshmi, Iyya,' she said, shyly joining him in laughter.

Zeruba did not like being called Iyya, sire, but he let it be for the time being. But after about a month he told her one day, 'Don't call me Iyya hereafter.'

'Iyya?'

'It sounds slavish,' he said. 'I don't like it.'

'But I'm your servant.'

'I make no distinction between the high and the low. So don't call me Iyya.'

'What shall I call you, then?'

The choice was between Mama, uncle, and Anna, elder brother. 'You can call me Anna,' he said.

She looked doubtful. It sounded too casual to her.

'Or you can call me Mama,' he said, seeing her hesitation.

'I'll call you Mama,' she said. The term was both respectful and affectionate. And it had resonances of intimacy, as girls often married their maternal uncles.

From that day on, the nature of their relationship began to change. Entirely comfortable with each other now, they soon developed a warm, easy intimacy, joshing each other and sharing their droll experiences. But Lakshmi was essentially a serious person, with a compulsive need to improve herself. And Zeruba, finding her keen and intelligent, took on himself the task of educating her. He taught her to read and write English, also arithmetic, while she taught herself to read and write Tamil with the help of a neighbourhood child. She spent every spare minute she had in practising reading and writing. A quick learner, with an exceptionally retentive memory, she became quite fluent in English in about four years, and began devouring the books in the cottage, especially biographies and books on religion and philosophy. But she had no interest in fiction. Nor did she have any aptitude for art. Her focus was sensibly on what she needed to learn to cope with life.

The Pygmalion-like transformation of Lakshmi from a dirty, dishevelled, illiterate slum girl, to a clean, well-groomed and gracious young woman, was rapid, almost incredible. Her wisdom was, however, innate rather than acquired from books, and her culture was essentially of character, not just a cultivated veneer.

Meanwhile, within a few months of she joining him, in fact, they had become lovers, sliding into that intimacy without deliberation or self-consciousness, as a natural expression of their deepening relationship. Lakshmi's sexuality was like cold fire, passion without heat. Her body was always cool to touch, wherever he touched her and whatever the season. Making love to her was something of a holistic experience for him, refreshing to the mind as well as to the body. And gradually, over the years, he came to regard her more as his helpmate and companion than as a servant, though there still remained a wide cultural gap between them.

Their beautiful relationship endured for six years, and those were the happiest years in Zeruba's life.

'I feel wonderfully rejuvenated,' he wrote to Mathu, without mentioning Lakshmi. 'This is the life for me.'

Then one day he ran into Aditi. And together they plummeted headlong into a living hell.

Aditi

1

By the mid-1960s, Zeruba, who was around thirty then, had become something of a celebrity in Madras, and was much lionized by society ladies. To have one or two of his paintings at home or office was considered a status symbol, especially as they were quite expensive. The media acclaimed his style as an exciting fusion of Western techniques and Indian imagination. One eminent art critic presumed to see his paintings as 'potent and thoroughly modern existentialist interpretations of ancient Indian mythologies, which are here shredded and then reassembled in the hellish electric forge of contemporary ontological angst'. Another critic wrote of the 'relentless, explosive missile lock on contemporary reality' in his paintings. These extravagant comments and his own sullen reclusiveness enveloped Zeruba in an aura of mystery, and fuelled public interest in him. He was thought to be an intellectual. And there were dark rumours about his private life.

Zeruba thus became a fixture at consular and high society cocktail parties, where he always took up his position near the bar, methodically fortifying himself with liquid nurture. He made quite a striking figure, standing there aloof, dressed in calf-length raw silk kurta and cotton churidar. His thick mop of hair, parted neatly in the middle, fell smoothly to his shoulders, and his full beard was neatly trimmed and brushed. Tall, a six-footer, he seemed even taller, huge in fact, because of his barrel-chested, broad-shouldered build and erect bearing. His light brown skin glowed with health. But he was by no means handsome, his face overlong and dominated by an immense, hooked Semitic nose, his eyes small and deep-set, his cheekbones so prominent as to seem like incipient tusks. His voice had a peculiar timbre, as if spoken from inside a deep well, and at parties he usually wore a sombre frown, which was taken by everyone as the mark of some awful and unspeakable inner turmoil.

Zeruba did not particularly enjoy these parties, of women synthesized in beauty parlours, and men hollow except for the stuffing of money in them. But these people were his patrons, and he had to cultivate them. Besides, though the guests were dull, and the conversation vapid—the highbrow babble of the no-brows, as he thought of them—the Scotch was always good. And sometimes, though rarely, he met someone interesting. And it was at one such party, a cast party thrown by a local amateur theatre group at the home of a socialite, that Zeruba first met Aditi. They were introduced by Mathangi, who had designed the stage set for the production.

'Here's someone desperate to meet you, Dada,' Mathangi said. Dada was her name for Zeruba, and it had caught on.

'Desperately drunk,' Aditi chortled.

'Watch out,' Mathangi warned. 'She's a maneater.'

'I am! I am!' Aditi burst out, waving her glass of gin and lime.

Zeruba looked her over sombrely. Her cheeks, he noticed, were heavily dimpled, the sure mark of a born liar. She was tall and well-endowed, a bit plump, but robust and shapely, with a burnt-gold complexion and glistening, pearly teeth. A trifle too oomphy. A trifle too fleshy. But voluptuous. And very vivacious. A whirling Aphrodite, crackling with brio! Aditi, Zeruba recalled, is the name of the great alpha female celebrated in the Rig-Veda as the mother of gods—the goddess of infinity, of the heaven and the earth, the goddess of inexhaustible abundance.

Aditi gazed at him with open, brazen lust. *Look at me, man,* her expression said. *See how desirable I am! Lush and full of juice. Don't you want to take me in your arms?*

'Eat me,' he said.

'Aaaaargh!' she snarled, baring her teeth.

She was dead drunk. And he himself was feeling a trifle reckless.

'Go for the jugular, kids,' Mathangi said. 'I'm going to get a drink.'

'So you're our resident Picasso?' Aditi teased.

'Dali,' he said.

'What?'

'Dali is the name.'

'Oh!' she said. 'Salvador?'

'*Si, senorita.*'

'*Comment allez vous, monsieur?*' she asked with a mock curtsy.

'You're cheating,' he said. 'That's French, not Spanish.'

'What do facts matter to a surrealist?' she scorned.

'*Touché!*'

'Doesn't anyone call you by your real name?'

'Only strangers,' he said. 'I don't like my name.'

'Oh, I love the name,' she said, roaring with drunken laughter. 'Sounds like so many bells ringing together. Zerubbabel-*bell*!' He then told her how he came to have his strange name, and she laughed some more.

'When do I get to see your paintings, Bell-bell?' she asked.

'Anytime,' he said. 'Whenever you want.'

'Today? Now?'

'Sure,' he said. 'As you wish.'

'You've a vehicle? Scooter?'

'I've a tin box,' he said.

'Fine,' she said, putting a hand over his shoulder and pressing her breasts against him. 'Let's ride the *dabba*.'

In the car, his hand on the ignition key, he asked, '*Chalen?*'

'Okay, let's rip,' she said, snuggling against him and clasping his arm tight against her bosom.

'Hey, let go,' he said. 'I'm a two-fisted driver.'

'You aren't going to kiss me, are you?' she taunted.

'Why not?' he asked, turning in the seat to face her.

'Don't,' she warned. 'If you kiss me, I won't be able to stop.'

So he kissed her, and she very nearly tipped the little car over in her desperate, convulsive response, latching on to his mouth like a vacuum cleaner gone berserk. And the seed of a faint doubt took root in his mind. What's wrong with her, he wondered. Why is she so desperate? But he said nothing.

2

Zeruba drove down Mount Road, the arterial road of Madras, which had a fair amount of traffic even at this time, though it was nearly midnight, but once he turned into Cathedral Road, he had the way virtually all to himself. He drove sedately through the rain-washed, slumbering city. The air was cool, and the city, though filthy and leprous in daylight, now seemed almost romantic in the faint glow of moonlight filtering through wispy clouds. Further down, Mowbray's Road, flanked by immense avenue trees, was a tunnel of green. Here there was no traffic at all. And the only sounds were the sibilant squelch of Zeruba's car tyres over the wet blacktop and the low hum of his perfectly tuned car engine. A great calm descended on Zeruba as he drove on, and for a moment he forgot Aditi sitting beside him, and was lost in the thought-free serenity of the still moment.

'Doesn't this jalopy go any faster?' Aditi asked, nuzzling his ears.

He pulled over to the kerb and stopped the car.

'This isn't a jalopy,' he said in mock anger, to conceal his real anger at her for fracturing the perfect moment. 'This is one of the most beautiful cars ever made. And it has been maintained beautifully.'

'My! My! Aren't we proud!' she laughed.

'I am,' he said.

The car was an early model Mayflower, manufactured by the Standard Motor Company of the UK, and was a family heirloom, which Zeruba had brought to Madras after his father, who never stirred out of the family compound anymore, stopped using it. It was a small, but uniquely elegant car, with contours of classic perfection, a work of art. Zeruba leaned over and lightly kissed its grooved steering wheel. 'It's a haiku of a car,' he said.

'Okay, okay, but let's go,' Aditi urged. '*Chalo!*'

He put the car in gear and drove on.

'Come on, Dada, go faster,' she said. 'Won't this go any faster?'

'It would,' he said. 'But Zeruba won't go any faster.'

'I'll help,' she said, and stretching a leg over his knees, slammed her foot down on the accelerator, sending the car into a wild skid on the rain-slicked road.

'You'll kill us both,' he said, struggling to regain control of the car.

'I will,' she purred. 'But not yet.'

South of Adyar, the car emerged from the cavernous belly of the city into the open countryside. Aditi sat morosely slumped in her seat, disgusted with his placid driving. He ignored her. A few kilometres down the Mamallapuram road, Zeruba shifted down to the second gear, and turned into a sandy path through a grove of casuarina trees humming to each other, passed a cluster of huts huddled in sleep, and drove into his compound and parked.

'Close your eyes,' he told Aditi, and, holding his hands over her eyes, led her blindly to the railing of his patio. It was a full-moon night, and the clouds had cleared.

'Look,' he said, taking off his hands.

As she opened her eyes, there suddenly rose before her the infinite, rippling, moon-bathed expanse of the molten silver sea, with the moon itself hanging a third way up the horizon, like a giant sandalwood-paste tilak on the bare, blue-grey vault of the sky. The suddenness of the scene was breathtaking, and Aditi let out a long, low whistle of entranced surprise. Everything was eerily still and quiet.

'This is out of the world,' she said, her mouth agape.

Zeruba, pleased with her enchantment, hugged her lightly from behind. Above them, the rain tree sighed, rustled by the sea breeze.

'It is,' he whispered. 'We're now one with Brahma. This is the moment to die.'

'Not yet,' she said, turning and putting her arms around him.

'Well then, later,' he said, laughing.

'Don't you ever get lonely here?' she asked.

'No,' he said. 'The sea is a good companion.'

'This place gives me the shivers,' she said. 'Let's go in.'

The moment they entered the cottage, her mood turned predatory again.

'Give me a drink, Dada,' she said.

'I've only rum,' Zeruba said.

'Any fucking thing,' she said.

'Neat?'

'Fine.'

He went into the kitchen and brought her a tot glass of rum. She drank it in one gulp and tossed the glass to him.

'One more,' she said.

He poured her another drink, and she drank that too in a gulp.

'I too have something very special to show you,' she said, handing him the glass.

'What?'

'Watch.'

As he watched, she stripped off her clothes one by one with flamboyant, drunken abandon, flinging away each piece with comic theatricality. Totally naked, she then unpinned her coiffure, shook loose her spectacularly abundant, knee-length hair, and struck a pensively alluring pose, with one hand lightly on her chest, and the other covering her pubes with the end of her cascading hair.

'Guess who?'

'Botticelli?' he asked. He couldn't help laughing. *'The Birth of Venus?'*

'Right,' she guffawed and flung herself into the bed.

'Come,' she said, holding both arms out to him.

'Give me a minute,' he said.

Fastidious and methodical, he put away the tot-glass, drew the curtains, brushed his teeth, undressed and got into bed with her.

'I've a confession to make,' she said.

'What?'

'I'm not a virgin.'

Zeruba chuckled.

'Nor am I,' he said.

3

The next morning, Lakshmi caught them in bed. Aditi slumbered on but Zeruba immediately got up, wrapped a lungi around his waist, lit a cigarette, and went and sat in the veranda. Lakshmi then brought him the newspaper and a cup of tea, as usual. She paused momentarily as she handed him the cup, as if about to say something, but checked herself. He himself said nothing. And she went about her work, calmly, quietly, showing no emotion whatsoever. She even made a cup of tea for Aditi, and brought it to her as soon as she woke up.

'Who's this?' Aditi asked, sitting up bolt upright in bed, her eyes popping.

'Lakshmi, my housekeeper,' Zeruba said evenly.

'Arre-wow!' Aditi exclaimed with a broad, leering smile. 'She's very, very pretty.'

'She's a wonderful person.'

'Do you screw her?'

'Pardon?'

'I asked, do you f.u.c.k her?'

34

'*Je ne comprends pas*,' he said. 'What's effuseekay?'

She threw a pillow at him. 'What time is it?' she asked.

'Quarter past nine.'

'Oh my god! I'm late. I've a meeting.' She was a PR consultant.

'What time?'

'At ten.'

She flung away the sheet covering her and pelted naked out of the bed into the bathroom, not minding Lakshmi dusting the furniture. Zeruba glanced at Lakshmi, but her sensitive face had turned into an impassive mask. She didn't say anything even when he returned to the cottage after dropping Aditi off at her flat. On the way back he had bought for her a thick string of jasmines, and he now went up to her as she stood at the kitchen counter rolling chapathis and fixed the flowers on her hair. She tensed at his touch, but went on with her work.

'Lakshmi,' he said, 'you knew that this had to happen sometime.'

At his words she broke down, and as he turned her towards him, she collapsed into his arms, sobbing inconsolably. He held her in a gentle embrace, resting his cheek on the crown of her head. Neither of them said a word. After a while she calmed down, wiped her face with the end of her sari, and smiling through tears said, 'I know my place, Mama. I know you have to find a mate from your own class to share your life.' Droplets of tears sparkled on her eyelashes.

'I was so unprepared,' she said. 'This was so sudden.'

'It was sudden for me too,' he said. 'I met her only just last night. What happened, happened only because we were both so drunk. I doubt whether it'll lead to anything. I don't even know whether we will ever see each other again.'

4

Lakshmi cried her heart out that night, but she was dry-eyed and calm when she came to the cottage the next morning. One phase of her life was now over, she knew. She had to prepare herself for another life now.

Later that day, around five in the evening, while Zeruba was at the easel, Aditi unexpectedly roared into the compound on a sap-green moped. He saw her through the window and went out into the veranda to receive her. She walked up to him briskly, with springy steps and a self-assured smile.

'Surprise, surprise,' she said.

'A pleasant surprise,' he said politely, but without enthusiasm.

'I've come to see your paintings, Dada,' she said. 'Yesterday I was too drunk, and so many things happened, that I didn't even look at them.'

He showed her his works.

'I see Lakshmi in some of these.'

'Yes, she has modelled for me.'

'You're very fond of her?'

'Yes, I am,' he said. 'She's the best thing that has ever happened in my life.'

'Where's she?'

'Gone home.'

'Where does she live?'

'Right behind the cottage.'

Aditi immediately took off to see Lakshmi—she had, she said, brought her a sari, to make up for the shock she had given her the previous day. And Zeruba, reconciled that he would not be able to work any more that day, cleaned his brushes and went and sat on the patio to wait for Aditi, vaguely wondering what she was up to. A pair of squirrels were playing tag on the rain tree, watched by a flock of cheering sparrows. When Aditi returned, she pulled out a deckchair from the veranda and sat next to Zeruba, her legs propped up against the railing of the patio.

36

'Got a cigarette?' she asked.

He lit one for her, and she sat there silently for a while, blowing smoke rings.

'I don't know what came over me yesterday,' she said after a while, flicking off the half-smoked cigarette over the railing.

'You don't have to explain anything,' he said.

'I was dead drunk. I'm not usually like this. It won't happen again.'

'As you wish,' he said.

But Aditi spent that night too in the cottage. Gradually, and somewhat uncomfortably, Zeruba found himself in a whirl with her. From the very beginning, she took over from him the patronage of Lakshmi, showering her with generous gifts. Both Zeruba and Lakshmi were uncomfortable about this, but could do nothing to stop her. Lakshmi kept out of her way as much as possible, intuitively sensing in Aditi's insistent and overwhelming generosity a troubled and secretly rapacious soul. It took Zeruba a great deal longer to realize the true nature of Aditi, and by then it was too late for him to save himself.

5

From the time Aditi spent her first night in the cottage, Zeruba and Lakshmi avoided any sexual intimacy. He still yearned for the soothing comfort of her lovemaking, and did once ask her to spend the night with him, but she said, 'It'll be wrong.'

'Why Lakshmi?' he asked. 'Why are you denying me?'

'I'm denying myself,' she said.

He did not press her. *Yes,* he thought, *this is the best way to end this relationship, nipping it off in its full bloom and saving the memory, before its fragrance turns stale*. But what lay ahead for him? He feared that his life, which had been gliding along placidly, was now, in his turbulent relationship with Aditi, spinning out of control and tumbling—into what fatality, he did not know.

Aditi pursued Zeruba relentlessly, giving him no time even to pause and think what to do. Her very vitality and high spirits, her flaming impetuosity, which made him shrink from her, also drew him irresistibly to her. It was as if he had bitten into something that was too sweet to spit out and too bitter to swallow—though, if anyone had asked him what was sweet about the affair, he would have been stumped for an answer.

Then one night, a few months after they first met, as they lay in bed, Aditi turned to him, and resting her head on his shoulder, began running her hand through the inch-thick mat of hair on his chest. This, he knew from experience, was her preliminary gesture before making some troublesome or time-wasting demand on him. He waited.

'You know, Dada, at one time I used to pity you, thinking who would marry a man with so much body hair. Ugh! Like a gorilla,' she said. 'I didn't like your dick either. Looked like a donkey's thing. I thought it'd be pink.'

'What's it, Adi?' he asked. 'What's it that you want to tell me?'

'I'm pregnant,' she said, tilting her head and looking into his eyes.

He relaxed. A manageable problem, he thought. There were only two options before them. Either they should now get married, or she should have an abortion. She would probably choose abortion, he believed, and that would be his preference too. But the choice had to come from her. He couldn't possibly suggest abortion to her.

'You've nothing to say?' Aditi asked, sliding off his chest and propping herself up on pillows against the headboard.

'We should get married immediately,' he said.

'Right,' she said.

Zeruba's immediate concern was to see Lakshmi settled properly, before he himself took the plunge. This was not merely a matter of sentiment for him, but of doing the right thing and being true to his word. But he was at a loss as to how to go about arranging her marriage. Fortunately, Aditi took the task upon herself, and set about it with her usual zest and resoluteness. She had many friends among Madras businessmen and industrialists, people known to her through her family and through her PR work.

'What's the dowry you're going to give her?' she asked Zeruba.

Zeruba had raised Lakshmi's monthly salary by fifty rupees every year, but she continued to take home only hundred rupees a month as in the beginning, so her savings, along with his matching contribution to her savings and the bonus she had earned, now amounted to a very substantial amount.

'I've worked it out,' he said. 'She would receive about thirty-eight thousand rupees.'

'Make it forty,' Aditi said.

'Okay.'

'That's a princely sum. With that dowry we should be able to marry her off very well.'

'It won't be a dowry,' he said. 'The money will remain in her name.'

'Leave it all to me,' she said.

Aditi did indeed find a perfect match for Lakshmi, a young man named Gopal, who had an engineering diploma and was a mechanic with a leading industrial house in the city. She made discreet inquiries about him with the personnel manager of the factory where he worked, and, on Zeruba's suggestion, also got a high-ranking police officer to order one of his subordinates to check out his family at their place of residence. All the reports about him were positive. The personnel manager was all praise for Gopal's integrity and hard work, and the police officer reported that his family, though poor, was held in high esteem by their neighbours. Gopal himself made a good impression on Zeruba when he came to see him. He had an open face, and was polite and mild-mannered.

'I'm endowing Lakshmi with a very large sum of money,' Zeruba told him.

'Amma told me, sir,' he said.

'It will remain her money, and will be held as a joint fixed deposit in a bank in her and my name. It can be withdrawn only by both of us signing the document,' Zeruba said. 'I'm doing this to make Lakshmi's future absolutely secure. You seem to be a decent young man, and I'm sure that you will take good care of her. Still, I've to take this precaution.'

'I understand, sir,' Gopal said.

'You're welcome to invest the money, but the investment will have to be made in her name. Have you given any thought to what you would like to do with the money?'

'Yes, I have, sir,' Gopal said. 'I plan set up a small workshop in her name, to do subcontract work for my factory.'

'You are planning to resign your job?'

'No, sir. Lakshmi can manage the workshop, and I'll work there after factory hours.'

'If everything goes well, you can resign your job later.'

'Yes, sir.'

'Well, first of all you and Lakshmi will have to meet and approve of each other.'

'I've asked him to come again on Sunday evening,' said Aditi.

'Fine,' Zeruba said.

Unknown to Zeruba, Aditi had already arranged a brief meeting between the two, and she had their consent to proceed with the arrangements. Lakshmi's mother was kept informed of the developments, but was not allowed to interfere in any way. On Sunday, Aditi herself dressed Lakshmi, and when Gopal arrived, she made him sit on a cane chair in the veranda and had Lakshmi bring him a cup of coffee in a silver tumbler. Later, she persuaded them to go and sit on the beach and have a chat. When

40

they returned, Zeruba noticed that Lakshmi's face was flushed, and he felt a momentary stab of jealousy. She immediately left for her house.

'Lakshmi is like a sister to me,' Zeruba told Gopal. 'Her happiness if of the highest importance to me.'

'May I say something, sir?' Gopal asked.

'Yes?'

Gopal looked at Aditi doubtfully.

'It's alright,' Zeruba said. 'We've no secrets between us.'

'Sir, Lakshmi has told me everything,' he said. 'I tried to stop her, but she insisted that I should know everything about her before making my decision.'

'Well, we had a different kind of relationship at one time,' Zeruba said. 'But now she is like a sister to me. Truly.'

'Who hasn't transgressed in life!' Aditi said.

'I too have sinned, sir,' Gopal said.

'The important thing is to put the past behind you and move on,' Zeruba said.

'I accept what happened,' Gopal said. 'And I know that you're an honourable man and you'll do nothing to harm my family, and that there'll be nothing between you and Lakshmi hereafter.'

'I'll give you my word of honour on that,' Zeruba said.

7

Uncharacteristically, it was Zeruba who broke down when Lakshmi finally took leave of him.

'You have always been strong, Mama, why are you distressed now?' she asked.

'I fear for my own future,' he said.

'Mama, you had taught me so much about Buddha,' she said. 'Why have you forgotten all that?'

True, Zeruba thought. All things pass. Despair is the shadow of hope, sorrow the inevitable denouement of every happiness.

Every bond ends in separation, and everything in life ultimately ends in desolation. Everything. It would therefore be wise not to have any strong attachments for anything or anybody. This was what Zeruba used to tell Lakshmi. And it was all true. But how hard it was for him to reconcile himself to this Buddhist wisdom in his own life!

'Our happiness together is now over,' she told him decisively. 'For you and for me.'

'Yes, you're right,' he sighed. 'Who knows what the future holds for us? Maybe it would be better. Maybe it would be worse. But let's not worry about it now.'

'You told Gopal that I'm like a sister to you now,' Lakshmi said. 'That's how I'll be to you from now on, Mama. A sister. And I'll be with you always.'

Then she embraced him for the last time.

Every detail of Lakshmi's wedding was arranged by Aditi, and everything went off perfectly. Lakshmi then moved in with Gopal and his aged parents in Ambathur, at the other end of the city from where Zeruba lived. Two weeks later, Zeruba married Aditi, at a quiet wedding in the presence of just a few friends.

Rama Durai

1

Aditi was an orphan, and was brought up by her aunt after her parents died in a car accident when she was around four. Theirs was a prominent zemindari family of Rajakottai, a middling town about sixty kilometres south-west of Madras. The family was said to be under a curse, as a result of which only daughters had been born there in the last couple of centuries, that too only two in each generation. The family's response to the predicament was to marry off the elder daughter with a dowry and send her off to live with her husband, and to adopt the younger daughter's husband, usually a close relative, into the family as the heir.

Aditi's mother was the younger of the two daughters of her generation, and she and her husband were a well-known and respected couple in Tamil Nadu, honoured as much for their cultural accomplishments as for their wealth and aristocratic lineage—she was a proficient Carnatic musician, and he a distinguished scholar. Aditi was the older of their two daughters. When her parents died, her mother's sister, who had no children of her own, came to live in Rajakottai to take care of the children and manage the family properties. She was an energetic and competent woman, and the affairs of the family ran smoothly under her care. But she had problems with her husband, Rama Durai. A colonel in the army, he had dutifully resigned his commission and had moved to Rajakottai to help his wife with her responsibilities, but soon got so utterly bored with the dreary monotony of small-town life that he grimly took to a life of sloth and effete debauchery.

The girls were sent off to a boarding school in Madras when they were about six, and were at home only during vacations, so the couple lived all by themselves in their immense four-storeyed family mansion in the town. Their living quarters were on the first floor of the building, where they had their bedrooms. On the ground floor were the kitchen, storerooms, servants' rooms and guestrooms, as well as a huge drawing room with a Mughal style canopied seat at the far end for the head of the family. The top two floors of the building were kept shuttered, and were opened only to put up relatives on special occasions.

Aditi was born in this house on Father's Day in 1943. And it was on a Father's Day fifteen years later that there took place the traumatic event that fissured her life and gradually turned her into the frenetic person that she eventually became. The two sisters were home for the summer vacation at this time. On that fatal Sunday in June, there was an important festival at the local Shiva temple, which was by tradition organized by the zemindar, so all the members of the family, including visiting relatives and all the servants, had gone to the temple for the evening rites—all except Aditi, who could not go because of a hip sprain, and Rama Durai, who paid his devotions only to the bottle. When everyone left, Rama Durai ensconced himself in bed, with a bottle of scotch and a soda siphon on the bedside table, and sat listening to radio music, which was his favourite pastime. When he saw Aditi limping past his room, he called her to him.

'How is the sprain?' he asked.

'It still hurts,' she said.

'Come and sit here,' he said, patting the bed beside him. 'I'm feeling sad and lonely.'

'Why, Uncle?'

'I don't know,' he said. 'I just feel miserable.'

She went and sat on the bed.

'You want a drink?' he asked.

44

'Goodness! No!' she said.

'Have just a little,' he said. 'It'll ease the pain.'

So she took a sip. Then some more.

'What are you doing for the sprain?' he asked.

'I apply the balm given by the *vaidyan*.'

'Don't you get it massaged?'

'No. I just apply the balm.'

'You must massage. You can do it yourself.'

'I don't know how.'

'I'll show you,' he said, sitting up against the headboard. 'It's on the right side?'

'Yes,' she said.

'Here?' he asked, pressing his thumb against her hip bone.

'Ouch! It hurts,' she cried.

'Have another sip,' he said, extending his glass.

So she took a couple more swallows of whisky.

'Don't you feel better now?'

'I feel drunk.'

'Good. It'll ease the pain,' he said. 'Come, I'll show you how to massage yourself.'

He massaged her hip gently with his fingers.

'Does it hurt?'

'It's nice,' she said.

As he went on massaging, she could see a tumescence rising mountainously from beneath his dhoti. She smiled shyly when he caught her looking.

'This is not the right way to massage,' he said. 'When you do it yourself, you should massage directly on the hip, not over the skirt.'

'Yes,' she said.

'I'll show you,' he said, slipping his hand under her skirt. 'Like this, see.'

The girl, quite drunk now, made no objection.

'It's nice,' she said.

There was still a trace of the medicinal oil on her skin, so his

45

hand slid smoothly on her taut young flesh, and every now and then his fingers strayed to her crotch, brushing against its silken, downy hair, or flitting over the labia. From the corner of her eyes she again glanced at his tumescence.

'I can massage you better if you sit in my lap,' he said.

Without a word she swung a leg over him and sat facing him in his lap. Now his explorations grew bolder, groping under her skirt, inside her blouse, and finally, meeting no resistance, he drew her over and gave her a long slobbery kiss.

'You're so beautiful,' he said. 'So very beautiful.'

With one hand under her skirt he now manoeuvred himself into place, and with the other hand on her bare, yielding buttocks pushed her firmly against him. But penetration of the pubescent virgin was not easy, so he placed both his hands on her buttocks, lifted her slightly and then pressed her down hard.

'Ouch! It hurts,' she cried. 'It hurts, Uncle.'

'There, there,' he said, pushing harder, deeper, rocking her back and forth in a pounding, rolling motion.

2

When the family returned from the temple they found Aditi asleep in her bed. Rama Durai was still at the bottle.

'Let her sleep,' the aunt said. 'She must have been in pain.'

That month Aditi missed her menses, but that was not noticed. However, when she missed it again the next month, inquiries were made. Aditi, when questioned, went into a tight foetal curl, sobbing paroxysmally, and no amount of coaxing or threats could make her open up. Her aunt had her own suspicions about what had happened, but she kept the thoughts to herself. It was finally decided that Aditi should have an abortion. The family doctor was taken into confidence in the matter, after swearing him to secrecy over an oil lamp in the puja room. But such things could never be kept secret in a small town, so that when a groom was sought for Aditi a few years later, all the promising proposals eventually fell through. There were, however, many suitors for her younger sister, Rupa, who was more beautiful than Aditi, besides being the heiress. It was therefore decided, against normal social conventions, to marry off the younger sister first. Aditi agreed to this readily and with seeming cheerfulness, saying that she wanted to continue her studies and did not want to get married just then, though deep down she was horribly lacerated by the disgrace of being passed over.

'There were so many suitors for me, top professionals and businessmen,' Aditi once told Zeruba, having over the years convinced herself that this was how it really was. 'But I refused them all because I wanted to study and I wanted to marry for love. Even this cousin who married my sister actually wanted to marry me, and married her only because I refused.'

Aditi indeed did exceptionally well in school and college, and won numerous prizes in academics as well as in sports. After graduating with distinction in commerce, she took a two-year postgraduate course at the Madras School of Social Work, and then set herself up as a public relations consultant in the city. Her natural effervescence and ease in dealing with people of every sort made her an ideal PR person, and her family contacts gave her easy access to a number of business houses. She was much sought after. Meanwhile Mathangi, who had been Aditi's schoolmate and boon companion, also established herself professionally, as an architect-cum-interior decorator, and Aditi moved in with her in her flat on Harrington Road, an upscale residential area of Madras.

They were something of an oddity among women in staid old Madras society, being smart, successful and thoroughly modern professionals, and on the whole they were highly regarded, though there was also some malicious gossip about their lifestyle. But the two were entirely unlike each other, in appearance as well as in character and temperament. Mathangi, unlike Aditi, was small-boned and delicately built, rather fragile, and was always dressed demurely in white. Calm, sober, level-headed. But there was also something brittle about her, and she was guarded in all her relationships. Not at all given to romantic fancies. So when Aditi told her about her plan to marry Zeruba, she considered it a crazy idea and tried to dissuade her.

'I thought you were just having a fling,' she said, pushing aside the drawings on which she was working at the dining table.

'This is serious,' Aditi said.

'Don't tell me that you have fallen in love,' Mathangi said.

'Love is the most important thing in my life.'

'You want to be loved, true,' Mathangi said. 'But that's entirely different from being in love.'

'Don't give me all this pop psychology crap,' Aditi said crossly.

'Does he love you?'

'Absolutely.'

'You're deluding yourself, Adi,' Mathangi warned. 'I know artists. And I know Dada. His devotion will be only to his work, not to you or anyone else.'

'Artists are great romantics,' Aditi said.

'Yes, but only in their art, not in their lives,' Mathangi said. 'In everyday life most artists are awfully crabby and egocentric. They take love: they don't give love. As the Chinese say, it's death to love an artist. Besides, there's absolutely no compatibility between you two.'

'What do you mean?'

'You are entirely different kinds of persons, Adi—you're an extrovert, he's an introvert; you love people, he hates people . . .'

'Okay-okay! He's constipated, I've diarrhoea!' Aditi laughed.

'. . . he's an incurable pessimist, you're an incurable optimist . . .'

'What the hell are you saying, Mats? These differences are irrelevant when you are in love. Opposites attract, haven't you heard?'

'That's bullshit. Pulp fiction fantasy. Marriage has to be based on harmony, not on contrariety.'

A few days later, when Mathangi ran into Zeruba at an art exhibition, she asked him: 'What's all this I hear about you two getting married?'

'It's time I settled down,' he said.

'Aditi is not the type that settles down,' she warned.

'Let's see how it goes,' he said.

'He sounded so casual,' Mathangi told Aditi that night.

They were in bed watching television. Aditi was furious.

'Why are you doing this to me, Mats?' she asked. 'Are you after him yourself?'

'Don't be daft,' Mathangi said. 'You know my sexual preference.'

'So that's it! You want to keep me chained to you as a sex slave.'

'That's not my style, and you know that,' said Mathangi. 'I never resented your affairs with men.'

'So why now?'

'Because I'm very fond of you. Both of you,' Mathangi said, taking Aditi's hand in hers. 'I fear that you're making a terrible mistake, Adi. I'm trying to prevent a calamity.'

'How generous!' Aditi mocked, pulling off her hand.

Mathangi ignored her taunt. 'You'll be destructive towards each other,' she said. 'You'll destroy him, Adi, and he'll destroy you.'

'You're a real Cassandra, aren't you?'

'Don't be cross, Adi,' Mathangi said. 'Please do think about what I've said.'

'Okay, okay! But let me sleep now,' Aditi said, turning her back to Mathangi and switching off the bedside lamp.

3

Mathangi, who had known Zeruba and Aditi much longer than the two had known each other, was certain that they were all wrong for each other, and she watched with helpless foreboding events rolling on inexorably. Aditi was too impetuous, and Zeruba too fatalistic, for Mathangi to make them change course, whatever she said or did. Zeruba, obsessed with his work, left it to Aditi to make all the marriage arrangements, laying down only that the ceremony should be kept as simple and private as possible.

'We need to have at least a few guests,' Aditi said.

'Keep them to the minimum,' Zeruba said. 'Not more than a dozen people.'

'What about Lakshmi?'

'No,' Zeruba said. 'It would be embarrassing to her and embarrassing to you. And how do you think our guests will treat her? It's out of question.'

'But how can you not invite her?' Aditi asked. 'She has been the one closest to you.'

In the end they decided to go and personally invite Lakshmi and Gopal, and leave it to them to decide whether to attend the wedding.

'Please excuse us, Mama,' Lakshmi said. 'We'll be misfits there. It'll be embarrassing to you as well as to us.'

'What nonsense,' Aditi said.

'No, Lakshmi is right,' Zeruba said. 'But do come to the cottage that evening. We will be alone then.'

A more complex problem for Aditi and Zeruba was to decide how to deal with their parents. There was no question of seeking their consent for the marriage—that would have led to all sorts of complications and difficulties. Luckily, they had a good excuse for rushing through the marriage without parental approval, for around this time Zeruba received a fortuitous invitation from a small American college to spend a couple of years there as an artist in residence. He had met the president of the college, Dr Russell, an India enthusiast, two years earlier when he dropped in at his studio on the way to Mahabalipuram. Russell was impressed by what he considered to be the synthesis of Christian and Hindu motifs in Zeruba's paintings, and he, back in Madras now for another visit, called on Zeruba and made him the offer.

'There is a problem,' Zeruba said.

'What?'

'I'm getting married.'

'Congratulations,' Russell said. 'Or should I say, good luck?'

'Wish me luck,' Zeruba laughed.

'You would certainly need luck in marriage,' said Russell, a happy divorcee.

'I can't leave my wife behind,' Zeruba said.

'Bring her along,' said Russell. 'We would be delighted to have two on the salary of one.'

They had to be in the US within two weeks, so there was really no time for any elaborate wedding arrangements. They briefly considered having a civil law marriage, but Aditi wanted at least the semblance of a conventional wedding, so they decided on an Arya Samaj ceremony, a shortened Hindu ritual with Vedic chants. Arya Samaj had no objection to the groom being a non-Hindu, but said that he would have to be converted to Hinduism before the wedding, by undergoing a purification ceremony and reciting the Gayatri mantra.

'They'll give you a certificate of conversion,' Aditi told Zeruba.

Zeruba refused to go through the charade.

'Nothing doing,' he said. 'I've no religion, and want to keep it that way.'

'But this is just a formality,' she said. 'It doesn't mean anything.'

'I know it doesn't mean anything,' he said. 'That's why I won't do it.'

'What shall I tell the pujari if he asks about your religion?'

'Tell him anything you like,' he said. 'I don't care.'

Aditi had initially wanted to hold the ceremony in Zeruba's cottage, but the priest said that it was too far for him to travel, so she decided to have it in Mathangi's flat. And Mathangi, once she realized that she could not prevent Aditi and Zeruba from taking the plunge, did everything she could to facilitate the ceremony. The moment of sunrise was chosen, in consultation with astrologers, as the *muhoortham*, auspicious time, for the wedding.

The pujari from the Arya Samaj, a young, bearded and rather effeminate gent in a kurta-dhoti ensemble, arrived astride a violently backfiring old motorbike. He wore a huge red *thilak* on his forehead, and he had a little tuft of hair at the back of his close-cropped head, but otherwise there was nothing particularly priestly about his appearance. He had brought with him all the requirements for the rite, a portable *homa-kundam* to set up the sacred fire, a few splinters of firewood, camphor, ghee, honey, rice-flakes, incense, *sindur*, *tambulam*, and so on, and these he unceremoniously dumped on the floor in a corner of the drawing room. All the furniture in the room had been shifted out for the ceremony.

The pujari looked at his watch and smiled eagerly at the small group of guests standing in a disorderly cluster in the room. They looked back at him blankly. 'Well, let's get this show on the road,' he said, rolling up his sleeves and speaking in imitation of the characters in American soap operas, of which he was an avid fan.

Zeruba was in one of the two bedrooms in the flat, lying on his back in bed in the yogic *savasana* posture, his eyes closed. Aditi was in the other bedroom, being dressed by Mathangi. They were now summoned for the ceremony. Zeruba wore an undyed new cotton dhoti and shoulder cloth with broad gold-lace borders, and had, on Aditi's insistence, daubed sandalwood-paste on his forehead, chest and upper arms. But he firmly refused to put on the gold chain that she wanted him to wear.

'No,' he told her. 'That would be vulgar.'

Aditi, though a Tamilian, was dressed like a traditional Nair bride of Kerala, in dhoti, blouse and *dhavani*, all of the same plain, undyed cotton as Zeruba's clothes, but with much wider gold-lace borders. Her jewellery was minimal, just a *poothali*— a multi-strand, delicately intricate gold necklace—a couple of broad, openwork gold bangles on each hand, and single-pearl ear studs. Her forehead was adorned with a short but broad and precisely applied band of sandalwood paste, and her eyes were lined with kohl. The whole effect was one of noble simplicity, and she looked absolutely radiant. Zeruba smiled with pleasure, looking at her.

4

'Groom's name?' the priest asked officiously, taking out a notebook and a ballpoint pen from his plastic shoulder-bag.

'Zerubbabel,' Zeruba said.

The priest frowned. 'Serupapel?'

'Yes.'

'How do you spell it?'

Zeruba spelled it for him.

'Initials?'

'T.'

'Father's name?'

'Tharakan.'

'Tharakan?'

'That's right.'

'What's your *jati*, man?' the priest asked testily, looking at him askance, with narrow, suspicious eyes.

'*Manushya jati*,' Zeruba said, enunciating each syllable clearly. Human caste.

The priest slammed the notebook shut and capped his pen. He didn't like Zeruba.

'I can't marry you if you aren't earnest,' he warned.

At this point Aditi intervened. She took the priest aside and spoke to him quietly, and he thereafter treated Zeruba with great circumspection and wariness. Zeruba was puzzled.

'What did you tell him?' he asked Aditi after the ceremony.

She collapsed in laughter.

'I told him that you are a little touched in the head,' she said. 'And also that you are prone to violence.'

'And I am,' said Zeruba, laughing.

The pujari had also wanted to know from Aditi whether Zeruba was indeed a Hindu.

'A Namboodiri,' Aditi had replied in awed undertones. 'But thrown out of the caste because of his occult practices.'

'He knows the Gayatri mantra?' the pujari asked

'Shiva-Shiva! He knows the whole Rig-Veda by heart,' she said.

Yet another contingency that Aditi and Mathangi had anticipated and provided for, was the absence of the parents of the couple. Again, Zeruba did not know anything about the arrangements.

'Where are the parents of the couple?' the priest asked.

'My parents are away,' Zeruba said.

'What about her parents?' the priest wanted to know.

'They are away too,' Zeruba said.

'Then who'll give the bride away?' the priest asked plaintively, inching away from Zeruba and turning to Aditi.

At this point there stepped forward, to the utter amazement of Zeruba, an imperious looking middle-aged woman, a total stranger, built exactly like the ancient Didarganj sculpture of *yakshi*, and she told the priest in a stentorian voice that brooked no counter, 'I'm Aditi's aunt. Her parents are abroad. I and my husband will give her away.' A tall, emaciated man in thick horn-rimmed glasses stood behind her, nodding at the priest encouragingly.

'Who is this woman?' Zeruba asked Aditi.

'Shhhh!' Aditi silenced him. 'Mats's aunt.'

The priest then set up the sacred fire and began the rites, chanting the Sanskrit hymns sonorously, and guided the couple through the ceremony with brisk efficiency, explaining each hymn and act in a running commentary in English. The ceremony was both instruction and sacrament. The bridal couple, wearing the thick jasmine garlands they had exchanged at the beginning of the ceremony, sat on low footstools before the sacred fire, facing east, the bride to the right of the groom. Zeruba sat in the yogic *sukhasana* posture, his body gravely erect, while Aditi sat relaxed, with her right leg tucked under her and her left leg drawn up against her bosom, and her hands laced demurely over the knee. The priest sat in front of them to their right, half-facing them. The guests paid no attention whatever to the ceremony, and stood about gossiping. Zeruba, following the pujari's instructions, tied the *thali*, the wedding pendant, around Aditi's neck and led her around the sacred fire. Then, as the final act of the rite, they took seven steps together, symbolizing the different facets of marital relationship, the first step for vigour and the seventh step for friendship. At the end of the ceremony, the guests showered the newly-weds with grains of roasted rice mixed with turmeric, as was the custom. The priest then doused the fire, packed the *homa-kundam* and left. The ceremony was over in about an hour and a half.

5

That evening, Lakshmi and Gopal visited them in the cottage, bearing two huge jasmine garlands.

'Lakshmi made them herself,' Gopal said. 'She didn't want to buy them in the market.'

Lakshmi lowered her eyes in shy acknowledgement.

'These are the most valuable gifts we have received,' Zeruba said, disconcerted by the rush of feelings in him.

'We have brought them for you to put on each other,' Lakshmi said.

'Of course,' Aditi said. 'Come on in.'

Lakshmi had brought a little brass lamp with her, and into this she poured a thimble of coconut oil from the kitchen, placed in it the wick she had with her, and lit it. Zeruba and Aditi stood before the lamp, facing east. Lakshmi gave one garland to Aditi, and Gopal gave the other to Zeruba, and the couple solemnly put them on each other while Lakshmi sounded the *kurava*, a throaty yodel, to mark the auspicious event and to drive off evil spirits.

Two days after the wedding, Aditi's younger sister Rupa and her husband Natarajan called on the newly-weds. They were a handsome, genial, cultured couple, and Rupa, it turned out, was familiar with Zeruba's work. They had a pleasant get-together over tea, though Rupa appeared a trifle preoccupied. She had the same build and complexion as Aditi, but her features were finer, and her manner gentle. When Aditi went into the kitchen with the tea tray, Rupa followed her.

'Rama-uncle says that if you haven't slept with your husband, you should leave him and come home,' she told Aditi.

Aditi gave her a withering look.

'Oh, he wants to know whether I'm still a virgin?'

Rupa blushed crimson.

'Why are you blushing?' Aditi asked. 'It's ancient history, Rupa. I've put it behind me. So let's not bring it up again.'

'Have you told *him*?'

'I told Dada that I was not a virgin. But I didn't tell him about my teen pregnancy. I haven't told even Mathangi about it. So don't go gabbing about it.'

'What shall I tell Uncle?'

Aditi looked at her levelly. 'Tell him to come and ask me the question himself,' she said.

'I'm only a messenger,' Rupa said.

'Alright. You've delivered the message. Now tell me what you think I should do?'

'I don't know. You've to decide yourself.'

'There's nothing to decide,' Aditi said. 'The marriage is my decision.'

'Uncle says that if you marry outside the community, you'll be an outcaste, and will lose the right to inherit the family property.'

'Tell him that my lawyer will deal with the matter.'

'I'm only a messenger,' Rupa said.

'Don't keep parroting the same thing, Rupa. Tell me what you think. Do you think I should be deprived of my inheritance?'

'I think you should have your rightful share.'

'Then let's leave it at that,' Aditi said. 'Uncle has no role in this.'

When they left, Aditi told Zeruba about her uncle's advice.

'I suppose his idea is that if you're still a virgin, the marriage can be annulled, and you can be married off to someone of your own community.' Zeruba said.

'Ha! A virgin indeed! What a joke!' Aditi laughed.

Devi

1

Zeruba now tensely awaited the reaction of his irascible and unpredictable father. To his surprise (and somewhat to his disappointment as well), Korah received the news of the marriage fatalistically, as if it was something predestined and which he had been expecting all along, knowing his son's wilful and rebellious nature. Besides, he no longer had the energy or spirit to assert his will. Though he was only fifty-eight, and would live for another thirty years, he was a forlorn old man now, crushed by the many misfortunes of his life.

'I only hope that this won't turn out like Devi's marriage,' he sighed.

Devi, Zeruba's younger sister, was Korah's favourite child, indeed the apple of his eye, and it was her scandalous elopement with a Chettiar film producer eight years earlier that had crushed Korah's spirit, and turned this once feisty man into a limp fatalist.

'She was like congealed sunlight,' Korah would often exclaim in his old age, remembering his long lost daughter. 'So radiant. But how dark her life turned out to be!'

As a child, Devi was everybody's favourite. Even Sarah— Korah's mother, who detested him—doted on her, and used to claim that she was the very spitting image of herself, though there was, in fact, no resemblance at all between them, except that they were both very fair complexioned. Devi was christened Rebecca, but became Devi, goddess, around the age of eight, soon after the family moved into their ancestral home, when servants took to calling her by that name, claiming to see a golden aura around her. 'When she comes into a dark room, the room lights up,' claimed the old maidservant who started it all.

'Bioluminescence,' Mathu laughed, telling this to Zeruba once.

Devi grew up to be a luminously beautiful young woman, slender as a sylph, vivacious, bright and accomplished, the pride of the family, indeed the pride of Azhiyur, their hometown. On her Korah exclusively focussed all his affection, and she luxuriated in his love. It was unimaginable that she would ever do anything that would hurt him in the least. But evidently people were attributing to Devi the ideal qualities that they wished to see in her, and not seeing her as she really was. They knew nothing of Devi's turbulent inner life, in which the *rajasic* energy of her father and the *tamasic* wilfulness of her mother had combined to give her a fatal polarity of temperament. Her elopement was a shock to everyone, and it devastated Korah, and to the end of his life his eyes would often cloud over thinking about her tragic fate.

'Karma,' he would lament. '*Thalayilezhuthu*!'

After finishing school in Azhiyur, Devi was sent to the Women's Christian College in Madras, where she did brilliantly as a student of English literature. She was also active in the college dramatic society, and it was at one of the college productions that she caught the attention of two young men studying in a neighbouring men's college—the Chettiar boy, Alagappan, and Ravi Menon, a scion of the former ruling family of a small kingdom in Kerala. Devi played the two of them beautifully, setting one beau against the other, to intensify the ardour of both.

Korah had absolutely no knowledge of these developments, so he was aghast when one day he received a letter from the principal of the college asking him to rush to Madras, as she had learned from a reliable source that Devi was intending to elope with a Chettiar boy. For a moment he was struck numb by the news. Then he exploded.

'I will kill her,' he roared, pacing up and down the portico, shaking with fury. 'I'll chop her up and feed her to the dogs.'

Mariam sat in a corner, silent and helpless. The hubbub brought Mathu rushing in from his room in the gatehouse of the mansion. On learning what the matter was, he managed to calm down Korah somewhat after a while, impressing on him that the situation required delicate handling, for the sake of Devi as well as the family. Korah finally agreed to let Mathu go to Madras, but insisted that he should bring Devi home immediately.

2

'I'm sorry about this,' the principal of the college said to Mathu when he met her in her office. 'Devi is one of the best students we have ever had.'

'Are you sure about this affair?' Mathu asked.

'My information is from a very reliable source,' she assured him.

'Let me talk to her,' Mathu said.

The principal then sent a peon with a note to fetch Devi from her class.

'Kochappa! What a surprise!' she exclaimed, seeing Mathu.

'We need to talk,' he said.

'Anything wrong? Is Appa alright?'

'He's not well,' Mathu said. 'That's why I've come.'

'Why don't you go into the garden and have a chat?' the principal tactfully suggested.

In the garden, they sat side by side on a green-painted, slatted wooden bench under a shady tree beside the clock tower. The ground was carpeted with the small yellow blossoms fallen from the tree. There was no one else around.

Devi looked at Mathu with a sly smile. 'I know why you have come,' she said, ostentatiously twisting the horseshoe shaped *navaratna* engagement ring on her finger. 'It isn't because Appa is ill. You have come to find out about me.'

'Yes,' said Mathu. 'So tell me.'

'I intend to marry Alagu,' she said levelly.

'That's not for you alone to decide.'

'Really? Who else should decide?' she challenged.

'Your parents.'

'It's my life you're talking about, Kochappa. My life!'

'But you also belong to a family,' he reasoned. 'Marriage is not just between two individuals. It's also an alliance between two families. It has to be seen in its social context.'

'Come on, Kochappa,' she said. 'Those are fuddy-duddy notions.'

'Breeding matters, Devi,' he said. 'Family matters. Don't forget that ours is an ancient family.'

'Every family is as ancient as every other family,' Devi said dismissively. 'What's this family pride you're talking about? There's a whole new world out there, Kochappa. Our family name means nothing there. In fact, it means nothing anywhere, except in our own inflated heads. We're irrelevant in today's world.'

'Our family means nothing to you?'

'Look, I wouldn't like to hurt the family in any way. Particularly Appa. But I don't belong to the family. I belong to myself. And I'm going to build my own future.'

'Isn't that rather selfish?'

'It is,' she cheerfully agreed. 'But that's the only way one can survive in the world.'

Mathu was struck by Devi's brutal practicality. She had always been a level-headed girl, but the three years in college, away from home, had given her character a steeliness that he found disconcerting.

'Your father has great plans for you,' he said.

'I've got great plans for myself,' she said gravely, looking at him intently, her eyes sparkling. She was dressed in plain, deep-purple cotton sari and blouse, with a small purple bindi, just a

61

dot, on her forehead, and wore a short, thin gold chain around her neck, and tiny, plain gold studs on her ears.

My god, she's so beautiful, so vibrantly alive, thought Mathu. *What right have we to snuff out this light by enclosing her in a drab, conventional marriage?*

'I want to belong to something new and vital,' Devi said, echoing his thoughts. 'Our mouldy old world would be death to me.'

'Look,' he said. 'I agree that it's your life, and you have the right to make your own decisions about it. I'm only pleading with you not to rush into this matter. Consider the feelings of your father. He's absolutely shattered by the news.'

'No, I'm not going to rush into it,' she said. 'I'm going to let it ride for a while. I've other options.'

'What?' He looked at her with surprise.

'There is this prince from Kerala who is pursuing me.'

'Who's this?'

'Ravi Menon. He's a grandson of the raja.'

'What about your engagement, then?'

'That stands. In all probability I'll marry Alagu. But I'm going to wait awhile and think it over.'

'Your father wants you to return home with me immediately.'

'The college closes next Friday. I'll go then.'

'We'll go together.'

'Alright,' she said. 'Would you like to meet Alagu?'

'Yes, of course.'

'When?'

'Any time. Let me see. Sunday evening?'

'Alright. I'll tell him.'

3

Mathu got Alagappan's address from Devi, but instead of waiting till Sunday, he paid him a surprise visit at noon the very next day, Saturday. He took an instant dislike to the boy. A corpulent youth, Alagappan already had, though only in his early twenties, a prominent potbelly, in which Mathu saw a life of sloth and indulgence. He was dressed gaudily in a flowered slack-shirt, white trousers and white shoes, and wore many gem-studded rings on his fingers, a gold wristwatch on one arm and a thick gold bracelet on the other. Mathu found him singularly vulgar. Worst of all, he found him with a bunch of friends, drinking beer. On realizing who Mathu was, Alagappan had the bottles and glasses hastily removed, and apologized for the scene, saying that since their exams were over, his friends had pestered him for a celebration. The friends sidled away.

Alagappan was courteous, but in a simpering, hypocritical manner that Mathu found distasteful. He offered Mathu tea, and when that was refused, served him a glass of chilled tender coconut water. His parents, Alagappan told Mathu, had gone away to their ancestral home in Karaikkudi for a few days. Mathu spent barely fifteen minutes with him, making polite, desultory conversation.

'There was no rapport at all,' Alagappan told Devi that evening. 'I'm afraid your uncle dislikes me.'

'What's your objection to Alagu?' Devi asked Mathu when they met again a couple of days later. 'Is it because he is a Hindu?'

'That's not the main consideration,' he said.

'But it is a consideration?'

'Yes, it is,' he said. 'As you know, I'm not a religious person. But religion is not simply a matter of faith in a particular god or rituals. It's also a culture, a way of life. So it would be difficult for a couple from two different religions to harmonize their lives.'

'That's true only in a rural environment,' Devi said. 'Alagu and I are city people. We share the same lifestyle. Besides, Alagu is not orthodox at all.'

'I could see that.'

'He has an occasional drink—you object to that?' she asked. 'I myself have a drink sometimes.'

63

He turned to face her directly. 'You trying to shock me?'

'Are you shocked?'

'You know how fond of you we all are at home, Devi. It would hurt us deeply if you become wayward.'

'What do you want me to do?'

'I've given some thought to this matter,' he said.

'Yes?'

'I believe that a person should be judged on his own merit. It's his personal quality that primarily matters. His wealth, religion, language and so on are only secondary considerations.'

'And you find Alagu wanting as a person?'

'I'm afraid so,' said Mathu. 'To be frank, I think that on his own he's an utterly worthless fellow. He has wealth, but no worth. All his great wealth pales into insignificance before that basic fact. Besides, he's so gross, repulsive. How can you bear to touch him?'

'Wealth is worth, Kochappa,' Devi said. 'All virtues are accessories to gold, haven't you heard? People will see Alagu as wise and noble and even handsome because he's wealthy.'

'You deserve someone better, Devi,' Mathu said. 'Alagappan is the last person I would consider a suitable match for you. Why, he even seemed rather stupid.'

'He may not be very bright,' Devi said, 'but he's a good and sincere person.'

'Being a simpleton isn't a redeeming quality.'

'Why don't you see him again? Spend more time with him.'

'I would rather not,' Mathu said.

4

Alagappan's father, Subbiah Chettiar, was a big time film producer and financier, and was called Emperor of Kodambakkam, the film production centre of Madras. A short, stout man with a bulbous nose and puffy, sensuous lips, he was usually dressed in silk kurta and dhoti, with a gold embroidered shawl thrown carelessly over his shoulder, and was always redolent with expensive perfumes. Diamond earrings adorned his pendulous ear lobes, and he wore a large and rare blood-red star-ruby on the second finger of his left hand. And he went about in a chauffeur-driven, pink Phantom IV Rolls Royce, looking very much like a Tamil film caricature of a bloated Croesus.

Subbiah Chettiar loved to flaunt his wealth. 'If I bundle up a lakh of rupees and throw it into the sea every day for the next twenty years, there would still be enough left for my family for several generations,' he often boasted to his sycophantic minions. Legend had it that he had a strong-room in his house in which currency notes were heaped like paddy in a granary, into which fresh sacks of money were emptied every now and then, and that when needed, money was just scooped into baskets and taken out, without counting. Chettiar was also proud of his deviousness in business. 'If I'm given the option of making a crore of rupees by fair means or by foul means, I would always choose the foul means,' he used to brag. Testing himself against the law was a thrill for him, and kleptomania a secret vice—he was once caught shoplifting a packet of expensive pipe tobacco from a tobacconist in New York, and had to save himself by buying the shop.

All this had something to do with the poverty and misery of his early life. He had come to Madras as a penniless youth, and had worked for years as the odd jobs factotum and pander of a leading film star-turned-politician, before moving on, after about two decades, to become a film producer and accumulate his great wealth. He then built for himself, in a suburb of Madras, a palatial Chettinad style mansion with three inner courtyards, each about half the size of a hockey field. In time, he also acquired several racehorses, a fleet of imported cars, and a string of starlets as concubines. His wife did not seem to mind his philandering, and never interfered with his life outside the home. A short, fat, mousy woman with an ashen face and scanty, moth-eaten hair, she always looked rumpled and slovenly, even when freshly bathed and dressed. Quiet and retiring, she was hardly ever seen in public.

Subbiah had no children of his own, and had adopted Alagappan, a nephew, as his son. The boy proved to be a disappointment as he grew up, being easy-going and feckless, without the grit needed to survive in the treacherous, high-risk movie business.

'I fear for the future,' Subbiah said to his wife one day.

'You should discipline him,' she said. 'Give him some responsible work.'

'You can't straighten a dog's tail by putting it in a tube,' he grumbled.

Mathu heard all this from quiet inquiries with his relatives and acquaintances in Madras. He also did a bit of personal sleuthing about the family the day after he met Alagappan, and what he found out distressed him greatly. He went to the Chettiar's office in the guise of a Malayalam film producer seeking finance, and spoke to the office manager there, a Tirunelveli Iyer with a simian face and arms reaching to his knees, a very Hanuman. He regaled Mathu with candid stories about the old man's exploits, to which Mathu pretended to show great awe.

'But how is it that he has no children of his own?' he asked. 'Is he sterile?'

'Sterile but potent,' said the manager, clenching his fist and pumping it up dramatically with a wild, leering grimace.

'What is his adopted son like?' asked Mathu.

'A wastrel, an absolute wastrel,' said the man. 'Chettiar knows how to make money and how to spend money, but the boy knows only to spend money. He'll come to no good.'

'There's a rumour that he's going to marry a Malayali Christian girl,' said Mathu.

'Oh yes. I haven't seen her, but I hear that she's very beautiful and very bright. The old man approves of her and thinks that she would be a good influence on Alagu,' the manager said, and then added in a hoarse, guffawing whisper, 'You know what I think? I think the old lecher fancies her himself.'

Mathu did not say any of this to Devi. Nor did they discuss Alagappan again till they reached Azhiyur.

5

When Mathu and Devi arrived home, Korah shut himself up in his bedroom and refused to see Devi. So she sat on the floor outside the room and told him through the closed door, 'Appa, I'm sitting here at the door, and I'll not stir from here till you come out and talk to me. Beat me if you want, but talk to me.'

The stand-off lasted a few hours, then Korah opened the door and stood in the doorway, his face dark and ominous, his eyes bloodshot. He was breathing heavily, and he seemed on the verge of doing something violent. But when Devi rose and fell at his feet, he lifted her up and burst out sobbing uncontrollably. But her own eyes were dry. She was not emotionally involved in the scene. It was just a situation to be managed.

'Men are such crybabies,' Devi later told Zeruba, recalling their father's crying binge.

Ever since Devi was nine, Korah had been putting aside some money every month to build a fund to be given as her dowry, and had by then accumulated a fairly substantial sum. He was certain that with this dowry, combined with the family's high name and Devi's beauty and talents, he would be able to arrange an excellent match for her within the community, and he now set about the task in good earnest. A series of prospective grooms now arrived at Azhiyur to see Devi, but she spurned them all one after the other. The first to arrive—and the first choice of Korah— was the son of a Syrian Christian cabinet minister of the Central government in Delhi. It was a match of double exigency, for the boy happened to be in love with his first cousin, a forbidden relationship, and his parents were trying to lure him away, just as Korah was trying to turn Devi away from Alagappan.

'What happened to the proposal?' Zeruba once asked Mathu.

'Not even Devi's beauty turned his head,' Mathu said. 'The cousins later married, but the marriage ended in divorce.'

Then came an IAS officer, son of an avaricious priest who wanted 50,000 rupees as dowry, a car and a house, all of which Korah promised, though it would have been nearly impossible for him to meet those commitments. But Devi rejected the boy outright saying that he was too short. The next to come was an engineer from a well-known family in south Kerala, who was going to Africa for a job with an American company. As soon as he came, he wanted to lie down for a while, saying that he was very tired. Later, over tea, he met Devi. He asked her what her hobby was.

'Cycling,' she said. 'I go cycling in Madras.'

'On the road?' he asked, startled.

'Yes,' she said. 'Don't you enjoy cycling?'

'Oh yes,' he said. 'But I cycle only inside our compound. I'm scared to go on the road.'

Out he went. To yet another boy Devi secretly showed the thumbs down sign with a grimace of disgust, and this was seen by the boy's mother, and they stormed out of the house in a huff. Korah then asked Devi to give him the exact particulars of the type of boy she would like to marry—height, weight, complexion, education and job—so he could ask Viswakarma, the divine all-maker, to create a youth of her specifications and send him to her. Devi laughed.

Korah finally gave up his matchmaking efforts, but still he absolutely refused to let her marry the Chettiar boy.

'Not this boy, never.'

'Why?' Devi asked.

'Ask your uncle what he thinks of him.'

'Kochappa met him for just fifteen minutes.'

'That was enough,' Korah said. 'Look, I'm willing to let you make your choice. But choose someone else. The Chettiar boy is out of question.'

6

Meanwhile, Alagappan kept bombarding Devi with letters, registered letters and telegrams, most of which Korah tore up and threw away without opening the moment they were received. And Devi's letters to Alagappan, which she gave to servants to post, were also torn up and thrown away on Korah's orders. When Devi came to know of this from one of the servants, she threw a fit and locked herself up in a bathroom with a razor blade, threatening to kill herself by slashing her wrists. It was probably a bluff, but Korah kicked open the bathroom door and took away the blade from her.

'Okay,' Devi said. 'Now tie up my hands and legs and throw me into a dungeon.'

'I'll kill you,' he said flaring up.

'Oh? Why not let me kill myself?' she mocked.

At this stage Alagappan wrote to Devi that he was coming to Azhiyur to take her away. This was too much for Korah. 'If he comes here, I'll kill him,' he snarled. 'I'll rip out his entrails and feed him to the dogs.' Prudently, Alagappan did not turn up. Instead, two of his friends flew down to Kochi and motored to Azhiyur to take Devi with them. 'I cannot stop you from going,' Korah told her. 'But if you go with them, you should go by the back door, and you should never-ever enter this house again.' Surprisingly, Devi heeded the warning.

As family tensions continued to mount, Mathu one day told Devi that Korah might agree to let her marry Ravi, though he still preferred her to marry a Syrian Christian boy. Devi smiled. She now knew that she was winning the tussle with her father, and would not have to hold out much longer to have her way all the way.

'I don't know,' she told Mathu. 'I don't think it'll be good for me to marry Ravi. I don't look forward to living in a joint family ruled by his grandmother, the Nethyaramma.'

'You've met her?'

'She summoned me to her palace in Madras during one of her visits to the city to look me over, ' Devi said. 'I didn't like it one bit. She was very condescending—this ex-princess of a defunct stamp-sized kingdom!'

'But you will be living in Madras with Ravi, while she'll be in Kerala most of the time,' Mathu pointed out.

'Ravi quakes before her,' she said. 'He's a wimp.'

'But they are a cultured people,' Mathu reasoned with her. 'Not like this vulgar film producer.'

'Maybe,' Devi said. 'Maybe Alagu is vulgar. But Ravi is effete. His is a vegetative feudal family. They've no future. Future lies in trade and industry. Alagappan is much, much richer than Ravi, and he will only grow richer.'

'Is money all that important to you?'

'It's everything, Kochappa.'

'It's new money. It stinks.'

'It doesn't,' she said gravely. 'I've smelled it.'

'What's made in an instant can go in an instant,' Mathu said. 'You yourself said that Alagappan is not very bright.'

'But I'll be there. I'll take charge.'

'The boy is so crude. He has no culture. What sort of life will you have with him?'

'The life I desire,' she said, turned abruptly and walked away.

7

In the end, Korah bowed to the inevitable as gracefully as he could, and let Devi return to Madras. He even promised to attend the wedding. As it happened, he could not do so, as Devi's letter about the wedding arrangements reached him only the day after the marriage, for she had purposely delayed posting it, fearing that Korah with his volatile temper might make a scene at the wedding. Not even Zeruba, who was then in Madras engaged in doctoral research, was informed in time.

The day after the wedding, the couple left for Kashmir for their honeymoon. When they were away, Subbiah Chettiar died suddenly of cardiac arrest, so Devi and Alagappan had to rush back to Madras. Soon Devi discovered that the affluence of the Chettiar was an illusion, and that all he had left behind were vast debts. But Devi also discovered that having huge debts was almost as good as having huge wealth. Devi and Alagappan continued to live opulently by borrowing money recklessly, travelling around India to attend horse races and betting heavily, contemptuously indifferent to their losses, and borrowing money still more recklessly to cover their loses, their very nonchalant extravagance giving financiers the confidence to lend them money.

During this period, Devi, with Alagappan in tow, did visit Korah a few times, demanding her inheritance. On one of these visits, as Devi importuned Korah for money, Alagu took out a revolver from his trouser pocket and sat there glumly twirling it, as though warning his father-in-law to take care. Korah ignored him.

'You've chosen your own future,' he told Devi with finality. 'I'll not help you.'

A few days later, Alagappan roared into the courtyard of the Azhiyur house in his car, brakes screeching, and stepped out at the portico, drunkenly shouting for Korah. As Korah approached, he put his hand into his trouser pocket, and Korah, fearing that he was going to take out the revolver, flung himself on him and pinioned him in a tight embrace, shouting for help. But it turned out that it was only a cigarette lighter that Alagappan had in his hand. As Korah released him, Alagappan puffed up his bloated body, hawked contemptuously and spat at him. Korah froze, taken aback by the sheer effrontery of the act, but only for a moment. Then he, a giant of a man, heaved and swung at Alagappan with all his might, flooring him, and would have probably killed him, if servants had not held him back. Devi, who was sitting in the car watching, then dragged Alagappan into the car with the help of their driver, and they drove off. That was the last that Korah saw of Devi.

71

Mathu

1

'What humiliations I had to suffer on account of Devi,' Korah would often bewail when he was in his cups.

It was one damned thing after another for Korah from then on. The trauma of Devi's outrageous and catastrophic marriage was quickly followed by the disgrace of Zeruba turning into an artist. Around this time, the family also lost a good chunk of its properties in the land ceiling legislation enacted by the communist government of Kerala. His younger son Chacko, the only remaining hope for the future of the family, was not doing well in college, and seemed unlikely to make a success of his life. And to cap it all, now there was this humiliating marriage of Zeruba with some Tamilian girl without as much as the courtesy of asking for his consent. All this was too much for Korah to handle. He was now like a punch-drunk boxer, his reactions befuddled, incapable of asserting his will. So all he did on receiving Zeruba's letter about his marriage was to send Mathu to Madras to find out what his renegade son was up to.

Mathu was the firefighter of the family, and was ideally suited for that role. He had a marvellously equable disposition, and was the only one in the family totally unaffected by the pervasive gloominess of the house, though he had more reason than anyone else to be gloomy. His was a singularly unfulfilled life. He had no family of his own, his wife having deserted him the very day after their marriage; he had no profession or job; and his literary and intellectual endeavours, though tireless, were entirely fruitless. Yet he was serenely contented. And his was a contentment that no external circumstance could subvert or diminish, for it was a self-subsistent state that arose from his disengagement from the world.

'I know life. I want no part of it,' he once told Zeruba.

This detachment did not, however, make him neglect himself or his social obligations. Rather, he cultivated himself with reverential care, took his familial and social responsibilities seriously, and did all that was expected of him as a member of the family, community and society. But he did all that without any emotional involvement. So he claimed.

'I'm not a victim of the senses,' Mathu said with a self-deprecating chuckle. 'I'm a spectator of life, not a participant.'

'Isn't all this just a rationalization, for you to live with your failures?' Zeruba challenged. He was quite attached to Mathu, and was closer to him than to anyone else in the family, regarding him as much as a friend and wise counsellor as an empathetic uncle. They were on the same wavelength, and were very free with each other.

'Perhaps,' Mathu agreed good-humouredly. 'But I've withdrawn from the world not in anger or contempt, but because of the knowledge of what life is all about—'

'—what your life is all about,' corrected Zeruba.

'What do you mean?'

'I mean, each of us makes up his own view of life to suit his particular predicament,' Zeruba said. 'No one has any final and definitive knowledge of the meaning of life.'

'True of course,' Mathu conceded. 'But my subjective knowledge is for me the final and definitive knowledge.'

Zeruba was tempted to ask whether it was not a single chance event, his wife's desertion, that warped his view of the world, but he checked himself. Mathu had been in his youth one of the most eligible bachelors in the community, the scion of an ancient and respected though somewhat impoverished *tharavad*. He had done brilliantly all through school and college, winning several gold medals, and was one of the very first persons in Kerala to acquire an American university degree, a masters in philosophy from Columbia University. A brilliant career awaited him, everyone was certain. His bride was considered a perfect match for him, pretty and well educated, a graduate, and from a well-known, rich and progressive family of Kottayam. The marriage ceremony, held in the ancient Cheriya Palli in Kottayam, was conducted by three bishops, and was a celebrated event in the recent history of the community.

Immediately after the ceremony, the bridal party left in a motorboat for Mathu's home, where a grand reception was held to celebrate the wedding. But the next morning, the bride disappeared. No one ever found out what it was that Mathu did, or failed to do, on his wedding night that sent her fleeing in wordless fury to her cousin's house in Azhiyur early next morning, before anyone else in the house woke up. There was no fuss, no noisy quarrel. Mathu followed her up to the portico of the main house, but neither of them said a word to each other. In the front yard, she picked up a broomstick that was lying there, broke it into two and flung it at Mathu with a look of utter revulsion, then turned and left the house. Mathu smiled and waved grimly. As soon as she left, he brought a pitcher of water and a broom from the kitchen and washed off the sandalwood-paste footprint that she had, according to the family custom, made with her right foot at the threshold to make her entry into the home auspicious.

She sent for her bags later that day, and in a couple of days her parents came and took her home to Kottayam. The family never heard from them again; there was no word of complaint or explanation, but her parents, using their considerable influence in the church, had the marriage annulled. There was a lot of whispered discussion in the family and the town about the unhappy affair, but no one said anything openly. Nor would Mathu ever speak about it. Once, a couple of decades later, when

Zeruba was thinking of getting married, he asked Mathu why he didn't marry again.

'Who would want to take a second bite of a bitter fruit?' Mathu replied, curling his lips in hawking distaste.

No amount of persuasion by his parents would make Mathu agree to marry again. He was equally adamant in refusing to take up legal studies, as his father wanted him to, or take to any other profession. Ever since then, he had lived cooped up in the gatehouse of their ancestral home.

Mathu never sought anybody's friendship, had no friends, in fact. But he was always friendly towards everyone he met, and everyone liked him, though he made no particular effort to make himself likeable. A good part of his charm was entirely physical, his appearance of radiant good health and well-being, and his open, pleasant demeanour. He was fair and tall and robustly built, and could be even considered handsome, though a slight overbite and a short lower lip gave him a somewhat rabbity look, and his cheeks were heavily pitted from a long ago bombardment of pimples. A physical culture faddist, he took excellent care of his health. He woke up at the same time every day, at five in the morning, did yogic exercises for an hour, and in the evening took a brisk walk for a couple of hours. Every now and then he took a ferry across the lagoon—beside which Azhiyur was situated— to the beach and went for a long swim in the sea.

He was a marvellous raconteur and conversationalist, and was the only one who could ever make Zeruba's melancholic mother laugh. His wit, however, was sardonic, with a cutting edge to it. Once when he and Zeruba were travelling by train, Mathu got into an elaborate theological discussion with a Catholic bishop in their compartment, addressing him with cynical reverence as Your Excellency. And when the bishop rose to get off at Thrissur, Mathu dropped to his knees and, as Zeruba looked on startled, kissed the signet ring of the bishop.

'Your Excellency, how I wish I were a Catholic!' he said, rising.

'Why, my son?' the bishop asked with a puzzled smile.

'Well . . . ,' began Mathu, his eyes crinkling, mouth pursed hard puckishly. 'Well . . . because the Catholic Church is the greatest and most successful racket in the world.'

For a moment the bishop's face darkened, but he recovered quickly, and chuckling indulgently turned and stepped off the train without a word.

2

For all his apparent good cheer and contentment, there was a faint undercurrent of despondency in Mathu. He, however, never indulged in self-pity, but kept himself forever busy with various creative pursuits, though no one in the family except Zeruba paid any serious attention to his work. He did not mind the indifference. He wrote poetry, which no one ever published, and he wrote innumerable articles on 'The Indian Predicament' and sent them to newspapers and magazines, all of which unfailingly came back with unsigned, printed regret slips pinned to them. He also conceived elaborate plans for starting various civic projects, none of which ever materialized. And finally, having failed in everything, he wrote a booklet titled *Seven Easy Steps to Success*, but could not find a publisher for that either. Still, he never lost interest or slackened the pace of his work.

The gatehouse was Mathu's sanctuary, and he spent nearly all his time there, going into the main house only to bathe and to have his meals. He was very industrious and disciplined, and was always hard at work, reading or writing, or pacing up and down the room with his hands clenched tight behind his back, devising his visionary schemes. He had a tiny, precise hand, and he wrote in black ink on thin blue paper with his fine-nibbed Parker pen. Everything he wrote was neatly logged in a leather-bound foolscap notebook, noting when each piece was written, where and when it was sent, and when it was returned. And he carefully saved the paper clips and pins with which the editors' rejection slips were attached to the returned pieces, storing them in a bottle, which was neatly labelled PRICK-PINS. In over four decades of tireless labour, he had nearly filled the bottle with pins, the measure of his literary oeuvre.

It depressed Zeruba that the total worth of his uncle's life could be measured in a few grams of metal pins. The futility and wastefulness of his life was appalling. But that was not how Mathu saw his life. He was, in his view, leading a fulfilling life, all the more creditable because it was entirely self-contained and was not dependent on anything or anyone in the world. He was totally free.

'What's the point of all this, Kochappa?' Zeruba once asked him. 'It seems to be an awfully perverse self-indulgence.'

'Oh yes,' Mathu admitted gladly. 'It is, it is.'

'So what keeps you going?'

'Because it indulges the self,' he said, spreading his arms magnanimously. 'Look, I'm not saying I'm indifferent to whether my articles get published or not. I certainly would like to see them in print. But as Tagore advised, if no one heeds our call, then we should walk alone. I'm content to walk alone.'

'But doesn't the isolation and futility depress you?'

'No at all. Writing is like talking to a friend, a good companion,' said Mathu. 'Besides, what else am I to do with my life?'

'How can you write living cooped up in this wooden crate?' Zeruba asked. 'Don't you have to experience life first-hand to write about it?'

'Of course experience matters,' said Mathu. 'But what you make of experience matters even more. In any case, I get all the experience I need right here in this crate. It's teeming with people, life, adventure. I have to only shut my eyes to see it all.'

'That's fantasy, not life.'

'Of course it's fantasy,' agreed Mathu. 'But fantasy too is life, life in another dimension. Experience is not confined to the things that happen outside you, son. The books you read and the movies you see are experiences. And the stories people tell you. Your reveries and daydreams are experiences. And so are your dreams and nightmares. This is meta-reality, son. Nothing like it.'

'Are you serious? You mean there's no difference between reality and fantasy?'

'Oh there is,' said Mathu. 'Reality is tedious, boring, limited. Not so the fantasized world, where the only limit is the limit of your imagination. There you can move freely, experience any kind of action exactly as you desire. You're in perfect control.'

'It's an alternate life?'

'Not an alternate life, but life's true fulfilment.'

3

Mathu saw his own restless creative impulse reincarnated in Zeruba, and hoped that it would in him yield luxuriant efflorescence in an early spring, unlike the promise of his own life that had frosted in an everlasting winter of waiting. But he now feared that marriage might prove fatal to Zeruba's career. So it was with considerable anxiety that he arrived at Zeruba's cottage.

Zeruba was delighted to see him, and was proud to introduce him to Aditi. She received him with her usual warmth and exuberance, and Mathu in turn was pleasant to her, though reserved. Over breakfast, he asked her a few questions about herself and her family, but more out of courtesy than interest, it seemed. He made no comments on their marriage. He then went off to take a nap on a camp-cot under the rain tree, saying, 'I didn't sleep well in the train.' He slept again after lunch. Later, after tea, he and Zeruba walked over to sit on the beach, and it was only then that he brought up the subject of the marriage.

'You know my views on marriage,' he said.

'You're going by your solitary bitter experience,' Zeruba said.

'No,' Mathu said. 'I'm being entirely objective about this.' The institution of marriage, he maintained, is pernicious, more so the nuclear family. 'It turns the husband and wife into psychic cannibals, feeding on each other. It's savage.'

'There are marriages and marriages,' Zeruba disagreed. 'If it works well, it can be wonderfully fulfilling.'

'If it works well, yes. But it seldom does. Tell me, do you know any happily married couples? Any one at all?' Mathu challenged.

Zeruba looked away. 'I can't think of any right away,' he admitted. 'I don't know that many people. But there must be millions of happily married couples.'

'Maybe one in ten thousand, maybe one in hundred thousand marriages works out,' Mathu said. 'In all other cases, marriages endure not because the couples are happy with each other, but because they lack the will and courage to separate. Or because they fear hurting their parents or their children. Or some such thing.'

'That one-in-a-hundred-thousand chance is worth taking.'

'Is it? Mind you, it entails a 99.99 per cent risk of lifelong misery,' said Mathu. 'The only rationale for marriage is that you need a family to rear children.'

'That's an important function, isn't it?'

'It is. But there are better ways of doing it,' Mathu said.

'Like what?'

'Like the old matrilineal system of Nairs in Kerala. It was an ideal system.'

'Ideal? But Nairs themselves are ashamed of it now.'

'That's progress!' Mathu scoffed.

The traditional Nair custom was for the girl to continue to live with her mother even after her marriage, and for her children in turn to live with her all their lives, taking her caste and her family name, and inheriting her family property. Her husband visited her at nights, or sometimes, if mutually convenient, moved in with her. This arrangement, according to Mathu, helped to preserve the aura of romance in marriage, by separating courtship and mating from the drab, soul-numbing responsibilities of maintaining a household. It was more like a romantic liaison than a conventional marriage, and the couple were free to quietly separate without any formality if they ceased to please each other. And if they separated, there was no trauma, either for the children or for the parents. The husband leaving the family was like a guest leaving the house.

'The arrangement served all the goals of marriage without any of its horrors,' Mathu said. 'It provided for happy companionship, for happy sex, and it provided a secure, tension-free environment for rearing children. And it left plenty of private space for both husband and wife.' It did not require the transplantation of the wife or husband from one family environment into another family environment. And, best of all, the relationship between husband and wife in this system was only one of the many strands in the complex web of relationships in the joint family, so the quality of one's family life did not hang on a single brittle thread, as it does in the nuclear family. 'It was a perfect blend of freedom and security.'

'If it was such a wonderful system, why didn't it endure?' Zeruba asked.

'Because it could exist only in a joint family set-up,' said Mathu, 'and the joint family itself could exist only in an agrarian society in which people lived rooted to a particular place.'

'So it's an archaic system?'

'Yes. But I think that there could be a revival of it in the future, when women gain full economic independence. And also because people in the future are more likely to live rooted in particular places.'

'Just the opposite is happening.'

'People today move from place to place mainly for the sake of their careers,' said Mathu. 'But I think that advances in communication technology and production automation will eventually make this unnecessary, and enable a good number of people to live in a place of their choice and work for an organization in another place, even in another continent.'

'You're talking of a past that's gone and of a future that's yet to come,' Zeruba said. 'Unfortunately, we've to live in the world as it is today.'

'Yes,' Mathu conceded. 'We're caught in an abominable in-between time.'

They sat in silence for a while. The dusk had fallen. The wind was up. To their left, south of the harbour, they could see a line of ships strung out loosely along the shoreline, their lights ablaze. There were a few catamarans of fishermen bobbing far out in the sea.

'You know, I think I can still swim out as far as those catamarans,' Mathu said.

'Please don't try,' Zeruba cautioned.

The catamarans were riding towards the shore, and fishermen could be seen in them as dark silhouettes, paddling languidly.

'There's something I want to ask you,' Zeruba said.

'Yes?'

'You haven't told me what you think of Aditi.'

'What I think is irrelevant.'

'Still?'

'Interesting person.'

'That's all?'

'She laughs a lot,' Mathu said, his eyes still on the fishermen. 'That's not a good sign. Something phoney there.'

'This is prejudice, Kochappa. Adi is just exuberant.'

'Maybe. But I sense an undercurrent of some disturbance or grief in her.'

'Adi grieving?' Zeruba laughed. 'She's the jolliest person imaginable.'

'Those are just surface ripples.'

4

Mathu stayed on in Madras to see off Aditi and Zeruba to the US. When they arrived at the airport, they found Lakshmi and Gopal, along with Mathangi, Rupa and Natarajan waiting for them. Lakshmi had brought a pinch of kumkum as *prasadam*— sanctified ritual offering—from her temple, and she now marked Zeruba's forehead with it, a liberty that he would not have allowed anyone else to take. Aditi looked away.

'Who's this?' Mathu asked Aditi.

'His former mistress,' she said crossly.

Mathu ignored her and turned to Zeruba. 'Keep writing to your father,' he advised as they said their goodbyes. 'He might not reply at first. But you must keep writing, and in the end it'll be alright.'

'I will,' Zeruba promised.

They were in a flurry at the airport, for they were late and were in danger of missing their flight. Zeruba was a stickler for punctuality, but Aditi was pathologically incapable of ever being on time for anything.

'What does it matter if we are a little late?' she would grumble whenever he tried to hurry her. 'No one minds it.'

'I don't care whether anyone minds it or not,' Zeruba would answer. 'But it matters to me. So please hurry.'

And she would just shrug her shoulders. In the age of nanoseconds, Aditi functioned to what Zeruba assumed was the peasant's unhurried seasonal rhythm of time, indifferent to hours and even days. He initially thought that this was because of her rustic childhood in an orthodox Hindu cultural environment, but he later realized that her problem arose from some psychological disorder. She was late because she needed to be late. 'Chronic lateness is a planned event,' a psychologist friend told Zeruba. 'It's a passive-aggressive act. And this personality trait indicates some mental disturbance.'

'Hmm!' Zeruba exclaimed.

'Don't feel smug about it, my friend,' the psychologist cautioned. 'Obsessive preoccupation with punctuality also indicates insecurity.'

'Punctuality isn't an obsession with me,' Zeruba said. 'It's merely a convenience.'

Zeruba liked to do everything unhurriedly, with deliberation and mindfulness, while Aditi's style was to think and act on the run. She was always in a mad rush, and always embarrassingly late for everything. When they invited friends home, it would be just when the first guests arrived that she would be rushing to have a bath to get ready to receive them. *Adi likes to be naked when guests arrive*, Zeruba would often reflect morosely. She was never on time for business meetings either. And on the day they left for the US, they just barely managed to catch their flight.

During the journey there was yet another problem. Though Aditi was quite her usual breezy self on the flight to Bombay, chatting with the airhostesses, charming the elderly gentleman who sat next to her, her mood changed inexplicably during the flight from Bombay to New York, and she curled up in her seat, sobbing violently.

'What's the matter?' Zeruba asked.

Instead of answering, she flung herself into a still more violent paroxysm of sobbing, each spasm looping into a higher and tighter pitch. It was awful.

'People are looking,' Zeruba cautioned her. 'Calm down. Whatever is the matter with you?'

But she just went on sobbing, her head buried in the *pallu* of her sari. Zeruba then decided to leave her alone to recover in her own time. He tilted his seat back, closed his eyes, and went to sleep. Later, she would accuse him of callousness.

5

She had, in fact, made that charge within a couple of days of their marriage, over his preoccupation with his work. Zeruba had begun a new painting the very day after their wedding, inspired by Mathangi's aunt, who, along with her husband and Mathangi, had called on them that day. He was once again staggered by the sheer physicality of the woman. She was so monstrously steatopygous that she seemed to be wearing a hoop-skirt under her sari, and her pillow-sized breasts seemed to belligerently thrust out of her blouse.

'Why are you staring at her like that?' Aditi hissed at him.

'She's the earth mother, Adi,' Zeruba whispered back. 'The great mother goddess.'

'You're embarrassing me,' Aditi cautioned.

He ignored her. And as he watched Mathangi's aunt, she swelled fantastically in his imagination into a primal, supernatural all-being, and out of that vision was born his most celebrated work, a huge, six-by-nine-foot painting titled *The Earth Mother*, which he completed in a sleepless, feverish rush in the fortnight before leaving for the US.

The painting showed a grotesquely, obscenely bloated woman of enormous breasts and buttocks, slender waist and capacious pelvis, the mother of all mothers, lying naked on her back, stretched out mountainously from horizon to horizon. Her legs were bent and spread out and straining, as if in birth throes, and she seemed to surge ominously from the bare, clayey earth—and also simultaneously decompose into it, her doughy flesh oozing viscously. Her eyes, huge and glazed like fine white china, with all-seeing black irises, sparkled with eerie, orgasmic ecstasy, as countless life forms, every conceivable species of plant and animal, pullulated frantically out of her fertile, putrefying flesh. It was an awful, revolting painting, and everybody loved it. And it won Zeruba the national Lalit Kala Akademi award a couple of years later.

Zeruba had little time for Aditi till he finished the painting. She resented this.

'We've just been married, and you've already started neglecting me,' she complained.

'I'm sorry,' he said. 'I didn't mean to. I just had to finish the painting.'

'The moment we got married, you changed,' she charged. 'You were so considerate and romantic before marriage, but the moment we got married you began to treat me indifferently, like some inconsequential appendage.' Zeruba had no idea what she was talking about. He could see no behavioural changes in himself.

Aditi's weeping episodes continued unabated in the US, became worse in fact, with the added aggravation of periodical suicide threats, usually by opening the car door when they were on the highway and threatening to throw herself out. On the first few occasions when this happened, he pulled the car over and tried to soothe her, but he soon realized that every time he did that, she demanded from him an ever greater degree of penitent compliance to her fancies. There would be no end to it, he felt, and decided that the only way to cure her would be to ignore her tantrums. The cold turkey treatment worked, and in time her weeping and suicide threats petered out. But she never forgave him. And she would wreak her revenge on him when they returned to India.

6

The two years that Zeruba spent in the US were singularly uneventful. They were in Crystal Lakes, a small town of many lakes in central Florida, in a small college whose main distinction was that it had the largest complex of buildings ever designed by Frank Lloyd Wright, structures that snugly burrowed into the rolling lakeside campus. It was the late sixties, and a gentle swell of liberalism had reached even the conservative nooks of America, and there was a growing interest in Indian mysticism everywhere. Aditi and Zeruba were, therefore, made much of by the cultural elite of the town, and Zeruba was even invited to be an honorary member of the Country Club.

It was a good life, but not very productive. Zeruba did only five paintings in the two years he spent in the US, which was a low output even by his leisurely pace of work. Those years were like an interregnum, a hyphen, in his life and work. The only really worthwhile thing he did in the US was to father Saumya, his daughter. Within a week of their arrival in the US, Aditi told him that she was mistaken about her pregnancy in India.

'I had missed my period, and I had morning sickness, so I was certain that I was pregnant,' she said. 'Are you sorry you married me?'

'Don't be ridiculous,' he said. 'Of course not.'

And that was the truth. They had, of course, inflicted a few bruises and gashes on each other in the course of the usual everyday aggravations of married life, but nothing very serious yet, nothing that portended a fatal denouement. And the birth of Saumya was for them compensation enough for all the shortcomings of their marriage. Zeruba was inordinately proud of the child, and cherished every memory about her, even the precise moment of her conception.

Aditi's sexuality had a fiercely gladiatorial quality about it. She loved to get on top of Zeruba, huffing and puffing and pounding him violently with her pelvis. Zeruba would usually lie inert, letting his mind wander, planning a painting or silently chanting a mantra, so as not to be gone before she came to. The trigger of ejaculation being in the head, he kept the connection insulated with other thoughts, so he invariably outlasted her in reaching the climax. She resented this. With her, sex was a combat, but how could she subdue a man who refused to join the joust? It was very frustrating. Also, she felt deeply hurt that he remained remote even in this most intimate act of their relationship. It was as if he was not there at all.

But on the particular Saturday night when Saumya was conceived, he was the satyr and she the cowering doe. That afternoon they had, along with several other faculty members, gone canoeing in a local river, which had rapids along part of its course. It was not particularly dangerous, but was nevertheless an adrenaline-pumping new experience for Zeruba, and he was still high on it when they got into bed that night. But she was tired and wanted to sleep.

'Get off me,' she cried. 'What's all this suddenly?'

But he kept her pinioned under him until he was done, then rolled off and fell asleep. The next morning she was sick. When she missed her period that month, she had a medical check-up, and it was confirmed that she was pregnant. This upset Aditi.

'I don't want a child just now,' she said. 'Let's get it aborted.'

The suggestion outraged Zeruba, and he eventually persuaded her to give up the mad idea. But she remained depressed throughout the pregnancy. However, once the baby was born, she transformed herself into a wonderfully caring mother. The child was born early morning on the Buddha Purnima day, the full-moon night of May. An attendant nurse showed the child to Zeruba through the glass panel of the nursery in the hospital, a little bundle of squirming flesh swathed in white sheets, her fists clenched tight and held close to her chin in a boxer's posture. There was already a fair length of hair on her head, and a tuft of it, a cowlick, stood up vertically, like the mast of a ship. Her eyes, screwed up against the glare of light, glinted. Zeruba fancied that she smiled.

7

Returning to his flat after the nightlong vigil in the hospital, Zeruba made himself a breakfast of scrambled eggs and toast, then took out a six-can pack of beer from the fridge and sat down at the window overlooking the lake, drinking and smoking and thinking about his daughter and about his own life. The birth of a human child, he reflected, was an event of absolute inconsequence in the cosmic scheme of things, or even in the earthly scheme of things, no more significant than the shifting of a speck of dust from one place to another by a random puff of wind. Yet how fundamentally important this was to him!

How did this being, this particular being, come to be? It was a chance convergence of opportunity and action, the odds against which were so great as to be incalculable. One day, in an hour of vagrant passion climaxing in a momentary and spasmodic ecstasy, a man ejaculated a glutinous white substance into the vagina of a woman through a distended tube of spongy tissue, depositing there some two or three hundred million microscopic sperms. Then the tube shrank, and the man slid off the woman and fell asleep. The woman too slept. But unbeknown to them both, at the far end of one of the fallopian tubes curling out from the woman's uterus like a Rajput's moustache, a tiny egg, smaller than a fine grain of sand, just a tenth of a millimetre in diameter, was lying in wait for this moment of destiny. The egg had a life of only about forty-eight hours—if a sperm did not mate with it within this time, it would perish. But it did nothing on its own about this. It just waited. The sperms had to find their way to it.

That was not easy. The sperms were fragile and infinitesimal, a mere one ten-thousandth the size of the egg. And they had to contend with surging vaginal and uterine currents that would flush them out. Now began a blind and desperate melee within the vagina, as the sperms, whipping their wispy tails, scrambled to get to the far, far away egg, driven by complex chemical impulses ingrained in them over aeons of evolution. Millions of them perished in the stampede, but many millions did finally manage to reach the egg. There the struggle continued. Only the fittest, or the luckiest, would survive. Of all the millions of sperms, only one, just one, could penetrate the egg. And penetration looked impossible, like trying to pierce an iron ball with a wet thread, for the egg was covered with an impervious protective membrane. Undaunted, the swarming sperms bombarded the egg with minute shots of enzymes, and this finally weakened the membrane and enabled one sperm to burrow into the egg and fuse with its nucleus.

It was thus that Saumya came to be. What would be the life of this innocent little baby he had brought into existence? What should he do to prepare her for life, Zeruba asked himself. In time she would have her own children, and these children would have children of their own, and the thread of life would keep on being spun out. But for what purpose and for how long? Surely not for ever. Everything ends in the end. The earth. The solar system. Even the universe. So what's the point of it all? For that matter, what's the point in thinking about it at all? One loves one's child without worrying about its fate or place in the cosmic scheme.

Two days later, Zeruba brought Aditi and the baby home. He was tense taking Saumya home from the hospital, especially while climbing the steep steps to their garage-top apartment, scared that he might accidentally drop her or that she might wriggle out of his hands. He could breathe easy only after he handed her to Aditi in bed. Saumya was a healthy baby, with a lusty appetite, and one of Zeruba's fondest memories was of her sitting in a canvas sling hung from the wooden lintel of their dining room door, being fed baby food by Aditi, gurgling happily with every spoonful she slurped.

They had, quite early in Aditi's pregnancy, decided to name their baby Saumya, if it was a girl. When Zeruba suggested the name, Aditi asked: 'What does it mean?'

'It means the gentle-natured,' Zeruba said. 'The word is also related to Soma, the sacred drink of Vedic Aryans, and to the moon.'

'Saumya Zeruba?' Aditi demurred. 'Sounds awful.'

'Saumya Tharakan,' Zeruba corrected her.

'Okay,' Aditi said. 'That's okay.'

A z h i y u r

1

The birth of Saumya finally mollified Korah and reconciled him to Zeruba's marriage. This was his first grandchild, so when Zeruba sent him a photo of the baby and mother, he wrote back asking him to go directly to Azhiyur on his return from the US, to celebrate the baby's first birthday there. Zeruba took a circuitous route on his way back to India, spending a couple of days in London and Paris, visiting museums, then going on to Amsterdam to breathe the air exhaled by Rembrandt, his favourite European painter, and finally to Moscow to see for himself the wretched reality of the imagined utopia of his childhood. From Moscow they took an Aeroflot flight to Delhi, where they landed in a summer dust storm.

Saumya was sick in Delhi, because of the oppressive heat, and she vomited a couple of times in the plane on their flight to Kochi, to the unconcealed disgust of the sullen airhostesses of the Indian Airlines. Aditi was tense throughout the flight, and would not even look out of the window when Zeruba pointed out to her the lush landscape of Kerala over which they were flying. And when they were disembarking in Kochi, she took an involuntary step back at the door of the plane, as if to get back into the plane and escape. She did not know what to expect from Zeruba's people.

She need not have worried. They were received at the airport by a troupe of his relatives, father, mother, brother, aunts and uncles and even a grand-aunt, and they were all very solicitous towards her. The grand-aunt had a lovely mansion in Kochi, where they had lunch. Aditi, once she was in the midst of people, quickly recovered her composure, and was warm and pleasant to everyone. All were already her friends.

In the evening they drove to Azhiyur, where, a couple of days later, Saumya's first birthday was celebrated on a grand scale, almost like a wedding. Korah, much to the relief of Zeruba, easily took to Aditi, and seemed to see in her his beloved daughter Devi returned to him in another mould.

When Zeruba mentioned this to Mathu one day, he asked, 'Any news of Devi?'

They were in the portico and Aditi was with them, dandling a squealing Saumya on her knees, and she said, 'We had a call from her just before we left for the US.'

'What did she say?' Mathu asked, continuing to speak to Zeruba, ignoring Aditi. 'Did you see her?'

'No,' Zeruba said. 'I asked for her address, but she said she was rather unsettled just then, and would call us later.'

'And she didn't call?'

'No.'

'It's very sad what has happened to her,' Mathu said.

'Maybe one day she'll return to us triumphant,' Aditi remarked.

Once again Mathu ignored her. 'Well, I've got to get back to work,' he said, rising.

When Mathu left, Aditi turned to Zeruba. 'Why doesn't your uncle like me?' she asked.

'What makes you think he doesn't like you?'

'I can sense it.'

'It takes him time to warm up to people.'

Aditi would not leave it at that. She handed the baby over to Zeruba and followed Mathu to the gatehouse. She found him sitting slumped at his desk.

'Why don't you like me, Kochappa?' she asked straightaway.

'Whatever gave you the idea that I don't like you?' he countered, averting his eyes.

'I'm no fool, Kochappa,' she said. 'I've a good feel for these things. So tell me.'

'I've nothing against you at all.'

'Then why are you aloof to me?' she asked. 'If I'm doing anything wrong, you should correct me. I'm family now.'

'Alright, I'll tell you,' Mathu said, turning in his chair to face Aditi. 'I'm worried about Zeruba. I've seen so many promising lives ruined by marriage. I would hate to see this happen to him.'

'Don't worry, Kochappa,' she assured. 'I'll take good care of him.'

2

When Aditi told Zeruba about her conversation with Mathu, he went to reassure him about Aditi.

'Of course we have tiffs,' Zeruba admitted. 'But that happens in every family. We'll be alright.'

'I hope so,' Mathu said. 'Anyway, she has perked up your father.'

'But how are you?'

'Great,' he said, as usual.

Later that day, Zeruba showed Aditi around the old wing of the house and told her something of the family history, but she had little interest in any of it, and he himself felt depressed by the dilapidated condition of the house. Every time he visited home, he found the house a little more dreary, a little more decrepit than before.

'It's so awfully gloomy,' Zeruba said to Mathu the next morning, when he went to see him in the gatehouse. 'It's going to tumble down one of these days.'

'Houses are like people,' Mathu said. 'They too have their allotted lifespan.'

The family pride that initially motivated Korah to venture on the renovation of the house had long since waned. Besides, he had no money any more. The house, even its new wing, was built in an age when only pedestrians and an occasional bullock-cart wended their way along the unpaved road in front of it, but the road was now macadamized and had heavy motorized traffic. And every time a bus or truck roared by, a tremor rattled the house. Though this did no damage to its central wooden structure—which, strange to say, stood rock solid—elsewhere in the house, the floor had buckled and cracked in several places, and tiles had fallen off here and there along the roof edges, giving the house a maimed, craggy appearance. A banyan seedling had taken root in a crack in the wall of the new wing. The smell of mould pervaded the house.

'Time has now almost run out for this house,' Mathu said. 'Yours will be the last generation to live here. So it has been foretold.'

'What do you mean?' Zeruba asked.

'I'll show you,' Mathu said. From his table drawer he took out a bunch of heavy, rusty keys on a metal ring, selected one, and with some effort opened one of the antique chests he had lined along a wall in his room, and took out from it a long, beautifully woven wickerwork casket with a vaulted lid. It was a manuscript box filled with old palm-leaf documents, and from the lot he took out one bundle, selected a strip and handed it to Zeruba. The leaf was covered with minute, closely written old Malayalam script, precisely inscribed with a very fine stylus. There were occult symbols on the margins of the leaf.

'This is the horoscope of our house,' Mathu said. 'Can you read it?'

'Difficult.'

Mathu took the leaf from Zeruba and, holding a large, round magnifying glass against it, chanted sonorously:

Eravi Shankaran eetradi Thingalam
Piraviyor Shankaran eetradi Thingalam . . .

93

'Doesn't make any sense to me,' Zeruba said.

'Nor to me.'

'Who wrote this?'

'The brother of Ittyachan who built this house. He was an occultist.'

Mathu showed Zeruba the name written at the end of the manuscript on the back of the leaf, beneath an elaborately flowery, illegible signature: Mathu Chacko.

'Your namesake!' Zeruba exclaimed.

'Yes. And here's the date: Karkadakam 8, 968.'

'968?'

'Of the Malayalam era. You've to add 825 years to it to get the English date. Karkadakam is August—the foundation of this house was laid in August 1793.'

'What's the prediction?'

'I know only its gist,' Mathu said.

'Which is?'

'According to an astrologer I once consulted, it says that four generations will thrive in this house, but the family fortunes will decline under the next three generations, and that the eighth generation will abandon it to ruin. Your generation.'

'I didn't know that houses had horoscopes.'

'Why not? Everything in the world rides on the energy of time,' Mathu said. 'The foundation of this house was laid at the worst possible time, in Karkadakam, the month of demonic influences.'

'But why?'

'Because of the arrogance of Ittyachan, who was the chief priest of our parish and thought that god himself rode on his shoulder.'

'And his brother was an occultist!'

'Yes, he was a Tantric. Was known as Chekuthan Mathu in his time.'

'Satan Mathu! God!'

'Actually, there was no evil in him,' Mathu said. 'He is said

94

to have been a very gentle, calm person, but he was a loner and kept very much to himself. People respected him, for he was a scholar and physician, but they also feared him, because of his occult powers. Young women were particularly kept out of his sight . . .'

'Pubescent women!'

'Yes, but how did you know?'

'I know it in my blood,' said Zeruba.

'He needed virgins for ritual sex in Tantric rites, not for carnal enjoyment,' said Mathu cuttingly. 'And he had the power to entice any woman on whom his eyes fell. He only had to beckon them, and they would run to him.'

'Really?'

'So it is said. Except for this quirk, he was a very kindly person. And a man of varied talents. When a European missionary brought into the town the first pendulum clock, he wheedled it from him for a few weeks and fabricated an identical clock made entirely of wooden parts, except for the spring.'

'He lived in this house?'

'No, no. The family ostracized him,' said Mathu. 'But that didn't bother him. He lived in a small cottage near the beach, with an Arayathi mistress.'

'Fisherwoman?'

'Yes. The legend is that she was golden complexioned, a real Aphrodite. Perhaps she had the blood of some ancient Greek or Roman trader in her veins.'

'Or of some European sailor of the recent times.'

'Maybe.'

'He was ostracized because he renounced our religion?'

'No. He remained a Christian.'

'How could a Tantric be a Christian?'

'Why not?' asked Mathu. 'Christianity has its own cabalistic sects with occult practices. So I suppose that in his own odd way Chekuthan Mathu was a Christian of sorts.'

The occultist, Mathu said, was in any case given a Christian burial, despite grumbling by some parishioners. But his funeral turned out to be as bizarre as everything else in his life, for when he was brought from his cottage to the church for the obsequies, it was found that he lay in the coffin with an erect penis, to the acute embarrassment of his brother, the priest, and the leering amusement of the congregation.

'I don't believe this,' Zeruba laughed.

'Such is the legend,' Mathu said.

He carefully replaced the palm-leaf bundle in the wicker box, returned the box to the chest and locked it. Then he opened another wooden box, and from it took out a small, fist-sized purple silk bag tied with a drawstring, pulled it open and tipped onto the table its content of divining cowries, brown with age.

'What's this?' asked Zeruba, stretching a hand to pick them up. Mathu slapped the hand away.

'Did you have a bath today?' he asked.

'Not yet,' Zeruba said.

'Then you can't touch these. These are sacred cowries.'

'These also belonged to Chekuthan Mathu?'

'I think so,' said Mathu, rolling the cowries in his palm. 'These are certainly charged with some mysterious potency. I can feel their vibration in my hands.'

'How strange all this is!'

'What?'

'The Christian-Hindu melange in our family.'

'It's not all that strange,' Mathu said. 'This sort of intertwining is there in several old Syrian Christian families. Our own family legend is that we were originally Uralars, Namboodiri trustees of the local temple, whom St. Thomas converted. The first named family to be converted.'

'There is not a shred of evidence for that.'

'True, there's no direct evidence,' conceded Mathu. 'But there is strong circumstantial evidence. You know that there were close contacts between West Asia and Kerala in the time of Christ, and there were Jewish traders settled here. So it is quite likely that the apostle came here in a trading ship to preach Christ's message to the local Semites. And he probably converted some prominent local families also.'

If St. Thomas did indeed come to Kerala, it is quite probable that he landed near about Azhiyur, Zeruba's hometown, which was directly across the lagoon from Kodungalloor, the ancient capital of Kerala and a world-renowned port city, the very hub of international spice trade. There was a fine all-weather harbour there in the lagoon, carved by the Periyar, the river of life of Kerala, which flowed down the northern flank of Azhiyur into the lagoon, and then into the Arabian Sea through an estuary just south of Kodungalloor. Ships were safe there even from the howling violence of monsoon storms. Phoenicians and Egyptians, perhaps even Babylonians before them, had traded there. Later came Greeks, Romans, Hebrews and Arabs, and many of them settled there. There was said to have been a Roman garrison in the town at one time, even a temple of Augustus.

Azhiyur, the twin city of Kodungalloor, was also a prosperous commercial centre once, extolled by poets as a town as permeated with the heady odour of money as a sandalwood forest with fragrance. The town was dominated by seven families of Jacobite Syrian Christian traders, descendants of ancient Semitic migrants or early Indian converts. When trade in Azhiyur slumped with the decline of Kodungalloor in late medieval times, these families took to agriculture, acquiring extensive tracts of land. And they continued to dominate the town. Zeruba belonged to this clan.

'Maybe all this is true, but it still doesn't make us Namboodiris,' Zeruba protested.

'Well, on this we have more direct evidence,' Mathu said.

'What?'

'Solid facts,' Mathu said. 'Don't you know that our family enjoyed certain rights in the Shiva temple here?'

'No.'

'Well, till about a century back, the silk umbrella to begin the temple procession used to be opened only in the presence of the head of our family, and the first sheaves of paddy harvested from the temple fields used to be brought to us as a symbolic tribute and fixed with cow-dung on the lintel of the main door of our house. It is said that there was an understanding that when we were in need, the temple would meet it, and when the temple was in need, we would meet it.'

'Do you really believe this?'

'It's not a question of belief,' said Mathu. 'These are facts. In any case, facts do not matter all that much, Zeruba. We are who we believe we are. That's what defines our sense of self, not what the facts prove.'

'Fantasies make us what we are?'

'In a way. Myths are the means by which individuals and families, even communities and nations, give themselves identities.'

'But they aren't real.'

'Real enough for those who believe in them,' Mathu said. 'And I believe that it's our high caste pretensions that turned us into a family of scholars. Why, even your great-grandfather, for all his wildness, was proficient in Sanskrit, Tamil and English, apart from Malayalam. He was one of the first persons in our town to learn English. I remember him sitting at this table, right here, with four Bibles open before him—Tamil, Malayalam, Sanskrit and English—and reading aloud each verse in each language.'

'There is a Sanskrit Bible?'

'Yes. Published in 1858,' said Mathu. 'We still have it—want to see it?'

'Some other time,' said Zeruba. 'I thought the old man wasn't religious.'

'He wasn't. The Bible was the only book in print those days, and he loved to read.'

Zeruba's ancestral home was on the main street of Azhiyur, directly facing the Shiva temple across the road and immediately to the left of the parish church. The house was built at the turn of the eighteenth century, on the site of a much older family home destroyed during the sacking of the town by Tipu Sultan, the Mysore ruler, during his brief foray into Kerala in 1789-90. A large, double-storeyed edifice, its main wing was built entirely—floor, walls and roof—of thick panels of jackwood, now black with grime and age. The core of this structure were two large strongrooms on the ground floor, which had beneath them an underground vault reached by a trapdoor in one of the rooms. The vault was empty now except for roaches and scampering rodents. Under the wooden floor of the vault—or perhaps elsewhere in the house or the compound, no one knew for sure—were said to be buried seven jars full of *varahans*, medieval gold coins, guarded by serpents or genies.

'Is this true?' Zeruba once asked Mathu.

'Possible, but unlikely,' Mathu said. 'Such stories are told of most old houses.'

'Why don't we dig up the floor and see?' Zeruba asked. 'We can do with the money now, with nearly all our lands gone.'

'It has been warned that we should look for the treasure only when the family has been reduced to an income of four coconuts and four measures of rice,' said Mathu. 'We haven't got to that yet.'

'It won't be long.'

'Then we will see.'

One of the strongrooms was open and was used as a junk room. Haphazardly stored in it were several huge cauldrons of copper and bronze, a few bronze piss-pots, spittoons and oil-lamps, all thickly covered with patina, several rusty tins, a pile of wicker baskets, a few China jars, bundles of old magazines, and amidst them, quite incongruously, a gleaming white Western style commode. There were also a few recent relics there—a broken-down radio, a bald car tyre, a couple of Zeruba's old badminton and tennis racquets, the tricycle on which Chacko used to tear around the house even as a teenager, several celluloid dolls of their sister Devi, their naked, pink bodies covered with grime. The other strongroom was kept locked with an elongated, kitten-sized padlock. The key to the lock had been lost, and the room had not been opened for three generations. No one knew anymore what was in it.

'Your father once engaged a blacksmith to open the lock,' said Mathu. 'He worked on it for a couple of days, then gave up.'

'When was this?' Zeruba asked.

'Twenty–thirty years back.'

'Why don't we try again?'

'Your father has given up on the future,' Mathu said. 'He won't do it.'

'Why don't you?'

'I? Oh no, not me,' Mathu said, laughing. 'I've given up on the world itself. But why don't you?'

'I don't belong here,' Zeruba said morosely.

5

The first floor of the wooden building consisted solely of a spacious but low-ceilinged hall, reached by a steep wooden staircase with narrow, widely spaced steps. Its roof of solid wood planks was overlaid with a three-inch thick plaster of crushed stone and lime, which kept the house cool in summer and insulated it from the risk of fire from the thatch of braided palm leaves that originally covered it. The thatch was replaced with tiles in the third quarter of the nineteenth century, in the same year when the local church and temple were tiled. It was the first house in the town to have a tile roof.

It was also the first house to have an electric connection. The news of this marvellous invention was first brought to Azhiyur by a grand-aunt of Zeruba, who as a child had gone to Madras to visit some relatives, and on returning told her mother and sisters about how lights in the houses there came on magically when the wall was pressed with a finger.

'C'mon, what lies you tell!' her mother scolded.

The entire wood-built wing of the house was unoccupied, and was unliveable. The family lived in the single-storeyed masonry wing attached to it at the back, consisting of four bedrooms, a kitchen and a dining room, all built along the narrow, parapeted veranda girding a small, bare inner courtyard. This wing of the house was extensively modified by Thoma Tharakan, Zeruba's great-grandfather, who was a man of taste and innovative ideas. The rooms there were originally very low, their flat wooden ceiling only a little over six feet high, because that was the traditional architectural convention, though people had grown taller over the centuries. Thoma had the floors there dug up and lowered, to give the rooms a height of nearly seven and a half feet. But he left the doors as they were, though they were only about five and a half feet high and were of an antique design, built without hinges, their panels of solid, single piece wood turning with explosive creaks on thick shafts fitted into sockets gouged into the door frame. Zeruba, six feet tall, had to bend double to pass through them.

Thoma Tharakan also built a new wing extending westward from the old building, with a large drawing room on the ground floor and a master bedroom upstairs, and he converted the porch of the house into a broad, sweeping portico stretching over the entire frontage of the house. He loved gardening, and planted, in neat rows along the borders of the front yard of the house, croutons of sun-blest colours and clusters of jasmine bushes, and in the yard itself a laburnum on each side, lush with golden chandelier blossoms. And he trained bougainvilleas over the roof of the portico, to relieve the severity of the house with their frothing crimson flowers. In time, the croutons and the bougainvilleas, untended, turned into untidy bushes, and the jasmine clumps became scabrous with age. But the laburnum continued to flower profusely every year around Vishu, the spring festival, in a fraudulent promise of rejuvenation.

6

For all the modifications that Thoma Tharakan made in the house, he did not himself live in the main building, but occupied the gatehouse. This structure had, on the ground floor, two disused masonry rooms flanking the gate, and above them, reached by a covered external staircase, a large, airy and pleasant room built of wood with many jalousied windows, and with narrow balconies at the front and the back, resting on slender wooden brackets. This was the lair of Thoma Tharakan.

And this was the room that Mathu now occupied, and he had turned it into something of a family museum, salvaging antiques from the junk room. The furniture in the room consisted of a bed, a table and chair, two glass-doored almirahs, and several old wooden chests of various sizes and shapes, all with brass knobs and fittings, some lacquered. All these were lined against the walls to leave a large open space in the middle of the room for Mathu to pace about, as he constantly did, working on his endless chimerical projects. The bed, formerly used by Thoma Tharakan, was an immense four-poster affair in rosewood, broad and high, with intricately carved trefoil designs and pierced volutes on its high headboard and footboard, which had taken, according to family records, a carpenter and his two assistants ninety-eight workdays to make. It was originally in the middle of the room, but Mathu pushed it to the far corner, and placed next to it the table and chair, which also belonged to Thoma Tharakan. Over the sides of the table were hung, on chains fixed to the ceiling beams with brackets, two large brass oil lamps, and there were on the wall alongside them clusters of oil smears, like tongues of black flame, where Thoma Tharakan had wiped his fingers after pushing the wicks in the lamps.

Like everything else in the room, the articles on the table were precisely arranged. Its centrepiece was an antique bronze standish, which now held the gold-capped Parker pen presented to Mathu by his father on his graduation. Behind the standish, on a polished wooden base placed against the wall, were four small cannon balls found in the compound after Tipu's raid on Azhiyur. On the wall facing the table, at eye level, was a large, plain *Malayala Manorama* calendar, and immediately above it, a well-preserved and elegantly proportioned halberd, its quarter-moon blade razor-sharp and its long rosewood handle gleaming with brass rings.

Above the halberd was an antique cuckoo-clock, its time frozen. Alongside it, over the headboard of the bed, was a muzzle-loading flintlock gun, its black stock decorated by some ancestor with crude silver inlays of birds and animals. On the other walls of the room were fixed several old and rusted swords, and between them a number of yellowing framed family photographs. The almirahs were crammed with books, arranged precisely according to their heights.

At the foot of the bed was a large wooden chest, elaborately adorned with brass inlays. This was a most remarkable piece, with numerous tiny drawers and boxes inside it, some thirty or forty of them, that fitted into each other in an intricate manner, and could be taken out only in a particular sequence, for otherwise everything in it would jam hopelessly. It evidently took great patience and skill to make the chest—and it required great patience and skill to use it.

'It would drive me nuts,' Zeruba said.

'It very nearly drove me nuts,' Mathu said. It took him several months of resolute application to learn how to take out the boxes and open the drawers, and fit them back.

Korah

1

Zeruba could well imagine his uncle working on the chest with cheerful diligence day after day, week after week. Nothing ever disturbed his equanimity, or tried his patience. Mathu was like a man living inside a mathematical theorem, the equation of his life entirely insulated from the buffeting of the world.

In contrast, his elder brother Korah, Zeruba's father, writhed and sputtered with every impulse of the world and forever seethed with discontent. He craved for status and power, but these eluded him, and he blamed everything and everyone but himself for his fate—his parents, his wife, his children, and, more than anything else, the changed times, Indian independence, democracy, the communists. Often, when acquaintances visited him, he would bring out and show them the *veera-shankala*, the hero-bracelet, which his father, Paulose, had received from the raja of Kochi.

'The rajas knew how to honour old families,' he would say. 'But the sons of bitches that rule us now . . .'

'Yes, yes,' they would agree hypocritically. 'Those were the days!'

'Gone! Everything gone.'

The bracelet was a chunky but delicately worked piece of solid gold jewellery, with two elephants interlocking their trunks at its clasp. It was presented to Paulose when he relinquished— forced to resign, in fact—his office as the chief of police of the kingdom. The raja had appointed him, a prominent Christian, to the post in the hope of pleasing the Resident, the British Viceroy's deputy in the kingdom, but he regretted the decision almost immediately, for although Paulose was well qualified for the job by his education as a lawyer and by his robust physique, he was temperamentally unsuited for service, being arrogant, short-tempered and wilful.

His first year in office was relatively uneventful, but he precipitated a crisis in his second year by arresting the head priest of a temple in Kochi for some misdemeanour and parading him handcuffed through the streets. This he did against the express wishes of the royal family, saying that a criminal was a criminal, whatever his caste and status. The incident caused a minor riot in the town. Paulose then set out to prove his impartiality by arresting the priest of a local church on some pretext and parading him too, through the town in handcuffs. This did not mollify Hindus, but infuriated Christians, and it nearly caused another riot. A few months later Paulose—Paulose *Superint*, as he would be known thereafter all his life—levelled the communal score by having a prominent Muslim merchant of Kochi's grain market publicly whipped, for molesting a Hindu woman worker.

When the complaint about the molestation was brought before Paulose, he used his magisterial powers to sentence the merchant to whipping, and himself went in his dog cart to supervise the punishment, dressed in full uniform, and wearing a huge gold-laced turban. At the centre of the bazaar, where the whipping took place, a multicoloured cap was placed on the head of the culprit and he was stripped to the waist and tied to a scaffold by hand and foot. Rules required that no more than twelve strokes should be given, and that the strokes should be moderate and administered on the back of the criminal, with a pause of a specified time between strokes. Punctilious about everything, though tyrannical by nature, Paulose interfered when lashes were struck too hard. The flogging was watched by a large number of Hindus and Muslims, and the air crackled with tension. A rash word or act by anyone there could have sparked a communal conflagration. Fortunately, the crowd dispersed peacefully after the whipping.

In all his actions, Paulose had done nothing outside the law or beyond his power, but his high-handedness was an embarrassment to the mild-mannered raja—there had been no public flogging in the state for years—and he desired to get rid of his overweening officer. But Paulose had the backing of the British Resident, and so was able to continue in office for some years, disdainfully ignoring the displeasure of the raja. Then one day, when Paulose was on his usual pre-dawn stroll through the town, he was set on with a sword by an unknown assailant, perhaps a henchman of the raja, as rumour had it. The blow was meant to sever his head, but at the precise moment it was struck, he stumbled on a stone and bent over, so the sword fell across his back, and that saved his life. But he was hospitalized for a couple of months, and the wound left a raised white welt diagonally across his back. When he recovered, he was persuaded by the raja to leave service honourably, and it was on that occasion that the raja ceremonially presented him the hero-bracelet.

After leaving service, Paulose continued to live in Kochi for some years, where he had built a house, and tried to set himself up as a lawyer. In that he was a dismal failure. He took up only such cases where he was convinced that his client had a just cause, and to convince himself of that he often put the clients on a private trial himself. Not many were willing to put up with such haughtiness. And even the few cases he took up, he lost, because he did not have the low cunning needed to manipulate witnesses and judges, but proceeded on the grand assumption that justice would inevitably prevail. It seldom did. Pretty soon no one turned up to consult him, and he returned home to Azhiyur.

2

By the time Paulose returned to Azhiyur, the family fortunes had sunk low, his father, Thoma, having sold the bulk of the family lands to finance his ruinous three decade-long feud with Vareed, his father-in-law, for supremacy in the church and the town. The clash between them was part of the larger conflict between conservatives and progressives in the Jacobite Syrian Christian community of Kerala, which began in the mid-nineteenth century and raged on for well over a hundred years. Thoma headed the younger group of reformists in the town parish, while his father-in-law, who was a trustee of the Kerala church, was the leader of the conservatives. One thing led to another, and presently the differences between Vareed and Thoma over public issues slued into bitter private hostilities, matters of absolute personal honour that had to be vindicated at all costs.

It was an uneven contest, for Thoma was no match to his suave father-in-law. A cultured and mild-mannered aristocrat, Vareed was accommodative throughout his clash with Thoma, always ready to forgive lapses and make compromises. But Thoma, irascible and bent on self-destruction, remained implacable. He sought absolute triumph or nothing. And, discomfited at every turn by Vareed, he grew increasingly virulent and reckless over the years, his frustrations fuelling his naturally violent temper. The conflict ruined Thoma, ruined his family too.

There is no rational explanation for the bizarre conduct of Thoma. He was not at all devout and had no real interest in religion—he went to church only for parish meetings, never to attend the mass. And he disregarded all the prescriptions and proscriptions of the church, and took vociferous delight in ridiculing saints and miracles. But church politics was quite another matter. This was his magnificent obsession, the battle for power. In another age he would have probably led a private army, but now his battles were fought mostly in law courts, where he filed case after case against the group headed by his father-in-law, to wrest the control of the church.

He lost all the cases and all the appeals. When the state high court gave the final verdict against the faction he led, he felt so humiliated by it that he waited until nightfall to return to the town, and even then took a back lane to go home, jumping over fences and hedges. He did not emerge from the house for several weeks, and entirely withdrew from public life thereafter.

'He was very quiet in his last years,' Mathu recalled. 'The fire in him had burned out.'

But Thoma in his durbar days was the uncrowned king of Azhiyur. That at least was how he saw himself. He used to sit on the balcony of his gatehouse, like a king on a throne, and all except his relatives were required to take off their turbans and fold their umbrellas while passing in front of the house.

'How did he get away with it?' Zeruba asked.

'Because people were timid,' said Mathu. 'He once scandalized the whole town by spitting in the face of a Brahmin pundit, his own guru, for not removing his turban while speaking to him.'

'Incredible!'

'There were many such misdeeds by him,' Mathu said. 'I suppose that in his view he was merely exercising the traditional privileges of the family, though he no longer had the kind of wealth and power enjoyed by his ancestors. In his early days, he used to go about in a twelve-oared boat like a king, and even the river patrol used to give him a wide berth. But all this changed when he lost his wealth.'

'He became meek?'

'Not really,' Mathu said. 'The elephant doesn't become a mouse because it loses weight. But he was devastated by the loss of wealth and power, and sort of shrank into himself. Once when I was going with him in a boat in the lagoon—'

'—In the twelve-oared barge?'

'No, no. All that was long gone,' Mathu said. 'This was just an ordinary country boat, propelled by a single punter. Well, grandfather swept his arms grandly at the islands and the coconut groves along the lagoon, and said to me, "Look son, all these lands that you see here, these are all lands we once owned. And all the families living there, hundreds and hundreds of them, were

our tenants or serfs. And all that was lost by me, all by myself."
He laughed saying this, but his eyes were moist.'

From several hundred acres of prime land, including some
islands in the lagoon, his wealth had shrunk to just a couple of
dozen acres. But he was absolutely scrupulous in his dealings.
Although some of his relatives advised him to transfer the
properties to his wife to thwart the creditors, he refused to do so,
saying that he would rather have his family driven into the streets
than cheat. He had to sell most of the family heirlooms too,
including the jewelled gold crowns worn by the brides and grooms
of the family at their weddings—he smashed them with a hammer
and sold them for their gold and gem value, even though the
buyer pleaded with him not to smash them and offered to double
the price. But he kept the two domed brass boxes in which the
crowns were kept, as hollow symbols of his lost power and
prestige.

'He even burned the *nilayangi*, the head to foot dress which
his ancestors had worn on ceremonial occasions,' Mathu said.

'Why?'

'How do I know!' said Mathu. 'It was awesome the way he
ruined the family in just a couple of decades.'

'Sad.'

'Well, that's life,' said Mathu. 'As the Persian saying goes,
the bucket of fortune that comes up full at one turn of the wheel
must go down empty at the next turn.'

'Sad all the same.'

3

For all the violence in his life, Thoma Tharakan died peacefully
in bed. He did not have to suffer even the humiliation of being
laid low by the infirmities of old age or by any lingering illness.
He just lay down in bed for his usual afternoon nap one day, and
didn't wake up. The servant who brought him his evening tea

found him lying stretched on his back in bed, his arms folded under his head on the pillow.

'*Muthalali*,' he called softly, unsure whether he was asleep or lying awake with his eyes closed. Not getting any response, he padded out quietly. He returned after a while with a fresh cup of tea, but found him still lying in exactly the same posture, so he looked at him closely and noticed that he was not breathing.

'When we saw him, he seemed just sleeping,' Mathu recalled.

'He died in this room?' Zeruba asked.

'Right on this bed. All the shops in the street closed immediately.'

'No one would give a damn these days.'

'Our only privilege today is to be buried in the second row of the church cemetery, immediately after the row for priests,' said Mathu. 'One day soon that too will be gone.'

On the death of Thoma Tharakan, the family responsibilities fell on his only son, Paulose. The general expectation was that he, because of his education and the high office he had held in government, would be able to shore up the tottering family fortunes. That did not happen. Outwardly he was still very much the lordly patriarch, but that was just a facade. He was really a broken man. All around him, the old families that had dominated the land for centuries were crumbling into debris in the flood of social change, and there was nothing that he or anyone else could do about it. Besides, he was ill most of this time, and died within three years of his father's death. So it devolved on his sons, Korah and Mathu, particularly on Korah, the older son, to take care of the family. Neither was up to it.

Korah, like his father, was a lawyer. He hated lawyering, but was forced into the profession by his father, for it was the career of choice of the ambitious those days, as lawyers enjoyed high incomes and were at the top of the newly emerging society. Korah didn't share his father's ambitions. He was poor in studies, and though he somehow managed to get through college and obtain a bachelor's degree, he adamantly refused to go on to study law.

'Then you must take up some other profession,' his father told him.

'I'll stay at home and manage our lands,' Korah said.

'What lands?' Paulose laughed. 'There aren't any lands left to manage.'

Korah then said that he would study engineering, but Paulose would not agree to that, for an astrologer he consulted at this time had predicted that Korah stood in grave danger from machines but would shine as a lawyer and would become a judge. A judge! This was the very thing that Paulose dreamed of for his son. The prediction sealed Korah's fate. Paulose now coerced him to join the Thiruvananthapuram Law College, and, on his graduation, had him set up his practice in Kochi.

Meanwhile, his marriage was arranged with a girl from a prominent family in a nearby village. Her great-great-grand-uncle was, in the early decades of the nineteenth century, the first Christian judge of Kochi, and Paulose saw in the marriage proposal a sure and lucky sign that the astrologer's prediction about Korah would come true. It was also hoped that the bride, Mariam, a calm and grave woman, would have a sobering influence on Korah.

4

The marriage turned out to be a disaster.

'It was the union of fire and water,' said Mathu.

'Ice,' said Zeruba.

'You know your mother better,' said Mathu.

Korah was mercurial, hot-tempered, gregarious and fun-loving, but Mariam was cold and humourless, and had no joy in other people. While he, for all the disappointments of his life, was an incurable optimist and compulsive adventurer, who ever surged towards what he thought was the blazing light at the end of the tunnel, she, an introverted pessimist, found nothing to look forward to in life and shrank ever deeper into the interior darkness of her life. In their whole life together, they had spoken very little to each other. They had no common life to share.

It is difficult to say who caused the greater misery to whom. Outwardly, Korah's frustration was greater—while Mariam curled up mute and aloof inside herself, as if in an iron shell, he kept hammering at the shell to get her to respond to him. Their early years together, when he was struggling to establish himself as a lawyer, were particularly vexing to him, because she offered him no solace at home to relieve his professional frustrations.

Korah was an utter failure as a lawyer. Though he had many boon companions and they sent several clients to him, he lost even the easiest suits. He did not have the mental discipline and stamina to think cases through, and, though quite loquacious in the company of his friends, he was nervous and tongue-tied in court.

'Have patience,' Paulose advised him when he wanted to quit practice and return home. 'You'll soon learn the ropes.'

'You never learned them,' Korah reminded him.

'It was different in my case. My mind was on other things.'

'So is mine,' Korah said. 'I want to come home and try my hand at some business.'

'Please wait awhile longer,' Paulose told him.

It is possible that Paulose genuinely expected his son to eventually succeed as a lawyer and fulfil the astrologer's prediction, but he certainly did not want him to take to business. Korah, he knew, did not have the caution and craftiness essential for success in business, and that it was more the restlessness of character than the passion for making money that made him think of a business career.

Paulose was also worried about something else—his wife, Sarah, disliked Korah and detested Mariam, and he feared that their presence at home would set off family tensions. Paulose, in sharp contrast to his arrogant public persona, was a lamb at home, and was besotted with his wife, a buxom, moon-faced beauty of the traditional type, and a most remarkable woman. She was calm and soft-spoken, like Korah's wife, but while Mariam was limp and passive, Sarah was imperious. She did not ever raise her voice because she never needed to—her quiet words were unquestioningly obeyed by everyone, by husband, children, servants, and whomever she dealt with. Mariam too obeyed her, but with what seemed to Sarah to be sullen resentment, instead of the usual high esteem she received from everyone else. She suspected in Mariam malice and ill will towards her. She did not like Korah either, because of his wild temperament.

'Why do you shout so much?' she once asked Korah, sending a servant and calling him to her, when she heard him yelling at a tenant for some offence.

'I can't tolerate the insolence of these people,' he said.

'When a dog barks at you, do you bark back?' she asked, closing the issue.

5

'I won't have them living with us,' Sarah flatly told Paulose when he suggested that maybe Korah and his family should return home.

Paulose demurred, but finally yielded to her will, as usual. However, since Korah had absolutely no earnings at all as a lawyer, Paulose sent him a small amount of money every month, just enough to keep him going. But when Paulose died bequeathing all the family property to Sarah, it placed Korah entirely at the mercy of his wilful and censorious mother. 'All things revolve round my little finger,' she said at a family gathering soon after the death of Paulose, looking pointedly at Korah and Mariam. 'Let all remember that.'

Sarah considered Korah to be a fool and a wastrel, and she now decided to bring him to some sense of responsibility by cutting off his allowance. 'We have given you all the education that you were capable of receiving, and we have supported you financially for several years,' she wrote to him in Kochi a few months after her husband's death. 'This dependency cannot go on—it is not good either for you or for our family. It is time that you stood on your own feet. So from the beginning of next year I won't be sending you any money.' This was written on a postcard, so it was read by the Azhiyur postmaster, who put a finger to his nose and commented to the clerk who showed him the card, 'What a shame!'

The moment Korah got the letter, he flew off the handle, threatening to kill his wife and children and commit suicide. Hearing of the crisis, an aunt of his, who lived in Kochi, rushed to Azhiyur with her husband to plead Korah's case, but Sarah calmly explained to them why she had done what she did.

'How long do you think the little land we still have will last?' she asked them. 'What'll happen in the future if he doesn't earn an independent living?'

'What if he does something rash?' they asked.

'He won't,' she assured them. 'I know my children. When you get back you'll find him in a different mood.'

And indeed that was how it was. 'Alright,' Korah said to himself. 'Even if I have to earn my living by working as a coolie in the market, I won't ever take another paisa from her.'

But how was Korah to live? A briefless lawyer, he had no income at all. The milk-woman threatened to stop her deliveries as he could not pay the seven or eight rupees he owed her, and the provision stores man threatened to take him to court to recover the eighty-five rupees owed to him. Korah somehow managed, selling or pawning his wife's jewels one by one, learning prudence and frugality in his adversity—the very lessons his mother wanted him to learn—hoping for some miracle to turn his fortune.

There were no miracles. And the worst was yet to come. The one advantage that Korah had at this time was that he did not have to pay rent for his residence in Kochi, as he lived in the house that Paulose had built there. Though Paulose had sold it to clear some debts, it was considered to be still virtually with the family, as it was one of his sisters who had bought it. Initially, when Korah asked for the house, she readily agreed to let him live there, saying, 'It'll at least be swept now and then.' But now, on the death of Paulose, she feared that if Korah was allowed to live there for long it would be difficult to get him to leave. She therefore asked him to vacate the house, saying that a bank wanted to rent it.

This was a totally unexpected blow. Where would Korah go? What would he do? He did not have the means to rent even a modest house. His mother did not want him at home. It was a particularly bad time for him, as Mariam was ill with typhoid then, and was hardly in a condition to move out. But self-respect required that he should not live on sufferance even for a moment. So he sold another one of his wife's jewels and moved into a tiny rented house, a hut, in fact.

'I put Amma in a rickshaw, took hold of Zeruba by one hand and Devi by the other hand, and slunk out of the house one early morning and went to live in the hut,' Korah recalled one day many years later. He was lying on the divan in the portico of the Azhiyur house, and Zeruba and Chacko were sitting on the parapet facing him. Mariam sat apart in a chair, silent, showing no emotion at all. 'Our little servant girl followed us holding a chicken in her hand, our sole possession in the world. That was the saddest day of my life.'

'I was born in the hut?' Chacko asked.

'Yes,' Korah said with a momentary flash of his old fiery temper. 'And don't you ever forget that, though you now preen as if you own the world.'

The hut was in a lane where pedestrians on the road stopped to urinate, and the stench there was suffocating. 'How can they live in this stinking place!' their relatives used to mutter to themselves, scowling and stopping up their noses while entering the lane.

'It was not our choice,' Korah continued. 'We were too poor.

I paid five rupees a month as rent for that hut. Its walls were plastered with mud, and it was thatched with coconut fronds. The roof leaked in several places. It was all very dreary.'

Korah and family lived in the hut for about three years. His woes ended only when he received his share of the family property on the death of his mother and was able to return home. Even that was not without a crisis. When Sarah was ailing and felt that she would not recover, she decided to write a will dividing the family property between her two sons, giving the bulk of it, including the ancestral home, to Mathu, her favourite, and only a subsistence portion to Korah. But Mathu, to whom she confided this, opposed the proposal.

'Do you want us brothers to live in amity after your time?' he asked her.

'Yes, that's my wish,' she said.

'If that's your wish, then you should divide the property equitably. The division you are proposing will result only in rancour between us,' he said. 'Actually I should get only a subsistence portion and Chettan should get the bulk of the property, for he is the elder son. And he has a family, while I've none.'

'You might marry again.'

'Impossible.'

'But how can I give it to him?' she asked. 'Whatever I give him, he will squander it all in no time in some hare-brained business.'

She had good reason to fear that. When Korah was in Kochi, unable to make a living as a lawyer, he had launched several madcap schemes—a company to make hair oil, another to make shoe-polish, another for rearing sheep—by raising money from his indulgent friends and relatives and by selling his wife's jewels.

All the ventures folded within a few months. But that did not dishearten him, and he did not consider himself a failure as a businessman.

'I lost only what I invested. I didn't get into debt,' he proudly proclaimed.

Mariam reminded Mathu about all this. 'He will only drive his family into the street,' she said.

'It's his insecurity that makes him do these things,' Mathu said. 'What he needs is sympathy, not reproach.'

'Sympathy would only reinforce his delusion that what he does is creditable,' she protested.

'Reproach would only lead him to more desperate acts,' Mathu rejoined.

'Either way he would ruin himself,' Sarah said.

'Look, Amma, even if you give me most of the property, I'll give Chettan his due share after your time, because I won't be able to live with that injustice on my conscience.'

'Alright,' she said. 'Then I'll put the property in a trust in the name of his sons.'

'Don't even think of it,' Mathu said. 'Don't you see how humiliating it'll be to him?'

Sarah finally agreed to a fair division of the property. Thus, Korah at last came to have a place of his own to live in, and a fair income to live on. But Mariam's fears about him proved true. Soon after settling in Azhiyur on the death of his mother, he launched a fresh series of businesses, a marine fishing company, a hospital, a coir factory, and so on. It was no longer financial exigency that drove him to launch these ventures, but the need to vindicate himself and prove that he was not such an improvident fellow as people took him to be. But his was a singular approach to business. 'Even if I lose, no one else should lose money on my account,' he once declared in all seriousness. 'This is my business principle.'

It was evident that old money could not make new money. Fortunately, Korah soon got disgusted with business. 'You can't trust anybody in the world these days,' he grumbled, as his partners and employees siphoned money out of his firms. He then bought an elephant, a mangy old elephant, remembering that his ancestors in feudal times had the privilege of keeping elephants. Mariam was dismayed by this, and feared that he would take it into his head to go riding about the town on the elephant.

'My god!' she whispered to Zeruba. 'If he does that I will never be able to show my face in public again.'

'Don't be silly, Amma,' Zeruba said. 'He won't do anything so ridiculous.'

Korah did not in any case have the opportunity to ride the elephant, for the wretched beast died soon after he bought it. Then he bought a car, though he had nowhere to go which he could not reach in a ten-minute stroll. Every morning the driver would start the car and move it from its newly built shed and park it at the portico of the house, where he washed and cleaned it. He would then go back to the shed to lie on a mat there and read pulp magazines till evening, when he would drive the car back into the shed and go home. The family used the car perhaps once in a couple of months.

7

People snickered at these fancies of Korah, though never to his face. They were wary of him, for he, like his grandfather, had a fearsome temper and was prone to violence. Mathu was the only one who was sympathetic to Korah and was supportive to him, even though he knew that his brother's schemes were all fatuous and that he was allowing himself to be exploited by others.

The problem with Korah, according to Mathu, was that their mother had given him a terrible inferiority complex by her scorn for him. He was, said Mathu, looking for some worthy role for himself, rummaging through the rubble of his life. He yearned to belong somewhere, to be somebody, but the old world, where he could have without ability or effort found a secure social position as a squire, had slid away from under his feet, and he did not have the skill or the strength of character to find his footing in the new world of professions and business. He was like Thrishanku, neither here nor there.

Korah felt hemmed in by life and circumstances. The old vaulting, self-destructive family pride had, in him, shrivelled into petty discontent. And his compulsive need to make his presence felt often led him to pick quarrels at family and social functions for some imagined slight or some inconsequential deviation from conventional practice.

'It's such a small matter, why do you make such a fuss about it?' people would ask him.

'Small things matter,' he would respond. 'If you let slip small things, then everything will be ruined.'

'But we must be pragmatic.'

'Pragmatic? I only know what is right and what is wrong,' he would say, and go on ranting.

He quietened down considerably later in life, though he still did occasionally erupt volcanically. He became resigned to his fate, and his only wish was to live out his remaining days with some semblance of dignity. He now spent most of his time lying on the divan in the portico, reading crime fiction, especially the works of Peter Cheney and Leslie Charteris, of which he had whole sets, and read them over and over again. Slim Callaghan, Cheney's tough, cool, chain-smoking, poker-faced and taciturn detective hero was his particular favourite—this was the man he imagined he would have been had his life been different.

8

'Nothing in my life turned out right,' Korah said to Mathu one evening when they were having a drink together. 'Nothing at all.'

He sat reclining on the divan, his eyes closed, lost in reverie. Mathu sat in a chair to one side.

'Does anything ever?' Mathu asked. 'For anyone?'

'Everything is out of control,' Korah said, pouring himself a consolatory second drink. 'The world has turned topsy-turvy.'

'We've to come to terms with the times.'

'It's too late for me to do that.'

'Your children are making the transition,' Mathu said.

'None of my children has turned out right.'

'Only if we judge them by our fusty standards.'

'By any standard,' Korah said. 'What a mess Zeruba and Devi have made of their lives!'

'Chacko is doing fine.'

'In politics! Phew!' snorted Korah. This was pretence. Korah was secretly proud of Chacko's success in politics, but he wasn't going to let it on. 'It's a crooked life.'

'That's the only way to thrive now,' Mathu said.

'By crookedness?'

'By competitive skills,' answered Mathu.

'This family,' said Korah, 'has endured for many generations without having to tell lies, cheat anyone, or grab anything from anyone.'

'Come on, Chetta,' rejoined Mathu. 'At one time our ancestors would surely have been grabbers and cheaters themselves. Otherwise how could they have initially acquired wealth?'

'Maybe. But that was a very long time back. It's not relevant to what we are today,' Korah said. 'At one time our ancestors would have been cave dwellers, but that has no bearing on what we are now. Politics is not the profession for decent people.'

'Decent people can't survive in India today,' chuckled Mathu.

'And you're happy with it?'

'I'm neither happy nor unhappy,' said Mathu. 'I'm simply stating a fact.'

The Cottage

1

Zeruba and Aditi spent a week in Azhiyur, then took a train to Madras, where Mathangi met them at the railway station and took them to Zeruba's cottage. Before leaving for the US, they had entrusted the cottage to her to add to it a studio and two bedrooms, and this task she had executed with her usual thoroughness and skill, taking care to consult them on all details by sending to them the blueprints of her designs along with elaborate notes and drawings. Everything was in perfect order when they returned to Madras.

Mathangi had used polished pale-grey granite slabs for flooring throughout the cottage, and these were pleasing to the eye and cool to the bare foot. The walls were all painted in a matte shade of old-ivory, and there were plain raw cotton curtains of the same shade on all the windows. A few of Zeruba's paintings were on the walls, two in the living room and one each in the master bedroom and the studio, just four in all, so as not to spoil the simplicity and quiet elegance of the rooms. All the furniture in the living room, the divans and chairs and tables, were made of the darkest rosewood in spare, clean lines, and all were kept low, none, not even the dining table, more than eighteen inches high, as Zeruba had specified according to his favoured Buddhist prescriptions. And they were arranged in such a way as to open up the interior in a fluent sweep of space. The deckchairs on the veranda were replaced with low, armless rattan loungers, specially designed by Mathangi. The general effect of all this was of serene, finely contained energy. Immense windows with broad plateglass panels opened up the field of view in all the rooms and let the sea breeze stream through the house. But the glare of the sun was cut by broad verandas all around, so the cottage felt cool, yet bright and airy. The small bedroom, meant for Saumya, was adorned with a large watercolour painting of scenes from the *Panchatantra*, painted by Mathangi herself, and there was a huge, cuddly teddy bear on the bed.

'These are my presents for Saumya,' Mathangi said.

'Wonderful. Absolutely wonderful,' Zeruba said, putting his arms around Mathangi and hugging her tight.

'Let go, you moron,' she cried, wriggling to break free. She was a slight, small-made woman, and Zeruba easily kept her pinioned in his arms. Aditi laughed.

'Oh Mats, Mats, you're my true heart-throb, Mats,' he whispered in her ear in a loud aside.

'What?' Aditi challenged. 'Ain't I your heart-throb?'

'You are, honey,' he said. 'You're the throb of my left ventricle, and Mats is the throb of my right ventricle.'

'I haven't done anything much with the studio,' Mathangi said when he at last released her with a light peck on her forehead. 'You can do any mad thing with the room.'

'Perfect,' he said, feinting to grab her again.

'Sod off,' she said. 'We girls want to talk.'

2

Later that week, they went to Rajakottai to spend a couple of days with Rupa and Natarajan. Zeruba was suitably impressed by the immense pile of their ancestral home looming over the town. He was even more impressed by the gargantuan bulk of Rama Durai, a colossus of a man, grossly fat and grossly potbellied, under whose weight their Ambassador car groaned plaintively when he stepped into it, as Zeruba noticed when they all squeezed into the car to go to the family temple for a special puja performed for Aditi.

Aditi was inexplicably out of sorts during their stay in Rajakottai, and was particularly uncivil to Rama Durai. This offended Zeruba's sense of propriety, but he put it down to her resentment over Rama Durai's threat to disinherit her, and decided not to say anything about it, thinking that the best thing would be to let her vent her anger and get over it.

Back in Madras, the couple slowly re-entered their old life. Zeruba had written to Lakshmi from the US about his travel plans, and he phoned her on his return from Rajakottai. The next day she, along with Gopal, visited him, bringing their child, a son, for Zeruba to name him. He named him Santosh, Happiness, and placed in his tiny curling hand a gold sovereign. And every year thereafter Lakshmi unfailingly visited Zeruba on his birthday, with an offering of pazha-pradhaman, his favourite pudding.

A month after Zeruba's return, Lakshmi and Gopal approached him with detailed plans for setting up a workshop, along with various quotations and estimates. Zeruba pushed the papers away.

'I've no mind for these things,' he told Gopal. 'I've to work on trust. And I trust you.'

He then signed the fixed deposit receipts and gave them to him.

'I'm sure you'll do very well,' he said.

Indeed, their business prospered beyond their wildest dreams, so Gopal resigned his job after a couple of years to work full-time in the workshop. In a few years he expanded the workshop into a small-scale industry, with the support and financial help of the industrial house where he had worked. They then moved into a house of their own, not a large one, but quite comfortable, and Aditi and Zeruba went for their house-warming.

This was only the beginning, Zeruba felt. They were now on

the first rung of the ladder of success. Imagine where they will be when they are at the top! A vast vista of opportunity lay open for them and their progeny, he was certain. In contrast, he found himself at a dead end. His marriage with Aditi had soured irreversibly. And his work had become stagnant and repetitive.

'You've done very well,' he said to Gopal. 'I'm very proud of you.'

'All by your blessing, sir,' Gopal said.

On their way back, Aditi remained aloof and grumpy.

'After all that I've done for them, they still think that you are their saviour,' she said. 'It's so unfair.'

'They are people of character,' he said. 'And they respect people of character.'

For Zeruba's next birthday, Lakshmi and Gopal arrived in their own car, an Ambassador, with Lakshmi driving. They still refused to sit in Zeruba's presence, but he insisted on it. When they left, Aditi found Zeruba sitting on the patio with tears in his eyes.

'What's the matter?' she asked crossly.

'I'm so happy for Lakshmi,' he said.

'You're still pining for her, you bloody blighter?' she asked contemptuously.

'No, I'm not pining for her,' he said. 'I'm just happy for her.'

3

The crisis in Zeruba's marriage had a slow fuse. No one outside would have sensed anything amiss in the beginning. Indeed, the first couple of years after their return to India were a time of relative contentment for Zeruba, the proverbial calm before the storm. He felt good at working in the studio that Mathangi had built for him, a spacious and airy room, with a glass-panelled bay window facing the sea, and equally large windows on the other two external walls. On the granite seat that formed the base of the bay window, Mathangi had placed a large desert-rose plant with blush-pink flowers, its mottled earthen pot concealed in an egg-white, cylindrical ceramic container. Zeruba was particularly pleased with the plant.

'I had to hunt a week to find it,' Mathangi said.

'It's perfect,' Zeruba said. 'Just perfect.'

'Rather sissyish, isn't it?' Aditi commented, pointing to its sinuous, velvety branches.

'Yes, it's a very feminine plant,' Zeruba said. 'That's why it's perfect for this stark, masculine room.'

Zeruba made no changes in Mathangi's arrangements in the room, except to replace the cloth curtains with vertical Venetian blinds, so he could precisely control the light in the room. The easel was placed crosswise against the inner corner of the room, with a cushioned metal bar stool on castors in front of it. Zeruba's old paint-encrusted small wooden table was set to its side, against the wall. Behind the easel, flush in the corner, was placed a tall wicker bin with rolls of canvas in it, and alongside it were stacked, against the wall, Zeruba's paintings. A two-tiered, L-shaped shelf was built into the wall in that corner at eye level, and this held an array brushes, several boxes of paints, a set of Time-Life Library of Art books, and a stereo tape player. In the diagonally opposite corner, placed against the walls at right angles to each other, were two low and broad cushioned benches, for visitors to sit on, or for Zeruba to take his siesta. The studio had a small attached bathroom, so it could double as a guestroom.

Zeruba always had the tape player on when he painted, continually playing Chaurasia on the flute, keeping the volume barely audible. He never tired of the tape, because he never really listened to it, but needed its soft, misty swirls of sound to create a pleasing ambience as he worked. Most of the time when he was in the studio, he had Saumya with him, playing with her toys or doodling with crayons on paper, in which Zeruba, like any fond father, presumed to see great talent. Often they just horsed around. When she was a little older, and could read and write, he made for her a large format hardbound notebook of thick bond paper and gave her a set of felt pens, and, to his delighted amazement, she in no time at all filled the book with poems, stories and illustrations.

A couple of years later, when she was around eight years old, Saumya made a large number of watercolour paintings, and one day, seeing the self-portrait of Van Gogh, she painted a similar portrait of Zeruba in striated flakes of colours. Zeruba had this painting framed, and hung it in the studio alongside his own painting, and these were the only decorations on its walls. Mathangi was ecstatic about Saumya's work.

'She's going to be a great artist,' she said.

'Who knows what she'll be when she grows up?' Zeruba said. 'I'm not going to push her in any direction.'

'She's wonderfully creative,' said Mathangi. 'What else is there for a creative person except to be an artist or a writer?'

'That's not true anymore,' Zeruba said. 'Today, the most creative people are in the sciences.'

'He wants her to fulfil his failed biochemist's dreams,' Aditi said.

'Not at all,' he said.

'If science is such an exciting field, why didn't you persevere in it?' Mathangi asked.

'I didn't have it in me to be a good scientist, Mats,' he said. 'For that you have to be both thoroughly methodical and freely creative. I didn't have that particular combination of complementary talents, or didn't have enough of those talents. I need immediate gratification, and that's not possible in science.'

'You don't get any immediate gratification out of your paintings either,' Aditi pointed out. 'It takes you aeons to complete a painting.'

'I don't have to complete a painting to get pleasure from it,' Zeruba said. 'Each brush stroke is pleasurable, like each note of a song for a singer.'

4

Zeruba thought of himself as a man possessed, but his self-exorcism through art was a sedate process. He worked all the time, but not feverishly. And Aditi, viewing him as too withdrawn to succeed in a competitive world, decided to take charge of his career.

'I can make you anything you want,' she said to him. 'Another Husain.'

'No, thanks,' he said. 'I just want to be myself.'

'Don't you want to be famous, make lots of money?'

'Yes, that'd be nice,' he said. 'But there's a problem.'

'What?'

'I will work only for my own pleasure, not for wealth and fame. If wealth and fame come to me as I go about pleasing myself, that would be wonderful. But I won't make any special effort for them.'

'You don't have to do anything,' she assured. 'I'll do everything. I'll promote you.'

'Promotion is for trade, Adi,' he said. 'Not for art.'

'That's rubbish, Dada,' she scoffed. 'In today's world creativity and promotion go hand in hand. That's the formula for success. You may be a genius, but without promotion you'll die poor and obscure. That's where I come in. Art has to be marketed, like any other product. Others are doing it, so you've got to compete with them to succeed.'

'I'm not a competitive person, Adi,' he protested. 'I don't want to get the better of others; I only want to get the better of myself.'

'Okay, forget money,' Aditi said. 'But don't you want to be famous?'

'Fame should seek me out,' Zeruba said. 'I shouldn't go seeking it. You can't tie a rope around fame and drag it home like cow.'

'Who says you can't drag it home?' Aditi challenged. 'I can.'

And she did. There was no stopping Aditi once she launched herself into a project. She would take any rebuff, any humiliation, and persist unswervingly till she attained her goal. Whenever she went on business trips to Bombay or Delhi, she now made a round of the galleries and art critics there, zealously promoting Zeruba. No one could resist her cajolery. And Zeruba's reputation, which had till then been largely confined to Madras, attained national recognition through her efforts, and he made a good amount of money from the sale of his paintings. But as she stormed ahead, he retreated further into himself, and now had to be dragged out reluctantly to attend even the parties at which he once used to be a regular fixture. He just wanted to do his thing, sitting in his little corner.

'You know what's wrong with you?' Aditi asked him one day.

'What?'

'You've no ambition.'

'I'm ambitious in my own way,' he said. 'Why am I working so hard otherwise?'

'Just self-indulgence,' she said scornfully.

'All true artists indulge themselves, Adi. Only the hack indulges the public.'

'You think you're the most important person in the world?'

'I am, for me, the centre of the world,' he cheerfully affirmed. 'Its very nucleus.'

'You don't care for what others think of you?'

'I do care,' he said. 'But they have to take me as I am. I can't pander to them.'

5

Zeruba's smug self-containment disgusted Aditi. For her, the world was a gladiatorial arena, where she exultingly performed for applause and rewards. Fiercely competitive, and blessed with phenomenal mental and physical resilience, she was never daunted by any problem or adversity, and was insanely confident of accomplishing whatever she set out to do. These qualities made her a remarkably successful PR professional, and her clientele expanded rapidly. Soon after returning to India, she discarded her moped and bought a small car—a Herald, which, Zeruba was pleased to note, was from the same stable as his own Mayflower—and was out in the city most afternoons on her assignments. She hated housework, and was generally content to leave cooking and housekeeping to servants, of whom they now had two, both young women, a part-time maid to sweep, dust and swab, and a live-in cook who also served as Saumya's nanny.

Once Saumya started school, Zeruba was quite often alone in the cottage with the cook. A plump woman with a fleshy mouth and bulging, asymmetrical breasts, she was not at all the type of woman to whom Zeruba was normally drawn, and he disgustedly ignored the coquettish glances that she shot at him now and then. But she was not discouraged by this. And one day, when Aditi and Saumya were away in Rajakottai for a two-week summer holiday, she boldly pushed open the bathroom door when Zeruba was bathing and entered with a mop, as if to clean the room, though this was not her work. And, instead of withdrawing immediately, she paused to apologize.

'Iyya, I didn't know you were here,' she said.

He didn't say anything and she left, closing the door behind her. The next evening, a Saturday, when Zeruba was getting ready for his customary weekly oil bath, and was sitting on a plastic stool in the studio rubbing his body with sesame oil, wearing only a short loincloth, she came in with a cup of tea.

'I've already had my tea,' he said.

'Oh, I forgot, Iyya,' she said. 'I don't know what's happening to me these days.'

As she stood hesitating, he asked, 'Yes?'

'Iyya, may I say something?'

'Yes?'

'Why don't you get someone to massage you? It'll be good for health.'

'Where would I find a masseur in this village!'

'I know massaging,' she said. 'I used to massage my husband.'

'And he ran away!' Zeruba laughed.

She tittered.

'Alright, massage me, then,' he said, stretching himself on the floor, face down.

She was good with her hands, kneading and teasing his limbs, every muscle and every tendon, and he dozed off under her expert ministrations. This disappointed her, for there was no sexual arousal at all in him. But that evening, while sitting out on the patio having a drink, he called her to him.

'The massage was good,' he said. 'What else can you do?'

'Whatever you want me to do,' she said coyly.

'Did you have a bath today?'

'Yes, Iyya.'

'Bathe again before you go to bed.'

'Yes, Iyya.'

This is all wrong, Zeruba said to himself when she left. *I'll not allow this to go any further*. But his mood changed again later that night, after he had had a few drinks. And when the cook came to him after her bath to ask whether he needed anything else, he asked her to switch off the patio light and got her to go down on him as he lounged back in the chair with his eyes closed.

Just this one time, he cautioned himself. *Something I had not experienced before*. But she had a ravenous mouth and he was vulnerable, so the act became a part of his daily evening routine on the patio for the next few days. *As they say, a starving tiger would eat even grass*, he said to himself. *I'll end this the moment Adi returns*. But he did not.

Zeruba knew that what he was doing was stupid and degrading, and was often racked by terrible feelings of guilt, but still was unable to break off the liaison, and sought excuses to exonerate himself. *This is a trivial matter,* he reasoned. *A purely physical affair, without any emotional involvement, no more consequential than, say, having a tot of rum or smoking a cigarette.* Indeed, in the initial stages of his philandering with servant women, he turned again to Aditi with impetuous ardour, as a result of which she became pregnant again. This time they mutually agreed to get the pregnancy terminated.

'We have a good child,' he said, concurring with Aditi's decision. 'Let's not take a risk with another child.'

Soon after Aditi had her abortion, Zeruba got himself sterilized, to avoid causing any accidental pregnancies. On his doctor's advice, the vasectomy was done at a local medical college hospital. The orderlies there shaved and sterilized his pubes thoroughly, and led him into the surgical theatre. The doctor, an elderly gentleman, smiled at Zeruba affably and made him lie down on the operating table.

'Relax,' the doctor said, covering Zeruba's face with a piece of cloth. 'It'll be over in no time.'

'Fine,' said Zeruba, his body going cold with anxiety.

'I'll give you an injection of local anaesthesia,' the doctor continued. 'It'll prick just a little, like an ant bite.'

'Fine,' Zeruba said again.

And he kept up this amiable response as the doctor went on explaining each step he was taking, till he heard a half-suppressed girlish giggle near him and pulled away the cloth covering his face—to find, to his utter consternation, a group of medical students standing around the operating table, many of them openly smirking. The girl who giggled had covered her mouth with her hand, but her eyes were sparkling with mirth. It was to the students that the doctor had been explaining the surgical procedure, which Zeruba had thought was for his benefit. He promptly covered his face again with the cloth. *Oh my god*! he cursed himself. *They have seen my dick shrunk to the size of a peanut*!

Later, he upbraided the doctor for not warning him about the demonstration.

'Routine,' said the doctor dismissively.

Erich

1

Zeruba's clandestine affair with the cook came to an abrupt end one day at breakfast, when Aditi correctly interpreted an exchange of glances between them. When challenged, he remained silent, confirming her suspicions.

'How can you bear even to touch these filthy sluts?' Aditi fumed, pushing away her plate of idli and chutney in disgust and knocking down a glass of water.

'I haven't touched her,' he said calmly.

'No?' she challenged, livid with indignation, her cheeks flaming red. 'No?'

'No. Not even with my little finger.'

'So you've now started telling lies also?'

'That's an art form that I've yet to learn from you.'

'You're lying,' she hissed through her clenched teeth, thrusting her head forward aggressively and glaring at him. 'I can see it in your eyes. You had sex with her. I know.'

'Depends on what you mean by having sex.'

'What do you mean?'

So he told her.

'My god! You filthy scum! Why are you telling me all these filthy, obscene details?'

'You asked me.'

'God! How could you do this to me?'

'It's just a passing incident,' he said. 'Don't get all het up about it. It's nothing.'

'Nothing? God!' she raged. 'You're like a pig that leaves a trough of grain to feed on shit. How could you do this to me?'

Zeruba shrugged his shoulders and went on with the meal. He had said all he had to say.

Aditi packed off the cook the same day, without asking or offering any explanation. She then phoned a domestic servants employment service and arranged for her to interview another cook the next day. The new cook arrived a couple of days later, and she, to the surprise of Zeruba, turned out to be young and personable, and so were most of the servants that Aditi subsequently employed. It was as if they were deliberately chosen by her to tempt Zeruba. Invariably he yielded to the temptation. And every time Aditi confronted him with her suspicions, his answer was always the same: 'It's of no consequence. Just a physical thing.'

And her response too was always the same: 'You bloody-bloody blighter! Filthy pig! You'll pay for this.'

2

'It's so humiliating,' Aditi bitterly complained to Mathangi, confiding in her what Zeruba was up to and seeking her help to make him desist. 'And this after all that I've done for him!'

'Probably a midlife crisis,' Mathangi consoled. 'It'll pass.'

'He's just a filthy pig.'

'Come on, Adi,' Mathangi reasoned. 'Don't get so worked up. You aren't blameless yourself.'

'That's different,' Aditi said. 'My affairs are with men of my own class. They aren't degrading.'

'Dada might see it differently.'

'He doesn't know anything about me. I don't think he cares either. He's so damn wrapped up in himself.'

'What do you want me to do?'

'Talk to him, Mats,' Aditi suggested. 'He has such high regard for you—maybe he'll listen to you.'

'I doubt it,' Mathangi said.

She was right. When she upbraided Zeruba on Aditi's behalf, he loftily raised the matter to a higher plane, claiming that having sex with low class women was spiritually liberating.

'It doesn't become so just because you say so,' she said.

'This is not just my fancy, Mats,' he said. 'It's Tantric wisdom.'

'What?'

'The Tantrics hold that intercourse without craving or emotional involvement makes a person stronger, stronger than he would be if he were to remain celibate,' he said. 'That's the way to overcome desire.'

'That's not Tantra,' Mathangi laughed. 'That's Oscar Wilde— the only way to overcome a temptation is to yield to it.'

'Universal wisdom, Mats,' Zeruba said. 'Sex liberates, love enslaves.'

'Rot,' Mathangi scoffed. 'How can you say that the sexuality that binds you actually liberates you?'

Of course it was rot, Zeruba knew. Desire is never extinguished by indulging in desire. But he wouldn't admit it.

'Sexuality doesn't bind me,' he protested. 'I can take it or leave it as it comes.'

'Then leave it. Don't you see how humiliating this is to Adi? She probably wouldn't have been so upset if your involvement had been with women of your own class.'

'That won't do at all,' he said. 'With women of my own class, I'm liable to get emotionally involved, and that won't serve the Tantric purpose.'

'You searching for the lost Lakshmi in these women?'

'No!' he said. 'That would be to put a romantic gloss on this petty affair.'

'Don't you feel any remorse at all? If not about your degrading affairs, at least for the pain that you've inflicted on Adi? I'm told that you were quite blasé about all this.'

'I'm not a demonstrative person, Mats.'

'How can you be so utterly self-absorbed? You know, what really hurts Adi is not your transgression, but your indifference to her feelings.'

'What can I do, Mats? That's the way I am. I didn't mean to hurt her.'

'At least look at this from the practical point of view. How can Adi have authority over servants when you're intimate with them?'

'I'm not intimate with them at all,' he protested. 'I just have sex with them. I allow them absolutely no liberties with me. And none would dare to show the slightest disrespect to Adi.'

'What should I tell Adi?'

'Look, this matter does not in any way alter my relationship with Adi,' he assured her. 'I'll do nothing to harm my family.'

When Mathangi reported the conversation to Aditi, she said, 'I don't buy all this Tantric crap. He's just rationalizing his weakness.'

'Well, higher the brow, lower the loins.'

'You serious?'

'So they say.'

'Just another alibi,' Aditi sneered. 'Men are pigs.'

'Look Adi, don't do anything rash,' Mathangi advised. 'You've to think of Saumya.'

'No, I'm not going to do anything rash,' Aditi said. 'But I'm going to have to make my own plans now.'

3

But why did Aditi, knowing Zeruba's weakness, continue to employ young maidservants? This puzzled Zeruba. Later the thought would occur to him that she was probably doing this as a pre-emptive gambit to defend her own infidelities, should they get exposed. In marital jousts, Aditi was a matchless strategist, who foresaw every contingency and prepared her counter-measurers well in advance. In contrast, Zeruba was a babe in the woods. He had on occasions, even before their marriage, noticed a certain glint in Aditi's eyes when in the company of some men, and this had troubled him, but he never suspected actual infidelities.

His first intimation of serious trouble came in the form of a phone call. Zeruba hardly ever picked up the phone, but let Aditi or the servants answer calls, though he had an extension of the line in the studio. But on that particular day, as the phone kept ringing without anyone answering it, he lifted the receiver, and just at that very moment Aditi too picked it up in the bedroom.

'Aditi?' the caller asked.

'Yes,' she said.

'Devilal,' the caller said.

'Hi, Devi. You calling from Bombay?'

'No, I'm in Madras. Staying at the Taj. Why don't you come over this evening? I've brought a bottle of champagne from Bombay. Dom Perignon. The best.'

'Well . . .'

She sounded so obviously embarrassed that the caller sensed that something was wrong.

'Anyone in the room with you?' he asked.

'No-no . . . yes,' Aditi fumbled, knowing that Zeruba was listening on the extension.

Zeruba quietly put the receiver down. He had heard enough.

'That was Devilal, a businessman I met in Bombay when I was there last month,' she told Zeruba, going into the studio immediately after the call. 'I like his gall, calling me to his hotel room! I gave him a piece of my mind.'

Zeruba went on painting.

'Now don't you go imagining all sorts of things,' she said.

'Okay,' he said, without taking his eyes off the painting.

'You're the sort that will see crocodiles in a drop of water.'

'He sounded intimate.'

'I flirted with him in Bombay, yes,' she said. 'It was just innocent flirtation, but you men have only one thought in your heads. Pigs!'

'Okay,' he said coldly.

'You can fantasize any damn thing,' she said, flouncing out of the studio. 'I don't care.'

4

Zeruba was quietly alert thereafter. When Aditi became aware of his vigilance, she, instead of turning cautious, began to aggressively flaunt her flirtations, virtually taunting him to try and stop her. But he kept his feelings to himself. He wasn't going to allow himself to be provoked into any precipitous action.

He would do what he needed to do in his own time, he decided—if he needed to do anything at all. One thing was clear to him: Aditi's flirtations were not in retaliation to his philandering, though she made it appear as if they were so. The trait was there in her even before their marriage. A highly combustible woman, a mere glance was enough to set her ablaze. He also suspected that she had some obsessive psychological need to continually attract men to her, and this he attributed to her suppressed rancour over having been passed over by her younger sister in marriage. 'When I was studying for school final, at the time of my sister's marriage, I thought I was going crazy,' she had once told Zeruba. Her flirtations, he believed, were her means of self-vindication. So he was not unduly perturbed by them in the beginning, and felt that there was no danger to the integrity of the family from them, just as there was no danger to the integrity of the family from his own straying. Most of the men Aditi flirted with were in any case old enough to be her father or even her grandfather. She had a fixation for father figures—probably looking for the father she missed in her life, Zeruba thought. He knew nothing of the trauma she had suffered at the hands of Rama Durai, though she had once dropped a broad hint about it, saying, 'He used to get drunk and do all sorts of mad things. Unspeakable things.'

Violated in sex, Aditi sought to redeem herself through sex. But soon the means became an end in itself, a helpless addiction. Like the ogre Baga-asura, whose appetite increased with every meal he had, the more men Aditi ensnared, yet more men she longed to ensnare. And she had, in the dozen odd years since her marriage, won a good many suitors, men of all sorts. She was omnivorous. This was another reason why Zeruba regarded her flirtations as harmless coquetries—with so many suitors around, he did not feel threatened by anyone in particular. But he did occasionally lose his temper, as he did with Sundaram Iyer, an industrialist in his eighties, with whom Aditi spent hours flirting on the phone. And one day when he phoned, she buzzed Zeruba in the studio.

'Sundaram wants to talk to you,' she said, when he took the phone receiver.

'Yes, speak,' he snapped into the phone, furious at being put to the humiliation of having to take a call from one of Aditi's beaus.

'Zeruba?' Sundaram asked.

'Yes.'

'Sundaram here.'

'Yes?'

'Aditi and I've become great friends.'

'Fine.'

'Hope you aren't one of those possessive types.'

'As a matter of fact, I am,' Zeruba said.

'So am I,' said Sundaram.

'Fine,' said Zeruba. 'May I ask you something, man to man?'

'Sure.'

'Can you still get it up?'

'Sometimes,' Sundaram chortled.

'Then I've a suggestion for you.'

'Yes?'

'Why don't you shove it into your granddaughter?'

At this Sundaram drew himself up. 'Who do you think you're talking to, you twerp?' he snapped.

'I know who I'm talking to,' Zeruba said. 'Shithead Sundaram, no?'

'How dare you?' Sundaram snarled. 'I'll pulverize you.'

'Really?' Zeruba asked. 'Send your goons. I'll be waiting.'

'I can break you like a dry twig,' Sundaram warned.

'Maybe,' Zeruba said. 'But you'll never make me bend my knees.'

'It's your funeral,' Sundaram said with finality.

'Oh, another thing,' Zeruba cut in. 'Lay off my wife. If I ever catch you phoning her again, I'll rip off your balls with my bare hands. In public. So bugger off.'

As soon as Zeruba rang off, Aditi came storming into the studio, so angry that her jugulars swelled as if about to burst.

'Are you mad?' she raged at him. 'He's old enough to be my grandfather. What can possibly be there between us?'

'I don't know and I don't care,' he said. 'I don't like the rheumy-eyed lecher. So this must be ended now. Right away.'

'You just killed off one of my best business contacts.'

'Good. Bury him deep.'

'He just wanted to be friends with you.'

'I know,' Zeruba mocked, mimicking Sundaram. 'Here are your horns Zeruba, my good friend. They would look nice on you.'

'You're just a filthy MCP, that's what you are,' Aditi said. 'Worse than the worst of them. You pretend to be liberal and progressive, but you're really a medieval creature. Out of the Dark Ages.'

'Maybe.'

'Don't you ever think of me and my feelings?'

'I'm too preoccupied with myself to think of other people.'

'I'm not other people,' she protested.

'Then why are you arguing with me?'

'You're crazy,' Aditi informed him. 'You know what?'

'What?'

'You're really a wretched creature who can be happy only if you're miserable.'

'Oh, I see,' he said. 'How very kind of you to give me this particular happiness!'

5

That was the end of the Sundaram affair. But unknown to Zeruba, something far more sinister was developing beneath the surface flirtations of Aditi, her liaison with a German diplomat, Erich Hoffmann. He was the consul general of Germany in Madras, and Aditi and Zeruba had often gone to his house for parties. Erich and his wife Greta were a weirdly mismatched couple. He was a big-made man in his late fifties, built rather like Rama Durai, but not quite so huge and rather more flabby, with a sickly yellow skin and several folds of dewlap. He looked, in Zeruba's eyes, like a hideously bloated bullfrog. Greta was the exact opposite of her husband in physique, a shrimp-like woman, very small and very thin, with a perpetually exhausted look in her deep-sunken, sleep-starved eyes.

'They're going to split,' Zeruba told Aditi one night when they were returning from a party at the Hoffmann's. 'I could hear the sputter of tension between them.'

'You're imagining things,' Aditi said, though she knew all about their impending divorce. 'They are quite happy together.'

'Mark my word,' Zeruba said. 'They're going to split.'

'Let them. What does it matter to us?'

Aditi uncharacteristically kept her growing intimacy with Erich a deep secret, taking only Mathangi into confidence. Her very secretiveness marked the affair as serious, unlike her open flirtations. Zeruba was conscious that there was something brewing there, especially after Greta left Madras, but he thought that it was just another one of her passing fancies. But Aditi was dead serious about Erich. Her marriage with Zeruba had not turned out quite what she had expected of it. He was a trophy she had won. Not bad. But not good enough to gratify her. He did not have the worldly ambition to suit her. Marrying a European, a diplomat at that, possibly a future ambassador, living in a palatial, centrally air-conditioned mansion in the priciest neighbourhood of Madras, instead of in a tiny cottage adjoining the slums in the suburb—that would be her ultimate revenge on Rama Durai, and on her sister too, and the means to finally and irrevocably redeem her self-worth. She knew that most Indians held the whites in fawning respect even after three decades of independence, and she knew that if she married Erich, people generally, even Rama Durai and Rupa, would bow and scrape before her and her husband, even if they talked ill of her behind her back.

And she was certain that this was her destiny, for a seer had predicted it for her. The prediction was, in her view, absolutely credible, for it was unsolicited and had happened by chance. She had on that day accompanied Mathangi to Pondicherry, to help her shop for some handicrafts, and, as it was late by the time they finished their work, they decided to spend the night there and drive back to Madras the next morning. They took a room in a hotel along the seafront, had a long shower, and later in the evening, it being an oppressively muggy day, they crossed the boulevard and went for a stroll on the broad and clean promenade along the beach. There they came across a small crowd gathered around an ash-smeared, cadaverous old man with long, matted, dirty-grey hair and beard, and they paused there for a moment to watch. The man spotted Aditi immediately.

'You, the one in orange sari, come forward,' he called out, pointing a spindly finger at Aditi. 'I've a message for you.'

Amused, Aditi pushed through the crowd to the front, as all eyes turned on her.

'Your life is about to be transformed,' the sadhu proclaimed, 'and your lustre that is now three will rise threefold to nine. You'll be a queen among women.'

'What sort of change?' Aditi asked.

'The man you're married to now is not your true husband,' he said. 'Your man of destiny will be from another land. And he will be a ruler of men.'

Aditi took out a hundred-rupee note from her handbag and laid it on the mat on which the man was sitting. She was very pleased with herself. She had never doubted that she would win Erich. Now she had an oracular confirmation of her destiny.

'You're crazy to believe him,' Mathangi warned her as they walked on. 'He was just reading your mind. Your cravings.'

'No, Mats, what he said will come true,' Aditi said. 'I'll have Erich. I know it in my bones.'

'What about Dada?'

'What about him?' Aditi sneered. 'He's just an egomaniacal monster stewing in his own shit, and he'll continue to stew in his own shit.'

'Don't be so harsh, Adi. You want to destroy him?'

'I want to save myself,' Aditi said. 'Anyway, why are you so concerned about Dada?'

'Because I'm very fond of him.'

'Is fond the right word?'

'Yes.'

Aditi stopped and turned to face Mathangi. 'Sure?' she asked, looking searchingly into her eyes.

'Yes,' Mathangi said firmly.

'Well, you don't have to worry about him,' Aditi said. 'My leaving him will have no effect on him.'

'I think you're wrong, Adi. He keeps his feelings to himself. But that doesn't mean he has no feelings.'

Aditi shrugged indifferently, and they walked on in silence for a while.

'I've a bad feeling about this, Adi,' Mathangi said as they

turned around at the end of the promenade. 'Erich is a cad. He just wants to screw you, not marry you.'

'You'll see.'

Mathangi then told her about a rumour she had heard, that Erich had taken a bet with Rami Reddy, a prominent lawyer and high-society playboy, about who would bed Aditi first.

'All lies,' Aditi said. 'Rami would never betray me.'

'You know he always boasts about his conquests when he's drunk,' Mathangi said. 'And you have slept with him.'

'Yes, I have. But he hasn't told Erich about it,' Aditi said. 'If he had, there would not be this bet, would there?'

'So you know about the bet?'

'Maybe,' Aditi hedged. 'But it doesn't matter. I'll have Erich.'

6

She very nearly had him. Erich did indeed at one time seriously consider marrying Aditi. But the prospect of getting involved in her messy divorce case, and the uncertainty about how it would affect his plans to remain in India after retirement troubled him. He also feared that Aditi would cuckold him, just as she had cuckolded Zeruba. More than anything else, Aditi's rampant sexuality intimidated him. Erich was a premature ejaculator, and on the first day they slept together, Aditi had drunkenly taunted him, 'You finished? I didn't even know that you were in! Let's do it again.'

'I'm not up to it,' he said, turning his back to her.

Aditi immediately realized that she had made a mistake.

'Hey, I was joking, yaar,' she said, hugging him. 'It was good. Really.'

But the jibe rankled, and made him change his mind about Aditi. He would just play her along, he now decided, and turned to another woman who had shown an interest in him: Parvathi, an obese and bespectacled spinster in her late forties, who taught

German in a city college. He felt secure with Parvathi. She was sexually and emotionally undemanding, and was grateful for whatever little attention he paid her. There would be no complication in marrying her. So he proposed to her, and she accepted.

But Aditi would not give him up without a fight. Erich's engagement, instead of disheartening her, spurred her into a high pitch of combative frenzy, and she now began to hound him relentlessly, bombarding him with phone calls and letters, often barging into his office and home. He then changed the telephone numbers at his home and office, but that was no use, for Aditi used her wiles to get the new numbers. She would not accept rejection.

'How can this woman compete with me!' she exclaimed indignantly to Mathangi. 'Once she sees me, she'll run away and hide somewhere.'

'Maybe what Erich wants is a doormat,' Mathangi said. 'You probably scare him off.'

'I'll eat him whole,' Aditi said.

As a part of her campaign, Aditi also began to harass Parvathi with phone calls, and once visited her at home to ask her to free Erich from his promise to marry her, as he was really in love with her (Aditi) and had slept with her. This created a scene between Erich and Parvathi, and she, timid though she was, threatened to break off their engagement unless he brought Aditi's harassment to an end.

Zeruba was blissfully unaware of all this. But one afternoon when Aditi was in the city for a business meeting, the German consular car drove up to his cottage and the chauffeur delivered to Zeruba an urgent note from Erich, which read: 'My dear Zeruba: It is imperative that I see you today. I would not ask you on such short notice were the matter not one of surpassing importance. I shall be at the house of our friend Rami Reddy at four p.m., which will be the most convenient place for us to meet. In writing this brief note, I want to stress that the matter we have to discuss is of the utmost importance. Sincerely, Erich.'

What could this be about, Zeruba wondered. Since they were meeting at Rami's house, he assumed, rather illogically, that this had something to do with Rami, who was going through a very bad phase just then, as his only son had a nervous breakdown and his only daughter's marriage was on the rocks. He had been drinking very heavily of late, and was often indiscreet in his words and deeds. It did not occur to Zeruba that the meeting had anything to do with Aditi.

When Zeruba arrived at Rami's house, he found Erich and Rami along with Rami's wife Shanta and another woman, all sitting stiffly and solemnly in the drawing room. The stranger was introduced as Erich's fiancée, Parvathi, and immediately Zeruba sensed that this had something to do with Aditi. Erich came to the point right away.

'This is an embarrassing matter, and there's no easy way to handle it. So it's best to deal with it head on,' Erich said in a thick voice which sounded like he was trying to swallow his tongue. 'Your wife has been pursuing me without any encouragement from me, and she has been harassing Parvathi. This has to stop.'

Zeruba, to his own surprise, took the news calmly, almost indifferently, as if it were an abstract problem for which he had to find a solution by and by. As Erich went on to narrate the details of the problem, Zeruba stopped him.

'I don't want to hear the details,' he said, getting up. 'I had no idea about this, but I assume that what you're saying is true. I'll see that this problem is resolved today.'

'Won't you have some tea?' Shanta asked.

'No, thank you, Shanta,' Zeruba said. 'I'm booked to leave for Kerala by the night train. And before I go, I've to deal with this problem. Excuse me.'

146

7

Even as he came out of the house, Zeruba's mind was made up about what he should do. From a shop on the way, he phoned Mathangi at her office, and told her that he needed to see her urgently, preferably in her flat. By the time he got to her flat, she was already there.

'What's wrong?' she asked, her eyes clouded with anxiety. She feared the worst.

As he began telling her about the development, he suddenly became overcome with emotion and fell silent, his head bent over his chest, grimacing and choking back his tears, unable to speak. Seeing this, Mathangi went over and sat beside him on the sofa and put her arms around him comfortingly, whereupon he broke down and wept convulsively, burying his head in her lap.

'I'm sorry for you, Dada,' she said, stroking his head tenderly. 'I'm sorry for both of you.'

In a while he regained his composure and sat up.

'I'm okay now,' he said. 'I've drained out the emotion. I feel nothing now.'

She brought him a cup of tea.

'Did you know of this affair, Mats?' he asked.

'Yes,' she said. 'I tried to warn her off. But she wouldn't listen.'

'Why didn't you tell me?'

'I couldn't betray Adi's confidence.'

'Of course. But if you had told me we could have probably avoided this embarrassment.'

'I'm sorry,' Mathangi said. 'What's to be done now?'

'The matter has to be resolved today,' he said. 'I'm leaving for Kerala tonight. My father has had a heart attack . . .'

'I'm sorry. Troubles never come singly.'

'It's a very mild attack. Not serious at all. He's back home from a hospital check-up. But it's my duty to visit him. I've to go. And this has to be resolved before I go.'

'Is Adi going with you?'

'No. Just Saumya and I. Adi has phoned Father to say that she can't go because she's down with flu.'

'Is she?'

'No. She lies all the time, you know.'

'That's her PR habit.'

'No. It's a character flaw.'

'Maybe. But what are we to do now?'

'I would like you to come with me now and tell Adi what Erich told me, and make her stop pursuing him. He says he'll take other measures if she doesn't stop.'

'What other measures?'

'I don't know, Mats. Maybe he'll lodge a police complaint.'

'He wouldn't dare do that,' Mathangi said.

'Why not? He's a diplomat. He has political clout.'

'He wouldn't risk a scandal.'

'Look, what he would do is not my main concern,' he said. 'Don't you see that for my own sake, and for Adi's sake too, this has to be stopped right away, to avoid further humiliation for both of us.'

'Of course I'll come with you and talk to her. That's the least I can do. But I doubt whether she will heed me. Or even believe me.'

'Here, here's Erich's note. That's proof.'

'Alright. I'll come. Give me a minute.'

'Mats, would it be possible for you to spend a couple of days at the cottage? Or bring Adi here to stay with you? I'll be back in two days. I would feel a lot easier in mind if Adi is with you, than being alone in the cottage.'

'No problem,' she said.

On the way to the cottage, Mathangi said: 'Look, Adi might make a scene. In fact, I'm certain she'll make a scene. It'll be terrible for Saumya to be involved with it.'

'I'll take her for a walk on the beach. How much time would you need?'

'About half an hour, I think.'

'Okay. We'll get to the cottage at about five-thirty, so you should be through with Adi by about six. That's fine. I've to leave for the railway station around six. My train is at seven-thirty-five.'

'What's now going to happen between you and Adi?'

'I don't know. I'll decide when I'm in Kerala.'

'You've to think of how this is going to affect Saumya,' Mathangi said. 'How old is she now?'

'Fourteen.'

'That's a most impressionable age. You should be very, very careful not to hurt her in any way.'

'Yes, of course. That'll be my prime concern.'

8

'This is a surprise,' Aditi said, greeting Mathangi, and then tore into Zeruba. 'Where have you been? I was frantic with worry. Couldn't you at least leave a message?'

'Something urgent came up,' he said.

'What?'

'Mats will tell you.'

'What's all this mystery?' Aditi asked, laughing.

'Have patience,' Zeruba said. 'Where's Saumya?'

'In her room.'

He fetched her and they set out to the beach.

'What's all this, Mats?' Aditi asked.

'Come into the bedroom. I've something very important to tell you.'

When Mathangi told her about what had happened, Aditi initially refused to believe it.

'It can't be,' she said. 'It's all lies cooked up by Dada.'

Mathangi then showed her Erich's note. On glancing through it, Aditi rend the air with a long, heart-rending howl of anguish and dismay, and sank to the floor sobbing, knocking her head repeatedly on the granite. Mathangi tried to lift her up, but Aditi flung her off so violently that she staggered back and fell against the wall.

'Why have you done this to me, Mats?' Aditi cried plaintively, looking up at Mathangi with tear-filled eyes. 'You're so envious of me?'

'You don't know what you're saying, Adi. Have I ever betrayed you?'

'I don't know what's happening to me, god,' Aditi moaned. 'Help me, Mats. Please help me.'

'Of course,' Mathangi said. 'That's why I'm here.'

She put Aditi in bed and gave her a Valium, talking to her softly all the while.

'Calm yourself,' she said. 'Tomorrow morning you'll see all this in a different light.'

'What'll happen to me, Mats? I'm lost.'

Mathangi caressed Aditi's head tenderly and kissed her lightly on the forehead.

'You'll find yourself in the morning. I'll be with you.'

'Help me, Mats.'

'Of course. I'll be with you, always. Rest now.'

When Zeruba and Saumya returned from the beach, he hurried Saumya to her room, saying, 'Go and get ready. We've to leave soon.' Then he turned to Mathangi and asked, 'How has Adi taken it?'

'Badly.'

'Hmm.'

'I've given her a Valium, and she is calm now. She is very resilient. She'll bounce back in no time at all.'

When he reached Azhiyur the next morning, he phoned Mathangi at her office.

'Adi's with me in my flat,' she said.

'How's she?'

'On the mend. She'll be alright. She is going back to the cottage tomorrow. She'll be there when you return.'

'Any problem that I should anticipate?'
'I don't think so.'
'Okay. I'll see you when I get back. Bye.'
'Bye-bye.'

Mathangi

1

On the way back from Kerala, Zeruba, unable to sleep, slouched chain-smoking all night long at the window of his train compartment, thinking about how he should handle the crisis in his life. He had deliberately put off the consideration of the problem for a few days, so as to review it calmly by distancing himself from its emotional stress. Now he had to decide. There were several aspects to the problem. One was the matter of personal honour. This mainly had to do with how he would look in the eyes of the world when the news about Aditi's affairs became public. But this did not unduly trouble Zeruba, for he lived by his own code and did not care much about what anyone else thought of him. What concerned him were the personal consequences of the crisis, the disruption of his life and work, and jeopardy to Saumya's future. He was most bitter about that. But there was no question of he taking revenge on Aditi, through some civilized variation of honour killing. Already his anger towards her had turned into cold, hard resentment. The family was lost, and he had to reconcile himself to that. Soon the three of them would scatter, each to a different place, with no live link between them.

That was inevitable. He had to consider only how to contain the damage. The most important thing was not to traumatize Saumya with the crisis. It had to be kept a secret from her till she was old enough to take it in her stride. This meant that he had to sit on the problem for a while, a couple of years at least, till she finished school. There was, therefore, no need to do anything immediately. He had to only keep things quiet, avoid confrontations, check further transgressions.

Saumya slept like a log through the entire night journey, lulled by the speeding train humming and rocking metallically on its cradle of rails, and Zeruba had to shake her awake in Madras. From the Central Station, they took an autorickshaw to their cottage, and there found Aditi in the midst of a spring-cleaning frenzy. The house was in a mess, with the furniture all clumped together and covered with sheets. The air was thick with dust.

'Oh, Amma, you know I'm allergic to dust,' Saumya wailed, pinching her nose to hold back an erupting sneeze.

'Go to your room and close the door,' Aditi told her. 'It has already been cleaned and aired.'

For all her disorderly ways, Aditi was a demon for hygiene and cleanliness. Servants were not allowed to enter the cottage without first washing their hands and feet and cleaning their fingernails at the garden tap, and she herself bathed at least twice a day, and was for ever washing her hands and feet. And every now and then she went about maniacally tidying up the cottage, whipping the servants around.

Amazing, Zeruba thought, looking at Aditi. She had entirely regained her normal self. There was no hint of any disturbance at all in her. He too did not betray any feelings. To an outsider, or even to Saumya, everything would have appeared perfectly normal with the family.

'Go and bathe,' Aditi ordered Zeruba. 'The geyser is on.'

Not a word was said throughout the day about the recent developments. But that night, after Saumya had gone to bed, Aditi went and sat in a chair next to Zeruba while he was sitting out on the patio with his leg up on the railing, smoking a cigarette.

'So what have you decided?' she asked.

'Nothing. For the time being,' he said.

'When, then? And what?'

'Let Saumya finish school, then we'll see.'

'Be realistic, Dada,' she counselled. 'I can do so much for you. We still have a great future together.'

'I'll think about it.'

'You ought to be ashamed of yourself,' she admonished.

'Why?'

'Why! Instead of defending your wife against Erich, you come away like a coward with your tail tucked between your legs. I'm ashamed of you.'

'Defend you? For what? For cuckolding me?'

'I never had sex with him,' Aditi said indignantly.

'Oh?'

'I'm not like you at all,' she bristled. 'All you care for is sex, all I care for is love.'

'Fine.'

'You don't know how starved I'm for love. If I turn to other people for love, it's all your fault.'

'Of course.'

'I was pure at heart and you spoiled me.'

'I know,' Zeruba laughed hollowly. *Every harlot was a virgin once*, he said to himself.

'Why are you laughing, you moron?'

'Nothing. I was thinking of something I had read somewhere. Blake.'

'You vandalized my love.'

'I know.'

'Still, I've no resentment towards you. I'm very forgiving by nature.'

'Unfortunately, I don't have a forgiving nature,' he said.

'There's nothing to forgive.'

'Oh?'

'Yes, I fell in love, it's true. And I did some foolish things blinded by love. Is that a crime?'

'No, it's not a crime,' he said. 'But it's not right for you to live with me when you love another man.'

'I don't love him anymore,' she said. 'That episode is over.'

'Look, I'm tired. I want to sleep now,' he said, flicking away the butt and getting up.

That night, he slept on the bench in the studio.

2

A couple of days later Mathangi came visiting them.

'You'll see me here quite often for a while,' she said.

'Good,' Aditi said. 'You might be able to drive some sense into Dada.'

'Drive sense into him?' Mathangi snorted. 'Mission impossible.'

'What work brings you here?' Zeruba asked.

'I'm doing Agarwal's house.'

Tarun Agarwal was a middle-aged Marwari businessman with intellectual pretensions, who had made quite a pile with his small pharmaceutical company, by manufacturing substandard drugs and through various frauds in the import of chemicals. Later he sold the business for a huge profit, married Beth, an English spinster, and built his neo-classical palace on a two-acre property right on the beach, next to Zeruba's cottage.

'Why do you waste your talent on these vulgarians?' Zeruba asked Mathangi.

'Tarun is not a bad sort,' she said.

'He's a lunatic.'

'He's a bit eccentric,' agreed Mathangi. 'But that's part of his charm. And he has fairly good taste.'

'Like your film star client?' Zeruba teased.

That incident was quite a laugh—when Mathangi suggested to the star that they buy some antiques for the house, he wanted to know what antiques were, and when she told him that they were old sculpture, furniture and things like that, he told her that there was no need to go in for any old stuff as he could afford everything new.

'This is business, Dada,' Mathangi said. 'I meet the needs of my clients. I can't impose my tastes on them.'

'Dada dreads the idea of having neighbours,' said Aditi.

'Oh, I don't mind them at all,' Zeruba protested. 'I just don't want to see them or hear them, that's all.'

Tarun had dropped by to make Zeruba's acquaintance some months earlier, when his house was under construction, but Zeruba politely discouraged further contacts, saying, 'I'm afraid I'm not going to be a good neighbour. Please forgive me. I'm something of a hermit.'

3

Often when Mathangi visited, Zeruba was alone in the cottage, so they had many opportunities to discuss his marital crisis. She was a sensitive and large-hearted soul, and he had total trust in her fairness and good sense. What he did not know was that those visits were deliberately planned by Aditi to get Mathangi to persuade him to turn away from the precipitous course he had taken.

'It'll be only natural that you should take the side of Adi in this matter,' Zeruba said to Mathangi on the first day she broached the subject with him. 'But you can't help her or me by encouraging false expectations.'

'I know that,' Mathangi said. 'I care for you both, and I would like to do what I can to help. And I'm terribly concerned about Saumya.'

'She knows nothing about this.'

'Sooner or later she will. Even before that, the tension in the house will get her.'

'We'll be careful.'

'However careful you are, this is going to mark her for life,' Mathangi said. 'She's an enormously talented and sensitive child, and it'll be a tragedy if this ruins her future.'

'In a couple of years she'll be old enough to deal with this maturely.'

'I was about her age when my dad upped and left my mom for another woman, and even now, after more than two decades, I still have nightmares about it. I can't even have normal relationships with men. You know, there are times when I crave to know the love of some good man, have a family of my own. But I'm scared. I'll die alone and miserable.'

'Don't be silly,' Zeruba said. 'You're a truly exceptional woman, Mats, and if you haven't found your man it's only because your standards are very high.'

'Stop it!' Mathangi said, laughing.

'No. I'm dead serious,' he said. 'How old are you? Thirty-one? Thirty-two?'

'There you go again,' she said. 'I'm thirty-eight. Same as Adi.'

'You don't look it, Mats,' Zeruba said. 'In any case, you're too young to give up on life.'

'I'm not giving up on life,' Mathangi said indignantly. 'I only wish I had a different kind of life. It'll be terrible if something like what happened to me happens to Saumya.'

'What do you suggest I do?'

'I believe that you sleep in the studio these days. Saumya will notice this and draw her own conclusions. She's probably on to it already.'

'I can't go back to the bedroom.'

'Why not? You've twin beds. It'll not be all that different from sleeping in another room.'

'Are you trying to get us together again, Mats?' Zeruba asked suspiciously.

'It'll be good for all if that happens.'

'But it won't happen. Unless Adi changes radically. And that's unlikely.'

'How about you making some radical changes yourself?'

'Like what?'

'For heaven's sake, keep off maidservants.'

157

'I didn't mean to be bad, Mats,' he said. 'I just couldn't help doing what I did.'

'Weakness is no excuse, Dada,' she said. 'But an even more serious matter is your casualness towards Adi. She craves for intimacy and you distanced yourself from her. That's the basic problem, Dada.'

'No,' Zeruba countered. 'The basic problem is our chemical mismatch. We're all wrong for each other.'

'Well, I had warned you about it, remember? I had warned you both.'

'I had warned myself about it.'

'But since you have anyhow got married, and you have a child, you have the responsibility to hold the family together.'

'Yes, I've the responsibility,' Zeruba agreed. 'But I don't have the means. I'm sad about it. But there it is. Life with Adi has become a living hell for me.'

'Living hell?' Mathangi scoffed. 'C'mon, Dada, have a grip on reality. This sort of thing happens in most families. It's just a storm in a tea cup.'

'Perhaps,' Zeruba said. 'But the storm in the tea cup is a most terrifying thing to those who live in the tea cup. Two people knocking against each other within the tight confines of a nuclear family. It's absolutely devastating.'

4

'You should give Adi another chance,' Mathangi urged another day.

'What's the point?' Zeruba asked. 'If I can protect my family by doing that, I would gladly do it. But there is no hope of that. If I condone this transgression of hers, it will only lead to a greater crisis later on.'

'Think of Saumya.'

'I'm not going to do anything right away. I'll wait till Saumya finishes school in a couple of years. She's keen to go to college in the US. After she goes . . .'

'You'll send her away at this young age?'

'That's the only way I can save her. The house is on fire, Mats. I should let her escape.'

'Even if she goes to the US, she would still need a home to come back to.'

'By then she would develop other affiliations,' Zeruba said. 'Her relationship with her parents will not be so crucial then.'

'You're wrong there. Having a secure family as the base is the most comforting thing in the world.'

'I agree. But already there's no family. It'll do her no good to have a snake pit as home.'

'But it doesn't have to be a snake pit. If you look at the situation objectively, it's evident that your infidelities cancel out Adi's infidelities. You're quits.'

'Objectively, yes. But that's not how it works in life. You can't decide these matters through an actuarial analysis. Besides, our offences are not the same.'

'What do you mean?'

'Look, Adi's affair with Erich was not just a matter of casual sex. Casual sex is a universal vulnerability. It's of little account,' Zeruba said. 'But that's not the case here. Adi's was a serious romantic involvement of calculated intent. She was scheming to forsake her husband and child and marry Erich, and now she's scheming to destroy me. But I won't let her destroy me. I'm determined to survive this.'

He could have perhaps forgiven Aditi for straying, for he himself had strayed. What he could not condone was that she was going to abandon him, for to accept that would have been for him to deny his own self-worth.

'You're reading too much into what happened, Dada,' Mathangi said. 'Another day you'll see it differently. It's all a matter of perspective.'

'There will not be another day,' Zeruba said decisively. 'This marriage is done for. It's like a plant whose roots have dried. It cannot be revived. It's all over.'

'No, it isn't over,' Mathangi cautioned. 'This wound will continue to fester in you both till the end of your lives. Even then it won't be over. It'll continue to hurt Saumya, and it'll affect her own married life. And that in turn will affect her children, and the children of her children. No, it's not over. It'll never be over.'

'You're over-generalizing, Mats. Of course, nothing is ever finally over. The consequences of even the most trivial events will go rolling on till the end of time, I know,' Zeruba said. 'But that's the cosmic perspective. I can't take the cosmic perspective in a personal crisis.'

5

Zeruba's mind was set. He had to free himself from the draining entanglement with Aditi. He was at a crossroads in life, and felt that if he did not now decide wisely and act resolutely, his whole future would be in jeopardy. He was only forty-eight. He still had much to live.

It mystified Zeruba how Aditi could possibly choose someone like Erich over him, a man who had no worth at all as a person, neither physical charm nor intellectual merit. There was no explanation. For that matter, why did he himself turn from Aditi to maidservants? There was no explanation for that either.

Who knows why anyone does anything! Zeruba mused. *Perhaps we have no real control over anything we do, but only imagine we do, while inexorable fate—or our genes— independently determines our actions. Or maybe it's all just a play of chance, random couplings of events. Would not life for me and Aditi have turned out altogether different if there had been a slight shift in the meshing of events, a slight shift in the tempi of the spinning gears of our lives? Who knows! And if we are all victims of fate or chance, aren't we all innocent in everything we do? What right do we then have to pass judgement on anyone? In any case, aren't all distinctions illusory, all values contextual, as sages claim, and nothing is in itself good or bad, right or wrong?*

Maybe. But we cannot live in a world without distinctions, Zeruba reasoned. *Even if everything in the world is provisional, transient and uncertain, within this objective world of uncertainties, each of us has to build his own private world of subjective certainties. Here there are values. Right and wrong, good and bad. An impersonal observer outside time and outside history—god, if you will—might judge Aditi innocent, but I myself cannot but find her guilty.*

Many people, Zeruba knew, saw Aditi as a golden girl, noble, compassionate, generous, and always helpful. Maybe she was all that, he reflected. But even a golden needle hurts if it pricks your skin. And Aditi was hurting him, ruining his peace of mind, affecting his work. He could not allow it to go on.

Zeruba was not sure whether he saw Aditi differently now because he had ceased to love her, or whether he ceased to love her because he now saw her differently. There was nothing about her that pleased him now. She was generous to a fault, and he did indeed find it a fault. Once when Anna, Zeruba's brother Chacko's nosy wife, came visiting and admired the gold bracelet Aditi was wearing, she immediately took it off and gave it to her.

'Why did you do it?' Zeruba asked Aditi after Anna left.

'I like giving presents,' she said.

'That was not a present. It was a bribe.'

'Bribe? Goodness! For what?'

'For her to think well of you. To spread the good word,' he said. 'Or for you to assuage some secret feelings of guilt in you.'

'God! How you twist everything I do into something ignoble!'

'There's nothing called a selfless act, Adi. For anyone. We're always looking for something in return.'

'Altruism is a form of selfishness?'

'Yes, it is. No one lives for another.'

161

'Then the most altruistic act is also the most selfish?'

'No, that's not the logic of it,' Zeruba said. 'The logic of it is that even the most altruistic act is in some way selfish.'

'You know, you are really a very perverse person,' Aditi said. 'You're evil and you see everything as evil.'

'True,' he conceded. 'I've this evil habit of looking truth in the eye.'

'You can never understand a highly evolved being like me,' she said loftily. 'I've reached the final stage of transmigration. This is my last birth.'

'I sure hope so,' he said.

Zeruba had apprehensions about Aditi's character right from the beginning, seeing ill portents in her inordinate fondness for romantic pulp fiction, Barbara Cartland and Mills & Boon novels. When they were in the US, she even got Rupa to send her cheap Tamil magazines and romances, and was forever lying about devouring them, and to this he attributed a certain coarseness in her character. He tried to wean her away from the trash, but it was no use.

'I'm just relaxing,' she told him when he once chided her. 'What does it matter what I read to relax?'

'It matters, Adi,' he remonstrated. 'What we read goes into the making of what we are.'

'I don't see how,' she protested.

'Because reading is like any other real life experience. It influences the way you think, what you dream about and aspire for. It shapes your values, defines your character. It changes the chemistry of your brain, your neural connections,' he explained. 'You are what you read, Adi.'

'What rot! I am what I am, not what I read,' she snapped and returned to her book.

6

The views of Aditi and Zeruba about themselves and about each other were entirely contrary. Rather than seeing Aditi as a highly evolved being, as she desired to be seen, Zeruba considered her to be quite a basic creature, an entry-level human being. She claimed herself to be compassionate, and was indeed always helpful to others, generous with her time and money. But he saw her in a different light. In his view, she lacked sensitivity and self-awareness to be truly compassionate. It was not empathy that made her run to the help of others, but a natural exuberance of character—that, and her anxiety to look good in the eyes of others.

Zeruba considered Aditi to be a deeply flawed and insecure person behind her facade of jaunty self-confidence, who sought to compensate for her insecurities by puffing herself up with delusions of grandeur. And so intense was the power of her fantasies that she convinced not only herself but also everyone around her too that her projected self was her real self. It was an amazing feat of self-mythification.

There were, in Zeruba's view, fundamental differences between him and Aditi. In any alphabetical list, Aditi and Zeruba appeared at opposite ends. They were the Alpha and Omega, the beginning and the end, the low and the high, of everything. While Zeruba was a sedate and deliberate person, for whom precision and control were matters of the highest importance, Aditi was capricious, wayward and restive, quite wild in fact, and hardly ever in self-control. Sometimes he even doubted her sanity.

Aditi was like a searing desert wind howling through his life. He, like his mother, never raised his voice, even in great anger, but she screamed even in normal conversation, and was hysterical when excited. At parties he could always hear her loud and clear at the other end of the room or in the far corner of the lawn. He was helplessly open and truthful, while she was a cunning and resolute liar; worse, she thought that he too was a liar. The good, as they say, can imagine evil, but the evil cannot imagine good.

Mathangi laughed when he told her this.

'Amazing!' she said. 'Your capacity for self-adulation is simply amazing.'

'But these are facts,' he said.

'Warped, subjective facts.'

'Maybe. But facts nevertheless.'

Zeruba saw Aditi as wedded to the temporal, and himself as wedded to the transcendental. She was of the earth, he of the spirit. He was concerned with well-being, she with comfort; he sought gnosis and beatitude, she sought material gain and sensual pleasures; he was a creator, she was a consumer; he had ambition, she had hungers. She was sly, clever and quick-witted, but shallow. All fizz and no substance, he said to himself. Froth without beer. Impressive in appearance, but insubstantial.

7

Such were his feelings. Aditi's view of Zeruba was equally uncomplimentary. She did not even consider him to be intelligent—maybe he was talented and was an intellectual, but he certainly was not intelligent, and had no survival skills. He didn't know how to get ahead in the world. That apart, he was, in her view, utterly selfish.

'You're just a selfish brute,' she told him.

'Selfish?' he challenged. 'What have I ever taken from anyone?'

'You may not take anything from anyone, but you don't give anything to anyone either,' she charged. 'You may not be the grabbing type, but you're so egocentric that it's worse than being selfish. Give and take is the process of bonding in society. You're antisocial.'

'Asocial,' he corrected her.

'Being asocial is being antisocial,' Aditi charged. 'You live just for yourself. I live for others.'

'Why don't you spare some of your grand generosity for your own family, for your husband for instance, before showering favours on others?' he asked.

'I can't live just for my family,' she said. 'I've wider concerns.'

'You've to earn the right to be generous, Adi,' he advised. 'And you should earn that right by fulfilling your duties to your own family.'

'You first practise a little generosity yourself,' she retorted, 'just a wee bit, before sermonizing me on generosity.'

There was no meeting ground at all between them. Still, he did esteem certain qualities in her. He admired her energy and gregariousness, and her irrepressible optimism about life. She was also good in bed, though rather ferocious, and she kept the cottage spotlessly clean and managed the servants well. She was a lousy cook, but that did not matter much, for she hardly ever cooked, though at times some atavistic urge would come over her, and she would banish the cook from the kitchen and prepare a couple of dishes herself. She did this once on their wedding anniversary—the date of which, for the life of him, Zeruba could never remember—spending a good part of the evening preparing dinner. But Zeruba, who was busy in the studio the whole day, did not know of this, so when she proudly served him some exotic meat dish she had prepared, he took a bite of it and gagged.

'What the shit is this?' he asked.

Aditi made a face.

'Fried shit,' she said.

Aditi's culinary misadventures did not trouble Zeruba, but her chronic lateness and her utter lack of truthfulness were matters of grave concern to him, especially her lack of truthfulness.

'Who doesn't tell lies?' she asked in self-defence. 'Don't you?'

'Yes. But there's a difference,' he said. 'Most of our lies are harmless and self-limiting. There's no aggression in them. But lies are battle weapons for you. Your primary battle weapon.'

'I'm not a saint,' she said. 'I'm just trying to survive in a harsh world.'

'You know, PR is a good profession for you, but you will do even better in politics,' he taunted. 'You've no scruples, no shame, and you're an inveterate liar. You would make a great politician. Try it.'

'I'll think about it,' she said icily.

It did occur to Zeruba now and then that he was probably making unrealistic demands on Aditi, wanting her to fit into his expectations of her in every detail.

'Don't pester me about small things,' she once told him. 'It's because you keep bothering me about small things that I can't do big things properly.'

And he said, 'Everything has to be done right, Adi. If you don't take care to do small things well, you won't take care to do big things well.'

'You expect me to be perfect, but are you perfect?'

'No, I'm not perfect,' he admitted. 'Nor do I expect perfection from you. But I expect both of us to strive to be better than we are.'

'You expect me to live the life of some imagined ideal,' she grouched. 'I can't do that. I've to live my own life. Let me be.'

8

Looking back, Zeruba could not think of any particular day or incident that marked the point of no return in his marriage. The Erich affair was only the proverbial last straw that broke the camel's back, the culmination of what had long become inevitable. The friction between Aditi and Zeruba was mostly over trivial and common and even ridiculous matters, but their cumulative effect was devastating. Most couples would have resolved those problems by making concessions to each other, but Aditi was too combative and Zeruba too adamantine to do that. In a way, Zeruba was more responsible than Aditi for the crisis, being too self-willed to make the compromises necessary to preserve the marriage. There was no give in him; he wanted everything to be exactly as he desired it.

Still, in the early stages of their marital crisis, his attitude towards Aditi was rather ambivalent. While outwardly he seemed obdurately resolved to end their marriage, there were also times when he vaguely hoped that something or other would happen that would enable them to pull back from the brink. He did not want to lose his family. At times he was bitter with resentment towards Aditi for vandalizing his life, but at other times he saw them both as unwitting victims of a capricious fate, and was awash with sadness. *Why have we done this to each other*, he often asked himself. *We could have been happy together.*

There were indeed times even now when he felt tender and protective towards her, and wanted to reach out to her. Weren't her desperate acts really cries for help? At times he thought that he could hear in her exuberant laughter a faint echo of some long ago pain. Didn't she then deserve understanding and sympathy, rather than reproach?

And there were times when he desperately needed her to reach out to him. To save him from himself. For all his cavalier defence of his philandering, Zeruba had awful feelings of guilt about it. He felt that he was sliding helplessly into these affairs. He prized self-control, and felt debased by his vulnerability. And he secretly hoped that Aditi would pull him out of the quagmire into which he was sinking.

Aditi and Zeruba needed each other's help and support to rise out of the mess of their lives, but unfortunately they were always out of sync with each other. Whenever he felt dejected and needed her sympathy and support, she was invariably indifferent, and whenever she felt tender towards him, he wanted to be left alone; and whenever she felt low, he was invariably indifferent, and whenever he felt tender towards her, she repulsed him. Their chemistry was all wrong.

167

B a b a

1

Mathangi completed the work on Tarun's marble palace by the end of August, and Beth and Tarun moved in there in the first week of September. A couple of weeks before that Mathangi phoned Zeruba to say that Tarun wanted to buy one of his paintings, and also invite him to his house-warming.

'Why doesn't he decorate the house with his wife's paintings?' Zeruba asked.

'He's doing that,' Mathangi said. 'But he wants one of yours for the drawing room.'

'A conversation piece?'

'Perhaps.'

'Okay. But no bargaining.'

'Fine. No bargaining,' said Mathangi. 'I've already told him that.'

'I'll add your commission to the price.'

'No. Don't do that. I'm working on a flat fee on this project.'

'Wow! How much?'

'Pardon? I didn't hear you.'

'I asked how much you are making from the drug peddler.'

'Sorry, I still can't hear you.'

Zeruba laughed.

'Look, Dada, don't be rude to him. He's paying me a very fat fee.'

'I won't bite.'

'No barking, either.'

'Okay.'

The deal went off smoothly. Tarun had read about Zeruba's *Earth Mother*, and that was the painting he wanted.

'That's an award-winning painting—it'll be too expensive for you,' Zeruba said.

'How much?' Tarun asked.

'Five lakhs.'

Tarun didn't bat an eye. 'I'll take it,' he said.

The sale made it unavoidable for Zeruba to attend Tarun's house-warming party. Actually he hugely enjoyed the party, a wild, drunken affair, quite unlike the decorous, boring, high society parties he was familiar with. Most of the guests were small-time Gujarati and Marwari businessmen, a boisterous crowd that grew rowdier by the second, voraciously guzzling the excellent Scotch that Tarun plied them with. There was a sprinkling of foreigners among the guests, Beth's friends, who moved about with frozen smiles wondering how soon they could leave the party without seeming impolite. Among the guests were also a Parsi couple, a tall, wiry, silvery-haired man, prissily dressed, and his slender, baby-faced wife with an incongruously huge overhang of breasts, the weight of which made her totter so awkwardly as she walked on her high-heeled shoes that she seemed ever in danger of tipping over and falling on her face. Most of the guests hovered around the bar, which was set in the atrium, from which rooms radiated in all directions, each a freestanding unit with no common walls.

'We used the symbolism of the sun,' Beth said.

'Literally!' Zeruba exclaimed.

'In architecture you can't use symbolism symbolically,' Mathangi cut in, giving him a nasty look.

'Oh, I didn't mean it as a criticism,' he quickly added. 'In fact, I quite like the house. You've done a marvellous job in doing up the interiors, Mats. I especially like the painting in the drawing room.'

Beth laughed. No offence taken. She had a degree in Sanskrit from Oxford, and had been in Madras for years trying to establish herself as a Bharatanatyam dancer. That dream did not materialize. Though she had worked very hard for many years, and was a competent dancer, she was treated condescendingly as a peripheral curiosity by the conservative dance establishment of Madras. She then took to painting, but had no luck with that either, as art critics savaged her impressionist works as conventional and imitative. As the doors of opportunity closed one by one for her, this once wasp-waisted and bright-eyed young woman grew dumpy, her rosy skin turned sickly yellow, and her eyes grew dull. She was at a dead end. Then someone told her about Sai Baba, and she went on a pilgrimage to Puttaparthi. That transformed her life.

'Do not be troubled,' Baba said, blessing her. 'A new life awaits you.'

And indeed on that very day at Puttaparthi she met Tarun, and in him found a modest future for herself.

Tarun considered himself a great sage in the making. He had earlier visited the Aurobindo Ashram in Pondicherry to check out the competition, and was now at Puttaparthi on the same mission. From these visits he had drawn the important conclusion that it was imperative for him to have someone to promote him, preferably a British or American lady. It was when he was thinking over this matter that he ran into Beth and struck up an easy friendship with her, and this he took to be a sign from the heavens. They got married the same month.

Tarun, though a school dropout, was rather well-read for a man of his background, and what he did not know he pretended to know, which he could do brazenly, as there was no one to call his bluff in the semi-literate group of traders and petty businessmen he moved with. He had made a lot of money, much more than any of the others in this group, and that in itself entitled him to their adoration. Besides, compared to them, he was a matchless scholar, who knew everything about everything. And, to cap his glory, he had a memsahib wife. So they venerated him as an omniscient yet worldly-wise sage, and sought his advice on everything from spiritual matters to business problems and sexual dysfunction. This adulation, and the easy success of crooks and charlatans in setting themselves up as godmen in India, gave Tarun the confidence that he would be able to establish himself as a spiritual leader, and thus earn a name for himself, which he desperately craved. And he genuinely believed that he had great wisdom to impart.

Tarun's ideal in this enterprise was J. Krishnamurti, the theosophist. He did not want to work among the masses, but yearned for high society devotees, like those of Krishnamurti, and it was his fond hope that Beth, with her fair skin and Oxford accent, would be able to catapult him into the rarefied world of the Madras elite. The beach setting of their mansion was specifically chosen to provide the ideal ambience for holding soirees, and the house was done up opulently so as to impress the elite and induce them to recognize Tarun as one of their own.

Zeruba thought that Tarun was crazy. But he was also fascinated by him, and found in him an excellent means to divert himself from the problems engulfing him at this time. Tarun had a floodlit tennis court at home, and Zeruba, who had been an avid player in his college days, gladly accepted the invitation to play there.

'Come every day,' Tarun said.

'I go for a jog on the beach in the evenings,' Zeruba said. 'I'll come on Sundays, if it's alright with you.'

'Sure,' said Tarun.

'You'll also come, won't you?' Beth asked Aditi.

'Delighted,' Aditi said.

'She's a tennis fanatic,' Zeruba said.

'Wonderful,' Tarun said. 'We'll have fun.'

2

On Sundays, there was always a small crowd at Tarun's place. The Parsi couple whom Zeruba had met at Tarun's house-warming party—Ratan Screwallah, a cloth exporter, and his wife Vira—were always there, and so was Ashok Kumar, a scruffy, profane and scatological gadfly journalist with a leading newspaper. Also fairly regular were Krishna Iyer, a magnificently white-haired advertising company director who lived nearby, and his frail, shy and enigmatic daughter Pratibha. Occasionally, Swaminathan, a professor at the Indian Institute of Technology, and his morose wife Surabhi, also dropped in. Mathangi joined them sometimes, but she never played tennis.

'I don't like blood sports,' Mathangi said, when pressed to play.

'This isn't a blood sport,' Tarun chided.

'Close enough,' she said.

Tarun was a clumsy but fiercely competitive player, and he usually won the sets, as hardly anyone else gave a damn about winning or losing but played just for the fun of it, and some of them, particularly Vira and Surabhi, were good on the court only for comic relief. The only one other than Tarun who took the game seriously was Aditi—she was as fiercely competitive as Tarun, but unlike him she was a graceful player, and she usually thrashed him, much to his mortification. Zeruba was also a good player, and had a deadly backhand drive, but he played only to indulge his body, not to win games. Ashok was equally indifferent to winning. Feisty and cynical, he would not take anything or anybody seriously, and was often caustic towards his host, but was nevertheless pampered by Tarun, who expected from him a bonanza of newspaper articles heralding him, Tarun, as a great new sage. Aditi detested Ashok as a thoroughly disreputable character, but mainly because he was immune to her charms, being infatuated with Pratibha, who had worked briefly with him at the newspaper and was now rumoured to be working on a novel.

The best part of the evening was the drunken bull session after the game, when they sat on the lawn guzzling beer. Its only shortcoming was that Tarun prohibited smoking and the use of obscenities in his house.

'Fuck you, Tarun,' Ashok cursed when he was told of this rule. 'We use expletives to establish sociability.'

'I don't like it,' Tarun said. 'So please.'

'Okay, okay,' said Ashok. 'I'll comply, since you're bribing me with hooch.'

Their discussions usually had no focus, and topics of conversation slithered over one other like rat-snakes in a slime pit, with everyone talking tangentially. It was fun. It was fun even when Tarun and Swaminathan engaged in solemn debates on such esoteric topics as entropy, the meaning of time, the big bang, whether there was god or not, and so on. On all these, Tarun had the final answer, to which the professor generally deferred respectfully.

'At the age of fourteen, I set out to discover god,' Tarun declared one day in his earnest, gravelly voice. 'I gave myself two weeks to find out the truth.'

'You gave yourself too much time,' Ashok scoffed.

Tarun took him seriously. 'Nonsense,' he said. 'This is a problem that sages have been grappling with for centuries.'

'So what did you conclude?' Swaminathan inquired.

'Can I have some more beer?' asked Ratan.

'I'll get it,' said Beth.

'Will anybody please listen?' Tarun growled in exasperation.

'Sorry,' said Beth. 'You were saying?'

'Dada knows the answer,' Ashok said.

'Okay. Let's hear him, then,' Tarun said.

'There's no god,' Zeruba said.

'Ah, but there's Sai Baba,' Ashok said, teasing Beth.

'A magician!' Tarun snorted.

'Baba may not be god,' Beth said. 'But that's not important. What's important is that he gives godlike solace to many.'

'But the solace that people get from Baba does not come from Baba,' Zeruba said.

'That's very illogical,' laughed Beth. 'How can what you get from Baba not be from Baba?'

'On the other hand, it's perfectly logical,' Zeruba rejoined. 'What I mean is that Baba is only a facilitator. The solace you receive is what you draw from within yourself. It's your faith that does the trick, not Baba. Any absolute faith in anything or anyone would work equally well. Even a rustic's faith in a tree or stone or anthill.'

'What nonsense,' Aditi exclaimed. She had been converted into a Baba devotee by Beth. 'You mean any faith can work miracles? Even faith in you?'

'Yes,' Zeruba affirmed.

'Fine,' Aditi said. 'Show me a miracle.'

'Show me some faith,' Zeruba countered.

'That's exactly the point, don't you see?' Beth said. 'You can't inspire faith. Baba can. And that makes all the difference.'

'I agree,' Zeruba said. 'He's undeniably a man of some special qualities or skills. But that doesn't make him god.'

'I'm reading a book on the octopus now,' Iyer cut in. 'What an amazing creature it is! It can change its colour at will, even change the colour of parts of its body. And it can change the texture of its skin from rough to smooth at will. Should we then worship the octopus as god, because it can do miraculous things which we can't do, which even Sai Baba can't do?'

'You're looking at this the wrong way,' Beth said. 'It's not Baba's magical powers that make him divine. He himself dismisses his miracles as mere hooks to pull you towards spirituality. He calls them his visiting cards.'

'But his devotees see them as real miracles,' Zeruba pointed out. 'That's the power of faith, don't you see?'

'The power of wizardry,' Ashok scoffed. 'I mean, would Baba still be Baba if he had a crew cut and wore a safari-suit?'

'He's in his seventies now, isn't he?' Iyer asked. 'Does he dye his hair, I wonder.'

'And if he is god,' pressed on Ashok, 'why did he have to run for his life when there was a murder attempt on him—he could have just raised his hand and vaporized the felons.'

'Exactly,' Zeruba said. 'He's powerless against the faithless.'

'What's your point?' Beth asked. 'That Baba by himself has no power?'

'My point is simply that it's the faith of the faithful that gives Baba the power to help them,' Zeruba said. 'If you don't have faith in him, he can do nothing at all for you. It is the same with gods—they exist only because there are people who believe in their existence.'

'Can we change the subject, please?' Ashok pleaded. 'I can't breathe.'

'My uncle Mathu once had an encounter with Sai Baba,' Zeruba said. 'This was aeons ago, before Baba became famous.'

'I didn't know this,' Aditi said. 'Was he a devotee?'

'Well, he told Baba that he would become a devotee. But on one condition.'

'What?'

'He said that if Baba could get his two missing front teeth grow back again, he would become a devotee.'

'Baba has missing front teeth?' Surabhi was incredulous.

'No,' said Zeruba. 'My uncle has two missing front teeth. He lost them in the college hockey field.'

3

Zeruba, despite his mocking tongue, actually had considerable admiration for Sai Baba, as he had for anyone who had done anything exceptional. Whether Baba was endowed with paranormal powers or only with magical skills, he certainly was doing much good through his medical and educational institutions. And he was as much a solace to his devotees as any god. Perhaps more so. So if he had to play-act god to accomplish all this, why should it be scorned?

'What puzzles me is that so many people, lakhs and lakhs of them, even highly educated people, regard Baba, a human being just like them, as god,' Ashok said. Here is a man who sweats in his armpits like us, has body excretions like us, feels hunger and thirst like us, gets tired and has to restore himself through sleep, gets sick sometimes and has to be treated by physicians, and once had to run for his life when attacked by assailants. And one day Baba will surely die. To accept a mere mortal as god is to violate the very concept of god, Ashok felt. 'It doesn't make sense.'

'Of course it doesn't make sense,' Zeruba agreed. 'Faith never does. What you've to bear in mind is that the potency of faith is not in the object of faith, but in the heart of the devotee. So it can't be shaken by the facts about the object of faith.'

Beth, however, had a different explanation for the god / man paradox in Sai Baba. 'Baba is not god himself, but an incarnation of god,' she said. 'He is in his body like any other human being, and has all the limitations and vulnerabilities of a mortal, but he is god on the spiritual plane.'

'But what's the need for divine incarnations?' Zeruba wanted to know. 'Why can't god do his stuff by himself, as himself?'

'I don't know,' Beth said. 'Why should we seek a rational explanation for everything? Can't we accept certain things as mysteries? You'll see it all differently when you see Baba.'

So Aditi and Beth one day dragged Zeruba to Sai Baba's ashram. They, along with thousands of others, squatted on the ground in the baking sun, facing the dais where Baba sat listening to the bhajans sung by his devotees. He was dressed in an ankle length ochre robe, and kept wiping the sweat from his face with a folded white handkerchief. He looked weary. It would be nice, Zeruba whispered to Aditi, if Baba would favour his sweltering devotees by lowering the ambient temperature by a few degrees. She hushed him with a withering look.

Sai Baba's features were crude, aboriginal. He certainly was no Aryan god. There was a mole on his left cheek, Zeruba noticed, and his Afro hairstyle enveloped his head like a black halo. His demeanour was modest and gentle, and a faint smile played on his lips, as if to say, *What's all this? All is maya.* Or perhaps the smile was an expression of compassion: *How you suffer, my children! And how I suffer with you!* He performed no miracle that day, and called no one to him for special blessings. But the devotees were content. The mere *darshan* of Baba was blessing enough for them.

On their return to Madras, Aditi for a while took to singing bhajans before a gaudy, gilt-framed colour photograph of Baba that she had procured in Puttaparthi. But her devotion, as in everything else she did, did not last long, though she continued to accompany Beth to Puttaparthi once in a while. On one such trip, she got a small pouch of sacred ash from Baba. And she wanted to ritually mark Zeruba's forehead with it.

'Go ahead,' he said, turning to her from the painting he was working on.

'Turn to the east, you idiot,' she hissed. 'Don't you know even that?'

'I thought god is there in every direction,' he said.

'Why must you argue at a moment like this?' she remonstrated. 'I've half a mind to throw this bloody ash into your bloody eyes.'

'Go ahead,' he said.

'Turn, you bloody blighter,' she said, and took him by the shoulders and turned him to face the east. Custom required that before any ceremony she should do obeisance to her husband as her living god, so she perfunctorily touched his feet with her fingertips, and then smeared his forehead with the ash.

'You're under Baba's power now,' she warned. 'So be good.'

'I will,' he said gravely.

She scowled at him, but walked away without another word, dusting her hands. And he went into the bathroom in the studio to wash off the ash.

Sometimes, after tennis and beer at Tarun's place, Iyer, Pratibha and Ashok walked over to Zeruba's cottage, to smoke cigarettes sitting on the patio, and on such occasions they often made fun of Tarun's eccentricities.

'He's neurotic, perhaps even schizophrenic,' Ashok observed. 'Sometimes his speech sounds like word salad.'

'I believe he's under heavy sedation most of the time,' Zeruba said.

'He talks to god every day to advise him on how to run the world,' Ashok quipped.

'I think what he really wants is to be accepted by the Madras high society as one of their own,' Iyer said. 'Unfortunately, that will never happen. I know that crowd very well. The old money in Madras would treat him with contempt.'

'And he will never be accepted as a godman, either,' Zeruba said.

'He's crazy enough,' Iyer remarked.

'That's not enough,' Zeruba said. 'You can't play a godman by dressing in safari-suits like a bank manager, as he does. You have to wear a toga or robe or something. Look a bit weird.'

'A greater problem is his physique,' Ashok said. Tarun was short and roly-poly and completely bald. 'I mean, we can't have a bald god, can we?'

Aditi was furious with them for making fun of Tarun. 'You're a bunch of ingrates,' she berated them. 'You drink his beer and Scotch, eat at five-star hotels at his expense, and then sit around and make fun of him behind his back. You should be ashamed of yourselves.'

'How do you think we talk about you when you are not here?' Ashok asked and howled with raucous laughter.

'You're the scroungiest of all,' Aditi screamed at him. 'I don't like you at all.'

'Thank god!' Ashok said, still laughing. 'I would be scared if you liked me.'

'Then why are you here?'

'You want me to leave?' Ashok asked cheerfully, getting up.

'He's just joking, Adi,' Pratibha said, speaking for the first time that evening. 'He teases me also like this.'

'You're drunk, Adi,' Zeruba chided. 'Go to bed.'

'Why shouldn't we speak ill of our friends?' Ashok asked defensively when Aditi stormed out. 'After all, they are our friends not because they don't have any faults.'

None of them particularly felt like spongers on Tarun, because none of them were particularly enamoured of the Scotch and five-star dinners he provided; they certainly enjoyed the Scotch and the dinners, but they did not crave for them and would not have missed them if they did not have them any more. They flocked to Tarun's place mainly for the fun of the evening, and part of the fun of the evening was having a little innocent banter at Tarun's expense. There was no malice in it.

'All day long I do nothing but think, think, think,' Tarun said to them one day.

'All day long he does nothing but fantasize, fantasize, fantasize,' Ashok responded in a stage whisper to Zeruba. 'I fantasize, *ergo sum*!'

'Adi does the same thing the whole day,' Zeruba whispered back. 'In fact, she's more practical. Scheme, scheme, scheme, is what she does all day.'

5

Tarun was a poseur, but an amiable poseur, a harmless lunatic, and his fantasies were non-aggressive and self-limiting. In his grandiose daydreams, he saw himself correcting the errors of Einstein, advising Bergman on cinematic techniques, Eliot on poetry, Sartre on existentialism, and Ambani on business strategy.

Ashok teased him endlessly, but Tarun took him seriously and gave earnest answers to the quaint questions that Ashok came up with.

'What's entropy, Tarun?' Ashok asked him one day with seeming earnestness. Tarun then launched into a long and baffling explanation, which absolutely thrilled Swaminathan. 'That's more lucid than anything I've read anywhere,' said Swaminathan. Tarun twinkled with delight.

'Yes, but what does it mean?' Ashok persisted.

'Tarun has just explained,' Swaminathan said.

'But I didn't understand a word of what he said.'

'Maybe that's because you're too dumb, Ashok,' Aditi snickered.

'Okay, you tell me, then,' Ashok said.

'Bugger off,' Aditi snapped.

All this was innocent fun. But one rainy day, when they could not play tennis and were drinking whisky in Tarun's drawing room, Ashok got drunk and mercilessly tore into Tarun, telling him bluntly that he suffered from delusions, and that his wise sayings were silly, childish and ludicrous. Tarun was so dazed by this that he staggered to a corner of the room and stood there facing the wall, shaking convulsively and hitting his head on the wall, all the while jabbering insanely to himself. It was scary. Beth went to him and held him from behind in a consoling embrace.

'I'm sorry,' Ashok said. 'I didn't mean to hurt you, Tarun.'

'I think everybody better leave now,' Beth said.

'I didn't mean to hurt the poor bloke,' Ashok said contritely, when the group reassembled in Zeruba's cottage.

'You're crazy, Ashok,' Aditi told him. 'You're crazier than he is.'

The next day Beth phoned Ashok at the newspaper office. 'I would like you not to visit us any more,' she told him.

'That's okay,' Ashok said. 'But I'm sorry that I've hurt him.'

'You've always been taunting him and making fun of him,' she charged.

'But you know very well that what I said is the truth,' Ashok said. 'He's suffering from delusions.'

'Maybe,' Beth said. 'But when a man has built his entire life on those delusions, you can't knock them off without destroying him.'

'But what are friends for if they don't tell each other the home truths?' Ashok asked.

'We can do without such friends.'

'Look, mental illness is like any other illness, Beth. The patient has to be treated, and not told that he's fine, as you're doing.'

'You're really very crude, aren't you?'

'And you're really very afraid of the truth, aren't you?'

'Yes, I'm afraid of the truth,' Beth said. 'I'm afraid that the truth might one day drive Tarun to suicide.'

'Surely not because of me,' Ashok said.

'Of course not because of you. Don't flatter yourself,' Beth snorted. 'But please don't visit us again.'

'Fine,' said Ashok and put down the phone.

Beth went to see Zeruba the next day.

'Tarun is a very insecure person,' Beth said. 'He's very, very sensitive.'

'I know,' Zeruba said.

'He has no skin. He was very hurt by Ashok's taunts.'

'He was only joking,' Zeruba said. 'He didn't mean any harm.'

'Perhaps. But he has done great harm. Tarun has taken it very badly.'

'How is he?'

'In bed. He refuses to get up.'

'I'm sorry.'

'Oh, he'll be alright in a day or so.'

'Please forgive me for saying this,' Zeruba said, 'but doesn't he show signs of manic depression?'

'I'm well aware of that,' Beth said. 'That's why I've to request all of you to be a little more considerate to him.'

'Of course,' Zeruba said.

Ashok

1

Ashok's expulsion took the life out of the weekend tennis parties, which had derived much of their energy from his frisky, feisty irreverence. Iyer and Pratibha, close friends of Ashok, dropped out almost immediately, and Zeruba and Aditi became occasional players. Of those who remained, only the Parsi couple were regulars, but they were not good enough either as players or as conversationalists to engage Tarun.

Tarun had regarded his tennis buddies as the nucleus from which would eventually grow a large devotee following, as friends of his friends and their friends in ever widening circles flocked to him. That did not happen. Instead, he found that even the small group of friends already with him was breaking up and scattering. He had been riding on a heady wave of optimism ever since he married Beth, but now he realized that the high society devotees whom he so ardently desired would never materialize, and he squarely blamed Beth's devotion to Sai Baba for her failure to promote him.

'In Indian culture you can be devoted to two different gods at the same time,' Beth pointed out. 'Or even to a hundred different gods.'

'Yes,' said Tarun, 'but you can't promote two competing products at the same time.'

'I didn't know that sages are products.'

'In a commercial society they are,' he said.

These disappointments of Tarun were exacerbated by the financial problems that engulfed him at this time. A very large investment that he had grandly made in a Chettiar finance company in the hope of gaining the attention of the Madras social elite proved to be a dud, as the company collapsed. Besides, he had been living far above his means, and was now beginning to feel the pinch. Slowly his world began to shrink and close in on him. And Tarun and Beth drifted apart.

Zeruba was shocked by the utter depletion of energy in their home when he visited them on a Sunday evening after a gap of many weeks. There were no guests there, not even the Parsi couple. The tennis court was untended, and was strewn with wind-raked dead leaves. Tarun and Beth looked glum and withdrawn.

'We don't play tennis anymore,' Beth said. She looked pallid, as if drained of all blood.

'Why, Tarun?' Zeruba asked. 'I thought tennis was the high point of your day.'

'I lost interest,' Tarun said tonelessly, sitting cocooned in a beanbag, limply hugging his legs, his chin pressed against his knees, his hooded eyes downcast.

'He has lost interest in life,' said Beth.

When Zeruba left, Beth walked with him to the gate, telling him what their life was like now. Tarun, she said, spent the entire day lying on the couch in the drawing room, shrouded from head to foot in a woollen blanket, with the air conditioner turned up so high as to keep the room frigidly cold. He was putting himself in deep freeze.

'He's resigned to realizing his dreams only in his daydreams,' Beth said.

'That's what we all will be ultimately reduced to,' Zeruba consoled.

'Sometimes he wakes up screaming at night,' Beth said.

'Nightmares?'

'He says he sees fearsome winged creatures hovering over him.'

'So how do you spend your time?' Zeruba asked.

'I play solitaire most of the time,' she laughed. 'And I cook. I love cooking.'

'What about painting?'

'Oh, I've given it up,' she said. 'What's the point!'

Beth was still devoted to Tarun, and took good care of him, as a mother would take care of a handicapped child. But they hardly talked to each other any more.

'Anything I can do?' Zeruba asked.

'Come more often,' Beth said.

'I will,' Zeruba promised.

2

That was a promise that Zeruba could not keep, for he himself was in a limbo at this time, having lost the focus of his life in the swirl of events of the previous couple of years, the crisis in his marriage. He too gave up painting now, as he found it suffocating to work in the studio. Instead, he took up sculpting in stone, thinking that the punishing physical labour of chiselling granite would be the means to calm his troubled spirit.

Zeruba had been planning for some years to do a series of large paintings on the Vedantic concept of the relativistic and illusory nature of reality, but he now decided to work out that idea on stone. This was not an impulsive decision. The sculpture that he planned to do was of epic proportions, and he was well aware that executing it would be an arduous endeavour that would take him several years to complete. He, therefore, had to make sure, before he took the final decision, that this was something that he could handle, and he spent several weeks mulling over the matter. During this period he was physically inert most of the time, just lying about on the bench in the studio, or on the beach in the evenings. Aditi, who knew nothing of his plans, attributed his lethargy to depression, and gleefully reported it to Mathangi.

'I feel sorry for Dada,' Mathangi said. 'Talk to him, Adi, and help him to get over it.'

'No, I'm going to let him stew for a while,' Aditi said. 'Let him realize that he cannot manage his life without me, and come crawling back to me.'

'Shall I talk to him?'

'No!'

Aditi was as usual audaciously taking her fantasies to be reality. Far from being depressed, Zeruba was now in an exhilarated state of mind, quietly but resolutely gathering and focusing his mental energy for what he knew would be the most important work of his life. Finally, when the concept of the sculpture crystallized in his mind, he ordered from a local quarry eight massive blocks of black Charnockite granite, each six feet high, six feet broad, and two feet thick, and had them set up on a bed of bricks under the rain tree. The blocks were arranged in the form of a swastika, the ancient Hindu mystic symbol of auspiciousness, so there were nineteen visible facets with a total area of 528 square feet for Zeruba to work on.

He titled the sculpture *Moon River*, but had initially thought of calling it *Yajnavalkya's Dream*, for he had conceived it as an interpretation of a text attributed to that Upanishadic sage, who maintained that there is no difference between the internally perceived world of our dreams and the externally perceived world of our wakeful hours. Both are imagined. Both are maya. 'In dreams man finds his joy, roams around, witnessing good and evil, taking his pleasure with women, laughing, or else seeing dreadful sights,' observed Yajnavalkya. 'Then he hastens back . . . to the realm of wakefulness . . . where too he finds his joy, roams around, witnessing good and evil, taking his pleasure with women, laughing, or else seeing dreadful sights. Then again he hurries . . . to the realm of dreams.'

Later Zeruba found the same idea expressed more poetically by the Chinese sage Chuang-tze. 'Once upon a time, I, Chuang-tze, dreamt I was a butterfly, fluttering hither and thither, to all intents and purposes a butterfly,' wrote the sage. 'I was conscious only of following my fancies as a butterfly, and unconscious of my individuality as a man. Suddenly I awoke, and there I lay, myself again. Now I do not know whether I was then a man dreaming that I was a butterfly, or whether I am now a butterfly dreaming that I am a man.' Zeruba was so moved by this passage that he got a calligraphist to inscribe it on a plank of wood, and set it up on a post under the tree, as an inspirational inscription.

Zeruba expected the sculpture to take him five or six years to complete, by which time he hoped to fully recover from his personal agonies. He let the stones stand untouched for about a month, but woke up well before dawn every day and sat in the veranda for hours together, contemplating the stones and carving them in his mind, inch by inch. And every day in the evening, he transferred these images onto paper, drawing with crayon on large rolls of handmade paper. When he was finally done with visualizing the sculpture, he organized the drawings in their proper order, and one Tuesday morning—he considered Tuesdays to be auspicious for him—woke up at three a.m., the hour of Brahma, to begin work on the sculpture. He leapt out of the bed at the first ring of the alarm clock, his mind tingling, quickly made himself a large mug of steaming lemon tea, and set to work in the soft glow of starlight.

'Hey! Heeey! What the devil are you doing?' Aditi screamed at him through the bedroom window. 'There're people trying to sleep here. Are you crazy?'

Zeruba did not even lift his head from the work, but went on chiselling. He was by nature an austere person, but many of his paintings were characterized by sly visual jokes, and were lush with seething, swirling images. This was so in his sculpture as well, in fact more so in his sculpture, for he worked in high-relief, carving images in two or even three layers. 'In the layers of the sculpture are layers of meaning,' he liked to joke.

While working on the sculpture, Zeruba often thought of

Tarun and his delusions. But what about himself? Was he—or anyone at all—ever free from delusions? Aren't we all in every way deluded in our view of the world and of ourselves? Especially if, as ancient Indian sages and modern neuroscientists maintain, the phenomenal world as we perceive it exists only in our consciousness? We all see the world as we need to see it to cope with life.

Wasn't this that Tarun was doing in his own way? His was, of course, an extreme case, in which delusions, instead of serving as the means to energize action, had become ends in themselves. And these were ends that he could attain without any effort at all. All he had to do was to lie back and close his eyes, and everything would immediately fall into its exact place, exactly as he desired it. In this vapoury world of memory and daydreams, everything was entirely pliant to his wish and will, freely and summarily alterable, and every incident could be re-lived repeatedly, in ever-enriched variations. Here space and time were relative; all space was one space, and all time one time, the past and the future having merged with the present. This was the idea that Zeruba wanted to convey in his sculpture—the ever mutable, transitory nature of reality. An amalgam of Vedanta, quantum theory, neuroscience and the psychology of fantasy.

3

'We are all to blame for Tarun's predicament,' Iyer said to Zeruba one day, when he came visiting along with Ashok and Pratibha. 'We pampered his fancies, instead of encouraging him to face reality.'

'Well, Ashok told him some home truths, and you know what happened,' remarked Zeruba.

'It was too sudden and too tactless,' Ashok admitted contritely.

'I'm not blaming you,' Zeruba said. 'But I wonder whether Beth is not right after all in holding that we have no right to take away his fantasies. If fantasy is better than reality, more enjoyable, why not live in it always? What's so hot about the real world anyway?'

'You aren't serious, are you?'

'I am. It seems to me that there's no single right way of coping with life, Ashok,' Zeruba observed. 'One person might gain control over his life by aggressively dealing with external reality and prevailing over his circumstances, but another might gain an equal control over his life by disengaging from external reality and retreating into his own inner space to live there cosily. Delusions serve the same purpose as cold logic and hard-nosed practicality, and are, in subjective terms, equally effective in coping with life. Maybe Tarun's fantasies are good for him. Who can say!'

'I think it was too easy for him to make money,' Ashok said. 'That turned his head and gave him his megalomaniacal delusions. Making money is such a sordid business.'

'Come on, Ashok. That's prejudice,' Iyer remarked. 'Dedicating oneself to making money is no different from dedicating oneself to anything else, say literature or art. I don't think any kind of activity has any intrinsic superiority over any other kind of activity.'

'The shoemaker is as good as Shakespeare, as Tolstoy said?' asked Pratibha.

'Did Tolstoy say that?'

'Something like that.'

'Great,' Iyer said. 'It's not the type of your work, but the quality of your work that makes the difference. And the level of your achievement. It's degrading to toil just to meet your subsistence needs, but once you cross that threshold, making money becomes an art form. Almost a transcendental thing.'

'I agree with Iyer,' Zeruba said. 'It's like dedicating oneself to art for art's sake.'

'Anything more than what is needed for bare existence is vanity,' Ashok scoffed.

'Maybe,' Zeruba said. 'But then, art is also vanity, isn't it? Art isn't necessary for bare existence.'

'And how do you define bare necessity, Ashok?' Iyer questioned. 'It varies from person to person and culture to culture.'

'In terms of psychological satisfactions, there's no difference between people living at different levels of material culture,' Ashok said. The coolie in his mud hovel sleeps as soundly on his grass mat as the tycoon on his feather mattress in his air-conditioned bedroom, Ashok argued; the coolie gets the same pleasure from whatever food he eats, as the tycoon gets from whatever food he eats; he enjoys his arrack as much as the tycoon enjoys his champagne, and gets as much sexual pleasure from his lice-ridden wench as the tycoon from his deodorized beauty queen.

'You mean that cultural differences make no difference?' Iyer challenged.

'I wonder,' Ashok said. 'I mean, do you think there's any difference between the satisfaction of a butterfly feeding on nectar and a fly feeding on excrement? Does the fly envy the butterfly?'

'That's a bad comparison, Ashok,' Pratibha said. 'The fly and the butterfly are two different species. But the coolie and the tycoon are of the same species. How can the coolie but envy the tycoon and want for himself some of those rich goodies?'

'Well, if the coolie is aware that he has the option to have the rich goodies, yes, he would want them,' said Ashok. 'Then he would lose the enjoyment of what he had been enjoying till then. But if he isn't aware of the option, he would be happy with his lot, and would not hanker for the rich goodies.'

'And it wouldn't make any difference to him?' Zeruba asked.

'What difference?' Ashok wanted to know. 'I mean, just because you feed on caviar and champagne you don't shit butterscotch ice-cream and piss rosewater, do you?'

'My, my!' Zeruba laughed. 'Aren't you eloquent today!'

'I would agree that contentment is in the passive acceptance of the conditions of one's life,' conceded Iyer. 'But such contentment leads to stagnation. In society as well as in the individual. You can't be contented and be progressive at the same time.'

'The progress you're talking about is external to man,' Ashok commented. 'Man's happiness doesn't depend on externals. It depends on his state of mind.'

'But his state of mind depends on the externals,' countered Iyer.

'No,' Ashok asserted. 'His state of mind doesn't depend on externals, but on his attitude towards the externals.'

Iyer was stumped. 'Maybe you're right,' he granted.

'What're you talking about?' Aditi asked, joining them.

'Butterscotch shit,' Ashok said.

And they all collapsed in laughter.

4

Aditi had been out the whole day and had just returned. She was hardly ever at home those days, but was away most of the time on her PR work, or attending the French and German language courses she claimed she was taking. Most of these, Zeruba suspected, were lies to cover up her trysts, but he was far too disengaged from her to care any more. He was only waiting for Saumya to finish school and leave for the US, before initiating divorce proceedings.

Zeruba himself hardly ever left the cottage anymore, partly because he had no desire to meet anyone, and also because he wanted to be at home when Saumya got back from school in the afternoons. Her future was his primary concern at this time, and he wanted to insulate her as far as possible from the turmoil at home. A self-motivated child, she needed no prodding or assistance from Zeruba in her studies, and had consistently topped her class. But he enjoyed being with her when she studied, and she was happy to have him around. She was now in the final year of school, and was also simultaneously preparing for the US college admission test. Often, while Zeruba worked on the sculpture, Saumya sat reading in a deckchair under the tree, on the windward side of the sculpture, so that the dust from the chiselling would not blow on her.

Saumya was the one thing that had worked out perfectly well in Zeruba's life, and she had never given him any cause of concern over her. She was, like her parents, very independent-minded, but she had none of the glum arrogance of Zeruba or the flightiness of Aditi. Rather, she had grown into a pleasant yet serious, responsible and self-reliant teenager, and Zeruba had taken special care, especially after his alienation from Aditi, to see to it that she had no dependency on her parents. He encouraged her to make by herself all the decisions about her studies and career, with himself playing only a consultative role. It was she who decided which school to go to, what courses to take, and now about her college education.

Saumya was too intelligent and sensitive a child not to notice that all was not well between her parents. But that did not affect her studies. Indeed, she did so well in her college admission tests that she received outstanding scholarship offers from a couple of American universities. Of these, she chose the University of Florida, for it offered her the highest scholarship, and the state's subtropical climate suited her—and also perhaps for sentimental reasons, the state being the place of her birth.

Here again the choice was entirely hers, though Zeruba would have preferred her to go to a more prestigious university. And, although she was only sixteen at this time and had never travelled outside Madras by herself, he left it to her to make all her travel plans, what flights to take, where to stop over, and so on. Because of all this, by the time she left for the US, he was confident that she would be able to stand on her own feet thereafter, capable of independently charting her career and life. She would turn out just fine, Zeruba was confident.

'So what're you going to be?' Mathangi asked Saumya one day.

'An astrophysicist,' Saumya said.

'My! A star child!'

'I want to look Brahma in the eye,' Saumya said with mock gravity.

Where did she get this poise, Zeruba wondered, looking at her.

The day Saumya left for the US, the Madras airport was closed to visitors, because of a terrorist bomb blast there a few days earlier. So the three of them, Saumya, Aditi and Zeruba, sat in their car in the parking lot for a while and chatted. Then Saumya looked at her watch and said, 'I better be going.' She hesitated for a moment as they stood beside the car, and Zeruba thought that she was going to say something, or maybe hug them, but she abruptly picked up her suitcase and walked towards the terminal without a word. But he could see from the tension of her raised shoulders that she was struggling to keep herself in control. She never once turned back. She didn't want her parents to see her eyes filled with tears.

They waited for the aircraft to take off, then drove back home in silence.

'Now what?' Aditi asked when they got back.

'Now we separate.'

'If that's what you want, it's okay with me,' Aditi said. 'But you'll regret it.'

'Maybe. But that's what I want.'

'Okay. We'll file for divorce by mutual consent. I'll talk to Sarada about it.'

Sarada was a lawyer friend of Aditi.

'Fine,' Zeruba said.

'What sort of settlement do you envisage?'

'I've no views on this,' Zeruba said. 'Whatever you and Sarada decide will be fine with me.'

'I don't want anything from you.'

'As you wish.'

'We'll have to live separately for some months before the divorce comes through. That's the law, I believe. Six months or so. I'll move out.'

'Fine.'

'When do you want me to go?'

'I suggest that we continue to live together for a few more months, till Saumya is well settled in college.'

'Okay. I'll move out at the end of the year. But Saumya does not have to be told of our separation till she comes to visit us next year.'

'Fine.'

'Not even then, perhaps. We can live together for the duration of her stay.'

'Yes, that'll be good,' he said.

'But from this moment on, you're not my husband,' she said, removing the *thali* chain from her neck and flinging it at him.

'Okay.'

'You've no business to ask where I go or what I do.'

'Okay,' he said, pocketing the chain.

A couple of weeks after this, Lakshmi came to visit them. Aditi was curt with her, barely returned her greeting, and drove off immediately for work.

'Everything alright, Mama?' Lakshmi asked as they sat in the drawing room.

'No, nothing is alright,' he said, slouching in the divan.

She went over and knelt before him and took his hands in hers.

'Is there anything I can do, Mama?' she asked. 'Anything at all?'

'No. There isn't anything you or anyone else can do,' he said. 'I have to find my own way out of this mess.'

'If there's anything you want me to do, anything at all, or just want to talk to someone, please do phone me, Mama,' she said. 'And I'll come over immediately, any time of the day or night.'

'I know,' Zeruba said. 'Thank you, Lakshmi.'

The Fissure

1

Recoiling from the trauma of Erich's rejection and the mounting tension at home, Aditi plunged into numerous rash affairs soon after Saumya's departure, in a desperate and perverse attempt to redeem her self-esteem and reclaim her right to be loved. And she was often recklessly and needlessly rude to Zeruba.

'What were you doing staying out so late?' he asked her one day when she returned home well past midnight.

'Out fucking,' she spat contemptuously.

Her affairs were scandalous, but there was nothing that he could do about it. Indeed, there was nothing that he wanted to do about it. What she did were of no concern to him, he told himself; they had nothing to do with him. She was just somebody; he had no relationship with her. He did not even feel any great anger towards her. But ever on the offensive, Aditi put all the blame for the crisis on Zeruba, and went about trumpeting his faults, while presenting herself as a frustrated wife with pardonable romantic susceptibilities. Sometimes she blamed him for being too harsh with her, and sometimes for being too lenient.

'It's your fault that you let things come to this pass,' she charged one day. 'You should've beaten me or at least shown some anger when I strayed. I thought you didn't mind my flirtations.'

'I know,' he said. 'It's all my fault.'

'Yes, it is.'

She was certain that she could cow him into crawling back to her, and she assured him that he was not going to amount to anything much in life without her help, probably not even with her help.

'I can make anything out of something,' she said, 'but I can't make something out of nothing. And you're nothing.'

'Yes, I know,' Zeruba laughed. 'A zero—Zero-baba.'

'That's right,' she went on grimly. 'Zero-baba—that's what you're. You're a cipher without me. Without me around, no one will even come for your funeral.'

'What difference would it make to me when I'm dead?' he asked. 'I won't even notice it.'

'Do you know what the problem with you is?'

'Tell me.'

'You aren't capable of loving anyone.'

'Maybe,' he said. 'But then, I'm not capable of hating anyone, either.'

'But you're hateful yourself,' she retorted. 'You're a hateful creature.'

As she went on ranting, he ignored her to watch with rapt attention a mosquito landing softly, weightlessly on his arm. He could identify it as an Anopheles from the way its body and proboscis angled, and it was no doubt a blood-sucking female, for the male of the species fed only on nectar. As the insect wriggled through the thicket of hair on his arm, its wings aquiver, and poised its body to plunge its proboscis into him, he swatted it with a quick blow of his hand, and turned to Aditi.

'Thank you,' he said. 'It's enough nagging for today. Now leave me in peace.'

'Yes,' she said. 'I'll leave you in pieces.'

2

They were still fighting with each other occasionally at that time, and that was a good sign. As long as they fought, there was some hope of sustaining the marriage, for it meant that they were still involved with each other, and it was to force changes in each other that they fought. But soon they gave up on each other altogether—at least Zeruba did—and there were no more spats. Then the marriage was irretrievably lost. He could not even bear to look at her anymore, and whenever she spoke to him, he looked to one side or dropped his eyes to the ground. Aditi, though about forty, was still vibrantly youthful and voluptuous, but the thought of physical intimacy with her repelled him, so they could not even mitigate their conflict through the diversion of sex.

They could probably have continued to live together if they could at least live in peace with each other, but that too was clearly impossible, for in the end the issue between them had gone beyond incompatibilities and infidelities, and had become a power struggle, a fight to the finish, in which Zeruba engaged in quiet but mulish resoluteness, and Aditi with bellowing aggressiveness.

'You started it all,' she said one day when they were sitting at breakfast. 'That too with slum sluts.'

'Yes, of course,' he said. 'It was all my fault.'

'How could you even touch these sluts?'

'My karma,' he said. 'I even married a slut, you know.'

That blow stung. Livid with anger, her teeth grit, eyes flinty, Aditi snatched her glass of water and raised it to hurl at him. He tensed glaring at her, but did not stir. There had not been any physical violence between them till then, despite the growing virulence of their conflict. This could have been the moment they crossed that threshold. But she, seeing the look in her eyes, checked herself.

'I'll make you pay for this, you bloody stinker,' she promised, slamming the glass down.

3

Aditi, for all her aggressive posture and callous taunting of
Zeruba, was secretly afraid of him, and was terrified of the
prospect of living separately. Her main worry was that people
might think that he had abandoned her, and that was something
she could not possibly live with, for nothing was more humiliating
to her than being a loser. She was, therefore, keen to preserve the
shell of their marriage, however hollow it might be, at least until
she could make some credible alternate arrangement. A marriage
in form but without any conjugal obligations and restraints would
have been ideal for her, for that would have enabled her to
maintain a respectable facade and yet remain free to live as she
pleased. She, therefore, wrote to Zeruba's father about the crisis,
requesting his intervention, and also sought Mathangi's help to
coax Zeruba to accept a semblance of reconciliation.

On getting Aditi's letter, Korah immediately sent Mathu to
Madras. His visit was a surprise to Zeruba, for he did not know
that Aditi had written to his father. Nor did Mathu say anything
about this, as Aditi had strictly warned him not to tell Zeruba
that he had come at her behest.

'I was desiccating in Azhiyur,' Mathu said to Zeruba. 'I wanted
a change for a few days.'

'It's wonderful to have you with us, Kochappa,' Zeruba said.
'Hope you'll stay for at least a month.'

'A month? That'll make me homesick.'

'What's there to feel homesick about that dead town and the
crumbling home?'

'I belong there. You're lucky to have escaped.'

'Stay for a couple of weeks, then.'

'Let's see.'

Mathu tactfully did not broach the subject of his visit the
whole day, but late that evening, when he and Zeruba were sitting
on the beach, he said, 'I see a lot of tension between you and
Aditi—what's happening?'

'Has Adi been telling you stories?' Zeruba asked suspiciously.

'What makes you think she has?'

'You're evading my question, Kochappa. That means she has been babbling to you.'

'You haven't answered my question.'

'Now that you've raised the matter, I'll tell you the truth. This marriage is finished. We're just waiting for the right time to separate.'

'What's the problem?'

'Our chemistry is all wrong,' Zeruba said. 'We don't inhabit the same world.'

'What do you mean?'

'Our orientations to life are entirely different, Kochappa. Adi is a social creature. She lives dependent on others, and she wants others to be dependent on her. I am a loner. I don't want to be dependent on others, and I don't want others to be dependent on me. She has no clue about what my life is all about.'

'And you've no clue about what her life is all about?'

'Probably.'

'Look, the kind of harmony you're dreaming about exists only in romantic fiction, not in life,' Mathu said. 'You'll never find anybody with whom you can share your life fully.'

'I'm not looking for perfect harmony,' Zeruba said. 'But I don't see how two lives can run together unless there's some synchronization of the gears of life. Here there's no synchronization at all.' The basic problem, he said, was that they did not form a family, working towards common goals, a shared life. They pulled in opposite directions. 'We clash over everything.'

'Maybe you're running together too close,' Mathu suggested. 'I think what you have is a space problem.'

'It probably was that in the beginning,' Zeruba reflected. 'But now the whole thing has billowed into something monstrous that darkens my whole world. It's an impossible situation.'

'It's an impossible situation only if you consider it as an impossible situation. People put up with much worse,' Mathu said. 'You've to work on your marriage to save it.'

'To do that I've to have something to work on,' Zeruba rejoined. 'There's nothing at all here to work on. You can't blow fire from fireflies.'

'What do you want Aditi to do?'

'Nothing. It's too late to think of saving this marriage,' Zeruba said. 'There're basic flaws in her character that makes her impossible for me.'

'She's flighty and impulsive, I know,' Mathu conceded. 'But character flaws are no different from physical flaws. We don't find fault with a person for being blind or deaf or lame. So why should you find fault with Aditi for her mental oddities?'

'I'm not condemning her for what she is,' Zeruba said, 'but only saying that it's impossible for me to share my life with a person like that. There's an awful mismatch here.'

'You should've thought of all this before marrying her.'

'It never works that way, Kochappa, and you know that. One thing I've learned about life is that in none of our major personal decisions we act with rational objectivity. These decisions are visceral. We might rationally choose our job or profession, the shirt we buy or the food we eat, but there's no rationality in matters involving feelings. I made a mistake in marrying Adi, now I want to correct that mistake.'

'But she has abandoned her family for you. How can you now abandon her? She seems devastated by the crisis.'

'I see that she has been emotionally blackmailing you. Adi is not the victim, Kochappa, she is the victimizer. I'm the victim. Take my word, she'll cope with this crisis quite well. Much better than I would. Whatever her faults, her resilience is truly remarkable.'

'She cried and cried before me. She seems to be drowning in sorrow.'

'It's all just play-acting. There isn't enough depth in her sorrow for her to drown in it.'

'You think that there's no way of saving this marriage?'

'No,' Zeruba said. 'I wish it had worked out differently. I really do. But there it is!'

'Well, we can't cheat fate, can we!' Mathu said. 'Look Zeruba, my concern is not about Aditi. I'm not trying to save her; I'm trying to save you.'

'I can save myself only by ending this marriage,' Zeruba said. 'It'd be calamitous to continue with it. Calamitous to both of us.'

'You know what I think?'

'What?'

'I think that you're under the same family curse that ruined my grandfather and father. And ruined my life too. And I fear that it'll ruin your life as well.'

'What curse?'

'The curse of being all-or-nothing men. Our inability to make compromises. We court disasters.'

'That's good,' Zeruba said. 'Disasters are aerobic exercises for the mind. We should court disasters, not evade them. They make us stronger.'

'Equally, they might destroy you.'

'Not if you are strong,' Zeruba said. 'The weak will go under, but the strong will emerge stronger. I'll yet make something out of my life. I promise you that. I'll not fail myself.'

'Okay, we'll leave it at that,' Mathu said. 'What should I tell your father?'

'Don't tell him that we are separating,' Zeruba said. 'Just tell him that there are some problems, as in most families, and that we are trying to sort them out. I would like to keep the separation thing as quiet as possible.'

'I can't tell him lies.'

'You don't have to,' said Zeruba. 'But you don't have to tell him the whole truth either.'

'I'll see,' said Mathu.

Mathu left Madras after three days. Then it was the turn of Mathangi to work on Zeruba.

'We've been over this ground before, Mats,' Zeruba said.

'Let's go over it once more,' Mathangi persisted. 'You say that Adi doesn't understand you, but have you made any effort to understand why she behaved the way she did? It could be that she, by her affairs, was trying to make you somehow respond to her, to get you to prove your love for her. To see whether she still had the power to hurt you. Because of your indifference to her. They were cries for help, Dada, and you didn't hear the cry.'

'What! She was cuckolding me to make me love her?' Zeruba was incredulous.

'Something like that,' Mathangi said gravely.

'Look, it did at one time occur to me that she might be trying to tell me something through her affairs,' Zeruba said. 'But I'm now certain that they were not reactions to my actions, but rose out of something within herself, maybe some childhood trauma. In any case, it's too late to save this marriage through reconciliation. The crisis has gone too far for that.'

'It's never too late,' Mathangi said. 'Something can still be done, if you have the will. As they say, even boiling water will put out fire.'

'There is no fire to be put out, Mats. The fire is long dead. The house has burned down completely,' Zeruba said.

'Please don't be precipitant, Dada,' Mathangi pleaded. 'Give yourself more time.'

'Look, I've thought over all these matters very carefully, before deciding on what I've decided. There's absolutely no question of I turning away from the path I've chosen.'

'Why are you so mulish?' Mathangi asked.

'Because that's the way I am,' said Zeruba.

In the end Mathangi gave up. Aditi then reconciled herself to separating from Zeruba, and characteristically took a nonchalant attitude.

'I belong to the world of business, not of art,' she grandly told Mathangi. 'I realize that now. I love wheeling and dealing. That's my high.'

'Artists are impossible to live with,' Mathangi said. 'You might admire them, you might even have affairs with them, but you can't live with them. They are demonic people.'

'Well, it's all over now. And I'm glad it's over. I feel like I'm reborn.'

'What will now happen to Dada?' Mathangi wondered.

'Who the shit cares!'

'You should care, Adi. He's a good man.'

Aditi looked at Mathangi sharply.

'If you care all that much for him, why don't you go and live with him?' she asked.

'Don't be crude,' Mathangi said.

What Mathangi did not tell Aditi was that she and Zeruba had almost become lovers at this time. Almost, but there was a curtain of reserve between them that they could not overcome. They hugged and kissed once, and even that threw Mathangi into a dreadful panic. When they broke from the clinch, she flung herself into a chair, burying her head in her hands and sobbing.

'No! No! No!' she moaned.

Zeruba went over to her and sat on the arm of the chair, nestling her head in his arms.

'What's the matter, Mats?' he asked.

'This is a terrible mistake,' she said, shaking her head. 'I can't betray Adi.'

'But she'll betray you without a thought.'

'Perhaps. But I can't do it,' she said. 'We're very good friends, Dada. It's a beautiful relationship. I cherish it. Let's not destroy it by becoming lovers.'

'You're right,' said Zeruba, getting up. 'I'm sorry.'

'It's not your fault,' she said. 'We were both lonely. I had wanted you so much, without realizing it. That's why I think I took up this mission of reconciliation for Adi.'

'It's alright, Mats. We've pulled back from the edge. We're safe now.'

'You know what? I think Adi was deliberately trying to push us into an affair.'

'Why?'

'I don't know. Maybe to test me. Or you. I really don't know. She's a very mysterious person.'

5

Aditi moved out of the cottage in the first week of January. For several days before that, she was busy tearing up and burning her papers, clearing her wardrobe, packing her things, and giving away old clothes to slum women. Then she and the servants set about cleaning the cottage thoroughly, from top to bottom and every nook and cranny, dusting and swabbing. Zeruba paid no attention to any of that, but kept himself busy with his sculpture.

'I'm leaving everything spick and span for you,' Aditi announced when she was done with the cleaning up. 'I've told the servants about their duties. They'll look after you.'

'Thank you,' Zeruba said.

The next morning, she loaded her suitcases into her car. Zeruba pretended not to notice.

'I'm leaving,' she said, going to him as he worked on the sculpture. 'Goodbye.'

'Goodbye,' he said, looking her in the eyes for the first time in very many months.

'Don't you want to know where I'm going?' she asked.

'Not really.'

'Don't I mean anything to you?'

'No.'

'Don't you have any feelings at all?' she flared up. 'You aren't even angry with me?'

'I'm not the angering type,' he said.

'Aren't you sorry about all this?'

'I'm sorry to lose my family.'

'It's all your fault,' she said.

'Of course.'

'You'll realize my worth when I'm gone.'

'Maybe.'

Without another word, she got into the car, slammed the door shut, and drove away. She had arranged to live with Mathangi in her flat, as she had done before her marriage.

'Welcome home,' Mathangi said, marking her forehead with a sandalwood paste tilak.

'I don't want you ever to phone or see Dada again,' Aditi told Mathangi that night as they lay in bed.

'Why? We can all be friends still,' Mathangi said.

'No. Please. It would hurt me very much if you keep in touch with him after what he has done to me.'

'As you wish,' Mathangi said. 'What about you?'

'I'll never ever again have anything to do with that bloody blighter,' Aditi said. 'Nothing at all.'

'Hmm!'

'Fuck the men!' Aditi said. 'Who needs them!'

'Yes,' Mathangi said wistfully.

Chacko

1

Zeruba had not been to see his parents for several years, during the crisis in his marriage and its aftermath. He knew that his father was upset about this, but he could not bear to face them till he had regained some balance in his life. So it was only about two years after Aditi moved out, when his life was once again running fairly smoothly, that he finally made it to Kerala.

The overnight train from Madras reached Aluva at about nine in the morning, and from there he took a taxi for the short drive to his hometown. At the outskirts of Azhiyur, as the taxi crossed a small bridge and entered the town, its path was blocked by a raucous political procession crossing the road. There were, Zeruba estimated, several thousand men and women in the procession, a surprisingly large number for that sleepy town, and many of them were carrying dark blue flags with a large white sun emblem at its centre, apparently of some new party.

'*Yem-yem-pee*: *zindabad-zindabad*!' the marchers chanted. '*Yem-yem-pee*: *zindabad-zindabad*!'

'What party is this?' Zeruba asked the taxi driver, getting out of the car to watch the procession.

'I don't know,' growled the driver. 'Each day some cheat or other starts a new party.'

Now the leader of the procession himself rolled on to the crossroads, standing in an open jeep in lone splendour, and Zeruba immediately recognized his brother Chacko, even though his face was almost entirely covered by the jasmine and marigold garlands that his admirers had put around his neck. Chacko was evidently enjoying himself hugely, waving and smiling at bystanders, nodding at acquaintances and bowing to them. As the jeep rolled on slowly, Zeruba thought that his brother's eyes rested on him for a moment, but he was not sure, for there was no sign of recognition.

'Who's this *netha*?' Zeruba asked the driver innocently.

'Oh-oh! That's Chacko. I recognize him,' said the driver. 'But I thought he was with the Congress.'

'Not any more,' Zeruba said.

'They say he'll be the chief minister some day.'

At home, Zeruba found his father, mother, uncle, and Chacko's wife Anna sitting in the portico, waiting for him.

'Was the train late?' Korah asked.

'No,' Zeruba said. 'I got held up by a procession on the way.'

'Adi didn't come?'

'No. She couldn't get away.'

'Hmm! We are getting old,' Korah said. 'You all should visit us more often.'

'Next time she'll come,' Zeruba said.

'Any news of Devi?' Mathu asked.

'I'm afraid not,' Zeruba said. 'By the way, the procession I saw was led by Chacko.'

'Oh, you saw him? He's his own leader now,' said Anna, laughing. 'He'll be here for lunch.'

'What's yem-yem-pee?'

'MMP? Malayalee Munnetam Party—that's the party he has founded,' Anna explained. 'Just last week.'

'How is Saumya?' Korah asked.

'She's doing very well in college, Appa,' Zeruba said, and turned to his mother. 'How are you, Amma?'

'Getting on,' she said with a wan smile.

'She hardly gets up from bed these days,' Korah said.

'Getting on in years,' she said.

'Would you have a cup of tea, Chetta?' Anna asked. 'And hot water for bath?'

'Yes, please,' he said, and followed her into the house.

'How are the children?' Zeruba asked her. Chacko had three sons.

'We've put them in a boarding school in Ooty,' she said. 'They were getting spoilt at home. Just won't study. How's Adi?'

'Fine.'

'You're very lucky.'

'Am I? Why?'

'I mean, to have a wife like Adi,' Anna said. 'She's one of the noblest human beings I've known.'

Zeruba looked at her quizzically, wondering whether she was putting him on, but she looked earnest and sincere.

2

Anna both fascinated and repelled Zeruba. Physically she was rather unprepossessing, buck-toothed and flint-eyed, with pendulous breasts and shapeless elephantine buttocks, but her homeliness was more than compensated by her energy, shrewdness and diligence. She was considered a brilliant lawyer, and was very ambitious. Chacko was entirely devoted to her, and she to him. And it was she who shaped and guided his life. She was always nice to everyone, and was full of conventional pieties, all of which were a cover for her unswerving and hard-headed pursuit of wealth and power for her family, always working quietly and patiently behind the scenes, sowing tiny, invisible seeds of stratagems, and waiting patiently for their fruition. Zeruba had no doubt that she was responsible for Chacko breaking with the Congress and starting his own party.

'What's the new party all about?' he asked her, as he sat at the dining table drinking tea.

'Chacko felt that we need a strong regional party to fulfil

people's aspirations,' Anna said.

'People's aspirations, of course,' Zeruba laughed. 'You behind this gambit?'

'Me? What do I know about politics?' she protested.

She was actually an expert political intriguer, having learned the ropes from her businessman-turned-politician father and her lawyer-turned-politician brother.

'Why don't you satisfy my aspirations by giving me another cup of tea?' Zeruba asked.

'Here you are,' she said, pouring him another cup.

'Which side of the political fence is he on now?' Zeruba asked.

'He's with the ruling coalition,' she said. 'He has two other MLAs supporting him, so there's a good chance of him becoming a minister. He'll be the first minister from this town.'

'What was the procession for?'

'There is a public meeting this evening,' she said. 'The CM is coming. He's coming here for tea.'

'Here? At home?'

'Yes.'

'Have you told Appa?' Zeruba asked. 'He might not like it.'

'Chacko will tell him when he comes,' she said.

'I hate politicians,' Zeruba said, 'but I'll make an exception for Chacko. And, of course, I'm proud that he is so successful.'

'This is a new world, Chetta, and we have to learn new tricks to survive in it,' she said.

'I know,' he said, getting up. 'I'll have a bath now.'

Later, sitting in the portico with his father and uncle, Zeruba said, 'Chacko is making a great success of his life.'

'Thanks to his wife,' Korah said.

'They make a good team,' said Mathu.

'But I don't like their politician friends,' grumbled Korah.

'They are the new class,' said Mathu. 'The future belongs to them.'

'What class!' Korah rejoined. 'They have power but not class.'

He was saying that from habit. Actually, he was proud of

209

Chacko's success, and was happy that his marriage, unlike that of his other two children, had worked well, though when the marriage proposal first came, he had rejected it outright.

'Never!' Korah had said. 'The family has no status, and the girl, I'm told, is ugly.'

Relatives eventually prevailed on him to give his consent, pointing out that the match would be an ideal arrangement from which both families would benefit—an alliance between the new poor and the new rich, but still within the community, and therefore marked by both continuity and change. Anna's father came from a humble family, and had begun his career smuggling rice from Tamil Nadu into Kerala in a ramshackle truck, which he drove himself. But all that was a long time ago. At the time of Chacko's marriage, he was a very successful businessman and a highly respected member of the community, and had been a minister in the state government for a term. He had lately curtailed his activities considerably, because of a heart condition, but the family's fortunes continued to flourish under his sons, with his elder son taking over his political mantle, and the younger running the family's businesses. And Chacko, hitching his wagon to their rising star, himself prospered beyond anybody's utmost expectations.

3

Chacko was eleven years younger than Zeruba. As the youngest child of the family, born when his father was nearly forty, he was much fussed over by everyone as a child, but was not spoilt for that reason, and grew up into an affectionate and easy-going youth. The only problem with him was that he, like his father, was indifferent in studies, and in a family that had been devoted to learning for generations, it was Chacko's proud boast that he had never read a single book in his life.

'I read people instead,' he would often quip, after he became a successful politician.

He was not interested in sports either, played no games in school, had no playmates, and never went roaming around with friends. What he loved to do was to stay at home and ride his old tricycle up and down the kitchen veranda at great speed for hours together—which he continued to do till he finished school—or badger his mother for snacks, or play childish pranks on his father. He seemed rather dull-witted, failed a couple of times in school and college, but finally managed to graduate with a bachelor's degree in psychology from a local college. But when Korah pressed him to join some professional course or other, he firmly refused.

'I'm done with studies,' he said with finality.

Chacko's future now became a major worry for Korah, as the little land that still remained with the family was being nibbled away by the government, tenants or litigants. He was relieved only when, with the help of some relatives, he managed to get him appointed as a sales executive with a tyre manufacturer in Madras. So Chacko left home for the first time at the age of twenty-one. This change—living away from home—transformed his whole personality. From a shy and gauche youth, he now blossomed into a fun-loving extrovert. And it turned out that he had a natural flair for sales. This, and his evident personal integrity, made Chacko the golden boy of the company, and he rose rapidly through the ranks to become, in about fifteen years, the sales manager of the company.

Then suddenly, at the age of thirty-six, soon after he became the sales manager, he chucked his job and returned to Kerala to go into politics. This dismayed Korah, but he could not prevail on Chacko to stay on in his job, for he had by then come completely under the sway of his wife and her father. Korah was, however, delighted when Chacko won the Azhiyur seat in the legislative assembly elections held the following year, and saw in it the prospect of the revival of the family fortunes. Zeruba saw Chacko in his avatar as a politician for the first time that day on his way home from the railway station.

Chacko arrived home around noon, looking rumpled, but

radiantly happy, his eyes bright with the pleasure of his new life. The white cotton kurta he wore was soaked with sweat, and through it shone a diamond studded gold cross on a rope-thick gold chain around his neck. The significance of the cross was political, not religious. Chacko was not at all religious—none in the family was—but had, under the influence of Anna, become a regular churchgoer, as that was considered politically beneficial. He also sported, in the prevailing political fashion, a broad but closely trimmed moustache, a mere shadow. His very gait, Zeruba noticed, had changed. There was an air of authority about him now, and he walked jauntily, with a confident (but not offensive) swagger. He was going bald, but that only enhanced his appearance of benign authority.

'I saw you,' Zeruba said to him when he came in.

'I saw you too,' Chacko said. 'But it wouldn't have been proper for me to stop the procession to come to you.'

'Of course.'

'We are the slaves of the public.'

'Indeed!' Zeruba said. 'I'm told you have your own party now. What's your ideology?'

'Ideology?' Chacko laughed heartily. 'That's nineteenth-century politics, Chetta. No one talks about ideology these days. Not even the communists.'

'So what's your politics about?'

'About capturing and retaining power.'

'No principles at all?'

'None,' Chacko said happily. 'We're pragmatic politicians. We have no principles.'

'But what's the purpose of capturing power?'

'Why! To enjoy power.'

Chacko had all the qualities required in a successful politician. He liked everyone, and everyone liked him, even his adversaries, as he took care not to offend anyone personally. He was never ever bored with people. He had no false sense of pride either, and would cheerfully perform any task assigned to him by his leaders. He never took any offence at any insult, and never felt disheartened by any rebuff. Sometimes he won. Sometimes he lost. But he never lost his verve. Nothing ever got him down.

'Never despise an enemy nor ever trust a friend, but keep everyone in good humour—this is my principle,' he expounded to Zeruba.

Chacko's only political disability, at least initially, was that he had scruples. He would not cheat and deceive people. But Anna gradually cured him of these inhibitions, and instilled in him the ability to tell lies without blushing, cheat without compunction, double-cross friends with a smile, ensnare and subdue adversaries. All the constraints and value distinctions imposed on him by family tradition and upbringing were now gone. Success alone now mattered to him. Any means was good means for that. This new Chacko was wholly the creation of Anna, but she never betrayed the slightest hint of her power over him, and always made a show of deferring to him, and gave the impression of being a humble and obedient wife, a posture that greatly enhanced her influence on him.

Amazingly, Chacko, despite his metamorphosis, remained a very likeable person, cheerful, generous and good-natured. There was still a pleasing air of innocence about him, and he came out smelling like roses even after wading through the foulest muck. He was in robust health, did not smoke or drink, and was not vulnerable to sexual temptations. He seemed in every respect a model householder and citizen. And yet, paradoxically, he was also a very successful politician.

Zeruba was impressed. He recalled once telling Mathu that the sustenance in the soil of their hometown had been exhausted for the family, and that they should now move out to survive. Well, Chacko had proved him wrong. There was still sustenance in the soil. There was no need to transplant oneself. One had to only change one's orientation to life. Change one's feeding habits. Chacko had done very well in coping with the socio-economic changes that devastated the family.

He was the only member of the family to do so. Korah had long given up his foolish struggle to hold down the world when it rolled away from under his feet; he had no hopes or aspirations any more, only regrets. Mathu made no effort at all to deal with the changes, but shut himself up in a world of abstractions, insulating himself from all disturbances. Zeruba chose to drop out, to find a place of his own outside society and outside time, a doomed quest. Devi leapt away, trying to save herself, but landed in another sinking ship. Chacko stayed on and coped.

4

After lunch that day, as Korah was retiring for his usual afternoon nap, Chacko broached the subject of the chief minister's visit.

'I should serve tea to this upstart? In my own house?' Korah asked with contempt. 'His father was a peon of my father.'

'Who cares for family status these days, Appa?' Chacko argued. 'Money and power are all that matter.'

'I don't have either, so I don't have to see him.'

'Please don't embarrass me, Appa—I have invited him. He's coming to our town to address my meeting, so how can I not invite him home?'

'I'm not saying that he can't come here. He can come. But I won't see him.'

'What should I tell him?'

'Tell him that I am ill.'

'He would still want to see you.'

'Then tell him that I'm dead,' Korah said, turning away.

Chacko laughed at this, and turned to Zeruba to ask whether he would join them for tea. The problem of how to handle Zeruba's presence at home was discussed at length by Chacko and Anna. Would it be good or bad to have Zeruba meet the chief minister? If the CM came to know that Zeruba was there, he would take it as an insult if Zeruba was not presented to him, especially as Korah would not meet him. In fact, Anna argued, it might even be good to have a slightly disreputable brother, for the CM to scoff at what the old families were coming to. Besides, there was the risk that Zeruba might barge into the party on his own. It was, therefore, decided to persuade him to meet the CM.

'Do I embrace him, or lick his bottom?' Zeruba asked.

'Chetta, please make an effort and treat him deferentially,' Chacko said. 'This is a turning point in my career, and the CM is the person who would determine how it turns out.'

Zeruba patted him on the shoulder. 'Don't worry,' he said. 'I was only joking. What about Kochappa?'

'He'll be there.'

'Amma?'

'She doesn't talk to anyone these days,' said Anna. 'The CM in any case wouldn't expect to meet her.'

The chief minister, as befitted his status, arrived an hour late, and the first thing he said on being received by Chacko was, 'This house is falling apart.'

'What to do!' Chacko said.

'We can have it declared as a heritage building and fund its preservation,' the CM said with his trademark buck-toothed smile.

'That would be nice,' Chacko said.

The old crook must be in some political trouble to coddle us, thought Anna, and made a mental note to look into the matter.

'This is my uncle Mathu—and my brother Zeruba,' Chacko introduced.

'Ah, the artist,' said the CM. 'You should do a portrait of me.'

'That would be an honour,' said Zeruba without cracking a smile.

'The party will pay for it,' the CM assured. 'And pay well.'

'Thank you,' Zeruba said.

The crook definitely wants something from us, decided Anna.

'Where's your father?' the CM asked.

'Sleeping,' said Anna. 'He's not well.'

'My father's an old foggy,' said Chacko. 'He thinks that we should still be ruled by kings.'

'We are the kings,' the CM chuckled in self-adulation. He had a whinnying laugh, a singularly unpleasant sound made by sucking air in through the nose and wheezing it out through his mouth.

'Well, let's have tea,' the CM said, grandly inviting the family to tea in their own house. 'Sit down, sit down.'

The CM sank into a sofa, looking around the room and clucking in sympathetic disapproval at its disrepair.

Anna served him a tray of cakes and sweets, and from this he took a small piece of cake, but refused everything else.

'Doctor's orders,' he said. It was fashionable among the newly rich in Kerala to have diabetes. If possible, also a heart condition. 'I asked him what was the point of living if one can't eat sweets. But he wouldn't listen.'

He took a cup of tea from Anna, took a couple of sips from it, and then got up.

'Got to go now. There's a relative in town I've to visit,' he said, then turned to Mathu and Zeruba to invite them to the meeting: 'You all come. It'll be a grand meeting.'

'Of course,' they chorused.

5

The next day, when Zeruba was sitting in the portico smoking a cigarette after breakfast, he was joined by Chacko and Mathu. Their conversation inevitably turned to politics, with Mathu unexpectedly siding with Chacko in advocating the need to bend principles to suit ends.

'I think we place too much emphasis on values, as if they've some absolute validity,' Mathu said. 'Principles and values are just tools, like a screwdriver or spanner. You choose your tools—

216

or your values—to suit your needs.'

'It's not principles that matter in politics, but performance,' Chacko added.

'Absolutely,' Mathu agreed.

'People don't care a damn for principles,' Chacko said. 'They just want their life to be better.'

'But their life isn't getting better,' Zeruba said. 'It's only you politicians who are fattening.'

'Why should we expect politicians to be different from other professionals?' Mathu wondered. 'One doesn't become a doctor to save lives, but to make money, to earn a living. It's the same with politicians.'

'Exactly. All this business of virtue and righteousness is rubbish,' Chacko snickered. 'In the evolutionary process, it was not the principled that survived but the cunning and the ruthless.'

'The need for survival doesn't justify crimes,' Zeruba argued.

'You thrash this out. I'm going to my room,' Mathu said, leaving.

'Don't get me wrong, Chetta,' said Chacko. 'I'm not evil. I haven't hurt or cheated a single person. I've only helped people.'

'But you are cheating the public.'

'That's different. That isn't cheating at all,' Chacko said. 'Where in the world would you find rulers who are not exploiters? To be a ruler is to manipulate and use people. There is no other way one can be a ruler. You might find this repugnant, but that's the natural order of things.'

'Who wants to be a ruler in that case!'

'I do,' said Chacko. 'Because I enjoy being a ruler. And because it gives me the opportunity to do a lot of good. Politics may not suit you. But it suits me fine. You deal with ideas and images; I deal with men. You are secure in isolation, I'm secure with people.'

'And you feed on people,' Zeruba charged.

'Yes, I do feed on people,' Chacko said, raising his voice. 'That's because I find nurture in them, in their affection for me. You desiccate because you feed on yourself. I care for others. I serve them and they serve me. It's a symbiotic relationship.'

At this point Anna joined them.

'Chettan isn't desiccating,' she said. 'He's thriving as an artist. And one day he'll be rich and famous.'

'Thank you for saving my life,' said Zeruba. 'Chacko was mauling me to death.'

'You should hear him in the assembly,' she said. 'There's pin-drop silence when he rises to speak.'

'And haven't you taken advantage of people?' Chacko asked, continuing his assault. 'Don't think that we don't know what's happening in Madras.'

Anna now began to scratch her nose vigorously. This was their agreed signal to caution Chacko to be careful about what he was saying. But he ignored her now. This was a family matter; it had to be thrashed out between the brothers. His legs, which he constantly joggled in restless energy, were now still, indicating an internal concentration of feeling. He looked at his brother appraisingly. *You're nothing compared to me*, his look said. *People know me and defer to me. Heads turn wherever I go. Who are you to sit in judgement of me?* Anna prudently got up and went into the house.

'What about your wife of twenty years?' Chacko challenged. 'You threw her into the streets, didn't you?'

'Seventeen years,' corrected Zeruba.

'What?'

'Wife of seventeen years.'

'You threw her into the streets, didn't you? Why?'

'Because she tried to destroy me.'

'So you try to destroy her! Very humane and compassionate!' Chacko said. 'And what about your philandering? All this is a great shame for us.'

'Adi has been telling you stories, I realize,' Zeruba said.

'What does it matter who said it? It's all true, isn't it?'

'Yes, it's all true,' Zeruba said. 'But creative versions of truth.'

'Look, Chetta, I'm not blaming you,' Chacko said, lowering

his voice and assuming a tone of sweet reasonableness. 'Everyone has some vulnerability or other. All I'm saying is this: please don't be judgemental about me. We are both trying to cope with life in our different ways.'

Tarun

1

On his return journey to Madras, Zeruba was dropped at the Aluva railway station by Chacko, who was on his way to Thiruvananthapuram in his car for the legislative assembly session.

'Take care,' Chacko said. 'And Chetta, please forgive me for being rude the other day. I was distressed about something else, and I'm afraid I took it out on you.'

'I understand,' Zeruba said. 'I wasn't upset, though I wondered why you were so harsh.'

'I'm sorry.'

'Forget it,' Zeruba said.

'Take care.'

'You too.'

Zeruba was now fifty-one. The passage through life was rapidly narrowing for him, his options shrinking, and his own will and energy waning. He had to now firmly decide how he should live the rest of his life, what he should do with himself. There wasn't much time left. And there was much to do. He couldn't afford to fritter away his time. There was absolutely no question of him living out his days insouciantly, to die having merely consumed a certain amount of food and drink, bedded a few women, fathered a few children. His life had to mean something.

'Mean what?' Mathu asked, when Zeruba said this to him when he was in Azhiyur.

'Something.'

'You're chasing a chimera, son,' Mathu told him. 'There is nothing to life except to live it.'

'I can't accept that.'

'If you accept it, there'll be peace and contentment for you,' Mathu said. 'You can then remain tranquil in the midst of all the convulsions of life, passively accepting whatever comes your way as your lot, without cravings or attachments.'

'But I don't want to be contented,' Zeruba protested. 'Contentment is death to the artist.'

'True,' Mathu conceded. 'But please bear in mind that your discontent does not arise from your artistic nature, but your artistic nature arises from your discontent.'

'Maybe. But that's the way I am.'

'It doesn't have to be that way with you. You can be contented and happy. Anyone can be. All you've to do is to let go and relax. It's so easy. That's the only sensible way to live.'

'No, that's not the way to live. That's the way to die. To be dead even when you're alive.'

'But why not? What's the point of struggling against your circumstances, against your own nature? It's all utterly futile. Life has no meaning or purpose outside itself.'

'That's not how I see it.'

'How do you see it?'

'Life is not for just living, but to advance life—that's how I see it,' Zeruba said. 'There is something more important than contentment and happiness.'

'What?'

'To fulfil oneself. To do something worthwhile with one's life.'

'Why trouble yourself?' Mathu asked. 'Your labours will make no difference whatever in the long run. Not even the achievements of Einstein or Shakespeare or Tolstoy have any enduring value, let alone your puny efforts, when this earth itself and the whole goddam spinning universe are set to perish in time.'

'Well, the universe might perish in time, but since I won't be around when that happens, it wouldn't matter to me,' Zeruba said.

'Be practical, Zeruba,' Mathu advised. 'Grab whatever little happiness that comes your way in life. Don't waste your life in pursuit of hollow achievements. Do you think it would make any difference to anyone whether you painted or not?'

'Maybe not. But it would make a lot of difference to me,' Zeruba answered. 'I paint to fulfil my nature. Because an artist is what I am. And painting is what I enjoy doing.'

'Oh, that's fine,' said Mathu. 'By all means indulge yourself. Do whatever, yes whatever, that gives you pleasure. But don't value your work for anything beyond the pleasure it gives you. And don't, don't ever sacrifice your pleasures for the sake of some will-o'-the-wisp achievement.'

'It's strange that you should say this, Kochappa,' Zeruba said. 'At one time you had wanted me to make sacrifices and achieve something in my life.'

'That was once, Zeruba,' Mathu said. 'I was young and foolish then. Now I'm old and wise. How long do you think anyone will remember me when I'm gone? Maybe half a dozen people, my close relatives, will remember me every now and then for a week or so after my death, then maybe a couple of times or so in the year, then maybe once in a couple of years or so, then not at all. Once these relatives themselves are gone, no one at all will ever remember me. It would be as if I had not existed at all.'

Zeruba could not deny the essential truth of what his uncle said, that in the long run all human endeavours are futile, but he also knew that he had to deny the relevance of that truth in his life for him to live on at all. Life, to be worth living, had to have a purpose, he told Mathu. 'Maybe life in general has no meaning or purpose, but my life has a meaning and purpose. For me,' Zeruba said. 'If my life has no purpose or meaning, why should I live at all?'

'Only because you were born,' said Mathu.

'That might be a good enough reason for most people to live, but not for me. In any case, I don't think you're right in holding that human endeavour serves no purpose at all,' Zeruba said, and went on to argue that the achievements of Einstein and others have had a transforming effect on human history, though not on ultimate cosmic destiny. 'Even my own work might make some difference, even if only just a little, and only for just a few people.'

'So you hope,' Mathu scorned. 'Hope is a barren crone, Zeruba, though she makes us all dance to her tune! To be free of hope is to be free of disappointment, to be free of misery.'

'But to be without hope is to be without life, don't you see, Kochappa?' Zeruba objected. 'I mean, the inertly contented life that you advocate is just vegetative existence, not life. There is no suffering for the dead, or the living dead—isn't that what you are saying in effect?'

'Yes, I suppose so,' Mathu conceded. 'To live is to suffer. But you've the choice. A contented non-life without hope and craving, or a miserable life with hope and craving.'

'I don't even know whether I've the choice,' Zeruba said. 'I can only be what I am, not what I choose.'

2

Mathu's gloomy ruminations about life kept swirling in Zeruba's mind when he returned to Madras and resumed his solitary life. What saved him from terminal depression was his work. He felt miserable on the days he could not work, but as long as he was immersed in work, nothing troubled him. He, therefore, worked on the sculpture even on rainy days, wearing swimming trunks and a broad-brimmed rain cap—this in fact was a particular pleasure for him, for the ruttish smell of rain-slaked rock dust awakened something elemental in him, a pleasant exhilaration of senses.

And one day, while he was thus working on the sculpture in

a blinding downpour, Tarun came to see him, materializing spectrally through the curtain of rain, barefooted, his silk kurta and pyjama soaked, water streaming from his head like from a tiled roof.

'I was taking a stroll, and I saw you,' he said, his voice a hoarse whisper. 'May I stand here and watch you?'

'Of course,' Zeruba said. 'But why don't you come in and dry yourself? I'll make you a cup of tea.'

'I'm fine,' he said. 'I just want to stand here and watch you.'

'As you wish.'

'It feels good to watch you working,' Tarun said after a while. 'How I envy you, Dada!'

'Envy me?' Zeruba laughed. 'Whatever for?'

'You've something to do in life.'

'My uncle Mathu says that this is all just a waste of time—that no human endeavour is of any value.'

'He's right,' Tarun said. 'The trick is not to think about it.'

'I know.'

'My problem is I don't know what to do with my time.'

'That too is a happy state, isn't it—to have nothing to do?'

'No, I'm not happy with it. There are so many things that I want to do, so many things worth doing, but they all seem impossible for me to do. So all I do is to just curl up in bed. When I wake up in the morning all I want is for the day to end, so I can go to bed again.'

'But you don't sleep much at night, do you?'

'No. But the night gives me the excuse to go to bed again.'

'I'm about finished for now,' said Zeruba. 'Why don't we go in?'

'Let's just stay in the rain for a while,' Tarun said.

They sat in silence for a while on the steps of the patio.

'My mother is dead,' Tarun said abruptly.

'I'm sorry. Where was she?'

'With my brother in Bhopal. She's the one that made me the freak that I am.'

'We're all freaks, Tarun, in our own ways,' Zeruba said. 'I haven't ever met a single truly normal human being.'

'But I'm more freakish than other freaks,' Tarun said. 'That's okay. But it's difficult for me to forget what Mother did to me.'

'Don't say anything you'll later regret saying, Tarun.'

'I want to say it, Dada. I want to get it out of my system.'

'Alright.'

'She was a sick woman,' Tarun said, his head bent over, examining his fingernails one by one minutely, as if they held some occult secret. 'Neurotic. She became almost deranged after my father's death. I was about seven or eight when she used to spread rat poison on bread like butter and show it to me and say that that was what she would eat if I didn't behave. And one day she locked herself in the bedroom and got on a stool and tied a rope to the ceiling-fan to hang herself, as I stood howling at an open window. The neighbours had to break open the door and take her down. It was hell.'

'Oh, that's terrible,' said Zeruba quietly.

'I was just a kid then,' Tarun said, rubbing his temples with his palms. 'Just a little kid.'

'I'm sorry.'

'I grew up with such awful feelings of insecurity. I tried to compensate for that by pretending to talents and qualities I didn't have. All the time I was cracking up inside.'

'Well, we can't do anything about other people screwing up our lives,' Zeruba consoled. 'But we can do something about our attitude towards what they do to us. Did I ever tell you what President Radhakrishnan once told Kennedy?'

'No.'

This was when Radhakrishnan was on an official visit to the US. The day he landed in Washington it was raining heavily, and Kennedy commented regretfully about the foul weather. And Radhakrishnan said, *Mr President, we can't do anything about the weather, but we can do something about our attitude towards the weather.*

'What's the relevance of this to my predicament?' Tarun asked when Zeruba told him the story.

'Events themselves are neutral, Tarun,' Zeruba said. 'We can make heaven and hell out of anything. Or remain calmly detached.'

'You can't remain calmly detached to the events that affect you personally,' Tarun said, shaking his head gloomily.

'I'm not belittling your suffering,' Zeruba said. 'I too have been hurt quite seriously in life. But I've developed calluses over my wounds. They don't hurt any more. I get on with my life.'

'Childhood traumas are different,' Tarun said, getting up to leave. 'They mark you for life.'

'There's no point in having regrets about the past, Tarun,' Zeruba said. 'What's before your eyes is all you've got. You got to accept that and move on.'

'What've I got before my eyes?' Tarun snickered. 'Nothing. Just void. I'm tired of living.'

That night Tarun took a full bottle of barbiturates over half a bottle of whisky before going to bed. He never woke up.

3

Zeruba did not attend Tarun's funeral, but kept himself busy with his sculpture. But as the months passed, he retreated ever deeper into himself and began to spend long hours idling, listlessly going through the motions of living and working, talking to himself, his mind filled with morbid thoughts. He even lost his sense of self. In the mirror he could see a vaguely familiar face, but had difficulty in recognizing it as his own.

It was as if Tarun's departing soul had left some miasma in the air, which infected Zeruba. He was not able to sleep well at night, and was haunted by nightmares. He had recurrent dreams of a lone and crippled pigmy struggling up the precipitous face of a desolate mountain, the Everest perhaps, the summit of which he would never reach, and in any case his lunatic reason for trying to reach the summit was only to throw himself off the cliff. The very monumentality of the sculpture he had undertaken depressed Zeruba; he did not know when he would be able to complete it, or even whether he would ever be able to complete it at all. Had he wasted his life for nothing? Were all the sacrifices he had made to stay focussed on his work, and the discipline that he had so assiduously cultivated, all to no purpose?

On the surface, everything seemed to be going fine with him. He had all that a man could possibly desire—enough money for his needs, a roof of his own over his head, and he had all the sex he wanted with the women of his choice. And the work he was doing was exactly what he most enjoyed doing. True, he was alone, but this too was his own choice, as he believed that this was the only way he could control his life. In all, the life he lived was precisely the life he desired and had chosen. Yet there was a void in him, and he often felt miserable and lonely.

'It's fashionable for artists to seem unhappy,' Ashok taunted him one day when he dropped in at the cottage. He was the only close friend Zeruba had at this time.

'To each his own daily dose of misery,' Zeruba said.

'Yes, but don't melodramatize your petty miseries,' Ashok chided.

Petty miseries? Zeruba smiled wanly and said nothing. Maybe his miseries were petty in themselves, but to him they were absolutely devastating. To each of us, he brooded, whoever we are, the hobo on the pavement or the sultan in his gilded palace, the most important thing in the world, the most important thing in the history of mankind, is what is happening to him.

Life, he felt, had dealt him an awful deal. Or maybe, as his uncle told him, he had dealt himself an awful deal. But there was a streak of mulish obstinacy in him, so rather than changing his lifestyle, he gritted his teeth and hunkered down. *Well, if this is to be my life, then this is to be my life*, he said to himself. *I can't do anything about the given circumstances of my life. But I'll prevail despite them. I'll not yield.*

He would not let his life get in the way of his work, he decided. Besides, he felt he had no choice. He had to do what was in his nature to do. These thoughts of Zeruba were reinforced by the teachings of the obscure ancient Indian sect of Ajivikas, to which he was strongly drawn at this time. He thus came to believe that a man's life is determined by his innate nature—his chemistry— and the potencies of the time and the environment in which he lives. The individual is just a particular chemical formulation in a particular chemical setting, undergoing a process of chemical changes. Human will is never free will, and we are in no way responsible for how we live and what happens in our lives. Man decides nothing, and cannot by will or learning or piety change his nature, control anything that happens to him, or alter the tempo of his life even by a millisecond. Life rides on contingencies. Whatever will be, will be.

4

'Like Eliot's fool, we imagine that we turn the wheel on which we turn,' Zeruba said to Pratibha one day when she, along with Ashok and Iyer, visited him.

'That's just poetic fancy,' she said. 'People do change their lives by will and effort.'

'But the very will and effort of the individual is determined by his innate nature,' Zeruba said. 'You really have no control over your actions, for all your decisions are made at the molecular level, by your chemistry. Character is chemistry, Pratibha. Destiny is chemistry.'

'Pop a pill and alter your character, what?' Ashok hooted. 'And pop another pill and alter your destiny?'

'It might come to that,' Zeruba said. 'The brave new world.'

'I can't accept this absolute materialism,' Iyer said. 'There's more to man than just the matter he's made up of.'

'There isn't,' Zeruba maintained. 'There's nothing to man other than his chemistry. Different lives, and different forms of lives, are just different chemical formulations. And all the things that happen in us—what happens in our stomach, lungs, heart, brain and in every organ—are chemical processes.'

'I've a friend in office who says that we're just chemical entities consuming chemical substances which we call food, and excreting chemical substances which we call faeces and urine,' said Ashok. 'Man is just a shit and piss producing bio-mechanical device.'

'Yes indeed,' Zeruba laughed.

'You are forgetting procreation,' Iyer said.

'Okay then, man is a self-replicating shit and piss processing bio-mechanical device,' Ashok cheerfully conceded.

'What about thoughts and feelings?' Pratibha asked.

'What about them?' Zeruba challenged. 'Thoughts and feelings and moods, even your sense of self, are just chemical states. Auden had wanted to know why loneliness was not just a chemical discomfort. The answer can be given now. Loneliness *is* a chemical state. If you pop a certain pill, your mood will immediately lift. A cool shower on a hot day will have a similar effect. Or saying a prayer. Or being with friends—your visit has changed my chemistry, and when you leave, it'll change again. Everything that we do and everything that happens to us cause chemical changes in us.'

'Maybe,' Pratibha said. 'But I still can't accept that we have absolutely no control over our lives.'

'Well, it's nice to think that we've control, but it's a delusion,' Zeruba said.

'A delusion instilled in us by our innate nature,' Ashok added gleefully.

'This is no laughing matter,' Pratibha protested.

'Of course it is,' Ashok said. 'All metaphysics is bullshit.'

Zeruba had always been interested in religion and philosophy, and now he read avidly and purposefully, to find the means to reassemble the fragments of his life into some semblance of order. In the process, he let his work on the sculpture languish. He still woke up very early in the morning, at four, as had been his habit for many years, but instead of getting up immediately, he now merely turned over on his back to lie inert and relaxed, his arms and legs stretched out, his eyes closed, listening intently to the bedside clock relentlessly ticking off his life, second by second. In the background he could hear the soft, forlorn moaning of the sea, calling to him. It would take him several minutes to muster up the will to get up and face the day.

Rising, he would go through his usual routine yoga and meditation, then pull on his swimming trunks and leave for the beach, to lie supine on the water's edge, as the sea curled up calm at his feet, like a pet dog, sighing softly, licking his feet. Everything was utterly still at this hour, except the white beam of the lighthouse mechanically sweeping the horizon like some robotic gizmo left behind by alien invaders on abandoning a dead earth. Above, the heavens too were still, the great galaxies and the winking stars, all riveted to their allotted places. Behind him the halo of streetlights arched over the city.

Zeruba's mood, as he lay on the beach, varied from day to day. Some days he felt wonderfully invigorated, but most of the days he was overcome with melancholy, as waves of regret washed over him, about all that he had done but should not have, and all that he had not done but should have, and he felt like a piece of decayed driftwood washed up on the shore of time. Even the happy days that were gone had all turned into griefs.

It was perversely pleasant for Zeruba to caress those fragrant griefs. A wonderful thing about the mind is that it can go anywhere instantly, sail into the past one moment and rocket into the future the next, go to any continent and any city, into any home, be with any person it fancies. And Zeruba now, like Tarun, promiscuously indulged in nostalgia and daydreams. But he was also aware that this quaint mood of his was a treacherous quagmire that would suck him in and destroy his life if he lingered there for long. He had to pull himself out and move on. And sometimes, as he lay there on the beach in the predawn half-light, seemingly the only being alive in the cosmos, he felt something new stirring within him, something that made him both happy and apprehensive at the same time—what was it? The first, faint breath of another spring? Was that possible? Do we get second chances in life?

He would lie on the beach till sunrise, thinking over these matters, dozing off now and then, till puffs of sea-breath caressed him awake. By then the sea would be astir, the giggly waves collapsing over each other on the beach, like schoolgirls on a picnic. The sun would be just peeping over the horizon, an angry red, like the devil's eye, but even as Zeruba watched, its colour would change to burnt gold and then to blazing white, and he would hurry back to the cottage for refuge from the rising heat. But instead of working on the sculpture as he used to do, he would then lounge about reading a book, and it would be only late in the afternoon that he would take up the chisel. This was his routine now, so the sculpture progressed very slowly.

6

Zeruba now stopped going to parties altogether, seldom answered the phone, never replied to letters, and curled up snugly into his loneliness. He regarded this self-exile from society as therapeutic, necessary for his mental health. He was equally careful about his physical health. This was particularly important to him, for he believed that physical health was essential for mental health, especially now that he was assailed daily by countless anxieties. Everything would be lost if he lost his health, he knew.

Fortunately, he had a robust constitution, and seldom fell ill.

But that summer, when heat-waves killed nearly a thousand people all over India, and in Madras the temperature rose to 45 degrees, the highest in the century, Zeruba fell ill with the flu. On the second day he had a temperature of 38.5 degrees, but that did not worry him, as it was only a little higher than the ambient temperature in the cottage. But as the fever rose and persisted, he grew very weak, and he thought he was going to die. Indeed, there were moments during his illness when he, feeble and depressed, felt like just curling up and dying. But his cook, totally loyal to him like most of his servants, nursed him with affection and care—she never left his side during his illness, and at night slept on a mat on the floor beside his bed, while her husband slept on the veranda. He recovered after a week, and one early morning woke up sweating profusely, his scrotum chill as ice and his penis stiff as an iron rod. He then knew he was going to live. With some effort, he propped himself against the headboard of the bed, and the noise of his stirring woke up the cook.

'You're alright, Iyya?' she asked anxiously.

'I think so,' he whispered.

She quickly made him a cup of tea, but he did not have the strength to take the cup from her, and had her place it on the bedside table.

'I'll make you some rice gruel,' she said. 'With a little milk.'

'Alright,' he said.

He lay very still, breathing slowly and deliberately, summoning will and energy to lift the cup and drink the tea. Presently, the cook brought him a bowl of rice gruel, and that put some strength into his limbs. By evening, he felt strong enough to walk up to the veranda and sit there for an hour, letting the cool, sea-fresh air work its restorative magic on him. But it took him well over a week to fully regain his strength. And he now for the first time began to discern the effects of ageing on him. Life was oozing out of him, like water from a cracked pot, he felt. As years advance, man retreats.

Around this time, a beauty-queen-turned-film-star with aquamarine eyes visited Zeruba, to buy one of his paintings. She was the very perfection of physical beauty, her skin smooth and luminous, her limbs spry with sap. But what he noticed most in her was the delicate web of wrinkles beginning to form at the corners of her eyes, and he saw the worm of time nibbling at her body, leaving its corrosive secretions on her. And before his very eyes she seemed to wither into an old woman, the light in her eyes fade, her face sag, her firm breasts turn into wrinkled pouches, her supple, baby-smooth skin become parched and crinkly, like coarse paper.

What'll you be like when you're eighty, honey? he silently asked the beauty queen. *That's not ages away, but the day after tomorrow. Years will be gone in seconds. Look at me—just yesterday I was a nutty college kid who roared with laughter along with a theatre full of collegemates watching Laurel and Hardy movies, and today I am a weary old man with no joy in anything. Time devours everything, even itself. The one incontrovertible fact about all the immortal heroes of history is that they all died. And most of them are forgotten. Gone, gone like the fireflies of yesterday. So take care, honey. Snatch the moment.*

'I didn't have the strength to fight for life,' Zeruba told Ashok during his convalescence. 'I thought I was going to die.'

'You still are,' said Ashok.

'What?'

'You're certainly going to die,' Ashok said. 'Where do you think you're headed to? You've been on the death-row right from the moment of your birth, and your executioner was born with you, right inside your body. Even as we talk, death is creeping on you.'

Zeruba laughed.

'Laugh, you moron,' Ashok said. 'What else can you do but laugh at such an obscene absurdity as death.'

'Yeah. But the question is, are we born to live, or are we born to die? That's the most important question in life.'

'No, that's not the most important question.'

'What, then?'

'The most important question is whether it was the chicken or the egg that came first,' Ashok said gravely.

234

Zeruba

1

When Zeruba recovered from the flu, his cook brought him some *prasadam* from the nearby Ganesa temple—a couple of plantains and *kozhukottai* dumplings along with a few coconut pieces, betel leaves and betel-nut chips, all on a strip of plantain leaf.

'I broke a coconut at the temple for your recovery,' she said. 'And I prayed every day at the temple for you.'

'I'm grateful,' Zeruba said, receiving the *prasadam* with reverence, careful not to hurt her feelings, though he would later secretly throw it away into the sea. He couldn't depend on gods to take care of him, Zeruba felt, when man had enough trouble taking care of gods. What he needed was human solace. With age creeping up on him, he had been feeling rather forlorn lately, and this feeling had become acute during his illness. He needed a helpmate, someone gentle and affectionate to take care of him and share his life.

But it was now too late for that, he feared. He was too old, his ways too set, for the life with him to be bearable to another person. Besides, there was no woman in whom he was even remotely interested. Aditi had offered to move in with him and take care of him when she visited him once during his illness, but he turned her down without a moment's hesitation. The more he suffered, the more he cursed her for putting him in that predicament, and the stronger grew his resolve never to let her into his life again.

Aditi had been phoning him now and then to find out how he was getting on without her, though she had, on moving out, sworn never again to set her eyes on him or speak to him. And one day when she phoned, the cook told her that he was ill, and she immediately rushed to see him.

'I felt sorry for you when I heard that you are ill,' she said.

'Thank you,' he mumbled.

She went over and sat on his bed. He closed his eyes.

'You want me to stay and take care of you?' she asked.

'No,' he said.

'I still love you, though you were so nasty to me,' she said. 'I feel sorry for you.'

'Thank you,' he said.

'What do you say? You want me to come?'

'No,' he said. 'I can manage.'

'There's still a future for us,' she said.

'Sure,' he said. 'But not for us together.'

'You'll stew in your own misery,' she warned.

'Thank you.'

'Rot here, alone, forsaken by all.'

'Fine.'

'Even Mats doesn't want to see you ever again.'

'Fine.'

'Because of what you've done to me.'

'Yes.'

'How did you fall ill, anyway?'

'Don't know.'

'You probably caught something from one of these slum women,' she said.

'Probably.'

'You still screwing these sluts?'

'Maybe.'

'You'll die fucking.'

'Yes,' he laughed weakly. 'I'll go when I come!'

2

For about a week after his recovery, Zeruba felt so utterly exhausted that he was unable to work on the sculpture or even read a book, and spent most of his time stretched out in bed, staring blankly at the ceiling. He would later say that it was during that fortnight of illness and convalescence that he finally understood what his life was all about. There was now a slight shift in his character, a touch of genuine sadness in the place of the sardonic bearing that he usually affected.

Zeruba often thought of Lakshmi at this time, and fancied that she would have made a good wife for him, and that he would have had a fair chance of finding enduring happiness with her. But that was not to be. Marrying her, a slum girl, would have meant instant and irreversible severance from his family, pulling out his roots from his native soil, and he was not yet ready for that.

But he courted a worse calamity by marrying Aditi. It ruined him. It ruined her. But why did he choose to marry her at all? He was drawn to her, and this he mistook for affinity; there was sexual arousal, and this he mistook for love. Zeruba, it seemed, loved Aditi without feeling any affection for her. Still, it was not all that bad a choice. Their contrariness was complementary, and if their marriage had worked out well, they would have potentiated each other marvellously. But it didn't work out at all.

'A good life, Dada, is a patchwork quilt, willing compromises turned into a pleasing design,' Mathangi had once told Zeruba, during her rapprochement efforts. 'You don't have to repudiate your dreams, but only patch them into the other bits and pieces that life offers you.' He was on that occasion startled by the wisdom of what Mathangi said, and had told himself that he should take her advice to heart and mend his relationship with Aditi. But it didn't work. Their marriage was too fissured to be patched up.

How essential and yet how futile it is for one to connect with another human being, Zeruba reflected. No one really knows another, because we know very little about each other, and what little we know is skewed by our memories and imaginings. The relationship between men and women is particularly complex and tortured. Even the most intimate act between them resembles a combat, a clash of bodies in thrust and parry, in which women are always the gainers, while men are drained out. The dimorphism between them is not just of sex organs either—they also think and feel differently, and their orientations to life are different. Women, perhaps because they are child bearers, are earthier, and are closer to the processes of nature. And nature is devious. Bloody devious.

In a way, therefore, to blame Aditi was to blame nature itself. Deceit and aggression, he knew, mark all life, even down to the molecular level. We deceive each other and ourselves all the time. The greatest among us, the noblest, are still human. We all have feet of clay. The chemistry of all is the same. Only the absence of activity, as Hegel says, is innocent. To act, to live, is to cheat, betray and transgress. So then, how could he condemn Aditi? Of course they were disappointed with each other in many ways. But it couldn't have been otherwise, could it? Experience, they should have known, always falls short of expectation. We court a dream and marry a reality.

It was in any case unrealistic for anyone to expect a couple to live in harmony with each other day after day for years together in the cramped cage called home. People need private spaces. The very institutions of monogamous marriage and nuclear family seemed perverse to Zeruba. His uncle Mathu was after all right, he felt—it would be more natural for a couple to be lovers, than to be husband and wife. Instead of living together, they should visit each other, with no binding relationships or expectations.

But wouldn't men still be sexually possessive? Wasn't the

problem with his marriage really that he was sexually promiscuous, but would not grant that freedom to Aditi? But that too was unavoidable, he told Mathangi when she raised this matter with him once.

'You see, Mats, genetically it doesn't make any sense for women to go philandering,' he said. 'But it's perfectly natural for men.'

Mathangi laughed. 'I can see why Adi calls you an MCP,' she said.

'I'm serious, Mats. Look at it this way. It would serve no genetic purpose for a woman to be promiscuous, for she can have only one pregnancy a year however many men she mates with, but a man can father hundreds of children in a year if he wants.'

'True, but how come that some societies grant sexual freedom to women?' Mathangi countered.

'Maybe there's a cultural override involved in this,' Zeruba hedged. There was, he knew, a Cossack saying that a woman is not like a jug of milk—others can have her, but she'll still be there for you. And there was a similar saying in the Buddhist *Jatakas*, that a woman is like a river from which many can drink without depleting her.

'You see, Dada, it's all a matter of mental attitudes,' Mathangi said.

'True. But I can't change my attitudes, Mats.'

'Of course you can. People do it all the time.'

'Only superficially. We can't change our nature.'

Zeruba could not forgive Aditi for ravaging his life, however much others reasoned with him and however much he reasoned with himself. 'My life would've been so very different but for this ruinous marriage!' he once told Ashok, during his convalescence. He lay propped up on pillows in bed, while Ashok and Pratibha sat in cane chairs brought in from the veranda.

'You really got your head up your own ass,' Ashok reproved. 'Would your worrying about it make any difference now? Forget

239

what happened, damn it. What's gone, is gone. Don't waste time thinking about it. Move on, man.'

'Easy to say, difficult to do,' said Zeruba.

But of course, Ashok was right. To move on, Zeruba had to lay down the crushing burden of memory and regret that he was carrying. There was no point in apportioning blame either. Neither Aditi nor he was guilty; they were only weak, being human.

4

Zeruba now moved into a new phase of life, taking his illness as a warning from the Almighty, the master chronometer, not to waste his life. *There is much unused life in me*, he reflected. *However insignificant I might be compared to great artists—a mere mustard seed beside the Himalayas—there is much that even I can do. I'll stop the drain of sap through the pores of self-pity. I'll make do with what I have, with what I am, and within that find the means to lead a fulfilling life, and achieve peace and contentment, perhaps even happiness.*

Mathu was wrong, Zeruba realized. Life mattered. His life mattered. Buddha too was wrong. Happiness was possible. And happiness could be enduring. But he had to find it in himself. Not in or through others. No one but himself could give him happiness; no one but himself could destroy his happiness. He had only himself to fear.

Just because he would die one day, and the universe itself would perish one day, it didn't mean that he had to deny life. In fact, precisely because he had to die, and death might come at any moment, he had to cherish every passing moment. The true centre of the universe—the universe that is infinite in all directions and has itself no centre—is the egocentre, Zeruba decided. But that did not mean that he had to curl up into himself. There was no need for him to be an anchorite. Ascetic self-denial would only lead to fresh anxieties and perhaps to ill health. Equipoise and self-possession could be achieved only by leading a natural life, satisfying one's natural impulses. But without excess. Through discipline, avoiding both self-indulgence and self-denial. Too bright a light blinds one as much as darkness. A bee can drown in the bowl of honey that would nourish it. Moderation is the only virtue. He would calmly accept all that life brings him, without any prejudice about high and low, noble and base, sacred and profane. And he would enjoy the pleasures of life without letting his cravings consume him.

Zeruba emerged from his convalescence at peace with himself. The air he inhaled felt cool and fragrant again, and he felt healthy, in mind and body. He now resumed the work on his sculpture with new vigour. Ashok and Pratibha dropped in to see him now and then, and he was glad to be with them. But he did not miss them if they did not visit him for a couple of weeks. His work engrossed him totally. And one evening, when he was thus busy at work, Devi, his long-lost sister, dropped in unexpectedly to see him, arriving in a chauffeur-driven, wine-red Mercedes. She had put on some weight, but not much, and was still startlingly beautiful.

'My! You're looking divine,' he said, beaming with pleasure.

'And you're looking devilish,' she said. 'I'm so disappointed.'

'Born like this. What did you expect?'

'I expected to see a broken old man, and here you are sprightly as the devil, your eyes sparkling.'

'Devil with his tail on fire.'

'Whatever is the matter with you, big brother? You in love or something?'

'With myself.'

'Good. Hope you won't be disappointed.'

'There's always that risk.'

'I hear that you and Adi have split. What happened?'

'Oh, that's ancient history, Devi. But how do you know so much about me?'

'I've spies.'

'You're in Madras?'

'Off and on.'

'What do you mean?'

'I travel around the world quite a bit,' Devi said.

'Really? What for?'

'I do a bit of import-export—and a bit of smuggling.'

'You're putting me on.'

'I'm serious,' she said. 'It's my profession.'

'Please don't tell me anything more,' Zeruba said. 'How's Alagu?'

'Dead.'

'I'm sorry.'

'I'm not. He was an awful drag on me.'

'Come on in. Let's celebrate the reunion.'

'Can't. Got to run. I'll come again and we'll have a long chat.'

'Why don't you ever go home, Devi?' he asked. 'Appa will be absolutely thrilled to see you. They're getting on in years.'

'Some other time.'

'They might not be around then.'

'You can't live in the past.'

'Yes, you can. That's the easiest thing. So is living in the future. It's to live in the present that's difficult.'

For a moment, Devi's face clouded.

'What's the matter?' Zeruba asked.

'Nothing,' she said, quickly recovering.

Yes, living in the present is not easy, she reflected. *Nor living in the past. And the future? God! Whatever has happened to the promise of my life?* She remembered with shudder the deprivations of her childhood during the humiliating poverty of her father. The awful bleakness of her crumbling old home in Kerala. But a bright new world of infinite opportunities had opened to her in Madras. Where did she go wrong? Should she have married Ravi instead of Alagu? That would have given her absolute security. Instead, she chose freedom and adventure. *But what a mess I've made of my life! Doesn't matter. I'll make it on my own,* she resolved. *I will yet prevail.*

'Your face darkened,' Zeruba said with concern.

'It's nothing,' she said. 'Maybe I'll come in for a moment.'

'Tea?' he asked as they went in.

'No. Let's just talk,' she said. 'I know that everyone is disappointed with me. I'm disappointed with myself.'

'But you're doing very well. Mercedes!'

'Belongs to a don.'

'Oh!'

'Don't you snicker at me,' she said with heat, shaking a finger at him. 'I must rise by that by which I fall.'

'Where did you learn this?' Zeruba was amazed. 'It's a Tantric saying.'

'I don't know any tantra or mantra. I just want to get on in life.'

'So?'

'My strengths are rather weak,' Devi said. 'They can't lift me up. On the other hand, my weaknesses are very strong. So I must use the strength of my weakness to survive. I'm absolutely clear about it.'

'Like a wrestler making his opponent fall by himself falling?'

'Something like that. I'll not be defeated. Don't you give up on your little sis!'

'Of course not. Where do you live? How can I get in touch with you?'

'I'm a little unsettled just now. I'll let you know when things even out a little.'

'Give me your phone number at least,' he said.

'Later,' she said, leaving. 'Better not get entangled with me now. I'll call you.'

But she never did.

Anjali

1

In over three years of toil on his sculpture, Zeruba had covered only about half the surface of the stone, but as the pace of his work had now quickened, he was confident that he would be able to complete it in another couple of years or so. He also did several paintings at this time, and these sold well. His life thus fell into a comfortable and busy routine.

At the end of the year, Ashok and Pratibha got married. They were an odd couple—while he was bawdy and forever sputtering with raw energy, she was shy and reserved, very quiet and rather remote, especially in the company of strangers. But presumably they pulsed to some common tempo in their private moments. Maybe, Zeruba thought, he provided her with the energy and spontaneity she secretly craved, and she provided him with the repose and stability he needed. It was a perfect yin-yang match, and their marriage proved enduring and happy.

Theirs was a conventional Iyer wedding, and Ashok, despite his wild bohemianism, had taken care to conform. He wore a *panchakaccham* dhoti in the orthodox style, with one end pleated and drawn up between his legs and tucked in at the back, and had even put on a sacred thread, which he had given up wearing long ago, having taken it off and thrown it away the day he graduated. His frizzy hair, which he usually never combed, was oiled and slicked down, and his forehead was marked with a broad band of holy ash and a large kumkum tilak. And he wore a suffocating rose garland around his neck. Pratibha too was dressed in the traditional style, in a nine-yard canary-yellow Kanchipuram silk sari richly worked in gold thread, and was heavily bejewelled. She sat before the sacred fire with her characteristically tense, brittle dignity, and Ashok sat relaxed to her left with a perpetual goofy grin.

Iyer sat in a chair at the far back of the marriage hall, a cigarette dangling from his lips as ever. He was a widower, and Pratibha was his only child, so he insisted on Ashok moving in with them after the wedding. This made Ashok and Zeruba neighbours, and they visited each other frequently. Within a year a child was born to the couple, a boy. Pratibha's broomstick thin body now filled out, and her pallid complexion took on a ruddy hue.

'Hmm! Look at her bottom!' Zeruba once remarked to Ashok, seeing Pratibha in jeans.

'She can't be bottomless for ever, can she?' Ashok laughed.

'Cut it out,' Pratibha cried, smiling happily, cocking her head and peering at them through her thick glasses. 'It's disgusting. I don't talk about your dicks, do I?'

'My! What language!' Zeruba exclaimed. 'Where did you pick it up?'

'Where do you think?' she shot back, darting a conspiratorial glance at Ashok.

Ashok shrieked with pleasure. He remained very much his old crazy self even after marriage, but there was a radical transformation in Pratibha. She had shed her shyness and had assumed a self-confident and cheerful demeanour.

'How's your novel shaping up?' Zeruba asked.

'It's in cold storage.'

'Why? I thought it was going well.'

'I've something far more beautiful now,' she said, nuzzling her gurgling baby. 'My little *pappa*.'

'It's said that the desire for children is a form of desire for possessions,' Zeruba said.

'And so is the desire to write or paint,' she retorted.

A few months after the baby was born, Iyer died of cardiac arrest, as his doctor had warned he would, telling him that each cigarette he smoked was another nail on his coffin.

'Smoking has been a lifelong pleasure for me,' Iyer told the doctor. 'I'm not going to give it up just to add a few days to my life. Whatever for? I've nothing to do in my days. I'm just killing time while waiting for time to kill me.'

2

Around this time, Beth packed up and returned to England for good, and Tarun's mansion was sold to a television soap-opera producer, who had the tennis court dug up to build a swimming pool there. He also set out to redecorate the house, and assigned the task to Mathangi, the most sought-after and expensive interior decorator in Madras. This enabled Mathangi and Zeruba to renew their friendship, and whenever she came to oversee the work at the mansion, she dropped in to see Zeruba. But she never entered the cottage, and always sat in the veranda or on the patio.

'Come on in. Let's have some tea,' Zeruba asked her the first time.

'No. Let's not do that,' she said.

'What're you afraid of?'

'I'm afraid of being weak,' she said. 'I'm afraid of us both being weak.'

'That was centuries ago, Mats. We're both free from those temptations now.'

'I've promised Adi that I won't enter the cottage.'

'Okay then, let's sit out here,' Zeruba said. 'But do drop in whenever you can.'

'Of course,' she said.

'How is your work going?'

'I don't want to even think about it. They insist on covering the drawing-room walls with scenic wallpaper.'

'And you're doing it!'

'Of course. It's my livelihood.'

'What about my painting?' Zeruba asked.

'That has been removed and stored away.'

'What are they going to do with it?'

'Don't know. I'll ask.'

A few days later she told him that they had offered the painting to her as part of her fee.

'What's the price they have put on it?' he asked.

She looked at him with a sly smile. 'Guess,' she said.

'Worthless? For free?'

'Not that good.'

'C'mon. Tell me.'

'Ten thousand. I'll take it and give it to you.'

'Don't do that,' he said. 'I want you to have it, Mats.'

'I would very much like to have it myself,' she said. 'But I can't steal it. Paying ten thousand rupees for it is like stealing it.'

'You're stealing it from the morons, not from me. Take it.'

'Okay,' she said. 'But please keep it with you till I decide what to do with it. I can't take it to my flat. That'll upset Adi.'

'No problem,' he said.

3

A few months after this, Zeruba had a phone call from Ashok saying that the features editor of his newspaper wanted to meet him to do an article.

'Who's this?' Zeruba asked.

'Anjali,' Ashok said. 'She's very bright. And pretty. You would love her.'

'Never heard of her.'

'She joined us just last month from a newspaper in Bangalore. Her parents live in Madras. You probably have heard of her father, Dr Ranga Rao, the neurosurgeon.'

'Oh yes. She's welcome.'

'When?'

'Any time.'

And that was how Anjali entered Zeruba's life. She came the very next evening.

'Hello,' she said, coming up quietly behind him as he worked on the sculpture.

Startled, he spun around, and was astounded to see standing before him a woman so very like Lakshmi in her youth, having the same stature and build, face and demeanour, and, most striking of all, the same eyes of hypnotic luminosity. A virtual clone, except that Lakshmi was dark while this woman was fair.

'Sorry I startled you,' the woman said. 'I'm Anjali.'

'Yes, of course.'

'Don't interrupt your work. I'll just stand here and watch.'

'Fine,' he said, and turned back to the sculpture.

She regarded him calmly, thinking of how she should describe him in her article. He wore a faded denim shorts and was barechested and barefooted, his skin the colour of tarnished copper. Dappled evening light filtering through the rain-tree danced on his back. She knew that he was in his fifties, but he looked years younger, despite his grey-streaked hair and beard. Physically, he was rather overwhelming, tall and robustly built, with a deep chest, broad shoulders and muscular arms. His calf muscles bulged like that of a sprinter. There was also something occult about him, a faintly Rasputinish look, because of his long beard and his narrow face with its rampant cheekbones and deep-set, piercing eyes.

Zeruba could sense her eyes probing him as she stood to a side behind him, and the skin on the back of his neck tingled under her gaze. He tried to ignore her and go on with his work, but gave it up after a few minutes, and tossed aside the chisel and hammer.

'Something wrong?' she asked.

'Can't work with you watching,' he said.

248

'Sorry.'

'My fault,' he said. 'You remind me of someone else. That disturbs me.'

'You looked surprised to see me. I wondered why.'

'Let's not talk about it.'

'Okay,' she said. 'May I ask why this sculpture is called *Moon River*?'

'Because it's the river of memory and dreams,' he said, reciting his carefully rehearsed lines. 'It flows on full-moon nights, when you're asleep but your subconscious is awake.'

'Yes?'

'Yes. Everything is sort of jumbled up in it, the past and the present and the future, and dream and reality and myth, in a sort of space-time continuum,' he said. 'It's about the variability of truth and transience of reality.'

Anjali looked at him quizzically, her eyebrows cocked. There was a suggestion of a smile at the corners of her mouth, a glint of mischievousness in her eyes. Was she mocking him, he wondered. 'That's my theme,' he added quickly. 'The sculpture reflects the theme, but does not illustrate it. It's more a stream of consciousness in stone.'

'You don't have a sketch for it?'

'I do,' he said. 'But when I sculpt, I work with the sketch in my head, not with the paper before me, which means that the design is freely alterable in the process of sculpting. I sculpt and paint from inside the subject, by merging with the subject. I see better with my eyes closed than with my eyes open.'

'Really?' she asked. Her smile had broadened.

He hesitated for a moment, scowling at her, then plunged on with his set lines. 'Yes,' he said. 'Because what I see with my eyes closed is not cluttered with sensory inputs. In any case, seeing with your eyes closed is not all that different from seeing with your eyes open. In both cases, the image is formed in the brain.'

'I've a feeling that I've heard or read all this somewhere before,' she said.

'Very likely,' he shrugged. 'These are my stock answers to stock questions.'

Anjali laughed. *It's alright then*, he thought; *she's just teasing me*. He relaxed.

'I'm afraid all this is a little beyond me,' Anjali said. 'I'm not an art critic, and I don't want to do a conventional art article. Aesthetics and all that sort of stuff. My focus will be on the artist and his life. I want to write a human interest story, about how you relate to the world, and how that is reflected in your work.'

'Suits me,' Zeruba said, leading her into the cottage. 'Most art criticism is bogus anyway.'

'My view,' she said.

Anjali was perfectly at ease with Zeruba, without the usual fawning nosiness of reporters. She was dressed simply but elegantly in a starched pale yellow cotton sari with a thin brown border, its *pallu* demurely wrapped around her shoulder. Her shoulder-length hair was pulled back tight and bound at the nape of her neck with a rubber band, giving her face an open, earnest, self-possessed look. She wore absolutely no jewellery, not even earrings or bangles, and the only make-up on her was a sandalwood-paste thilak on her broad forehead, and the kohl lining her immense black eyes. Anjali listened with her eyes, exactly as Lakshmi did.

'Please,' he said, waving her to the divan.

'Very nice,' she said, looking around.

'Give me a minute,' he said, and went into the bathroom to wash up and pull on a T-shirt.

'Will you have some tea?' he asked, returning to the drawing room.

'That would be nice,' she said. 'May I help you?'

'You want to snoop in my kitchen?'

'Yes,' she said cheerily.

Anjali was a very beautiful woman. More than that, she had *isvaryam*, lustre. Her voice was a soothing, mellow contralto, whisper-soft, and she had a light, tinkling laughter. Perfect aural eroticism, he thought. In the kitchen she stood very close to Zeruba, almost touching him, as they waited for the water to boil. He could hardly breathe. *This is all wrong,* he said to himself. *She's just a slip of a girl, young enough to be my daughter. I should not allow myself to be distracted.*

'You're a very orderly person,' she said, looking around the kitchen.

'I am.'

'You do all your meals yourself?'

'A cook prepares my lunch. I make breakfast myself. I don't eat dinner.'

'So you lead a self-sufficient life?'

'Sort of.'

4

Back in the drawing room, Anjali sat on the divan, leaning snugly against bolsters, her feet tucked up sideways. Zeruba sat on a chair to her left.

'Shall we?' she asked, taking out a micro tape recorder from her handbag and placing it on the low teapoy between them.

'Fire away,' he said.

'Let's just talk,' she said. 'I don't want to do a formal interview.'

'Fine.'

'Tell me why you chucked science for art.'

'This is more me,' he said. 'I didn't have it in me to be a good scientist.'

'But you've it in you to be a good artist?'

'I don't know. All I can say is that I feel better at this than at science.'

'What does it take to be a good artist?'

'The ability to see what others don't see, the miraculous in the ordinary,' he said. 'And to transform the ordinary into the miraculous. It requires sensitivity and imagination, skill and discipline.'

'And you have them?'

'I'm trying my damnedest to acquire them.'

And so it went. She was a good interviewer, unobtrusive, letting him do the talking, only occasionally throwing a question or seeking some clarification. He liked talking to her.

'What's your creative impulse?' she asked. 'Why do you paint?'

'I don't know,' he said. 'It's my nature, I suppose. Why does the wind blow?'

'They say art is therapeutic—is that how you see it?'

'Yes, of course,' he said. 'Art is a good means to make one pure by purging oneself of the toxins of life.'

That was one of his favourite made-up sayings and it had never before failed to impress journalists. But Anjali laughed. 'Wow!' she said.

'You're making fun of me, are you?' he growled. But she could see from the smile puckering at the corners of his mouth that he was not offended, but just playing along.

'Cut the bull,' she said.

'I'm serious, Anjali,' he said. 'I would be a vicious or miserable creature if I didn't paint.'

'And you're a virtuous and happy person because you paint?'

'My work is a good substitute for happiness.'

'A good enough substitute?'

'Maybe not,' he said. 'But this is what I have, and I have to make do with it.'

'So we see your psyche in your art?'

'Yes. Every painting is a self-portrait, even a landscape.'

'It's rather exhibitionistic, isn't it?' she asked.

All art, like all creative writing, involves self-exposure, he said. But it's also a sharing. And if the artist is any good, his experience becomes the experience of the viewer and enhances his life.

'But this can't be true of abstract art, can it?' she asked. 'How can abstract art be life-enhancing when it says nothing about life?' Of course it enhances life, he said. But its effect is subtle, like that of music. 'It doesn't make sense to most people,' she objected. It doesn't have to make sense to work its magic on you, he said. A symphony doesn't make sense. 'I prefer realistic art,' she said. There's no such thing as realistic art, he said. Nor any realistic literature. No artist, as Nietzsche says, tolerates reality. The artist doesn't hold a mirror to life—he transfigures life. 'In any case, what do you mean by reality?' he asked.

'What I can see with my eyes,' she said.

'But what you see, what you take as reality, is actually a mirage, just images created in the brain by neural activity,' he contended. 'The eye looks, the brain sees. It's all virtual reality.'

'So you look within yourself to find truth, as the sages say?'

'That too is an illusion. Whether your eyes are turned inward or outward, your vision is always distorted. You can never see or know anything as it really is.'

'I can see you clearly. I can describe you clearly.'

'The person you think you see is a phantom that you yourself have created. It isn't really me,' Zeruba said. 'You see, Anjali, the image that you're forming of me now, and how I'll be presented in your article, depend as much on what you are as on what I am. Every image is crafted in the mind, and it will be re-crafted every time you summon it from memory, re-imaged according to your prevailing mood and environment. Your image of me will change between now and the time you write this story. And, of course, your readers will reconstruct it in their own minds, each reader a separate image.'

'You a Vedantist?' she asked.

'Sort of,' he said.

'What do you mean?'

'I'm more inclined towards the Buddhist view,' he said. The temporal world exists. The individual exists. But we can never have an objective and true perception of the world or of any individual or of anything else in the world, because everything in the world is a compound of different elements, and these elements are ever in flux and are continually reconfiguring. Neither the object observed, nor the subject observing, is the same from moment to moment. Nothing can be pinned down, even for a millisecond.

'You look the same to me as you did a minute ago,' Anjali laughed.

'That's an illusion,' he said. 'The stable world and the continuity of individuality that we see around us is something we create out of memory and imagination. The world we see ceases to exist at the very moment of our seeing it. And since each individual constructs the world in his mind according to his disposition, what we have is not a single, common reality, but multiple realities.'

'So we are all creative artists, what? World creators, in fact!'

'Yes, of course.'

'So what distinguishes the artist from the common folk?'

'The intensity of his vision, and his skill to transform that vision into a work of art.'

'Yes, but what makes his vision so intense?'

'His imagination,' he said. 'Intelligence is common, but imagination is rare. It's imagination that makes the artist creative, makes him leap from the edge of the mind into the unknown.'

'And that's what makes artists such crazies?'

'We aren't crazies. We are uncommon people, but we aren't crazies.'

'Maybe not crazies, but artists are generally eccentric, aren't they?'

'That's another way of saying that they are uncommon people.'

'And most of you are loners, aren't you?'

'Not by choice,' he said. 'But loneliness is the usual predicament of the artist. Look at it this way, Anjali. The artist's vision is unique. Another cannot see what he sees. So he is by nature a solitary.'

'But he's human, isn't he? Doesn't he need love and affection and companionship?'

'Alas, yes. You're right,' he said. 'And that's the most terrible thing about his life—he needs others, but he cannot share his life with others.'

5

'What about you, personally?' she asked. 'Don't you feel lonely living here like a hermit?'

'Will you have another cup of tea?' he offered.

'No, it's getting late,' she said. 'You haven't answered my question.'

'Well, I've a fair amount of self-sufficiency.'

'You were married once—what happened?'

'I would rather not talk about it.'

'You like being alone?'

'No, I don't like being alone,' he said. 'It'd be nice to have someone to share my life. But I can manage without it.'

'You have a reputation of being a womanizer—are you?'

'I won't say that. A sensualist, maybe. But I don't think I'm much different from most men in this,' he said. 'The only difference perhaps is that I'm not a hypocrite.'

'Isn't it another way of saying that you aren't ashamed of being a rake?'

'Well, isn't it another way of asking whether I'm not ashamed of being honest?'

'What turns you on sexually?' she asked, her tone casual, her eyes direct, as if she was asking what his favourite colour was.

'Lustrous eyes. And slender waist. And . . .'

'And?'

He smiled into her eyes. 'You really want to hear this?' he asked.

'Yes. I'm not a prude.'

'And deep, softly rounded navel,' he said.

'Gosh! You do have some weird fetishes, don't you!' she said, involuntarily pulling her sari tighter around her. 'Deep navel!'

'I suppose it reflects my subconscious desire for foetal security in the womb,' he said. This was a thought that occurred to him just then, for his normal image of the deep navel was of an inverted nipple to explore with his tongue.

'People say you're arrogant,' she changed the subject. 'Are you?'

'That's absurd,' he said. 'One can be arrogant only by comparing oneself with others. I don't make such comparisons. I live in a world of my own.'

'That's the ultimate form of arrogance, isn't it? To deny value to everyone else.'

'You're looking at it the wrong way, Anjali,' he said. 'It's true that I take myself out of the context of other people. But I do it humbly, without any feeling of superiority. Or inferiority. It's an acceptance of my solitariness, not a rejection of others. In any case, it's more important for me to be a good artist than to be a good man.'

'No social commitment or concerns?'

'I'm an observer, not a participant.'

'Why should anyone pay any attention to your self-indulgent work?'

'If my work is any good, sooner or later it'll receive public recognition. If it's no good, well, that's life.'

'That sounds fatalistic—are you a fatalist?'

'How can any artist ever be a fatalist?' he asked. 'Every work of art is an expression of hope, that things could be different, better. But, of course, the artist is never satisfied. Dreams never materialize. So there's always an element of despair in him. But it isn't fatalism.'

'When would you finish your sculpture?'

'In a couple of years,' he said. 'I've been at it for over three years now.'

'Isn't the pace of work rather slow?'

'Slow for what?' he asked.

'Hey, don't try to throw me,' she laughed. 'Slow in itself.'

'I suppose it is,' he said. 'Ashok's wife Pratibha says that what I'm doing is like trying to empty the sea with a ladle.'

'That's clever. I haven't met her.'

'What one achieves depends on the circumstances of one's life,' Zeruba said, thinking of the life he had wasted in his conflict with Aditi. 'As they say, a lamp can light up a small room or a big room. A big ship will flounder in a small canal just as a small boat will flounder in a great ocean.'

'Are you a big ship in a small canal, or a small boat in a big ocean?'

'You decide,' he said.

6

It was nearly night by the time Anjali was done.

'May I drop you home?' he asked.

'The company car is waiting at the gate,' she said.

'I didn't see. Hope you got what you wanted.'

'I've got to let it all sink in.'

On the steps of the patio, she turned. 'Well, goodbye,' she said, folding her hands gracefully into a lotus calyx.

'Are you a dancer?' he asked.

'No. Why?'

'Your movements are so like a dancer's.'

'Natural grace.'

'Of course.'

'My mother was a dancer, and I know a little,' she said, and did an *addami*, fluidly sliding her head to the right and the left on a stiffened neck, holding her face straight up frontally.

Zeruba laughed. 'I've always been fascinated by this gesture,' he said. 'What does it mean?'

'It's the opening movement of Bharatanatyam,' she said. 'It denotes affection, love, contentment, adoration, and so on.'

'Well, it has been wonderful meeting you, Anjali,' he said, attempting an *addami* himself.

It was comical. She laughed.

'Mind telling me whom I reminded you of?' she asked.

'Some other time.'

'I know a lot about you,' she teased.

'Really? But I don't know much about myself,' he said. 'So tell me.'

'The next time we meet.'

'Let's do it soon.'

She smiled, but didn't answer. And then she was gone. He didn't hear from her for a week, and her article on him didn't appear in the Sunday edition of her paper either. But later in the week she phoned him.

'Sorry I couldn't write the article,' she said.

'Subject no good?'

'Not that,' she said. 'I need to distance myself from my subject to write. I wasn't able to do that with you.'

'That's a new one,' he laughed. 'I haven't heard this dodge before.'

'It's not a dodge—it's the truth.'

'I would have loved to see what you had to say about me,' he said. 'But I'll survive.'

'I'm sorry I wasted your time.'

'I'm not sorry at all,' he said. 'The time I spent with you is the best time I have had in a very long while.'

'That's a new one,' she said, chuckling. 'I haven't heard this put-on before.'

'No put-on,' he said. 'Honest. Please do come again.'

'We'll see,' she said.

Ranga Rao

1

A fortnight after their first meeting, Anjali and Zeruba met again during an exhibition of his paintings in a city gallery. There she introduced him to her father, Dr Rao, a tall, wiry old man of aristocratic bearing and precise manners, dressed in dhoti, silk kurta and shoulder-cloth, in the traditional Andhra style. A pair of deep vertical creases marked his forehead, and this gave him a scowling, stern appearance, which was reinforced by the relentless look of his eyes as he scrutinized Zeruba intently through thick, horn-rimmed glasses. But his fingers, Zeruba noticed, were delicate and long, rather feminine, with immaculately manicured light pink nails. And his voice was soft. He was, as Zeruba would later discover, actually a gentle and compassionate man, and his look of severity was a mask deliberately put on to conceal his softness of heart and prevent people from exploiting him.

'If you are free this evening . . . I would be delighted . . . if you would drop in at home . . . for drinks,' Rao said to Zeruba. He spoke gravely and with deliberation, dividing and spacing out the sentence into even clauses, carving each word with a mental scalpel.

'My pleasure,' Zeruba said.

'Well then, we will see you in the evening. Six-thirty.'

A while after they left, Anjali phoned Zeruba at the gallery.

'This is the first time that Nana has invited home anyone other than his old friends,' she said. 'So please do come.'

'Of course,' Zeruba said.

'Another thing, Zeruba: please come on time. Nana is particular about punctuality.'

'So am I.'

'You offended?'

'Don't be ridiculous.'

'Alright. See you in the evening. Bye.'

At home, Rao was an altogether different person from the persona he affected in public, and even the furrows on his forehead seemed softer. He was a genial host, and Zeruba was pleased to find him to be a man of wide intellectual interests and liberal views. His wife, Uma, taught English literature in a city college, but her real interest, Zeruba learned, was in nineteenth-century Russian novelists, Tolstoy especially, and this was a passion he shared with her. A gentle, cheerful, plump woman, she had probably been a great beauty in her youth, and had the same eyes as Anjali, with long, curling eyelashes stretching out like awnings under narrow, elegantly arched eyebrows.

The Raos lived in an old but well-maintained colonial style bungalow in central Madras, with a large, spruce garden. The furniture in their drawing room was all very old, antiques in fact, and there were on the walls a couple of original Ravi Varma paintings. Rao was an Andhra Brahmin, whose ancestors had settled in Madras in the eighteenth century, and had over the generations distinguished themselves as professionals, mainly as doctors and lawyers.

'Let's sit out in the garden,' Rao suggested when Zeruba arrived. 'It's more pleasant.'

They sat in reclining cane chairs on the lawn, and were served by a mannerly old servant, a family retainer. Uma and Anjali, to the surprise of Zeruba, joined them for drinks, whisky and soda on ice. Rao was a serious drinker and kept urging Zeruba to keep pace with him, but the women had only one small drink each, which they nursed through the evening, munching pistachio nuts.

Anjali had an elder brother, Prabhakar, the black sheep of the family, who ran a shady finance company. He came in just as Zeruba was leaving, and greeted him with a sour smile that parted his lips but did not light up his eyes. There was something faintly unpleasant about him—his eyes were shifty, his hands clammy, and he moved slyly, like a cat, alert and cautious, but not timid. Zeruba took an instant dislike to him, but otherwise found the Raos very pleasant and congenial company, almost a surrogate family, and he visited them whenever he drove into city, which was now nearly every week, instead of once a month or so, as he used to do previously. Rao no longer practised medicine, so time weighed heavily on him, and he was glad to have Zeruba to talk to.

The Raos were patrons of a major cultural *sabha* in Madras, and Zeruba often accompanied them to classical music and dance performances—there were always four seats reserved for the family in the front row of the *sabha* auditorium, and since Prabhakar never joined them on these occasions, there was always a seat for Zeruba.

'I know nothing about music and dance,' Zeruba confessed on their first day at a concert. 'My enjoyment is entirely on the sensual plane.'

'You're lucky,' Rao said. 'We know a little about these things, so rather than enjoy a performance, we tend to pick flaws in it. The critical eye kills enjoyment.'

It was December, The Season in Madras, the only time of the year when the old rich of the city came alive and were visible in public, women resplendent in heavy Kanchipuram silk saris and diamonds, and men in diaphanous, superfine white muslin dhotis and kurtas. They trooped solemnly to the various *sabhas* in the city in this high winter ritual, as much to enjoy music and dance as to exchange gossip and to look over prospective brides and grooms.

Sometimes, when Rao and Uma had other engagements, Zeruba escorted Anjali to the *sabha*. Afterwards they would have dinner out, and then go to the Marina Beach to sit on the sands for a while, chatting. Anjali was a vegetarian and a light eater, and Zeruba was indifferent to food, so having dinner out was for them more a ritual than a celebration, something to be got over with as a prelude to the pleasurable high point of the evening, the hour or so they spent on the beach.

2

Anjali was a completely open person, with no pretence or deception, and there was an engaging simplicity in everything about her. She was serious yet playful, and had a fine sense of humour. These were qualities that Zeruba cherished, and in no time at all the two of them slid into a relationship of cosy, pleasant intimacy. They had many common interests, particularly in religion and philosophy. Besides, they were both recovering from woeful personal adversities at this time, both their marriages having ended at round the same year, though in entirely different circumstances.

Anjali had coped well with her loss. It cast no shadow on her, and she never talked about it, except once, to tell Zeruba the bare facts about what happened. She had, soon after taking her Masters degree in English literature, married her maternal uncle, Venugopal, though he was some eleven years older than her. Such close consanguineous marriages were common among Telugu Brahmins, but in this case their parents were initially uneasy about the match, as an astrologer had predicted that Anjali would lose her husband shortly after her marriage. But Anjali and Venu had been in love with each other for many years, and they persuaded their parents to agree to the marriage, pointing out that the same astrologer had predicted that Venu would never cross the seas, while in fact he did go to the US for higher studies and had been living there for years. A professor of sociology at the University of Chicago, Venu was particularly scornful of astrology as a medieval superstition.

Anjali joined Venu in Chicago soon after her marriage, and there, encouraged by him, she enrolled for doctoral research at the university, choosing Buddhist influence on classical Sanskrit literature as her subject, and took courses in Pali and Sanskrit in preparation for her work. They also decided to put off starting a family till she finished her studies. During the early months of their marriage there was some niggling, subconscious anxiety in them about the astrological warning, though neither of them ever spoke about it. They were relieved only when two years passed without any mishap, and when yet another year passed, they were certain that the prediction was false. Then, when they were least expecting it, tragedy struck. Venu died in a plane crash early in the fourth year of their marriage.

Anjali then returned home to her parents, and entirely gave up wearing ornaments and make-up. After a year of mourning, Rao tried to persuade her to marry again, but she refused, saying, 'I had married Venu because I loved and admired him. I'll marry again only for love, and only if I find someone whom I can truly admire.'

'Look, Anju, you are now nearing thirty. It'll be more and more difficult to find a suitable match for you from now on,' Rao warned.

'I don't mind remaining a widow all my life,' she said.

Rao then prevailed upon her to take up a job to keep herself occupied, and sent her to Bangalore, thinking that a change of place would be good for her. She worked there for four years, then returned to Madras, and there met Zeruba a few weeks later. It was a providential meeting for both of them. The chemistry between them, despite the great difference in their ages and their widely different lifestyles, was excellent, and they were entirely at ease with each other, as if they had grown up together since childhood. But there was nothing particularly romantic about their relationship—there was no flirtation, no sexual intimacy whatever. They were just good friends. They did hold hands sometimes, but casually. Secure with each other, they didn't feel the need to be demonstrative.

But gradually, over several months, there came about a subtle but discernible change in their relationship. And one summer evening when they were sitting on the veranda steps of his cottage, enjoying the sea breeze, Zeruba asked Anjali, 'Why don't you call me Mama?'

'Why?'

'Don't ask me why,' he said. 'I'm old enough to be your uncle anyway.'

'But my feelings towards you are not that of a niece,' she protested.

He turned to look at her with a scowling grimace, and she impishly grimaced right back at him.

'What'll you call me, then?' he asked.

'What I call you now—Dada. That's what all your friends call you.'

'But you're not like my other friends.'

'So what should I call you?'

'Mama.'

'Tell me what's special about that.'

So he told her about Lakshmi, and when he finished, she turned to him and took his hand in hers. 'I had known about Lakshmi all along, Mama,' she said gravely. 'But I'm glad you told me.'

'Anju . . .' Zeruba started, but he couldn't make himself say what he wanted to say.

'What?'

He looked at her hands. She had smooth and beautifully tapered ivory fingers, with the merest suggestion of creases at the knuckles.

'You have the hands of an angel,' he said.

'Because I'm an angel,' she said laughing. 'But what was it that you really wanted to say?'

'Oh, something you already know.'

'What?'

'That I love you,' he said.

I love you—he felt strange saying that. This was the first time that he had said that to anyone. Anyone at all. Ever.

'I know,' she whispered back, resting her head on his shoulder and nibbling at his neck. 'I love you too. But you know that, don't you?'

And he kissed her for the first time, just a peck on the forehead, cupping her face in his hands.

'You're restoring my life to me, Anju,' he said. 'But I'm also afraid.'

'There's nothing to be afraid of, Mama,' she said. 'We're safe with each other.'

'I'm old enough to be your father, Anju,' he said. 'You're thirty-three, I'm fifty-two.'

'I know, and I like it that way,' she said.

'You're a young woman, and you should enjoy the pleasures of youth,' he said. 'For me, companionship is now the most important thing in a relationship.'

'Companionship is by far the most important thing for me too,' she said.

'What about your parents?' he asked. 'I would hate to hurt them in any way.'

'They would bless me in whatever would bring me fulfilment and happiness.'

'Let's not rush into anything, Anju,' he cautioned. 'What we've between us now is precious and beautiful. It would desolate me if I lose it.'

'How would we lose it? We won't lose it.'

'It might get burnt out in the abrasions of our everyday life together, the wear and tear of marriage,' he said. 'I'm too old for another catastrophe, Anju. I won't be able to survive it.'

'We would never lose what we have,' she assured him. 'But we'll take the next step only when you're absolutely ready for it. There's no rush.'

Anjali was frank with her parents about her growing intimacy with Zeruba. They respected her feelings, but also cautioned her about the perils she faced. 'You know I'm very fond of Zeruba—he's one of the very few truly genuine persons I've known. But you must remember that artists are very difficult persons to live with,' Rao told her.

'But Mama and I are good friends, Nana,' she said. 'We get along very well. There has never been any problem.'

'But the situation will be different when you live together, Anju,' he warned. 'You see, making compromises is the essence of a successful marriage, as of everything else in life. But artists are usually stubborn monomaniacs, so you'll be the one who'll have to make all the compromises.'

'I don't mind making compromises,' Anjali said. 'I'm not an artist.'

'I'm not trying to dissuade you, Anju, but I want to make sure that you realize what you're getting into.'

'Don't worry, Nana. Everything will work out fine.'

'Are you trying to fulfil through him something you miss in your own life?'

'Perhaps. But wouldn't it be wonderful if I can help him to fulfil himself, and I'm able to fulfil myself through him!'

Anjali was clear-headed about what she wanted and what she should do. But Zeruba was assailed by uncertainties.

'What troubles you, Mama?' she asked him one day, seeing him moody.

'I'm worried about where this relationship is going to take us,' he said.

'Wherever you want it to take us,' she said. 'I'll go with whatever you decide.'

'You know how I feel about you, Anju. There is no uncertainty or hesitation there,' he told her. 'But I'm afraid that something might happen between us and I might lose you. And if that is to happen, I would prefer it to happen now, so I would have time to recover.'

'You won't lose me, Mama,' she said. 'I'll never betray you or forsake you.'

'There can be no absolute certainty about anything in life, Anju,' he said. 'Especially in human relationships. We think we know each other well, but do we? The man you imagine you love isn't the real me, Anju. Another person will see me differently, and you yourself will see me differently in another time. Even our direct communication is fraught with hazards. When I put my feelings in words, they come out differently, and you hear and understand them yet more differently. And what I want to do comes out a little different in the process of doing it, and you perceive it yet more differently.' Every word spoken, every action performed, involves a risk of missing its intent. Nothing comes out right. Nothing will ever come out right. And everything is transient. Nothing lasts.

'True,' she said. 'But are we then to do nothing at all? Retreat into ourselves? Not have any linkages with other people? Renounce all experience? Not enjoy the passing moment, for fear that it'll not last?'

Zeruba had no answer.

'I think you're inhibited by your past experience,' she said. 'The future might be entirely different, though we can't be certain.'

'There's something else.'

'What?'

'I've often felt that everything I've done in life other than my work has been a waste of time. Socializing, entertainment, sex— they've all been causes of regrets. The pleasures were momentary, the regrets are permanent.'

'What're you saying, Mama?'

'I mean, my work will always have primacy over everything else in my life,' he said. 'Even over you.'

'I'll have it no other way,' Anjali said.

'I don't want you to regret it later, Anju,' he said. 'So take

267

time and think it over deliberately.'

'I haven't decided this on impulse, Mama,' she said. 'I've thought and thought about it for months. About what it would mean to you and what it would mean to me. So I'm absolutely clear in my mind about this. But if you have any doubts, any doubts at all, we will break clean and never see each other again. Is that what you want?'

They were on the Marina Beach. People were milling all around them, children playing tag and kicking sand into the wind. She sat cross-legged to his side, calm and relaxed, while he reclined on his elbows, his eyes closed, trying to harness his thoughts.

'Look, Anju, this is the most important decision in our lives,' he said. 'So I think we should now pull back from each other a little before we make a final decision.'

'As you wish,' she said. 'You're under absolutely no obligation to me, Mama. You can make your decision in complete freedom. I value our relationship greatly. But if you have the slightest doubt about this, then there is no relationship, and it's better for us to break clean.'

'Let's give ourselves a couple of weeks,' he said.

'Fine,' she said.

4

Two weeks, he said to himself when he went to bed that night; *I'll put this matter out of my mind for two weeks.* But the very next morning, without any conscious deliberation, he woke up with absolute clarity in his mind about what he should do.

Zeruba, despite his saturnine pose, was really a dreamer. He had not, however, ever dared to trust his dreams. But that morning, as he lay in bed looking out through the window at the lambent predawn vista spread out before him, he felt certain that his fears were groundless. *Anju might be young enough to be my daughter*, he said to himself, *but she's mature enough to be my mother. I'll be safe in her care.*

He lay awake in bed for a long time that morning, savouring the epiphanic moment. Then he put the matter aside, and worked for a while on his sculpture. Now that everything was clear and everything was decided, there was no hurry to do anything. So it was only in the afternoon, after he woke up from his nap, that he phoned Anjali at her newspaper office.

'Anju, can I see you today?'

'Of course.'

'I'll pick you up at your office. We'll go some place. I've to talk to you.'

'Why don't I come to the cottage, Mama?' she asked. 'You can drop me back.'

'But how will you come?'

'Ashok is in the office. I'll take a lift in his car.'

'Okay, then,' he said. 'And Anju . . .'

'Don't say anything now, Mama. Please.'

'Okay,' he said. 'When will you come? Around six?'

'Before that, I think. I'll bring you some snacks. What'll you have?'

'Paruppu-vadai with mint chutney,' he said, knowing that this was her favourite savoury.

'For me or for you?' she laughed.

On the way, Ashok asked Anjali, 'What's the codger up to?'

'How do I know?' she said. 'Ask the codger.'

'I'm an investigative reporter,' he teased. 'I'll investigate.'

'Fine. Investigate.'

'You're tense. What's up?'

'Something,' she said.

When he dropped her at Zeruba's gate, he asked, 'Can the investigative reporter come in to investigate?'

'Scoot,' she said, waving him off.

Meanwhile, in the cottage, Zeruba had solemnly set the stage for the planned ceremony. He had, soon after phoning Anjali, gone to Adyar and bought two large jasmine garlands. Returning

269

to the cottage, he poured some coconut oil into the top tray of the waist-high antique bell-metal oil lamp that stood in a corner of his drawing-room, put a wick in it and placed it in the middle of the room. He then took a bath, changed into fresh clothes, and when he heard Ashok's car stop at the gate, lit the lamp, and waited for Anjali on the patio steps. She looked at him anxiously, but he took her hand without a word and led her into the drawing room, made her stand before the lamp, facing east, and gave her a garland.

'This is your *svayamvaram*, Anju,' he said. 'Make your choice.'

'You sure you want to do this?'

'Absolutely,' he said.

And so, with only the lighted lamp as witness, they exchanged the nuptial garlands.

'You may kiss the bride now,' Anjali said.

He kissed her forehead, then both her eyes lingeringly, and finally her tremulous lips. Later they sat on the veranda steps for a long time, with their arms around each other, talking. They decided that there was no need for any public ceremony or reception to mark their marriage. There were no legal steps to be taken either, no registration of the marriage, as Zeruba had not yet obtained a formal divorce from Aditi. Anjali said she would move in with him on an auspicious day, in consultation with her father.

'I've to phone and tell my parents now,' she said.

'They're happy,' she said returning to the veranda after the call. 'Nana says that the time we exchanged garlands was auspicious. He wants us to go home now.'

5

In Rao's house, they were received by her parents ceremonially, with *aarati*. They were then taken into separate bedrooms, to bathe and change. There was a new set of clothes for Zeruba on the bed, a *zari* bordered dhoti and upper cloth, and Rao told him to wear these after having a bath. When he was ready, Rao took him to the drawing room, where a sacred fire had been meanwhile set up, with their family priest in attendance. Anjali, wearing an antique diamond necklace, a family heirloom, and looking gift-wrapped in a cobalt-blue silk sari, was now brought out by her mother, and the couple went through a proper ritualistic Hindu marriage. No one except Rao and Uma were present at the ceremony, not even Prabhakar.

'Now that this is over, I want to tell you something truly marvellous,' Rao said after the ceremony, making the couple sit side by side on a sofa and handing to Anjali an yellowed piece of paper, its corners daubed with turmeric. 'When Anju was born, her horoscope was cast by our old family astrologer. He was a man of great learning and intuitive power, and these are his predictions. As you will see, this second marriage was destined. It has even been foretold who the groom would be, what would be his age, religion and language, and in which year and under what stars this marriage would take place. And since all his predictions have so far come true, I am confident that the further predictions will also come true. You have a very bright and happy future together.'

Anjali started crying. 'It's good that you should cry now,' Rao told her, 'for in future you'll have no occasion to cry.' Then he turned to Zeruba. 'I know you have had an unhappy life. But that's now behind you. I say this not because you've married my daughter—it has been predicted so. Fame and fortune will now come seeking you.'

'I don't know about fame and fortune,' Zeruba said. 'But I'm certain of happiness with Anju.'

Zeruba had always assumed that happiness, or even peace of mind, was not fated for him, and that it was his karma to suffer and create. He had even believed that it was good for him to suffer. There had to be some discontent in one, some hollow within oneself, for one to be creative, he had held, for the contented person would have no need to look beyond the life he had, and would have no need to create. He was wrong, of course. One didn't have to be in torment to be creative. Indeed, the happy man would have freer imagination, not being oppressed by his own anguish. Then painting, instead of being a means to escape from pain, would be the play of imagination delighting in itself. Zeruba now entered the most creative phase of his life. The brooding pessimism about life that had oppressed him for long now lifted. He felt cheerful, sprightly. The bells he had heard tolling for him now receded. Yes, he thought, Tolstoy is right: love hinders death.

'I had once thought that as an artist I should isolate myself from the world,' Zeruba one day told Anjali. 'I was wrong. It's one's integration with one's fellow beings that energizes true creativity. In isolation one desiccates.'

As Zeruba's attitude towards the world changed, the world's attitude towards him changed too. He was now generally received with warmth and affection by people, and he felt good about it. Even his physiognomy changed, and he gained a mellow look. 'The cosmic forces are working on you,' Ashok mocked.

6

Anjali moved into Zeruba's cottage three weeks after their marriage.

'Amma says that on the first three nights we shouldn't make love,' she said when they were retiring to bed that night.

'That's an old custom, Anju,' Zeruba said. 'Its purpose was to enable the couple to get to know each other before sexual intimacy. It doesn't apply to us.'

'I would rather . . .'

'Of course, Anju. We will respect her wishes,' he said. 'There's no rush. We've very many nights ahead.'

On the fourth night, when they were getting ready to go to

bed, a thunderstorm auspiciously broke over the land, and it was in the light of a flickering candle on the floor that they made love for the first time. For all his varied experiences with women, exploring Anjali's body was for Zeruba an odyssey of discovery. Her complexion was like old ivory soaked in honey, her skin so clear and soft that it seemed translucent. She was slender and wasp-waisted, her breasts modest but firm and beautifully proportioned, her mouth small, with soft, dewy lips. And Zeruba, for the first time very many years after Lakshmi left him, truly enjoyed making love that night, and was suffused with a warm feeling of total well-being, not just physical pleasure. Anjali was exquisitely responsive to him, not savagely like Aditi, but with ardour, moaning softly.

Later, after their unhurried lovemaking, as Anjali lay snuggling against him with her head on his chest, she lifted her face to look into his eyes.

'Mama,' she called.

'Yes, Anju?'

'Is there a third in bed with us, Mama?'

'No,' he said. 'Absolutely not. There'll never be a third.'

She then heaved herself over to nuzzle him, her lips hovering flutteringly over his lips, barely touching, teasing him happily. She liked playing sexual games with him, and often pressed herself against him tauntingly to feel his stiffness.

'Just checking,' she would say, pleased with his instant arousal.

Anjali took a month's leave after her marriage, but resigned her job after that.

'Wouldn't you get bored here?' Zeruba asked.

'With an octagonal husband like you?' she laughed. 'My hands will be full.'

'You shouldn't feel that you've wasted your life.'

'There is nothing that I want to do more than just be with you, Mama, and look after you.'

'But I'll be busy with myself most of the time. You might feel neglected.'

'I'll just sit around watching you work,' she said. 'And I would read. Maybe I would write. I had at one time wanted to write a biography of Buddha. Maybe that's what I'll do.'

'Excellent,' Zeruba said. 'Is there enough material on his life?'

'Plenty,' she said. 'But I'm thinking of an imaginative re-creation, stretching facts to fill the gaps.'

'Wonderful,' he said. 'I'm an admirer of Buddha myself. I know something of his philosophy.'

'Don't I know that!' Anjali laughed. 'How you lectured me on it the first day we met!'

'Yes, I remember,' he said. 'Why didn't you stop me, you wretch?'

'I didn't want to spoil your fun,' she said. 'I was your captive audience.'

So they bought a computer and set it up in the studio, and she worked on her book when he painted, or sat under the tree and read when he sculpted.

7

Zeruba's life at last settled to an even keel. He no longer roused himself compulsively at four a.m., but got up whenever he woke up, letting his body set its own pace. He felt relaxed, contented. *This is my life now*, he mused. *There will be no further changes. A wife, the sages say, is half the man, and it's only in concert with her that he can achieve the three goals of life—dharma, artha and kama—and fulfil himself as a human being. No man by himself can do this. That'd be like a single hand trying to clap.*

One day, a couple of weeks after Anjali moved in with Zeruba, Aditi breezed into the cottage, having heard about Zeruba's marriage through her grapevine network.

'So you're his new mistress!' she said to Anjali, laughing.

Anjali flushed, then smiled.

'Yes, I am,' she said. 'And whose mistress are you?'

'Who do you think you're talking to?' Aditi flared up, taking a couple of threatening steps towards Anjali.

'I don't know,' Anjali said sweetly, standing her ground. 'That's why I'm asking whose mistress you are.'

Aditi reddened. She was going to make a scene, Zeruba feared. But instead of erupting, she sank into a chair and buried her head in her hands, sobbing. Anjali went to her.

'I'm sorry,' Anjali said. 'I didn't mean to hurt you.'

'Yes, you did,' Aditi said into her palm. 'But I deserve the insult. I've done so many foolish things in life.'

After a while Aditi composed herself, and the three of them sat chatting for some time. When she left, Zeruba walked her to the car.

'I've come to say goodbye,' she said, starting the car.

'Where're you going?'

'My uncle passed away last week, and my sister wants me to go and live with her in Rajakottai. I'm leaving tomorrow. You'll be at last rid of me. We'll not see each other again in this life.'

Suddenly Zeruba was awash with tenderness, with pity for himself and for her, their wasted lives.

'I'm sorry that things did not work out for us,' he said, touching her hand on the car window.

'I'm sorry too,' she said. 'We could've had a beautiful life. But it's too late to think about it now.'

'I'm sorry.'

'It's alright,' she said. 'I'm not angry with you. It was all my fault. But I couldn't help being the way I was. There were awful disturbances in my childhood of which you know nothing. But it's alright now. I'm finally at peace with myself.'

'Let's keep in touch,' he said.

'Maybe. Maybe not,' she said. 'Well, goodbye.'

She engaged the clutch and let the car roll. She did not wave or look back.

8

A few days later, Lakshmi, who had heard about Anjali from her relatives in the slum—many of whom she was helping financially—also came visiting. Zeruba was not at home this time.

'I recognize you by your eyes,' Anjali said, greeting her. 'Mama has told me everything about you.'

'Yes, we were lovers once,' Lakshmi said with a contented sigh. 'It was something very beautiful, so don't expect me to feel ashamed or guilty about it.'

'Of course not,' Anjali said. 'I've no resentment about it at all.'

Lakshmi seated herself on the divan carefully. She had put on quite a lot of weight lately and suffered from arthritis. She was a grandmother now. Gopal, her husband, had died a few years back, and her son, Santosh, a brilliant engineer, now ran the family business, which had, over some twenty years, grown from a small workshop into a well-established factory.

'Those were the happiest years of my life,' Lakshmi reminisced about her life with Zeruba. 'But then I've been very happy with my husband too. And now I'm happy with my children and my grandchildren.'

'You've been very lucky,' Anjali said.

'Mama had told me that our happiness is entirely in our own hands, and is not dependent on others,' Lakshmi said. 'Happiness is not in what happens in our lives, but in what we make of what happens. We cannot control events, but we can control our responses to them. The choice is ours. I could have been devastated by my separation from Mama, or by the endless financial hassles in the initial stages of setting up our business, or during the long and painful illness of my husband. But I chose to be contented with whatever fate brought me. I chose to be happy.'

'But Mama himself chose to be unhappy,' Anjali said.

'Yes, he was never entirely at peace with himself,' Lakshmi said. 'Maybe because of his artistic temperament.'

'You've known him for so long—has he never been really happy?' Anjali asked.

'I don't know,' Lakshmi said. 'Difficult to say. There was always an undercurrent of something dark in him. But I think that in the years I was with him, he was relatively at peace with himself. Perhaps even a little happy.'

'Then there was his disastrous marriage.'

'Yes. It was heartbreaking to see what they were doing to each other,' Lakshmi said. 'In their different ways they were both good people, but they were absolute poison to each other.'

'I think Aditi was more at fault,' Anjali said. 'But then, my view is biased.'

'So is mine,' Lakshmi said. 'But I'm trying to see them as others saw them.'

They sat abstracted for a while.

'Mama has been hurt badly in life, and he has not been able to forget those hurts,' Lakshmi said. 'This is his problem. Only love can heal him. We all need love to survive, Anjali, just as our bodies need food. And now that he is getting old, he also needs someone to take care of him.'

'I'll take good care of him,' Anjali said firmly.

'I hope you'll do more than that,' Lakshmi said, her eyes suddenly moist and her voice aquiver. 'I hope you'll give him happiness. Everyone deserves a little happiness in life.'

'I'll do nothing, absolutely nothing, to hurt him ever.'

'That's not enough, Anjali,' Lakshmi said. 'You should make him happy with you. You should anticipate his desires and fulfil them before the desires turn into discontent.'

'Of course,' Anjali said. 'But his primary devotion is to his work, and he'll be happy only if he's happy with his work.'

'They go together, Anjali,' Lakshmi said. 'He'll be happy with you only if he's happy with his work, and he'll be happy with his work only if he's happy with you.'

'That's how it's working out, I think,' Anjali said. 'He's doing excellent work now, and I think he's happy with me.'

'How about you?'

'This is my life. I wouldn't have it any other way.'

'Look, Anjali, I'm old enough to be your mother, so don't be offended if I presume to advise you.'

'Of course not,' Anjali said.

'It's important that you should be contented in yourself, Anjali,' Lakshmi said. 'If you're discontented, everything will be ruined. There's a certain fatality in all our lives. We've to make do with what we have. Don't expect everything to be rosy.'

'No, I don't expect everything to be rosy.'

'Shadows fall into the life of even the luckiest of us,' said Lakshmi. 'Maybe they are even necessary for us to really enjoy our good fortune. That's what Mama used to say—if we don't have shadows, who'll see the light?'

'I can see why Mama was so much in love with you. You're so wise.'

'Wise?' Lakshmi shook her head. 'I know only what life has taught me.'

'Tell me how things are with you now,' Anjali asked. 'How's you son? Santosh, no?'

'He never comes here anymore,' Lakshmi said sadly. 'He knows that what we're today is entirely because of Mama's help. But he doesn't want to be reminded of it.'

'That's alright,' Anjali said. 'Why should anyone remain tied to the past?'

'But I'm tied to the past,' Lakshmi said. 'There is not a day, not a single day, when I don't think about Mama and pray for his happiness.'

'With you it's different,' Anjali said. 'It was a direct experience for you. For him it's only something he has been told about. He cannot possibly be sentimental about it.'

'Santosh is a good boy, and he isn't ungrateful.'

'I'm sure,' Anjali said.

When Zeruba returned to the cottage, Anjali told him about Lakshmi's visit.

'You were really happy with her, weren't you?' she asked.

He frowned, trying to focus his mind on the fugitive memory. 'I was, I think. But it was so long ago that it's difficult for me to recall its flavour now,' he said, folding her in his arms. 'But it doesn't matter. I don't have to live on memories anymore, Anju. The happiness I now have is real, and that's the only thing that matters.'

Saumya

1

In 1993, ten years after she left for the US, Saumya returned home for the first time. She had by then become almost a stranger to her parents, having steadily distanced herself from them over the years. She phoned them fairly regularly, but her tone was usually aloof, at times even a trifle hostile. Zeruba was puzzled and hurt by this. Even though this attitude of emotional detachment from her parents was precisely what he had hoped that she would develop in the US—to avoid getting sucked into the vortex at home—it was hard for him to face its reality. But he kept his feelings to himself, and took care not to give her any hint of what he felt.

What Zeruba did not know was that the change in Saumya's attitude was a direct consequence of the estrangement between him and Aditi—the crisis at home, as Mathangi foresaw, had reached across the continents to traumatize her. For quite a while he was not even aware that she knew that Aditi and he had separated—he had not told her about it, and he assumed that Aditi had not told her either. In the beginning, when he phoned her, he tried to give excuses for Aditi not being at home, but one day she said, 'Look, Appa, you don't have to cover up for Amma. I know that you are separated.'

'You do? How did you know?'

'Amma had written to me.'

'When?'

'Oh, quite sometime back. But please don't tell her that I told you this, because she had asked me not to tell you.'

'And she had made me swear not to breathe a word about the separation to you!'

'Please don't make an issue of this.'

'Of course not,' he said. 'I presume she has written to you her version of what happened. I'm not going to dispute that. But do keep in mind that what you've been told might not be the whole truth. Might not be the truth at all.'

'I know,' she said.

'Be open with me if you want to ask me anything,' he said. 'Don't distance yourself. Treat me as a friend.'

'Look, Appa, I've plenty of friends,' she said. 'What I need in you is a father.'

'Alright,' he said, taken aback by her cutting tone.

'I'm sorry, I didn't mean to put it that way,' she said contritely. 'You know I love you.'

'I'm not upset,' he said.

But he was. He was certain that Aditi would have told her all sorts of lies about him, and that was estranging Saumya from him. Yet he decided against telling her his side of the story, fearing that it would only make matters worse by making her a direct participant in the marital wrangle. He was, however, anxious, for her sake and for his sake too, that she should visit him early, so that they could open up to each other and clear the air. Also, she could then see for herself, instead of imagining the worst, that the separation of her parents was a bloodless operation, and that they were both doing fine independently. But he did not want to press her on this, and only once, some three years after she left, did he ask her about when she planned to visit Madras. Her reply was evasive.

'Let me first get somewhere with my studies, Appa,' she said.

'When, then?'

'Give me a couple of years more. I want you to be proud of me.'

'I'm proud of you now. Have always been.'

'That's sentiment. I'm talking about real achievement.'

'You decide,' he said.

'I'll come as soon as I can.'

But another seven years passed before she finally made it to India. She, however, did brilliantly in college, and graduated summa cum laude. Her interest had meanwhile shifted from astrophysics to neuroscience, and it was in this field that she took her Masters and PhD degrees. She then joined Yale University for post-doctoral research. There she met Dr Martand Singh, a medical researcher at the university working on *in vitro* organogenesis, and moved in with him, and it was with him in tow that she arrived in Madras.

2

Anjali and Zeruba met them at the Madras airport. Saumya, twenty-six years old now, was the spitting image of her mother at that age, though she looked somewhat taller, dressed in salwar-kameez. Martand Singh—Marty, as he was introduced—was a Sikh by birth, but was clean-shaven and short-haired, and wore no turban. A strapping young man, well over six feet tall and robustly built, he beamed at Zeruba and Anjali with open pleasure, and was entirely relaxed and spontaneous with them. But Saumya seemed tense, though Anjali tried to put her at ease by chatting with her as with an old friend.

'So you're into cloning?' Zeruba asked Marty as they were driving towards the cottage.

'Not really,' he said. 'Our project is to develop human organs as spare body parts, from precursor tissues.'

'I thought you did it with stem cells removed from embryos.'

'No, there're legal restrictions on it in the US.'

'Is there any work done on cloning people?'

'No. That's illegal,' Marty said. 'Actually, I'm not all that hot on cloning.'

'Why?' Anjali asked. 'It would be nice if we can create a whole lot of Einsteins and Leonardo da Vincis, wouldn't it?'

'Genetic identity doesn't mean identity of character or skills or achievements,' Marty said.

'Why not?' Zeruba asked. 'Identical chemical substances will behave in an identical manner.'

'Yes, but only in an identical environment,' Marty said. 'And since we won't be able to replicate the exact circumstances in which Einstein lived—the material, social, familial and cultural circumstances—we'll never be able make another human being exactly like Einstein. An identical genetic entity, yes, but not an identical man.'

'So what's exciting in your field?' Zeruba asked.

'What's really exciting is the prospect of improving our species through genetic engineering,' Marty said.

'Stop the lecture, Marty,' Saumya said.

'Good to hear your voice at last, Saumya,' Zeruba said.

'I'm very tired, Appa,' she said. 'Didn't get a wink of sleep on the plane.' As a child, Saumya had been quiet, and now she had become a grave young woman.

'You were saying?' Anjali prodded Marty.

'Cloning can only duplicate what already exists, but we can improve our species through genetic engineering,' said Marty. 'You know, in the last five million years or so since hominids separated from apes, our DNA has evolved less than two per cent. But now we can ourselves alter the DNA, and alter it precisely as we want, instead of depending on haphazard, unpredictable, and millennially slow evolutionary process.'

'Play god?' Zeruba asked.

'Why not, if we can by that improve the health and intelligence and well-being of man?' Marty rejoined. 'But it'll be a long, long time before we're allowed to do that kind of research. Even as it is, all sorts of people are up in arms against what we're doing.'

'The Bible Belt?'

'Not just them. There's a general anxiety among common

283

people about what they call tampering with nature. That's ridiculous. Man has been tampering with nature for thousands of years. The stone-age man who used tools, instead of his teeth and claws, was tampering with nature. And so is the man who ploughs the field. Taking any kind of medical treatment is tampering with nature. Cross-breeding animals or grafting plants is tampering with nature.'

'Absolutely,' Zeruba agreed. 'We are interfering with god's work when we trim our hair, shave our beard or pair our nails. Or wear clothes.'

'Yes,' Marty said. 'I don't see why genetic engineering of man should be considered any different from the genetic engineering of animals or plants. Aren't they all god's creations?'

'You see, ours is a homocentric view of nature,' Zeruba said. 'That's why we consider only the killing of man as murder. The killing of insects we don't even think of as killing. But if you look at all this from nature's or god's point of view, there's really no difference.'

'I think that the objection to tampering with nature is just a pretext,' Marty said. 'What's really involved is intellectual timidity. Fear of the unknown. This is something that has always been there. Would you believe it, a treatise on public health published in Germany in the eighteenth century—1795, I think— had warned people that excessive reading caused arthritis, asthma, indigestion, and so on, even epilepsy!'

'Really?'

'Yes. And people were warned not to read immediately after eating, and to read only when standing up.'

'But isn't there a danger in genetic engineering?' Anjali asked. 'We might end up creating monsters.'

'It's all a matter of perspective,' Marty said. 'Apes probably consider men as monsters. What you'd call monster is what I'd call superman. It took billions of years for the earliest, single-celled life forms to evolve into man, but from man to superman it would be but one short step, taken in just a couple of centuries.'

'He thinks he's already a superman,' Saumya said.

'I am! I am!' Marty laughed.

'And you are a supergirl,' Anjali said to Saumya.

'She is! She is!' said Marty, cuddling Saumya. 'My very own supergirl.'

'What exactly is your field of research, Saumya?' Anjali asked. 'I know that your general field is neuroscience, but what's your special work?'

'I work on certain functions of the hypothalamus.'

'The supervisor brain!'

'Yes,' Saumya said, surprised. 'Are you a biologist?'

'Afraid not,' Anjali said. 'I'm a student of literature.'

'Anju's father is a neurosurgeon,' said Zeruba.

'I would love to meet him,' Marty said.

'And wouldn't he love to meet you!' Anjali laughed. 'He loves chatting with bright young people.'

'It's wonderful that you both are at the very cutting edge of science,' Zeruba said.

'And you're at the cutting edge of art, Appa,' Marty said. 'We went and saw your sculpture in Bombay. We had a few hours between flights.'

'It's beautifully presented, Appa, in a rolling parkland, with a sweeping view from all sides,' Saumya said. 'We were there at noon in the blazing sun, but there were still some people going around it.'

'Probably lechers looking for what the morons call pornographic figures,' Zeruba scoffed.

He had sold the sculpture five years earlier through Mathangi to a newly risen industrial conglomerate for fifty-four lakh rupees—one lakh for each year of Zeruba's life—and it had immediately set off a controversy, which had not yet died down.

'No, they were discussing it seriously,' Saumya said.

'I don't know much about art,' Marty said. 'But the idea you have presented there fascinates me—that there are many versions of reality, all equally real or equally illusory.'

'He's stealing my words, Appa,' Saumya said, stabbing Marty sharply in the ribs with her elbow. He cried out in mock pain. They were kids having fun. Wonderful, thought Zeruba.

'It's an old Indian mystic concept,' Zeruba said.

'But it agrees with some of our latest scientific theories,' Saumya said. 'In quantum reality, for instance, it's considered plausible that different versions of the same reality can exist simultaneously in other universes existing in other dimensions.'

'The different universes are right here on earth,' Zeruba said. 'Each man is a different universe in himself. And each has a different version of reality.'

3

That night, after Marty had gone to bed soon after dinner—'Got to get my beauty sleep,' he said—Saumya went and sat with Zeruba as he sat smoking a cigarette on the patio.

'You still haven't quit smoking?' she asked.

'Just one a day,' he said. 'I like Marty. He's such a lively and spontaneous person.'

'Yes, he's great fun to be with. But he's also one of the sharpest minds in his field,' she said. 'How's Amma?'

'Doing very well, I'm told,' he said. 'I'm not in contact with her, but Mats says that she's empowering women in Rajakottai, spreading literacy, getting them to ride bicycles, that sort of thing. And she helps people with money and advice. I believe she has quite a few devotees in Rajakottai.'

'Devotees?'

'She's considered to have some sort of spiritual or clairvoyant power.'

'As long as she's happy, it doesn't matter what she does.'

'Of course,' he said.

'How are Uppappa and Ummamma?' she asked about his parents.

'Bad,' he said. 'I was there last year for a couple of days. Amma has slid into total dementia. And Appa has lost all his energy and cheerfulness.'

'Sad.'

'That's life. So what are your plans?'

'We would like to spend a few days with Amma, then a couple of days in Azhiyur—'

'That's not what I meant. What about you and Marty?'

'Marriage is only a formality, Appa,' she said. 'We might go through it sometime. No sweat. But you can introduce us to people here as husband and wife.'

'How long have you been living together?'

'Ever since I joined Yale.'

'Two years?'

'Yes. The funny thing is that after we decided to live together, we didn't talk to each other for a week,' Saumya said, laughing.

'You're joking!'

'Honest.'

'Really? Why?'

'Because we spent that week at a Buddhist retreat in San Diego, where we were required to break off all personal relationships.'

'Good beginning,' Zeruba laughed. 'I hope everything works out well for you.'

'We get along very well,' she said. 'We have the same goals in life and the same lifestyle.'

'The best thing is that you're both self-reliant,' he said. 'You don't have to feed on each other. Ultimately, the quality of our lives depends on ourselves, not on anyone else. If one is lucky, everything works out fine, but invariably there're problems.'

'Of course,' she said. 'One has problems with oneself, so how can one not have problems with other people!'

'That's why it's important that you should set clear goals about what you want to do in life, and not allow yourself to be distracted by what others do,' he said.

'Don't worry, Appa,' she said. 'We're both mature, serious

people. We won't do anything rash or foolish.'

The next day Mathangi, who was distantly related to Anjali, came to see Saumya. Zeruba and Mathangi had not seen each other for quite some years, though they often spoke on the phone. She looked weary, defeated, though she put on a brave front of cheerfulness. She was phasing out her business, and when Zeruba asked her about it, she said, 'Remember I once told you that I'll die lonely and miserable? Well, I'm preparing myself for that finale.' She said this laughing, but the spirit was clearly dying in her.

'Nothing is over till life is over,' he told her.

'Maybe for you,' she said. 'But I'm done with dreams.'

Saumya was thrilled to see Mathangi.

'I still have the teddy bear you gave me as a child,' she said.

'Really?' Mathangi was surprised. 'You took it with you to the US?'

'Of course. It's my security blanket.'

'I've now a present for you that you would value even more.'

'What?'

'Your father's painting. *The Earth Mother*. It's in the van.'

Saumya was touched. 'Why are you so good to me, Aunty?' she asked, hugging her.

'Because you're my child—the child I should've had,' Mathangi said. 'But let's not talk about me. Boring subject. What about you? It's so good to hear that you're doing brilliantly at the varsity. Have you at last found Brahma?'

Saumya laughed, remembering what she had told Mathangi while leaving for the US. 'Yes, indeed. And I've brought him with me,' she said, and dragged Marty out of the bedroom where he was taking a nap, and introduced him to Mathangi. 'This is my Brahma.'

'Hey! Who took my other three heads?' Marty cried, whirling around.

When Mathangi left, they all walked to the gate to see her off. She waved cheerily as she drove off, but Zeruba could see that she was biting her lips to fight back tears.

'So many people are unhappy in so many ways,' Anjali said to Zeruba as they walked back to the cottage.

'Mats certainly deserved to be happy,' Zeruba said. 'She's such a wonderful person.'

'Fate,' Anjali said.

4

When Saumya and Marty returned from Rajakottai, Zeruba took them to Azhiyur. Anjali went with them in the guise of Saumya's friend, as Korah had not been told about Zeruba's second marriage, out of regard for his age and sentiment. Meanwhile, Saumya had shed her reservations about Anjali, seeing her to be a genuine and warm person. They had become friends. And it was Saumya who shielded Anjali from embarrassments in Azhiyur.

'I want to close my eyes seeing you and Aditi living together again happily,' Korah said to Zeruba when they were all sitting in the portico soon after their arrival.

'Don't worry Uppappa,' Saumya said, as Anjali turned pale with mortification. 'They are both happy with their lives. There's no problem at all.'

'Hmm,' said Korah.

Marty and Saumya were then taken to see Zeruba's mother, and they examined her thoroughly with the help of the nurse attending on her, and went through all her medical reports.

'I'm afraid there's nothing we can do about this,' Marty said finally. 'All we can do is to keep her comfortable.'

'It's not life threatening?' Zeruba asked.

'Not in the short term. She doesn't seem to have any serious health problems other than the degeneration of the brain,' Marty said. 'You see, the brain is like any other organ. If you don't exercise it, it atrophies, though of course there are other major causes also.'

Later Zeruba showed Marty and Anjali around the old wing of the house, and then they all had lunch together. Anjali, Saumya and Marty were vegetarians, and the cook had been told about it, so they sat on mats on the floor and had a traditional Kerala vegetarian meal of rice and curry served on plantain leaves, with erusseri, pulisseri, kaalan, olan, thoran and so on as side-dishes, topped off with pazha-pradhaman as dessert. The smell of hot rice and ghee on freshly cut tender plantain leaf brought tears of nostalgia in Zeruba for his lost childhood.

'What's the matter, Mama?' Anjali whispered.

'Steam in my eyes,' he said.

After the meal they all retired for the mandatory afternoon nap, then gathered for tea in the portico. Marty was keenly interested in everything, and wanted to be told all about the family and the strange Syrian Christian community, of which he had never even heard till he met Saumya.

'Saumya tells me that you people were Christians centuries before Europeans became Christians,' he said.

'Well, we were Christians for about two thousand years, right from the very beginning of Christianity,' Mathu said. 'At least such is the legend.'

'How come?'

'St. Thomas, one of the apostles, arrived in Kerala soon after the crucifixion of Christ and converted a few Namboodiri families to Christianity,' said Korah, warming to his favourite subject.

'Who are Namboodiris?' Marty wanted to know.

'The highest caste of Brahmins in Kerala. Ours was one such family that St. Thomas converted. He landed in Kodungalloor, right across the lagoon from here.'

'Just a legend,' Zeruba commented.

'But the legend is entirely plausible,' said Mathu.

'This is a small community, then?' Marty asked.

'There are some five million of us around now,' said Mathu. 'We probably started with maybe forty or fifty families, but we proliferated like weeds.'

'And there would have been conversions,' Anjali said.

'Hardly,' said Mathu. 'We are a non-proselytizing community. There is certain caste exclusivity in us. Family pride. Most major Syrian Christian families are interconnected.'

'It's a devout community?' Anjali asked.

'It varies from family to family,' Mathu said.

'What about your family?'

'Oh no!' Mathu said. 'That's the only idiocy this family is free from.'

5

The next day they visited the famed Krishna temple at the nearby town of Guruvayur, where Anjali, an ardent Vaishnavite, was keen on offering worship. As they were waiting for the tourist taxi they had booked, it began to rain heavily, and in no time at all the air became so swollen with moisture that it seemed it might condense into rain within the house itself.

'Why should you go in this rain?' Korah asked. 'Go tomorrow.'

'Suppose it rains tomorrow also?' Mathu asked. 'And they're leaving the day after.'

Zeruba had, the previous evening, confided in Mathu that Anjali was his wife, and had told him how important the Guruvayur trip was for her.

'It's considered auspicious if it rains when you set out,' said Anjali.

'Indra's blessings,' said Zeruba.

Just then the taxi arrived, and the four of them, along with Mathu, squeezed into it and set out, with the rain pelting on the car like berries.

'Drive carefully,' Mathu told the driver. 'There's no rush.'

Even in the heavy rain there were a good number of people going about in the streets of the town, most men dressed in white shirt and dhoti tucked up to their knees, and women in saris bunched tight and lifted demurely up to their calves, all huddling under huge black umbrellas held low over their heads. Despite the blinding rain, cars, buses and auto-rickshaws tore down the narrow streets furiously, splashing muddy water on pedestrians, who defended themselves by wielding their umbrellas like shields.

'Drive carefully,' Mathu cautioned the driver again.

Out of the town, they drove through a narrow macadamed road slithering like a black snake under a dense, rain-drenched canopy of trees, their leaves glistening like they were oiled and polished. The countryside was suffocatingly lush and everything seemed to be at one and the same time rotting and sprouting and burgeoning frenziedly. The overpowering smell of compost pervaded the air, and the earth itself exuded a pungent odour.

'Kerala has an earth presence like nowhere else in India,' Zeruba told Anjali.

'There's a curious smell in the air,' she said.

'That's the smell of oestrous earth seeking its mate, Anju,' Zeruba said. 'You city people know nothing about it.'

'I know all about it,' Marty said. 'What you smell are the volatile chemical compounds released by streptomycete bacteria. There are about a million of them in a gram of soil, and they release the compounds when rain wets the ground after a long dry spell.'

'Very illuminating!' Saumya scorned. 'You just wrecked Appa's erotic fancy.'

'Tell me, Marty, is there anything you don't know?' Anjali teased.

'I don't know,' Marty said, and everybody had a good laugh over that.

Now they crossed a bridge and entered an island in the broad spread of the lagoon, and stopped at a tollgate. As they drove on, Mathu shook his head and chuckled.

'What?' Zeruba asked.

'I was just thinking how times have changed.'

'What do you mean?'

'This island was once our family property,' Mathu said. 'Now we have to pay toll to drive through it! We used to own several of these islands, some quite small, but others much larger, like this one.'

'How did we lose it?' Saumya asked.

'Well, nearly all the property was lost by my grandfather. My father bought some of it back, but when the communist government in the state introduced land ceiling, we lost a large chunk of it all over again.'

'Weren't you compensated for it?' Anjali asked.

'Yes, we were. Very generously! I think we got about ninety rupees for an acre of prime land, that too after a wait of some nine years. Then another law required us to give one-tenth of an acre to each of the tenants who lived in huts in our properties, so we lost about a third of what little land remained with us. For centuries we had owned a solid chunk of land in these parts, but nearly all of it was gone in just a few decades. We're nothing now.'

'Marx says that he who has nothing is nothing,' said Zeruba.

'So here we are, with our family name as our only asset, and just enough income for subsistence,' said Mathu. 'Till a few decades back, our old serfs in these lands used to come home for Vishu presents and to wail at our funerals. That too stopped after the death of my grandfather. We are relics of another time.'

'The feudal system had to go,' Zeruba said.

'I'm not complaining,' Mathu said sternly. 'But let's not be contemptuous about those days. There was certain expansiveness and grace about the life of those days. It is not even a memory now. My father probably had the last whiff of it in his youth. The last one to enjoy it in its full bloom was my grandfather, that too only in the early part of his life.'

They drove on. The rain had ceased. The road was now flanked by swaying emerald-green paddy fields and ran over countless gurgling streams bridged by culverts. In the distance, blue-grey hills seemed to vaporize into the sky in the early morning light.

'So *this* is god's own country!' Anjali said.

'And every man here thinks he's god,' said Zeruba.

'Actually this is one of the poorest states in India,' said Mathu. 'But it has the highest literacy rate, and a life expectancy similar to that in the US.'

'The people look cheerful and healthy,' Marty said. 'Well-nourished.'

'They thrive on air and sunlight, by photosynthesis,' said Zeruba.

'They thrive on tapioca, fish and toddy,' corrected Mathu. 'The soil here is so fertile that you've just got to scratch the surface for it to yield rich crops.'

'Yes, look at this vegetation,' Zeruba said. 'If you lie down here on the ground for a moment the plants will grow over you and smother you before you can get up!'

'In the backyard of nearly every cottage they grow tapioca,' continued Mathu. 'And fish like mackerel and sardine are cheap and plentiful, and there are toddy shops everywhere. No one dies of starvation in Kerala.'

'*Oru chaya, oru bidi, oru inquilab*—a cup of tea, a bidi, and a revolutionary slogan—that's all that the Malayali needs for his well-being,' Zeruba said.

'I must warn you young women that this is the land of lechers,' said Mathu. 'One of our rajas in the seventeenth century even issued an order permitting any man to kill any woman who refused him kindness.'

'Kindness?' Anjali asked.

'That's how the raja kindly put it.'

'Great,' said Marty. 'I think I'll move in here.'

'This is also the land of crazies,' Zeruba said, as he and Anjali got off the car at Guruvayur to go to the temple for worship. 'Kochappa, please tell them about that weird suicide here.'

Mathu chuckled, and took Saumya and Marty to the celebrated pipal tree near the main entrance of the temple.

'This happened a few years ago,' Mathu said. It was, he told them, a Friday evening, so the place was crowded with devotees, which was the reason why our hero chose that particular day for his bizarre spectacle. And he himself was dressed outlandishly, like a harlequin, with a dunce-cap on his head and a thick marigold garland around his neck. Taking his position under the pipal tree, he began beating the drum he had with him, playing a popular tune with aplomb and finesse. Soon a crowd collected around him, eager for any diversion, and he got them to form a circle around the tree.

'Now I want you all to be absolutely still and silent for a few minutes,' the man told them. 'I'm going to show you a great miracle.'

He then placed the drum on the ground, bowed to the crowd with folded hands in each of the four cardinal directions, and climbed up the tree, slowly and carefully, carrying a small cloth bag. On reaching a high branch of the tree, he took out of the bag a short rope with a noose at one end, shook it free and tied it to the branch, and tested its firmness by tugging it hard a few times. All this he did with calm deliberation—ceremonially, in fact. When everything was arranged to his satisfaction, he once again bowed to the crowd, and asked them to clap, setting the beat himself. And as the clapping reached a crescendo, he put the nose around his neck and plunged from the tree.

'Suicide as theatre!' Marty guffawed.

'Performed to public ovation,' Mathu said.

'And you have a communist government here!'

'Yes. The first-ever democratically elected communist government anywhere in the world.'

'I don't understand how such an oddball, individualistic people can elect totalitarians to rule them.'

'That's part of our craziness,' Mathu said.

6

Saumya and Marty spent five more days with Zeruba after returning from Azhiyur. He offered to take them to see the ancient monuments around Madras, but they said that they would rather stay at home and spend the time with him. The only time they ventured outside the cottage was to visit Anjali's parents, with whom they spent a whole evening.

The day after visiting the Raos, Saumya and Marty left for the Mudumalai wildlife sanctuary, to spend a couple of days there before leaving for the US. On their way to Bombay from Mudumalai, they phoned Zeruba from Bangalore, the two of them together on a speakerphone.

'We have had a most wonderful time,' said Marty.

'I've never been to Mudumalai,' said Zeruba. 'But I'm told it's a great place for holidaying.'

'I was talking about the time we spent with you,' said Marty.

'It was wonderful for us too,' said Zeruba. 'When will you come again?'

'You both come and stay with us for a while, Appa,' Saumya said. 'That would be wonderful for us.'

'I'm too old to hop across continents, Saumya,' Zeruba protested.

'Nonsense,' Marty said. 'You should definitely come. We'll fix up something in a couple of months.'

'We'll see,' said Zeruba.

'Well, goodbye,' Saumya said.

'Goodbye,' he said.

'May I speak to Anju?' she asked.

'She's right here,' he said, and handed the phone to Anjali.

'I'm so relieved, Anju, that you're there to take care of Appa,' Saumya said. 'He has had such a loveless life. I could see that you've brought a little sunshine into his life. That's wonderful.'

'Don't worry about anything,' Anjali said. 'Everything will be just fine.'

'I'm not a demonstrative person,' said Saumya. 'But I love him very much.'

'We know,' Anjali said.

'Goodbye, then.'

'Goodbye.'

They phoned again from Bombay, and again when they reached home in the US. And each time they phoned, Zeruba broke down after the call, sobbing into Anjali's bosom as she held him tight. Rivers that branch seldom meet again, he knew. His family has broken into fragments and scattered. What had he done with his life?

'I'm there for you, Mama,' Anjali said. 'I'll be both wife and daughter to you.'

N e i g h b o u r s

1

A month after Saumya and Marty left for America, Mathu came to live with Zeruba and Anjali. They had talked to him about this when they were in Azhiyur.

'I'm entombed here, my child,' he protested when Anjali tried to persuade him. 'Not even god almighty can resurrect me.'

'Please do think about this, Kochappa,' she said. 'It would mean so much to us.'

So he came, saying that he would stay only for a month. He stayed for nine months. And he fell in love with Anjali.

'If I were forty years younger, I would be desperately in love with you,' he told her when the three of them were sitting at breakfast one day. He was eight-two years old, and Anjali forty. 'In fact, I'm desperately in love with you now.'

Zeruba looked at Anjali. She was beaming happily, basking in Mathu's affection for her.

'Look at Anjali,' Zeruba said to Mathu.

'I'm afraid to look at her,' Mathu said, covering his eyes with his hand and peering at her through his fingers. 'Just kidding, child,' he added.

'Kidding? How you disappoint me now, Kochappa!' she said, trying to dam up her mirth with puckered lips. 'I thought you were serious.'

Mathu settled in Saumya's room comfortably. He had brought with him the old wooden chest of palm-leaf manuscripts, and this he placed at the foot of the bed. And on Saumya's roll-top desk he neatly arranged his personal files and notebooks, as well as his bottle of bell-pins and paperclips, and placed alongside them a large blue-leafed letter-pad with his old Parker pen next to it.

'What do you plan to work on now, Kochappa?' Zeruba asked him.

'Nothing. I'm done with writing,' he said. 'See this bottle. It's full. My life's work is complete.'

'So what're you going to do for the next hundred years?'

'Let me get through this year, then I'll decide.'

'You'll be lost if you don't write.'

'To write one has to burn a little within oneself,' Mathu said. He took off his glasses and examined them carefully, wiped them with delicate distaste with the edge of his kurta, and then put them on again, pressing their bridge against his nose with a twisting motion, as if screwing it into his face. 'The fire in me is dead.'

'You're going to work on the palm-leaves?'

'No,' Mathu said. 'I brought them for you. This is the only remaining legacy of the family. Keep it safe.'

'What do you want me to do with them?'

'I had hoped to transcribe and translate them. But now time has run out for me. See what you can do with them.'

'I'll have to engage some Malayalam pundit for that.'

'You'll find one in Madras.'

'Don't give up writing, Kochappa,' Anjali said.

'What should I write?' Mathu asked. 'I've nothing to write about.'

'Continue whatever you were working on,' Anjali said. 'I believe you were writing a book on the occult practices of Kerala. That would be fascinating. Why not complete it?'

'I gave it up long ago,' he said. 'It was driving me crazy. My last project was to write a pornographic classic.'

'Goodness!'

'Yes,' Mathu continued with a twinkle in his eyes. 'I had titled it *The Pecker's Pick*, and it had Mahalingam as its chief character.'

'Shiva-Shiva!' Anjali said, stopping up her ears.

Mathu laughed. 'Shiva's semen is said to have the fragrance of jasmine—did you know this?' he asked her.

'Never heard such nonsense,' she said.

'Read the Puranas,' Mathu said.

'Anju is a devotee of Vishnu,' said Zeruba. 'So you may say any wicked thing about Shiva.'

'But I've only good things to say about Shiva,' Mathu said gravely.

2

Mathu was something of an authority on Hindu mythology, which he had studied as an extension of his interest in Indian philosophy. He was also a rigorous practitioner of yoga, and even in his eighties spent a full hour every morning practising the asanas. Its health benefits for him were evident for all to see—he radiated energy, and his skin glowed like that of a young man in the full bloom of youth. But he himself considered it essentially as a mental discipline.

'It soothes the mind,' he told Zeruba one day. 'You know, the senses send millions or hundreds of millions of bits of information to the brain every second, and there are some hundred billion or so neurones scrambling to deal with this data blitzkrieg. Hundred billion—that's about twenty times as many neurones inside your head as there are people on earth! You can imagine the frenetic neural activity this involves! Yoga calms this process.'

'But the ultimate goal of yoga is spiritual, isn't it?' Anjali asked.

'Its ultimate goal is for you to achieve stability and serenity as a person,' Mathu said. 'Instead of being a seething victim of the flux of circumstances.'

'It also promotes health,' said Zeruba, himself a yoga enthusiast.

'Yes. And that's very important, because good health is essential for the tranquillity of the mind,' Mathu said. 'You can't have a calm mind in a tortured or sick body. The purpose of the asanas is to achieve the stability of the body, but the purpose of achieving the stability of the body is to achieve the stability of the mind. This is the ultimate goal of yoga. In fact, it is its only goal.'

'Really?' Anjali asked.

'Absolutely. *Yoga is the stilling of the fluctuations of the mind-stuff*—that's what Patanjali states at the very opening of the *Yogasutra*.'

'For most people it's just a set of physical exercises,' Zeruba said.

'Beneficial in itself. So why not?'

The beachside location of Zeruba's cottage was a particular pleasure for Mathu, and the three of them spent long hours on the beach every evening, lounging on the sands and talking. Mathu believed that he had a special relationship with the sea, and in Azhiyur he used to go for a swim in the sea at least once a week, taking a boat from the town to the Vaipeen island on the southern side of the disused Kodungalloor harbour.

'The tides of the sea are one with the flow of my blood,' he once told Zeruba. This was many years ago, in Kerala. They were, after a long swim in the sea, sitting on the sandbar jutting into the harbour, watching the blood of the dying sun redden the sea.

'Nice poetic fancy,' said Zeruba.

'Not fancy at all,' said Mathu. 'That's exactly how I feel in my blood. There is some collective unconscious or racial memory in me of riding the monsoon winds across the Arabian Sea many centuries ago, sniffing the wind for pepper and cinnamon and cloves, and then being shipwrecked and washed ashore here, right here, on a stormy night. I see it in my dreams often. It was to these very coconut palms, or their parents, that I clung as waves rolled over the land. Then the storm subsided, and it was morning, and people from across the harbour came in canoes and carried me to safety. I see it all very vividly in my dream.'

'Freud would have a different interpretation for it,' Zeruba said.

'Maybe,' Mathu said. 'But my own interpretation suits me fine. There is certainly something special between me and the sea.'

'Maybe it's a family trait,' said Zeruba. 'I myself can't think of living anywhere except on the beach.'

In Madras, Mathu went for a swim in the sea every day, after tea in the afternoon. Sometimes Zeruba went with him, if he was not occupied with painting. Anjali would join them on the beach later, and this was the most pleasurable part of the day for them. But time weighed heavily on Mathu the rest of the day, when Anjali and Zeruba were busy at work in the studio. So he started going for long strolls, in the beginning just to have something to do, but later because he found the experience amusing. He usually went early in the morning and was back for breakfast, but sometimes he went in the evening, or, if it was a moonlit night, after dinner, which they usually had around seven. He was gone for hours, just wandering wherever his feet and whim took him, along the beach or through the slums and fishermen's colonies.

'This is life at its irreducible minimum,' Mathu said one day when Anjali asked him how he could bear all that filth and ugliness in the slums. 'Just birth, procreation and death. Nothing non-essential whatever goes on in the slums. None of this nonsense about art and culture.'

3

Everything fascinated Mathu. Often, on returning to the cottage from his roaming, he would regale Anjali and Zeruba with accounts of his experiences. Buffaloes particularly intrigued him. In Azhiyur there were no buffaloes, and his first encounter with them in Madras was one of sheer terror. He had gone for an evening walk that day and had just turned the corner of a slum street, when down the road there came charging at him in blind fury a phalanx of huge and wild-eyed buffaloes, jet-black and slime-covered, a devil's squad of storm-troopers, their heavy, hard hoofs hammering the macadam road, their necks stretched out, snouts thrust forward and heads thrown back menacingly, cavernous nostrils flared, and enormous steel-grey sabre horns flung over their shoulders poised to strike. Mathu lifted his dhoti and leapt away from their path. Imagine his surprise on finding that these terrifying animals were being driven by an emaciated old man on a creaky bicycle, twirling a long twig and barking '*Trsh-trsh*!'

'Their horns are good only for scratching their backs,' Zeruba told Mathu.

'How was I to know!' Mathu said.

Later, when he became familiar with these timid and awfully dumb creatures, he developed a certain contemptuous sympathy for them. On his evening walks he usually came across lines of buffaloes trekking back home forlornly at dusk, their shoulders stooped, their heads hanging low, their steps leaden, their low, throaty bellowing disgustingly plaintive, and this, he thought, was one of the most mournful sights he had ever seen.

'Where did these creatures come from?' he asked.

'They originated in India,' Anjali said, consulting an encyclopaedia.

'I should have guessed,' Mathu chuckled.

Mathu had to pass by the TV serial producer's house on his walks, both while going and returning, and at its gate there was always a watchman sitting on a red plastic stool, the same man always, a stout, dark man with a grey handlebar moustache. Every day and all the time he sat in exactly the same place in exactly the same posture, without the slightest sign of animation in him. What was going on in his mind, Mathu often wondered.

'Probably his mind is as vacant as that of the buffaloes we see standing still on the roadside for hours together without stirring,' Zeruba said.

'Maybe he has attained Nirvana,' Anjali laughed.

'Of course,' Zeruba said. 'And so have the buffaloes.'

The suburb where Zeruba lived was largely open land, and had only some half a dozen bungalows and a couple of slum colonies. 'Here on my early morning strolls I can hear the call of nature—and also see men and women answering the call of nature,' Mathu liked to joke. In the open field, men and women could be seen through the morning mist, squatting in separate clusters and companionably evacuating. But a giant black man always sat aloof from these groups. He was the most regular of fellows, and came precisely at sunrise every day to squat under a particular palm tree. He sat there with bovine contentment for long, for something like a quarter of an hour, occasionally bending his head to examine with intense curiosity the golden pile rising beneath him, or throwing his head back and hawking to shoot phlegm at the sun in a wide arc. The sight of this lone man—he was the village headman, Mathu learned later—under the palm tree every morning reassured Mathu that all was well with the world, and that the sun and the moon were on their proper courses.

Further down, the fishermen colony was enveloped in the halo of smoke from hearths curling up though thatched roofs. A line of silent women ambled down the street, with water-pots on their sinuous hips. Others sat on the roadside washing clothes, slapping them rhythmically on stone slabs, and hanging them on lines along the huts, bright, colourful saris that fluttered in the breeze, prettier than the pennants of five-star hotels. Alongside the labouring women, men sat sunning themselves, wrapped in sheets against the winter morning chill, looking like roosting chicken. Packs of dogs were on the prowl. In front of one hut, busy hens clucked and scratched the ground viciously, watched over by a lordly strutting, red-plumed cock. Phlegmatic cows stood about passively, chewing cud.

The scene was different in the evenings, which was the time for slum spats. There was, Mathu noticed, an operatic quality about them, with shrill voices of different timbres weaving into each other in dramatic patterns, the women advancing on and retreating from one another like waves breaking on the shore, their voices rising and falling. Then suddenly there would soar the strident voice of one woman, a leader of some sort, her voice clear as a bell, to silence all. The crowd would hear her out, and then surge up again with jangling howls of protest. And this would go on and on. One day Mathu saw a lone woman walking about ranting incoherently at the top of her voice, with no one paying any attention to her—she was speaking not for anyone to hear her, but just to vent her frustration. Sometimes there were scuffles, women tearing at each other, yanking hair, ripping clothes, rolling in the mud, with men trying to untangle them.

At other times the slum scene was convivial, with several clusters of women, often in groups of three or four, sitting behind one another on the dirt road outside their huts, picking lice from heads and grooming each other, like monkeys. On Friday evenings, the women of the nearby slums congregated at the little Ganesa shrine under a hysterically chattering pipal tree at a road junction near the beach, all bathed and dressed in their Friday-best, with marigold or jasmine wreaths on their oil-slicked heads, and squealing babies on their hips. This was their one escape from the daily grind of their lives. Occasionally Mathu came across funeral processions, led by drums and pipes, with drunken men singing and dancing wildly around the bier and strewing flowers on the road. And early one morning, when he was strolling through the shopping area of the slums, he saw, on the veranda of an abandoned shanty shop, a man labouring over a woman on the floor, under the cover of a soiled, tartan-patterned sheet. A little girl sat nearby, next to a stack of blackened aluminium cooking pots, watching with dull, unseeing eyes. A family with women and children passed by, but they paid no attention to the roadside action, nor did the couple pay any attention to them. But when Mathu paused for a moment to watch, the couple too paused and turned to look at him. He guiltily quickened his steps.

On the weekends, pornographic films were screened in the tin-roofed theatre in the suburb, and one day Mathu bought a ticket—it cost ten rupees, an awful lot of money, he thought—and went in. At the back of the hall there were a few rows of rough wooden planks fixed on casuarina frames, but these were already taken by the time Mathu got in. The rest of the hall had only a sandy floor for the audience to sit. There was a narrow enclosure on the left side reserved for women, but there were no women for this show. On the floor, men sat cross-legged or sprawled, many of them drunk, smoking bidis. Mathu joined them, an odd figure in spotless white dhoti and kurta in that scruffy crowd. The show lasted barely an hour, and till the interval, and even a little beyond it, they showed bits pirated from various general release films, mostly fight scenes, and then the porno film for about twenty minutes, an Indian film, with a cast of scrawny men and fat, uncouth prostitutes, indulging in frantic simulated sex, with snatches of Hindi film songs as background music. None of the men in the film could get it up on cue. The movie was revoltingly obscene and badly filmed. But the audience, who had whistled and howled derisively during the fight scenes, went absolutely still and quiet, holding their breath, the moment the porno section started. This was a deadly serious matter for them.

When Mathu narrated these incidents, adding many colourful frills, Anjali teased him saying that at his age he should be thinking of the welfare of his soul and not the pleasures of his body.

'Doing research for my book,' he said solemnly.

Mathu was quite a hit with Zeruba's friends. 'My god, this uncle of yours is incredible,' Ashok said. 'He's like a cross between an Old Testament prophet and a Renaissance man, with a bit of Charlie Chaplin thrown in.'

'Yes,' said Zeruba. 'He's really extraordinary. But he has no achievement to show for his talents.'

'What're you saying?' Ashok admonished. 'The man is the message. His very persona is his achievement.'

Mathu liked to describe himself as a serious person who was not serious about being serious. A brilliant conversationalist, he always had something interesting to say, whatever the subject, and his views were unusually perceptive, though sometimes he also made up comments to amuse or shock people. He was a superb mimic, and once, when Ashok was there, he gave a side-splitting imitation of Shivaji Ganesan, the Tamil film actor, delivering the to-be-or-not-to-be soliloquy from *Hamlet*, arching his eyebrows fantastically, popping his eyes, twitching his facial muscles convulsively, twirling and flapping his arms, and prancing back and forth like a megalomaniacal lunatic. 'We reduce everything to parody,' Mathu said, catching his breath. 'And tragedy into comedy.'

'By sheer excess,' said Anjali.

Weekends were the best of times for Mathu, as Zeruba invariably had visitors then, and he revelled in their company. There was always plenty of alcohol—beer, whisky and rum—to enliven the spirits. Mathu himself hardly ever drank, but he was a diligent host who loved to see everyone have a good time. 'Enjoy yourself,' he would urge. 'There is so little time in life.' Dr Rao and Ashok were weekend regulars, and so was Narasimhan, a deeply conservative senior colleague of Ashok, who blamed all the ills of India on the quirks of the Kali-yuga, the present age of wrath in Hindu mythology.

'People will be so evil in this age that the dead will turn pale as death at the sight of the living,' Narasimhan said solemnly one day, high on several pegs of rum and cola. He was addicted to alliteration, and spoke in a sing-song voice. 'Ghosts are now mortally scared of the mortals!'

A pleasant-mannered old-world gentleman in his late fifties, Narasimhan was always dressed in crisp, white, khaddar dhoti and kurta, and wore a precisely drawn Iyengar caste-mark on his broad forehead. Every morning he spent a couple of hours performing puja at home before going to the office, and he attributed his good health and successful career entirely to this. 'It's all the Lord's boon,' he would say to anyone who complimented him. 'I'm nothing by myself.' But he had, despite his orthodoxy, a weakness for liquor, which he was not allowed to drink at home, having failed to convince his wife and mother that it was a perfectly proper Vedic practice, and that rum was in any case a pure vegetarian drink.

'I know something about the Kali-yuga concept,' Mathu one day said to Narasimhan. 'But I've a doubt about it.'

'Yes, Mr Mathu?'

'Is the Kali-yuga for all people?' Mathu asked. 'Or is it just for us Indians?'

'Of course for all people,' Narasimhan said.

'Then how is it that many countries in the world are now advancing in prosperity and culture, while we are declining?' Mathu asked slyly.

'A single firm in the US, one single bloody firm, Microsoft, is worth far more than the total GDP of India,' added Ashok.

Narasimhan was not flummoxed. 'What you call progress has been achieved by sacrificing spiritual values and mental peace,' he said. 'It's not a gain: it's a loss. Americans may have more material comforts, but they also have more mental misery.'

'I agree. Wealth doesn't mean happiness,' Mathu said with sweet reasonableness. 'But then, nor does poverty mean happiness. Misery is our common lot. But you know what, it's easier to endure mental misery when you're ensconced in material comforts.'

'The reverse is also true,' Anjali countered. 'We can endure any material discomfort if we have mental equanimity.'

'Absolutely,' agreed Narasimhan.

'But our reality is that we have neither material comfort nor mental equanimity,' Ashok commented.

'What else do you expect in the Kali-yuga?' asked Narasimhan. 'Everything gets inverted. Topsy-turvy and turvy-topsy.'

Awakenings

1

The freewheeling weekend sessions in Zeruba's cottage came to an end when the monsoon broke over the land and virtually marooned the cottage. Mathu now began to show signs of restlessness. He could not even go for long walks any more. For hours together he sat in the veranda looking out blankly, tilting his chair back with his legs on the parapet.

It was late July, not the main monsoon season in Madras, but it rained torrentially and incessantly that year. From where he sat, Mathu could hear the sea raging and bellowing, hidden behind the silver-grey veil of the driving rain. Mountainous thunderclouds loomed overhead, rumbling menacingly. The rain tree, whipped by the gale, tossed like a dervish. Close to the veranda, a drenched barn owl, shrouded in speckled white plumes, sat on the temple-tree, glowering at Mathu with unblinking eyes. The spray from the rain angled sharply into the veranda, soaking Mathu's legs, but he didn't seem to mind or even notice, as he sat gently rocking in the chair. Anjali and Zeruba noticed his listlessness and tried to keep company with him.

'What're you doing, Kochappa?' Anjali asked him one day.

'Watching the rain,' he said. 'I like watching the rain.'

'Shall I sit with you?'

'No. You go on with your work. I'm fine.'

Around this time, Mathu went for a medical check-up, and was pleased to find that he was in perfect health. 'The whole system is ticking just fine,' he told Zeruba, proudly flourishing the medical report. 'I'm in perfect shape to end my life.'

'To end your life?'

'Yes,' said Mathu. 'According to yogic teaching, the body should be in perfect health should one desire to end one's life.'

The rain abated by the first week of August, but the sky remained overcast and there was a steady drizzle most of the time. Then one early morning, Mathu knocked at Zeruba's bedroom door and called out to him.

'What's this, Kochappa? Let me sleep,' Zeruba grumbled, opening the door.

'It's the Independence Day, and the sun is out,' said Mathu. 'Let's go for a walk.'

'Let's at least have a cup of tea first.'

'I've already made it,' said Mathu. 'Come.'

Zeruba hurriedly changed into shorts, slipped on a pair of loafers, and they set out along the beach. The sand, smooth and wet, crumbled softly under their feet as they walked. Mathu was in an exuberant mood, and remarked on everything he saw, as if he were seeing them for the first time—or for the last time.

'Why are you in such a good mood today?' Zeruba ribbed, pleased that his uncle's gloominess was gone. 'Because the sun is out?'

'Partly. I feel that one must treat every day as the last day of one's life, savouring every sight, every smell, every touch,' Mathu said. He scooped up a handful of slime from the water's edge and smelled it. 'Even clay would smell like roses on the last day of your life.'

'And any day could be one's last day,' Zeruba said.

'Absolutely,' said Mathu. 'That's why we shouldn't miss the enjoyment of even a single day.'

'Well, it's hard to find any enjoyment at all in life,' Zeruba said. 'Our world isn't a particularly hospitable place to live.'

'Have you ever thought of committing suicide?'

'Who hasn't?'

'The question is, should we allow death to creep on us secretly like a timid thief, or take the matter into our own hands,' said Mathu. 'Death as an act of will, under one's own control, is an attractive idea.'

'People in control don't commit suicide, Kochappa,' Zeruba said. 'They commit suicide when they are not able to cope with life, or when they find no purpose in living.'

'Most people have no purpose in life other than to just exist,' said Mathu. 'I suppose that's why they go on living. If you look for meaning and purpose beyond mere existence, life would seem intolerable.' And this predicament gets worse with the progress of civilization, Mathu remarked. While the number of things in which man finds happiness multiplies as civilization advances, unfortunately, the number of things that makes him miserable also multiplies by the same measure. 'Deprivation and loss is the umbra of every gratification.'

'Yes, of course,' Zeruba said. 'But that equivalence existed at every stage of civilization.'

'No, things are worse now.'

'How can that be?'

'Because life has become more nuanced,' Mathu said. 'And the minimum conditions under which life is tolerable to man has become too exacting with the advancement of culture. That's why Kerala, our most literate state, has such a high suicide rate.'

'But it's cowardly to commit suicide,' Zeruba said. 'Death is not the challenge. Life is the challenge. Anybody can kill himself with no effort at all. But to cope with life is quite a task.'

'You're wrong,' said Mathu. 'Death is easy, of course. But so is life. It's sensible life that's difficult. And sensible death is as difficult.'

'There's nothing called sensible death, Kochappa,' Zeruba said. 'And suicide is an entirely negative act. I see no merit at all in it.'

'Suicide is not necessarily a negative act,' said Mathu. 'It could be an assertion of freedom rather than an acknowledgement of futility.'

'There is no freedom outside life.'

'Maybe,' said Mathu. 'But taking one's own life is the ultimate liberty one can take with oneself.'

'Why should we die?'

'The right question is, why should we live?'

'Because life is all that one has,' said Zeruba.

'Yes, but what is there in life? Just a mouldy store of memories and regrets. You're born alone and you die alone, and in most of the in-between time you're alone with the loneliness of spirit. Somewhere along the way, usually when you're well past your middle age, you discover who you really are, but by then it's usually too late to do anything about it. As Sophocles says, we cannot call a man happy until he is dead.'

'We all have regrets, Kochappa. But I'll never take my life. Will you?'

'Maybe not. Maybe yes,' said Mathu. 'You're afraid to die?'

'No, I'm not afraid to die,' Zeruba replied. 'But I don't want to die before I'm done with living.'

They walked on in silence for a while. The sea lay becalmed and quiet, weary after weeks of torment. The air was crisp, bracing. Gay, fluffy white clouds raced each other across the clear blue sky. On the way, Mathu found a large, black plastic carry-bag rolling gently along the beach in the breeze, and bent down to pick it up, but the instant he reached for it, the bag, lifted by a sudden gust of wind, puffed itself up angrily and went flying across the sands.

'The damn thing is alive,' laughed Mathu. 'If, as the Jains say, there's no great difference between the living and the non-living, then there can be no great difference between life and death.'

'Right. Except that when you're alive, you're alive, and when you're dead, you're dead.'

'You know, the death of a man, any man, is an utterly trivial incident in the cosmic scheme of things. Even the death of millions. Hiroshima wouldn't have caused even a teeny-weeny ripple in the cosmos, if anyone out there noticed it at all. So what can you say about my life or your life?'

'The trick is not to think about these things.'

'We don't choose to think, Zeruba. The thoughts come by themselves,' Mathu said. 'I don't know whether we should feel wretched about our insignificance, or feel happy that we exist at all.' There are some 125 billion galaxies—billion, not million; and galaxies, not stars—in the universe, and in our Milky Way galaxy alone there are about 150 times as many stars as there are people in India, Mathu observed. And there is a star out there somewhere that is four million times brighter than the sun. So you can well imagine the size of the universe. And the measure of our earthly insignificance. There might be hundreds of millions, or hundreds of billions heavenly bodies teaming with intelligent life infinitely superior to ours. 'Our life is momentary and utterly inconsequential, on an insignificant little planet in an insignificant little galaxy, in a universe that is itself transient. So what is there to cherish about your life or my life?'

'Because it's the only thing we have,' Zeruba said.

'Human life is entirely insignificant even on this planet,' Mathu went on. 'Do you know that there are some fifty thousand bacteria on every square inch of your skin? Fifty thousand! Man is significant only in his own self-adulatory view. For all we know, the frog in the village pond might be thinking the same about itself.'

'What are you leading to, Kochappa?'

'Nothing. As you say, let's not think about these things.'

Mathu, despite his bleak words, was in high spirits during the stroll, telling himself, and telling Zeruba, to treasure every momentary joy in our transient and ultimately worthless lives.

2

They returned to the cottage in time for breakfast. Throughout the morning, Mathu was busy in his room, sitting at his desk, writing and organizing his papers. After lunch he took his usual hour-long nap, and they all had tea together, with Mathu regaling them with family anecdotes from his childhood. Then Zeruba and Anjali went into the studio, and Mathu returned to his room. An hour or so later, he went into the studio. This was unusual, for he was normally careful not to disturb Anjali and Zeruba at work.

'Hope I'm not disturbing you,' he said.

'Disturb? You're our inspiration, Kochappa,' said Anjali.

'Oh, how I love you, my child!' he said, smiling happily and shaking his head. 'But tell me, why have you married this baboon nephew of mine?'

'I hope to teach him a few tricks,' Anjali said.

'You be good to each other,' Mathu said. 'And don't you ever give up on each other, whatever happens.'

'Of course not,' Zeruba said.

'You're at last at peace with yourself, and that's a wonderful thing,' Mathu said to Zeruba. 'Thanks to Anjali.'

'Why are you coddling me, Kochappa?' Anjali laughed.

'Because I'm in love with you, my child.'

'And I'm in love with you,' Anjali said.

'You know, you're the only woman who has ever said this to me.'

'And I mean it,' Anjali said.

'Of course,' Mathu chuckled. 'Well, I think I'll go for a swim now.'

'Wait for a while,' Zeruba said. 'I'll join you.'

'You go on with your work,' Mathu said. 'I want to go for a long, long swim. It's such a fine day.'

'Are you sure?'

'Of course,' said Mathu. 'I belong to the sea. Don't forget.'

Mathu then did something strange. Though he abhorred touching people, anyone at all, he now went over to Zeruba at the easel, and planted a kiss on his forehead, then turned and kissed Anjali too on her forehead. She noticed his eyes were moist.

'What's the matter, Kochappa?' she asked anxiously.

'Nothing,' he said. 'I'm just happy for both of you. Well, goodbye.'

The months that Mathu had spent in the cottage were the happiest in his life. There he had at last emerged from the abstract world he had shut himself in, and had bonded with Zeruba and Anjali in love. His life, he felt, has at last been consummated. Fulfilled.

'Goodbye,' he said again at the door of the studio.

3

'Something's wrong,' Zeruba said when Mathu left.

'Why don't you go with him, Mama?' Anjali asked.

Zeruba placed the easel and brushes on his worktable, and went over to the window. He could see Mathu in his blue swimming trunks striding towards the beach, his posture erect.

'I don't know,' said Zeruba. 'He might not like it.'

'I've a bad feeling about this, Mama,' said Anjali.

'If he swims out, I'll never be able to catch up with him.'

'Please go to the beach and see,' said Anjali. 'Please.'

'Alright.'

By the time he changed into swimming trunks and got to the beach, there was no sign of Mathu. This did not unduly worry him, for Mathu was a strong and experienced swimmer and he sometimes went far out into the sea, where he was barely visible, especially in poor light. So he sat on the beach to wait. In a while Anjali joined him.

'Where is he?' she asked.

'I think he has swum far out,' he said.

'Did you see him?'

'No.'

'What shall we do?'

'We'll have to wait.'

So they waited.

'Maybe he has gone for a walk,' she said.

Zeruba didn't say anything to it. There were no footprints on the sands, except the one pair leading into the water.

'Maybe he's back in the cottage,' she said. 'I'll go and see.'

Again he didn't say anything. And when she returned he was still sitting in the same position, staring into the sea. But now there were tears rolling down his cheeks. They sat there for a long while in silence, with their arms around each other, till it was dark, and there was no point in waiting any more.

'What shall we do?' she asked when they got back to the cottage.

'He was trying to tell me something when we went for the walk in the morning,' Zeruba said. 'But I didn't realize its significance.'

'What did he say?'

'About suicide being an act of affirmation. I thought it was his usual mental play.'

'But he looked so happy and full of life today,' she said.

Zeruba nodded.

'Shouldn't we call the police?' she asked after a while.

'Let me talk to Chacko,' Zeruba said. 'He would know what to do.'

Chacko was at home in Thiruvananthapuram when Zeruba phoned.

'We must keep this out of the newspapers,' Chacko said. 'That's the first priority.'

'What're you saying?' Zeruba shouted at him. 'The first priority is to find Kochappa.'

'Of course,' Chacko said. 'But let's keep this quiet. One has to be careful about image in public life.'

'What shall we do?'

'Leave it to me,' said Chacko. 'I'll talk to my CM right away and get him to talk to your CM. Leave everything to me. I'll call you back.'

'When?'

'Later tonight. Leave everything to me.'

'Alright,' said Zeruba, and rang off.

Around midnight Chacko called to say that the Tamil Nadu Home Minister had ordered the police to conduct a discreet inquiry about Mathu's disappearance.

'Are you coming?' Zeruba asked.

'Let's see what the police come up with,' Chacko said.

4

The police swung into action early next morning. The inspector, because of orders from his superiors, was deferential towards Zeruba, and was apologetic in asking whether the missing person had left a note. The thought of looking through Mathu's room had occurred to Zeruba, but he couldn't bring himself to violate his uncle's privacy. But now, with the inspector in tow, he and Anjali entered the room. Everything there was in perfect order, as usual. But on the roll-top desk, the letter-pad was open, and on it was a two-line note in Mathu's minute but calligraphic hand: 'Please don't wait for me for dinner. I might be gone for a long while.'

'What does it mean?' the inspector asked.

'He used to go for long walks,' said Zeruba. 'And sometimes he got back late.'

'He usually leaves a note?'

'No. This is the first time he has left a note.'

'How old is he?'

'Eighty-three.'

'And he swims in the sea?'

'He is very vigorous for his age.'

The inspector wanted a photograph of Mathu, and when this was given, he politely took his leave, saying, 'Don't worry, we'll find him. He probably got confused and wandered off. It sometimes happens to old people.'

Most unlikely, Zeruba wanted to say, but held his tongue. The inspector took off with a couple of constables in his jeep towards the fishermen's colony, but returned after about an hour to report that no one had seen Mathu. 'We'll come again in the evening. Some of the fishermen have gone to the sea, we might get something from them when they return.' But the evening inquiry also yielded no result. 'We have alerted all the police stations in this area. We'll know if anything turns up,' the inspector said. But nothing turned up the next day either. In the night Chacko phoned. He had already received a report about the futile police inquiries.

'I understand that Kochappa has left a note,' Chacko said.

'Yes,' said Zeruba. 'But it merely asked us not to wait for him for dinner.'

'Don't fool yourself,' Chacko said. 'You know very well what the note means.'

'I do,' Zeruba said. 'But it's difficult for me to accept it.'

'We've lost him.'

'Probably.'

'But we'll keep this to ourselves,' said Chacko. 'He could have gone to an ashram. He has always had an inclination for monastic life.'

'Don't fool yourself,' Zeruba said.

'I'm not fooling myself,' Chacko said curtly. 'I'm just looking for a way out of this embarrassment.'

'Embarrassment?' Zeruba asked, lowering his voice in anger. 'Is that how you feel about of Kochappa's death?'

'We have to think of the family honour,' Chacko said.

'And of course we have to think of your career too.'

'Yes. I'm not ashamed to say this. We, the living, have to carry on somehow.'

'Appa has to be informed,' Zeruba said.

'I'll take care of it,' Chacko said. 'I'll go home tomorrow. I won't mention suicide to him, but only that Kochappa has gone into an ashram.'

'Fine,' said Zeruba.

After Chacko called off, Zeruba and Anjali went into Mathu's room again, and searched thoroughly through all the papers and files on his desk for some clue to his disappearance, and there discovered a second note in the letter-pad, on the sheet of paper beneath the first note.

'My dearest Anjali & Zeruba: Think of me with happy thoughts always,' the note said. 'I'm now truly your guardian angel.'

The Finale

1

For a week after Mathu's disappearance, every morning and evening, rain or shine, Zeruba kept vigil on the beach for an hour. Late one evening when he was thus sitting slouched on the beach, hugging his knees, Anjali went to him. The sand was wet from the afternoon rain, and a fine drizzle was falling. Everything was still and quiet on the beach, except for the hushed sighing of the ocean. She knelt behind him and hugged him gently, pressing his head against her bosom.

'He's gone, Mama,' she said. 'What're you waiting for?'

'I'm not waiting for anything,' Zeruba said. 'I'm just keeping vigil.'

'You've done it for a week. It's enough,' she said.

'I loved him more than I loved my father,' he said.

'I know. I too loved him dearly,' she said. 'But we have to let go sometime. Come away now to your own life.'

So he got up, dusted off the sand from his clothes, and returned to the cottage. He never spoke of Mathu again. But he often thought of him, and wondered what his suicide meant. Was it an act of romantic despair? There is, he reflected, for each of us, a promised land of contentment and happiness beyond the tomorrow mountain. Our private utopia. But we never attain it, as the zillion tentacled everyday reality pinions us, breaks our spirit, destroys our dreams. What should we do, then? Resign ourselves to our drab existence in this imperfect world, which yields not one thing exactly as we desire it? Or go for the dark victory of suicide, in which the deceitful promises of the tomorrows and the hereafters are finally repudiated?

Mathu had told Zeruba that suicide was an act of affirmation. How could that be, Zeruba wondered. Suicide seemed to him to be a self-contradictory act—it affirmed the potential of life by rejecting life! If life didn't have the potential for happiness or achievement, there would be no hope and therefore no despair, so no one would want to kill himself. On the other hand, if life did indeed have the potential, should not one go on striving, instead of killing oneself? Either way, suicide made no sense.

The suicide himself knows this, and dies with a lump in his throat. He kills himself, not because he wants to die, but because he finds it intolerable to live. There simply aren't present the minimum conditions to make life bearable to him. Was this the case with Mathu? Couldn't be, Zeruba felt. There was no indication of any despair in him, though of course Zeruba could not be certain of what went on beneath the cheerful demeanour of his uncle. Zeruba preferred to think of Mathu's suicide as an ascetic act, like that of Jain saints starving themselves to death. He killed himself because he was done with living. But unfortunately, death has finality only for the person dying—for those who live on, the consequences of his death continue to roll on through their lives.

These gloomy ruminations of Zeruba did not last for more than a few weeks. If happiness, as Buddha says, does not last, nor does sorrow last. Time not only heals, but also replenishes. But the vacuum that Mathu's disappearance left in the life of Anjali and Zeruba led to an important decision—they decided to have a baby.

'There's something missing in our life,' Zeruba said to Anjali one day.

'What?'

'We've to have a child of our own,' he said. 'Three make a family, not two.'

This surprised Anjali, for Zeruba had, before their marriage, told her about his vasectomy, and when she told him that the operation could be reversed, he had said that he was too old to bring up another child. But now, nine years later, he wanted a child.

'It would be wonderful for me to bear your child,' she said. 'But let's do this only if you're absolutely certain of it. Don't do it for my sake, Mama.'

'I want it,' he said. 'But I want to talk to Saumya about this first. I don't want to upset her in any way.'

'Of course,' said Anjali. 'If she feels the least bit awkward about it, we won't do it.'

This, they felt, was a matter that had to be discussed with Saumya in person, not over the phone or by letters. So about a year after Mathu's disappearance, they went to the US to visit Saumya, for which she had been pressing them for quite a while. When Zeruba tentatively mentioned to Saumya his thought of having a baby, not only were she and Marty enthusiastic, but they insisted that the vasectomy reversal should be done at their university hospital. And when Anjali conceived soon after, they would let her and Zeruba return to India only after making absolutely certain that everything was fine with the pregnancy. So they stayed on in the US for nearly six months.

While they were in the US, Zeruba's mother died, and within a couple of months of their return to India, his father too died. Zeruba was having an afternoon nap one day when Chacko phoned him to say that their father had had a serious heart attack. He immediately set out for Azhiyur, leaving Anjali with her parents.

2

At home in Azhiyur, Zeruba found Chacko holding court in the portico, surrounded by a number of local political leaders and a few government officers. Several cars were parked in the courtyard, including Chacko's new white Mercedes. On seeing Zeruba, Chacko rose deferentially and took him inside. Korah's condition had stabilized, he told Zeruba.

'Doctors say that there's no immediate danger,' Chacko said. 'But given his age, nothing is certain.'

'How's he?' Zeruba asked.

'He's conscious and cheerful,' Chacko said. 'Anna is with him. Rest a while, then we'll go and see him.'

As Zeruba was changing to have a bath, Chacko rushed into his room.

'Anna phoned just now. He's sinking. Let's go.'

Chacko's Mercedes sped, its horn blaring continually, through the narrow streets of the town to the hospital barely a kilometre away, but Korah was gone by the time they got there.

'Appa is gone,' Anna said, standing at the door of his room.

He was, Anna said, conscious till the last moment. 'His teeth were chattering, so I asked him whether he was feeling cold and whether I should get some tea for him. He said yes. But when I was pouring the tea from the flask, I heard him call me. So I went to him, but he was gone by then.'

Korah did not know he was going to die, for the doctor had told him that he was doing fine and there was no need for anxiety. But his feet were cold, and he felt a chill creeping up his body. He needed a thicker blanket, he thought. And yes, a cup of hot tea would be nice. He watched Anna pouring the tea, but she seemed to take ages over it, and he wanted to hasten her. There was also something else that he wanted to tell her. 'Anna,' he called, his voice a barely audible whisper. But she didn't seem to hear him. So he called again, this time soundlessly, with his mind's voice. What was it that he wanted to tell her? Something important, but he couldn't remember what. An incident from his childhood now flashed through his mind—he, as a twelve-year-old boy, saving an unstoppable goal kick on the school football field, and the crowd roaring. 'Yes, I was good,' he thought happily, and closed his eyes. Then he stopped breathing. It was thus with a smile on his face that Korah died. But the smile seemed like a bitter grimace to Zeruba when he saw the body. What have you done to me, the dead man seemed to ask. And why have you done this to me?

This was Korah's second heart attack. Fifteen years earlier, at the age of seventy-three, he had had a mild heart attack. But he recovered well from it, and remained in good health till the death of his wife. Then a rapid slide began. Though there had been no harmony at all between the two of them, she was a familiar part of his life, an essential appendage, and in her death he heard the muffled tolling of the bells for him. He now shrank into himself. His body shrivelled, his skin turned leathery, and the light in his eyes faded. He hardly ever spoke to anyone anymore.

Zeruba, as the eldest son, had the duty of closing the eyes of his dead father. The body was then given a sponge bath in the hospital and draped in fresh white sheets, and taken home in an ambulance. Chacko and Zeruba travelled with the body. At home, a barber was summoned to shave Korah, and trim his fingernails and toenails. The body was then washed and dressed in white silk dhoti and kurta, and placed in the coffin set up on a low bench in the drawing room. His head was placed to the west, so he faced the east, the direction from which Christ in his Second Coming was expected to come. His hands were folded over his chest in an attitude of prayer, and in them were placed a small wooden cross and an unlit candle. A bottle of attar was procured and its contents poured all around the body along the edges of the coffin. A three-foot high, baroque gold cross on a polished rosewood stand was brought from the church and placed on a table at the head of the coffin, with two large candles on ornate silver stands flanking it. Two multi-tiered brass oil lamps, brought out from the old wing of the house and polished with tamarind to shine like gold, were placed on the floor on either side of the cross, with a single wick burning in each. A number of small, lit candles were placed all around on the frame of the open coffin.

Zeruba took no part in these preparations, but merely hovered about. He had no knowledge of the ceremonies, and did not know what was expected of him. Around the coffin sat the relatives of Korah, mostly women. One of them stood over the coffin with a palm-leaf hand fan, to whisk away the flies that landed on the corpse. Someone was reading the Bible aloud. Zeruba sat near the coffin for a while, then went and sat in a corner of the portico, where, having nothing else to occupy him, he read the day's newspaper twice over.

Outside, workers with spades and hoes were clearing the weeds and shrubs that had grown over the neglected courtyard. In no time at all, a large, particoloured canvas shamiana was erected there, and in it were arranged, in neat rows, a couple of hundred folding steel chairs brought in a truck. Every detail of the funeral preparations was looked into and taken care of by Chacko and Anna, and their minions ran here and there to execute their urgent orders. By noon, the house began to fill up with relatives and visitors. The chief minister arrived in the afternoon, and along with him several ministers, each bearing immense wreaths. Wreaths were also brought by MLAs and local party functionaries, as well as by government officers. But the largest wreaths were brought by the heads of private firms, who were no doubt beholden to Chacko for many favours. The drawing room was so full of wreaths by late afternoon that there was little space for people to move around the coffin. Men milled about everywhere, in the house and in the courtyard, even in the inner courtyard, traditionally the preserve of women. Zeruba knew hardly any of these people, and he had nothing to do either. So he took from Anna the key of the gatehouse, saying that he was tired and wanted to lie down for a while.

This was Mathu's old sanctuary, and evidently the room had not been opened since his departure for Madras. Zeruba closed the door behind him, opened a couple of windows, shook out the dust from the sheet on the bed, fluffed the pillows, and then lay down and closed his eyes. He felt absolutely no emotion at all at the death of his father, though Anna and even Chacko had wept in the hospital room. And when the body was laid out in the drawing room, several of his relatives had tears in their eyes. But Zeruba was dry-eyed. This man was a stranger to him. He had no feelings for him. In the vastness of the cosmos, on a mote of coagulated dust called earth, in a wretchedly backward country crawling with men like termites, an insignificant incident in an obscure little town—an old man who was nobody had died of old age. What had this got to do with him!

He would take a nap, Zeruba thought. But he could not sleep, and he kept thinking about his father. In another few years if he looked into the mirror, it would be his father's face that he would see, he knew. In physical appearance, they were virtual clones. He looked at the back of his hands—they were exactly the hands folded on the chest of the corpse, even in the shape and texture of the nails, in the wrinkles of the skin. Every feature of his body was exactly like that of his father. But the body, as the sages say, is just a garment the spirit wears. *My body might be my father's,* Zeruba thought, *but my self is my own. I might walk with my father's feet, eat with his hands, but I don't see with his eyes, think with his mind, speak with his voice. I am myself.*

But if the body is only a garment for the self, why all the ceremony about death? A dead body is just biodegradable garbage. One moment, even to the very last breath, you are a person. Then the last breath goes, and you are just dead meat. But what has happened to the self? What about the mind, its thoughts and feelings—do they also perish? In the Tibetan *Book of The Dead*, the priest tells the departed spirit: 'You are now a body of thought impressions.' But this seemed a mere fancy to Zeruba. Isn't mind just body thinking, and not something apart from the body? Obviously then, the self (or mind or soul) perishes when the body perishes. The belief that the self or soul would endure through transmigration or would resurrect in the hereafter is just a myth invented by man to reconcile himself to his mortality. Death is not just a stage in the cycle of life. It is not a transition. It's the end. There's absolutely nothing beyond it. There is no hereafter.

Is this really so? Or do we merely think so, because of our imperfect knowledge? When you die the neurones in your brain are turned off and do not any more drive the pistons that activate your body, and the light in your eyes goes out, so you no longer see the world. Nor can you hear, or smell, or feel the world. There are no sense perceptions at all. The world has ceased for you. But have you ceased?

'Die and become what you are,' the mystics tell us. As sleep refreshes man, death renews life—is that it? Why do we then mourn the dead? Rather, shouldn't we mourn the living, because they have to go on living and suffering? All this was confusing to Zeruba. It's all just sophistry, worthless nonsense, he finally decided. No, nothing survives death. This life is all there is to life. Someday, sooner or later, something will get him too, Zeruba knew, something so small that it could not be seen even under a microscope, but would be stronger than him and strong enough to kill him. And thinking of these matters, he slowly dozed off.

4

He was awakened by a loud knocking on the door. It was Gopi, his school friend, whom he had not seen for nearly forty years.

'I wanted to have a *darshan* of the great man,' Gopi said.

'At last!' Zeruba laughed.

'At last what?'

'At last I've someone call me great.'

It was amazing, Zeruba thought—in forty years Gopi had not changed at all, except that he had lost a couple of teeth. He was as ruddy and rotund as ever, his long hair and beard untouched by grey. And evidently he was still, as in his youth, very much a jolly, irreverent nihilist, who lived cheerfully sponging on his friends and relatives. No one could resist his daft charm, and all indulged him as they would a naughty child. Gopi did not have his head screwed on right, everyone said, and this he took as a high compliment.

'Amazing,' Zeruba said. 'You haven't changed at all in all these years.'

'That's an awful thing to say to an old friend whom you haven't seen for decades,' Gopi said, hopping on to the bed with youthful agility to sit cross-legged facing Zeruba, who lounged wearily against the headboard.

'Can't you take a compliment, you nut?' Zeruba scolded.

'That's not a compliment I'm going to return,' Gopi said. 'You're completely transformed, da. Remember what the oracle had said, that it's life that you have to fear, not death. Well, it looks like you have defied fate and prevailed over life.'

'It's been a long and painful struggle, Gopi, but I'm at last content and at peace with myself,' Zeruba said. 'But what about you? What have you done with your life?'

'Nothing, da,' said Gopi cheerfully. 'Absolutely nothing. I haven't even lived.'

'Then there's no death for you.'

'Thank you for that boon,' Gopi said. 'But what're you doing here when everyone is busy burying your father?' Gopi asked.

'Thinking,' Zeruba said.

'About what?'

'Death.'

'I didn't know you were that close to your father.'

'I wasn't thinking about Father, but about death in general.'

'Yes, it's humiliating to be dead, isn't it?'

'Yes. People do things to you when you are dead,' Zeruba said. 'They strip you naked and wash you like washing meat, and shove you into an oblong black box. Then they pour oil on you, even into your eyes and nostrils, and finally dump you into a pit and cover you with mud. Humiliating.'

'At least in your community they don't burn you,' Gopi said.

'I prefer to burn,' Zeruba said. 'I'm determined to exit through an incinerator.'

'Let's change the subject, please,' Gopi said. 'Your gloom is killing me. I hear that you're happily divorced.'

'No,' said Zeruba. 'I'm happily remarried.'

'What? To the same person?'

'No. To a different person.'

'How come I haven't heard about this?'

'Because I haven't told anyone.'

'And it's this new wife that has transformed you?' Gopi asked. 'From a miserable idiot to a happy imbecile?'

'Yes,' said Zeruba happily. 'Come and spend a few weeks with us in Madras.'

'Never,' Gopi said. 'I'm determined to die having never once stepped out of the municipal limits of Azhiyur.'

'But what's there in this dead town? Nothing ever happens here.'

'That's what I like about this place,' Gopi said. 'Well, some days it rains here. And every now and then babies are born and men fall sick and die. Those are enough happenings for me. You'll have to put a rope around my neck and drag me to get me out of this town.'

'Well then, I'll go and get a rope,' Zeruba said.

Just then one of Chacko's sons came into the room to call Zeruba to the main house. The bishop had come, he said, and Zeruba's presence was required for a ceremony.

'We'll meet again,' Zeruba said, taking leave of Gopi.

'No, we won't,' Gopi said.

'Why not?'

330

'Let's not pretend,' Gopi said. 'We won't see each other again. Not in this life anyway. So this is farewell.'

5

The funeral was arranged for the next morning. From the house to the church it was barely a hundred metres, but a hearse was called to take the body. A young boy carrying the gold cross led the funeral procession, and he was followed by two boys holding the candles on silver stands, and by a man carrying a blue ceremonial umbrella embroidered with silver crosses and decorated with tassels. Behind them, and immediately in front of the slowly rolling hearse, walked three priests, chanting dirges. Zeruba and Chacko followed the hearse, along with many relatives and townspeople.

In the church, the bishop took over the ceremonies. The coffin was placed on a bench, with the body facing the east, and the usual obsequies performed. Then holy anointing oil was poured on the body by the bishop in the form of a cross, once each on the face, chest and knees. Zeruba and Chacko stood on either side at the head of the coffin. The final rite was to cover the face of the corpse with the *mukha-seela*, a face cloth with an embroidered cross on it. When this was about to be done, Chacko said, 'Wait,' and bent over to kiss Korah's forehead. And Zeruba, puzzled, also did the same. But as he touched with his lips the dead, chill flesh, he was overcome with revulsion, and vomit came retching up in him, so he had to pull himself back hastily for fear that he might throw up on the corpse. Anna, noticing his grimace, was surprised by what she thought was his show of emotion.

The body was then taken to the cemetery within the church compound, where the grave was already dug. After further ceremonies at the grave, the coffin was lowered into it, and the priests scooped fistfuls of mud and flung it into the grave chanting, 'Dust thou art, to dust thou return.' Chacko, and Zeruba closely following him, also threw earth into the pit, and so did the others at the grave. Then the grave was covered with earth, with Chacko taking a shovel himself and working alongside the gravediggers. Finally, the funeral mound was patted down smoothly, and the wreaths brought from the house arranged all round it.

After the ceremony at Korah's grave, they all moved to the adjacent grave of his wife for prayers. Here all that remained of the wreaths were their bamboo ribs, the flowers and leaves having rotted into the ground; and the grave itself had subsided into a squat, rain-eroded mound. As Zeruba stood at her grave, a flood of memories came rushing to him. The lullaby she used to sing to him, she dressing him for school, cleaning his slate, sharpening his pencils. Teaching him to read and count. But most of all, he remembered her drained eyes that had no tears to weep. How was she as a child, he wondered. There were no photographs of her childhood. What about her school friends? Did she have any? How different her life would have been if she had not married Korah! Well, Zeruba would not have been born then!

But he had been born. And he has lived a life. Now he stood in the sun, smelling flowers and incense, while she lay under the rain-soaked ground, helplessly letting the earthworms feed on her. On her death, Chacko told him, she had regained her youthful body, her cheeks had filled out and her skin had smoothened. 'Her last breath left her like a thin whistle,' he said. Well, Zeruba thought, Appa and Amma have now merged their time with all time.

When they got back home, Zeruba asked Chacko when he could return to Madras. 'There's a special service in the church for Appa to mark the end of the mourning period,' said Chacko. 'You have to stay for that.'

'When's that?' Zeruba asked.

'Traditionally it's on the fortieth day,' said Chacko. 'But nowadays it's held on any day that is convenient to us. Let's do it on the third or fourth day, because I've to return to Thiruvananthapuram as soon as possible, and you're eager to return to Madras early.'

'Fine,' said Zeruba.

'There are also matters about the will to be settled.'

'You take care of it, Chacko,' Zeruba said.

'There is nothing much to be taken care of,' Chacko said. 'There are only some four acres of land left. These are given to me. You get this house and compound.'

'What am I going to do with this house?' Zeruba asked.

'It's yours, to pass on to the next generation of the family,' Chacko said.

'The next generation? I've nobody to pass it on.'

'To Saumya and her children.'

'It is most unlikely that she and hers would ever again visit this place, or even visit Kerala.'

'What can I say? You have to decide.'

'You don't want this?' Zeruba asked. 'I'll sell it cheap.'

'I don't think so,' Chacko said. 'I can't live here. I now belong to another world, Chetta.'

'So do I,' said Zeruba.

'It would be too much trouble to take care of it.'

'You can tear it down and build anew.'

'Don't even say that,' Chacko said, shocked. 'This is our ancestral home. We can't demolish it. Appa will turn in his grave if he hears about it.'

For three days, till the special church service for the departed soul, an oil lamp was kept burning day and night in Korah's bedroom, and his bed was kept covered with a white sheet. And every morning Chacko and Anna and other close relatives went to the church to attend service and to pray for Korah's soul. Zeruba stayed at home. But he attended the special service on the morning of the third day. When they returned home, the oil lamp was snuffed out, and the white sheet on the bed removed. A feast was then held at home, to which all the relatives and a number of townspeople were invited. After that, the relatives staying in the house since Korah's death left for their own homes. That evening, the old retainers and servants of the family were paid off with liberal gratuities. Only Chacko and his family and Zeruba were now left at home.

Early next morning, Chacko and his family left for Thiruvananthapuram. His Mercedes stood gleaming at the steps of the crumbling old house, with his official chauffeur, resplendent in white uniform and cap, standing in attendance beside it, with one hand on its rear door handle, ready to snap it open the moment Chacko took a step towards the car. In front of the car was parked a police jeep, with officers standing beside it. A couple of white Ambassador cars of government officers were lined up behind the Mercedes. Zeruba and Chacko stood on the steps, with Anna and the children behind them.

'I got to go,' Chacko said, holding out the keys of the house.

'You sure you don't want the house?' Zeruba asked.

'Absolutely,' Chacko said. 'It's all yours.'

'Any news of Devi?' Zeruba asked.

Chacko shrugged. Zeruba took the keys.

'Got to go,' said Chacko, turning. 'Take care.'

Then he was gone, his car taking a tight turn in the courtyard and purring away, with the jeep in front and the Ambassadors trailing. Zeruba then locked the house and went into the gatehouse to lie down on his great-grandfather's bed. Presently he dozed off. When he woke up, he closed all the windows and locked the gatehouse, and went into the main house. Here he looked through all the rooms thoroughly and systematically. All the internal windows and doors were open, yet everything seemed closed. Silent, dead. Its walls stained with ancient memories. And he himself felt like a forlorn spectre haunting an abandoned home. There was an awful smell of mould everywhere. In the old, wooden wing of the house, Zeruba pushed open the trapdoor at the head of the staircase, and climbed into the hall on the first floor. This was where he and Devi, as children, used to scream and scamper around during the rainy season, when it was impossible to step out of doors.

Whatever has happened to Devi, he wondered. No one knew. The three of them—Devi, Chacko and himself—were on entirely different orbits now, and their paths would never again intersect, Zeruba knew. Each has cut loose and drifted away.

As he stood there chewing the cud of memories, a sudden gust of the foul odour of bat droppings hit him like a slap on the face, so he hastened back downstairs, bolting the trapdoor behind him. He then went from room to room in the old wing, carefully closing all the windows and doors. After that, he went into his parents' room in the new wing, and ferreted in the table there for his mother's old fountain pen, a Waterman, and clipped it into his pocket. He also took for himself an old walking stick with an ivory bulldog head, perhaps his grandfather's, which he found in a corner of the room.

Then he switched off the electricity at the junction box, picked up his shoulder-bag, closed and locked the main door, then the door of the portico, and stepped into the courtyard. The laburnum was in full bloom there. He plucked one flower from a bunch on the tree and put it in a side pocket of his bag.

At the gate he found Chathu, the old family retainer, waiting for him. Chathu had joined the family as a servant boy and had been with them ever since, for well over seventy years, and had served them with absolute loyalty through all the misfortunes of the family and the social upheavals in Kerala. He was now past eighty.

'Kochu-muthalali is leaving?' Chathu asked.

'I've to go,' Zeruba said.

'All gone,' Chathu said, his nearly blind eyes filling with tears. 'I used to massage Valia-muthalali with oil and steam his body till just a few days back, and he used to say, "When Chathu does this it is a *sukham*, a particular pleasure."'

Zeruba took five hundred-rupee notes from his purse and gave it to Chathu.

'Chathu doesn't need this,' the man said. 'Chathu has his memories. That's enough.'

Zeruba pressed him to take the money. Chathu's hands were like dry coconut husk, callused with age and toil.

'Amma was also very kind to me,' Chathu said. 'She used to scold me for not marrying, and tell me that a man without a wife was like a bird with its wings chopped off.'

'Well, that's life,' Zeruba said. He closed the gate and locked it.

'I've to go now,' he said.

'Don't forget old Chathu, Kochu-muthalali,' the man said.

'I won't,' Zeruba said.

Zeruba took a taxi from the town to Aluva. Just outside Azhiyur, as he crossed the rivulet that marked the end of the town, he stopped the taxi and stepped out for a moment, to look back at the town. This, he knew, would be the last time that he would set his eyes on Azhiyur.

'Let's go,' he said, getting back into the taxi.

At the bridge across the Periyar on the outskirts of Aluva, he paid off the taxi and walked over to the bridge. For a while he stood there, leaning over the river, with his elbows on the parapet of the bridge. The river was so still and clear that he could see the grains of sand at its bottom, though it was over six feet deep there. Snowy cirrostratus clouds in an azure sky floated in the river, and peering through them was his own reflection. The river was narrow under the bridge, flowing through a gorge, but upstream it was wide and shallow, and there the family once had a riverside bungalow, to which everyone—all the aunts and uncles and cousins—used to troop in summer. From where he stood, he could not see the house hidden behind trees, but he could see the broad sandbank alongside it, where he and his cousins used to play tag. Once.

'Got to go,' he muttered to himself.

He now leaned the walking stick against the parapet and took out the *tharavad* keys from his shoulder-bag. For a moment he dangled them over the parapet. '*Kleelaathi moraan,*' he softly chanted. This was a snatch from the Syriac church service that he remembered from his childhood. He had no idea what it meant, but those were the words that mysteriously came to his mind as he held the keys over the river. *Oh yes, in my end is my beginning—that would be the proper meaning,* he said to himself. *Kleelaathi moraan,* he hummed. Then he dropped the keys. As they hit the water, the clouds in the river shivered, and his own image vanished. The key-bunch angled slightly as it slid to the bottom and embedded in the sand, with the huge main-door key sticking up from the river bed like the stern of a sunken toy ship. Even as Zeruba watched, the slow current began to cover it with sand. No man will ever again hold that key. The lock will never again be opened.

Zeruba waited for the ripples to fade. In a while the river once again turned smooth and clear, like glass, and his own image, wreathed in feathery white clouds, reappeared in the water. Then he straightened up and looked at his wristwatch. Three fifteen. There was plenty of time for him to catch the train. There was no hurry. From a public phone booth he called Anjali in Madras.

'I'm coming home, Anju,' he said.